The Alchemist Who Survived Now Dreams of a Quiet City Life

Usata Nonohara

Illustration by OX

02

YEN ON

New York

The Alchemist Who Survived Now Dreams of a Quiet City Life 02

Usata Nonohara

Cover art by **OX**   Translation by Erin Husson

IKINOKORI RENKINJUTSUSHI HA MACHI DE SHIZUKANI KURASHITAI
Volume 2
©Usata Nonohara 2017
First published in Japan in 2017 by KADOKAWA CORPORATION, Tokyo.
English translation rights arranged with KADOKAWA CORPORATION, Tokyo through TUTTLE-MORI AGENCY, INC., Tokyo.

English translation © 2019 by Yen Press, LLC

Yen On
150 West 30th Street, 19th Floor
New York, NY 10001

Visit us at yenpress.com ★ facebook.com/yenpress ★ twitter.com/yenpress ★ yenpress.tumblr.com ★ instagram.com/yenpress

First Yen On Edition: December 2019

Yen On is an imprint of Yen Press, LLC.
The Yen On name and logo are trademarks of Yen Press, LLC.

Library of Congress Cataloging-in-Publication Data
Names: Nonohara, Usata, author. | ox (Illustrator), illustrator. | Husson, Erin, translator.
Title: The alchemist who survived now dreams of a quiet city life / Usata Nonohara ; illustration by ox ; translation by Erin Husson.
Other titles: Ikinokori renkinjutsushi ha machi de shizukani kurashitai. English
Description: First Yen On edition. | New York : Yen On, 2019
Identifiers: LCCN 2019020720 | ISBN 9781975385514 (v. 1 : pbk.) | ISBN 9781975331610 (v. 2 : pbk.)
Subjects: | CYAC: Fantasy. | Magic—Fiction. | Alchemists—Fiction.
Classification: LCC PZ7.1.N639 Al 2019 | DDC [Fic]—dc23
LC record available at https://lccn.loc.gov/2019020720

ISBNs: 978-1-9753-3161-0 (paperback)
978-1-9753-3162-7 (ebook)

10 9 8 7 6 5 4 3 2 1

LSC-C

Printed in the United States of America

The Alchemist Who Survived
Now Dreams of a Quiet City Life

02

Hey!
The Japanese edition
of this novel begins with a
manga section. To preserve the
right-to-left reading orientation of the
material, we've moved that section to the
back of the book, so flip to the end,
read that first, then come back
here to enjoy the rest of
the story!

The Alchemist Who Survived Now Dreams of a Quiet City Life

O2 Contents

PROLOGUE   A Howl Signals the Beginning   001

CHAPTER 1   Peaceful Days   035

CHAPTER 2   The Deluge   087

CHAPTER 3   The Meat Festival   143

CHAPTER 4   The Path Toward Reclamation   187

CHAPTER 5   The Beautiful Blue Sea   247

CHAPTER 6   At the End of an Eternal Sleep   289

EPILOGUE   What Flows Through   357

BONUS CHAPTER   The Flickering Shadow   381

APPENDIX   391

PROLOGUE

A Howl Signals the Beginning

01

The moon was out.

The perfect circle floated in the cloudless night sky. It freely lavished the world below with light so bright it almost might have made you think it was daytime. However, most of that light was obstructed by thick trees, and it only slightly illuminated the open road as it filtered through the branches.

The forest trees, seemingly full of life in the middle of the day, stood out black in the moonlight, and the tips of the branches that extended to the road looked like the figures of people stretching their arms out to embrace travelers, their bodies writhing in anguish. In truth, these branches blocked the path of carriages resembling iron boxes that careened through the forest in the summer. It was as if they were trying to provide prey to the monsters in the forest.

This was the Fell Forest, an area crawling with beasts. In these woods, which remained dark even in daytime, the shadow of death loomed darker still than the silhouette of trees in the moonlight.

Two cavalrymen and three armored carriages rushed between the trees of the Fell Forest, cutting through the darkness.

These were the armored carriages of the Black Iron Freight Corps. Its members had traversed this road countless times. The cavalrymen and carriages would run through the forest, shaking off pursuing monsters and striking down only those who blocked their path.

That was how they always did it.

However, this time was different.

"Maaan, these monster-warding potions are craaazy effective! There's hardly any monsters on our tail," said Lynx from atop a raptor. This time, they had monster-warding potions at their disposal. No particularly strong foes typically appeared on the road connecting the Labyrinth City and the imperial capital—just forest wolves, black wolves, goblins, and an occasional orc or orc general. If only a handful of these creatures showed up, B-Rank adventurers could handle them with no trouble. However, since they attacked in large numbers both day and night, you'd need to be A Rank in order to travel through the forest alone.

The Black Iron Freight Corps employed two cavalrymen serving as outriders, who forced their way through with their thick armor, so slow monsters like goblins and orcs presented no problems. Instead, lupine monsters like forest wolves and black wolves proved to be more trouble. They chased the Corps in packs and relentlessly attacked the raptors' legs and weak points in the carriages' armor.

However, after the Corps gave the monster-warding potions a try, lupine monsters sensitive to the odor stayed away. Sometimes, a goblin unfamiliar with the smell would end up falling down in the road and be splattered into bits by the carriages.

Until now, dealing with these lupine monsters had been incredibly time-consuming, and a trip through the Fell Forest would take the Corps two and a half days. More recently, however, they'd made it through within two. Now that the heavy equipment they'd been using was no longer necessary, they'd lightened the carriages' armor and their own equipment for the return trip. As a result, the Corps traveled faster and faster, and they were set to complete the trip in a day and a half and arrive in the Labyrinth City that evening.

"Don't get careless, Lynx. The monster-warding potions only work on small fry. Once you're talking B-Rank monsters, they won't work even on whelps." The other cavalryman, a dual wielder named Edgan, spoke up.

"Ugh, Ed, you jinxed us. Look, now we gotta fight these rare ones."

The two cavalrymen, Lynx and Edgan, increased their speed and slashed at the three dark red masses that came rushing at them from the front. Edgan took on two, and Lynx one.

One of Edgan's swords caught the mouth of a monster baring its fangs and snapping at him and sliced it open from the palate to the back of its head. His left-hand sword firmly stabbed at the other monster, but it used the sliced body of its kin as a foothold to bound past his attack.

Lynx's foe dodged three of the five daggers he threw at it and bit into the fourth one. The fifth grazed its body, but the dark red miasma coating the creature's skin prevented the blade from landing a mortal blow.

"Whaaa...? It dodged 'em?"

Lynx jumped down from his raptor and confronted the monster. It would be easier to fight this way. The raptor rushed back to the iron carriages.

"Bring it on, pup. I'll finish you off in no time."

The monster snarled.

Though it looked like a large wolf, the surface of its body was completely covered by a dripping, dark-red vapor, which made it look like it had been dipped in gore. When the oozing miasma came in contact with the ground, it wriggled eerily like buzzing newborn flies before disappearing. The creature's bloodshot eyes darted around as if quivering in fear, making it impossible to know what it was looking at. Its mouth, oddly large compared to its body, contained sharp fangs across multiple rows, and bloody saliva dribbled from it.

A black death wolf.

The evolved form of a black wolf that had consumed human flesh.

Come to think of it, Lynx heard a foolish merchant from the imperial capital had entered the Fell Forest about a month ago without sufficient equipment and been annihilated. He'd taken several slaves with him instead of guards.

So these things had eaten their corpses...?

At Lynx's provocation, the largest of the three black death wolves bared its fangs. It turned to face Lynx and rushed at him like a powerful wind.

Chomp.

The black death wolf's gaping maw took off Lynx's head and left shoulder in a single bite, and in that instant, Lynx's body vanished in the creature's shadow.

"GROAR!"

The wolf, which should have had Lynx in its jaws, let out a yelp, and its entire body shook. Countless daggers sprouted from its belly to its back.

Lynx rose from the shadow of the convulsing body as it fell to the ground.

"Nice work, Lynx. You've upped your game," said Edgan, who'd safely dealt with the remaining black death wolf.

"It's not good enough, Ed. I wanna be able to beat one with just my sword, without using skills. Uh, whoa!" Lynx, who'd replied casually in one moment, jumped two yards back the next.

Edgan retreated at the same time.

"Yikes, now we've got one of these things? No way I can take it down. How 'bout you, Ed?"

"I can't either. I'd die."

What had appeared in front of the pair was a wolf, tall as a bear, walking on two legs. A werewolf. An A-Rank monster.

Moreover, it seemed to be the evolved form of a black death wolf, as its entire body was hazy with the dark red miasma rising from it.

"GHHHAAAAA......"

Although it possessed vocal cords more like a human's than a wolf's, its howl sounded as if it came from a beast writhing in a fire. The air, even the moonlight itself, seemed to warp from the screeching cry.

"How many people d'you gotta eat in order to turn into *that*?"

"Hell if I know. I bet they'll even eat each other. Look, it's doin' that now."

Although they both cracked jokes, cold sweat dripped down their backs, and their legs wouldn't move, as if sewn to the earth. They couldn't tear their eyes from the werewolf, which now devoured the black death wolves they'd taken down. If it considered those things prey, B-Rank individuals like themselves wouldn't stand a chance.

"Ed, wanna try fightin' it just a li'l?"

"Pass. Wouldn't even last a second."

"Yeah, why bother."

""Caaap, you're up!""

The two of them shouted in unison, and the door to one of the armored carriages opened to reveal a single man. Neither fear nor agitation showed in his movements as he descended from the carriage.

"You got it," he replied. The strongest member of the Black Iron Freight Corps, the A-Rank adventurer Captain Dick, alighted from the armored carriage.

With a single black spear in hand, Dick approached the werewolf. His armor was a similar black hue and worn in. Brimming with silent bloodlust as he calmly approached the beast, the captain was the very embodiment of the phrase "Black Iron."

The Black Iron Freight Corps made a lot of money in their line of work. Over half of the Corps were former members of the Labyrinth Suppression Forces. They didn't look like merchants, but transporting cargo was their job. They contracted goods for distribution the yagu merchant caravans couldn't provide at a high price. Because of the highly dangerous nature of their work, they paid up front for the cargo when they received it before delivering the goods to a preassigned buyer.

Over the course of three days, the crew had taken turns riding the raptors through the forest.

Things were just getting a little boring with nothing but small fry.

Grinning broadly, Dick pointed the tip of his spear at the werewolf.

"Sorry to interrupt your meal, but we're in a hurry. You can continue enjoying it in the afterlife."

Hooowl.

The werewolf, who'd just been on all fours like a beast while devouring the black death wolves' remains, vanished, then immediately reappeared right in front of Dick and swung its claws downward.

"Too slow!"

However, the werewolf's claws glanced off the tip of Dick's spear. No matter how many times it swung at him with both arms, his spear kept the beast at bay, never letting those claws reach him.

With a *wham*, Dick's foot struck the werewolf's stomach. The creature staggered backward.

"You know you can't stay on your feet forever, you mutt."

"RRR, GHHHAAAA……"

Dick's taunt made the werewolf's hair stand on end. With both hands on the ground, miasma rose from its quivering body like a vortex. The corners of its mouth spread open so far that its entire upper body looked like just one disgusting maw. New fangs sprouted and pierced the torn corners, and a dark red liquid that was neither blood nor miasma trickled out of its mouth.

The werewolf lunged toward Dick and closed in on him in less than the blink of an eye to try and sink its teeth into his left shoulder. Dick dodged half a step to the left before lopping off its right arm as it passed by.

"RRRRRRRAGGGGHHHH……"

As if having no sense of pain, the werewolf didn't appear to flinch from losing its arm, but instead launched itself at Dick again as soon as its feet touched the ground. In an instant, the flesh at the end of the severed arm bulged, and even the wound itself ripped open and sprouted fangs like a mouth that could tear into him at any moment.

The werewolf grasped Dick from the front with its fangs. The strange severed arm-mouth had sprouted enough sharp fangs over its entire surface to devour a large man in a single bite, and there was no doubt it could overwhelm any sword or even a spear. The werewolf's remaining left arm and the severed arm-mouth both rushed at Dick, trying to pierce him anywhere they could.

However—the black spear penetrated the werewolf's arm-mouth. Dick's single lance pierced the creature's arm-mouth, torso, left arm, and both legs *at the same time* as if he were attacking with an entire fleet at his disposal. He was much faster than the werewolf's healing capabilities, and not a moment later, the creature was rendered into lumps of meat. Finally, he pierced its heart and called to Lynx and Edgan, "I'm done!" as if he'd just finished up some chores.

"That's our captain," Lynx marveled with sincerity. "Too bad Amber's not here to see this. She'd totally fall for ya."

That last part was pushing it, though.

"Amber already knows how good I am. She ought to," replied Dick, pausing in an odd spot.

"So you're sayin' you tell her to 'watch my spear technique' at night?"

"Huhhh......?"

"Hold up, you serious? He actually said that?"

"Geez, captain! Come on! That's gross!"

As he teased the captain, Lynx quickly recovered the materials from the fallen werewolf. He aspired to be like Dick someday. Lynx found him competent, including the way he could take in insult, even if it was just a joke. Today he got to see the captain fight for the first time in a long while. The way he handled his spear and felled the werewolf with such ease—it made Lynx proud to be a member of the Black Iron Freight Corps.

He harvested a suitably large magical gem from the werewolf. The creature was relatively small for an A-Rank monster, probably because it hadn't been very long since it had evolved. The three black death wolves also had magical gems, and he was able to procure a certain material from the one he'd defeated.

"Ooh, a ley-line shard. If we were anywhere else, it'd be worth something, but not here."

Ley-line shards were transparent, pale golden fragments about the size of a fingernail. On rare occasions they could be found in relatively strong mid-grade and higher monsters and sold at a high price as materials for special-grade potions. Supposedly, they got their name from how they immediately shrank and disappeared when taken too far from the ley-line region they were drawn from. As there were no alchemists in the region, these shards weren't worth much in the Labyrinth City, but rather were purchased for cheap by the Aguinas family as research materials.

If the Aguinas family was just going to drive a hard bargain for it, giving it to someone who'd be delighted by such a "pretty stone" would be much better.

"Guess I'll give this to Mariela as a souvenir."

Lynx tossed the shard into ʿhe air, caught it, then casually tucked it into his pocket.

Just a little longer until they reached their destination.

After burning the corpses of the werewolf and black death wolves, the Black Iron Freight Corps resumed their journey to the Labyrinth City.

02

Malraux, lieutenant of the Black Iron Freight Corps, recalled a lone girl his group had once encountered as they neared the Labyrinth City.

It was autumn now. The Fell Forest had completely changed colors over the last three weeks, but soon they'd emerge at the spot where they'd first met her.

Dick originally mistook the girl named Mariela for a "forest spirit," but Malraux felt it was a surprisingly apt expression. And not just because of the grass skirt she'd been wearing when they'd met her.

The girl had used a monster-warding potion on mere forest wolves.

Given the scarcity of potions, it was an unthinkable decision.

The ley line in the Labyrinth City's region had been the monsters' domain ever since the Stampede, and alchemists could no longer connect to it through a Nexus. The resulting lack of potions had been a major concern during the post-Stampede restoration, and the margrave overseeing the City at the time responded to this problem with the development of magical tools. The margrave had the remaining alchemists create a large quantity of potions that were then maintained in a giant storage facility.

If the Labyrinth could be destroyed, the Labyrinth City would become the domain of humans once more. Alchemists would be able to connect to the region's ley line with a Nexus and provide potions again.

It was said that the vault had been constructed to store a large number of potions, enough to destroy the Labyrinth, as estimated by scholars at the time.

In general, magical tools for storing potions delayed their deterioration by means of an engraved magic circle. So as long as you didn't open the stoppers, these tools prevented any deterioration from taking place for several days at a time, even when they were taken outside the region they had been created in. The magic circle engraving made the tools a bit expensive, but wealthy families owned them as "substitute medicine kits."

Naturally, a potion's efficacy couldn't be preserved for more than a hundred years.

On the other hand, Malraux had heard that the storage facility, developed over a period of about ten years, was a substitute that incorporated many magical tools. It managed to suppress the deterioration of potions by convecting the source of the potion's magical effects, Drops of Life, inside of the facility, while continuously dispensing something similar to the alchemic skill used at the final step of making a potion, *Anchor Essence*. The amount of magical crystals required for this storage was huge and not something that any one person could possess.

The Aguinas family, who had been the head alchemists in the Kingdom of Endalsia, managed the potions in the Labyrinth City. The potions they supplied to the army on a regular basis were extremely expensive in order to cover the storage facility's high maintenance costs. Other influential families residing in the

Labyrinth City such as the margrave's family or the aristocracy had their own small-scale potion storage facilities, and they regularly replenished their supplies from the Aguinas family.

Apart from that, rumors abounded of potions buried in the Fell Forest.

It was more of an urban legend for children: Over a century ago, the alchemists who'd filled the storage facility with potions had disappeared. Apparently, some eccentrics used to live in the Fell Forest during the time of the Kingdom of Endalsia, and some say the alchemists followed suit and fled to the forest after becoming fed up with all the potion-related bureaucracy in the Labyrinth City. Rumor had it, they built a storage facility like the one in the City while living in the Fell Forest and left potions there for future generations.

Surely the idea of "buried treasure" in the Fell Forest was just a story to entertain the minds of young children. Even if alchemists had lived in the Fell Forest, what would they do about the magical gems needed to maintain the storage facility? Not to mention such a place couldn't be maintained without management at a city level.

However, against the backdrop of this urban legend, a certain phenomenon was taking place: The types and quantities of potions regularly provided to the Labyrinth Suppression Forces and aristocratic families had increased.

And, at that time, Mariela had used a potion that ought to have been scarce.

03

"I need money, so I was on my way to sell them."

Malraux didn't buy that explanation. Why did she have potions in the first place, and why had she purposely used one for the Black Iron Freight Corps as if flaunting it?

When Dick had offered to buy them all, she'd readily accepted, as if she really had meant to sell them. Her clothes were worn and covered in dust, and the way she looked, spoke, and acted was no different from other girls in the area. Could a girl like that have stumbled on the treasure of Fell Forest?

She'd shown disapproval when Dick proposed half the market price for them, so it wasn't as if she didn't know their value.

Everything she'd told Lynx after they purchased her potions seemed to indicate she wasn't a resident of the Labyrinth City. She said she lived in the Fell Forest. Given the way she'd turned pale at the sight of the ruins of the old city, it looked like she was seeing place for the very first time.

Was it really true that a bunch of world-weary alchemists had secluded themselves in the Fell Forest over a hundred years ago? Maybe this girl was their descendant; someone who didn't know how to use the potions those alchemists had left behind, but had inherited them and was now in charge of them. If that was the case, she undoubtedly had more than what she'd sold to the Corps.

Upon reaching this conclusion, Malraux directed Lynx, who was close to Mariela's age, to keep watch over her.

Even if she looked like a normal girl, she'd lived in the Fell Forest. She might have special abilities. Malraux was sure she must have come out to meet with the Black Iron Freight Corps after learning they had connections in potion sales.

But Malraux had been reading too much into things.

"Sell him to me!"

Mariela had demanded to buy a dying slave with half the money she'd received from selling the potions. It was plain as day that the likes of mere low-grade potions would do nothing to improve his condition. Was she using him for information? It couldn't have been a simple act of compassion. And even if it had been, wasn't she being a little too hasty?

Somehow, she's a lot like Dick. How interesting.

Malraux had grown tired of exchanges rife with trickery. He had little interest in nimbly evading questions or trying to discern the other party's true motives. It only brought the most unseemly people into stark relief and left him feeling empty. However, Dick wasn't like that. He was straightforward, simplistic, and to put it plainly, foolish. Dick didn't have a cunning bone in his entire body. His pure might, honest ambitions, and ability to know his place made Malraux come to believe perhaps that's how people should be.

Dick wasn't the type to simply watch from the sidelines, but comrades with the ability to enjoy life were difficult to come by.

Perhaps Mariela and Dick are cut from the same cloth. Just as Dick possesses incredible strength, she most likely has some sort of merit as well...

*   *   *

After arriving at the Yagu Drawbridge Pavilion, Malraux had proposed a business deal at what seemed to be a suitable time after Mariela had finished gathering whatever information she'd needed, and the discussion had progressed without a hitch.

There were probably all sorts of people who would have tricked her into telling them where she'd stored the potions before swiping the whole stock, but the Black Iron Freight Corps was not a band of robbers. Things acquired through force would be subsequently taken away by those with greater power; that was how the world worked. Potions had that much value. Acquiring a good business partner seemed like it could be reward enough.

Mariela agreed to the deal under three conditions:

First, she would decide the types of potions sold.

She couldn't sell stock she didn't have, so that was reasonable.

Second, she would occasionally need part of the compensation paid up front in the form of goods.

A girl who'd been living in the Fell Forest probably required special items. In exchange for goods that were hard for her to come by, she'd supply potions, thus further solidifying business relations between her and the Black Iron Freight Corps. If anything, this was desirable.

Finally, assistance from the Corps should her secret ever be exposed.

Anyone who couldn't provide this service shouldn't be dealing with potions in the first place.

From Malraux's point of view, Mariela's stated conditions were a matter of course. He even felt uncomfortable that they hadn't started with price negotiation up front.

"Then, isn't a thirty percent commission too low?"

"Eh?"

And yet, Mariela had suggested a price reduction.

She'd said she wanted strict confidentiality and extra support in the unlikely event her secret was leaked. Perhaps she was just a prudent person by nature, or maybe this was a bribe. Either way, both Dick and Malraux were a little tired of their life of back-and-forth trips through the Fell Forest.

This odd girl who brought omens of change with her gave Malraux the vague feeling that things were going to get interesting.

04

It was evening when the Black Iron Freight Corps arrived back in the Labyrinth City.

They'd reached their destination an entire day earlier than usual. The city's outer walls were bathed in the light of the setting sun, and combined with the purplish-red bromominthra growing around its environs, it gave the impression that the City was on fire. As those making their return to the Labyrinth City were full of a sense of security, it reminded them of the ephemerality of peace in this town at the same time.

As always, when they requested the southwestern gate to be opened, a Labyrinth Suppression Forces soldier who was a former subordinate of the two men was waiting to greet them.

"Lord Dick, Lord Malraux, the general urgently requests your presence at his estate."

Perhaps it was a matter concerning potions. The general must have ordered the guards to lead Dick and Malraux there as soon as they arrived.

After asking Grandel and Franz of the Black Iron Freight Corps to deliver the goods, Malraux and Dick urged their raptors to the estate of the Gold Lion General, Leonhardt Schutzenwald.

Aside from the young Lynx, as well as Franz and Yuric, whom they'd met in the imperial capital, all the members of the Black Iron Freight Corps were originally part of the Labyrinth Suppression Forces. Malraux had called people together under so-called special circumstances to form the group.

The Gold Lion General, Leonhardt Schutzenwald, was deeply trusted by his men. Despite their differing social positions, he treated Malraux and Dick, who were close to his own age, as friends. Even when this pair of commanding officers had no choice but to leave the army, he spared no effort in helping them form the Black Iron Freight Corps. And even after they'd left, they hadn't broken ties with Leonhardt. Rather, when the Black Iron Freight Corps received a request from the Labyrinth Suppression Forces, they would undertake it even at the expense of other jobs.

Leonhardt was the eldest son of the current Margrave Schutzenwald. Along with his younger brother, Weishardt, he managed the Labyrinth City and strove toward subduing the Labyrinth.

Margrave Schutzenwald's family had vowed to seize control of the Labyrinth. Regardless of the ups and downs of succession rights, those with brawn battled the monsters, and those with brains focused their efforts on stabilizing affairs within the

Labyrinth City. Because they were born and raised under the fear of death from the nearby Labyrinth and Fell Forest, they spent no effort on pointless matters such as fighting over succession, and thus had been able to govern the area over the last two hundred years.

Even among generations of Margrave Schutzenwald's family, Leonhardt possessed especially superior fighting ability and was an incredibly popular general. He'd dared to subjugate the Labyrinth countless times, and his younger brother often supported him with his exceptional wisdom.

The suppression forces would probably soon reach the fiftieth stratum. Based on the damage done by the Stampede two hundred years ago, scholars had estimated this would be the Labyrinth's final level.

The Labyrinth became exceedingly difficult after the fortieth stratum. The deeper levels were full of terrifying, formidable monsters, but the Gold Lion General Leonhardt was undoubtedly capable of taking them down. Surely the Labyrinth would be destroyed in his lifetime, ushering in a new era for the Labyrinth City.

The Labyrinth Suppression Forces—no, everyone who lived in the Labyrinth City believed as much.

"This way, please."

A genteel white-haired old man led the way through the margrave's Labyrinth City estate. By all rights, Malraux and Dick shouldn't even be there given the state they were in: still in their traveling clothes and without a bath for several days. However, no one stopped them, and they were shown to Leonhardt's bedchamber.

"Malraux, Dick, it's good to see you."

Both Malraux and Dick stared wide-eyed, flabbergasted at the sight that greeted them. No— It couldn't be—

The Gold Lion General Leonhardt was stretched out on his bed, half his body petrified.

"How... How did you, of all people...?"

At his older brother's side, Weishardt explained a basilisk had gotten the best of Leonhardt.

Basilisks were formidable foes. They possessed thick scales, powerful claws, and a terrible petrification curse. This curse was so powerful that it persisted even after the basilisk that inflicted it had died. Healing magic would cure an ordinary petrification, but in a case like this, only two solutions existed: a high-grade potion especially for removing curses, or a spirit-assisted curse-removal rite in the land where the victim was born.

The latter option wasn't feasible since Leonhardt was born in the Labyrinth City region where humans couldn't communicate with the spirits endemic to the area. The only way to save him was to use a potion.

The petrification's slowness was thanks to the healing spells cast by Weishardt and other sorcerers. If they stopped using this magic on him, Leonhardt would very soon turn completely to stone.

"Let's head to the imperial capital immediately," proposed Malraux. If they could get there, they could obtain a specialized potion for curse removal.

"There's no point, Malraux," replied Leonhardt. "We already confirmed with the capital that they don't have enough materials. Besides, even with more healing magic, this body of mine only has about a day left."

Weishardt clenched his teeth.

"Don't despair, Weis. We're taking over the Labyrinth. We should've assumed something like this would happen and planned accordingly. I'm passing the reins to you. Dick, I know you've got Amber to think about, but come back to the Suppression Forces. We don't have the leisure of letting someone with A-Rank chops go idle. You, too, Malraux. Weis'll pull some strings for your family."

Malraux and Dick looked grief-stricken as Leonhardt continued.

"Listen up. The Labyrinth Suppression Forces are on stratum fifty-two right now. Turns out that Labyrinth's a den of evil beyond fifty strata."

It couldn't be.

Malraux and Dick's eyes bulged from their sockets in shock.

No labyrinth in existence went beyond fifty strata. That was impossible.

The deeper the labyrinth, the stronger the boss monster residing in its utmost depths. The biggest labyrinth said to be manageable by people is fifty strata. Any more than that and the labyrinth boss is beyond anyone's capabilities. Hence, this was why every labyrinth was checked thoroughly for its boss's location, and depending on the labyrinth, it might be sealed off to prevent it from becoming overgrown with monsters. Then, before the labyrinth can grow to fifty strata, the boss was defeated, thus destroying the place entirely.

Originally, a fifty-strata labyrinth in itself was considered enormous and rarely seen in history. Scholars estimated it as the largest of its kind based on the scale of the damage inflicted on the Kingdom of Endalsia.

To think the Labyrinth was deeper than fifty was madness.

"The potions you guys gave us were a godsend. Without those, we would've been slaughtered. I was just too eager for success and let the basilisk get the best of me. Malraux, Dick—bring the army some potions. House Schutzenwald's supply is mostly gone, even the other clans'. The Aguinas family only gives us new medicine and other low-quality stuff. It's likely their storage facilities are running low, too. After all, no one expected the Labyrinth to go beyond fifty strata. I know it's not nearly enough in terms of compensation, but I'd like to arrange a reward for the owner of your potions."

"Wait, General." Dick let Leonhardt finish his speech before speaking up. "There may be a curse-removal potion."

"Impossible!" retorted Weishardt.

Curse-removal potions required special materials, things like rare moss that grew only in particular environments, or the petals of a flower that bloomed once every one thousand days.

None of these rare materials—particularly the moss—ever appeared on the market even in the Labyrinth City. If they could just gather the materials and hurry them through the Fell Forest, then perhaps it might be possible to save his brother. Weishardt clung to a shred of hope, desperate to find a way. The Labyrinth City storage facility itself had had only around ten specialized curse-removal potions, and those had been used decades ago. But what if there were still some left?

"I don't want to get your hopes up too much, but I can't just give up like this. Please, give me at least one more day." Dick bowed deeply.

Looking slightly concerned, Leonhardt simply replied, "I'll hear your answer tomorrow, then."

(Lynx, can you hear me?)
Malraux contacted Lynx via telepathic communication, a

skill used to convey information to prior registered parties. Once a connection was established, both parties could communicate back and forth, but the transmission could only be initiated by Malraux. Though a bit inconvenient, this skill proved very useful in the army, something only few people possessed.

(Loud and clear, Lieutenant.)

(We are heading to Mariela's location immediately. It's likely we'll be followed, so create a diversion.)

(Roger. Mariela's in the center of the northwestern district, in a house with a sacred tree growing in the yard.)

Malraux and Dick mounted their raptors and departed the Margrave Schutzenwald estate, heading southwest toward the Labyrinth City.

The night sky was strikingly different from the previous night: It was cloudy and moonless. The two riders, including their raptor mounts, were black like shadows. The southwestern gate to the Fell Forest was already firmly shut. As they passed by, the pair dropped their speed a little and then headed for the west gate, a small one, perhaps to exit from there.

The person following them was on foot, yet didn't fall behind the speed of the raptors, staying closely on their tail. After reaching the west gate, the two riders continued to the northwestern, north, and northeastern gates in turn before entering the Black Iron Freight Corps's usual lodging, the Yagu Drawbridge Pavilion.

The lights of the inn illuminated the two raptors, revealing their bare, riderless backs.

While the raptors and the person tailing them had been making the rounds in the Labyrinth City, Malraux and Dick reached Mariela's shop on foot.

The shop had long since closed for the night, but they knocked on the front door.

"What could someone want at this hour?"

Siegmund, now so muscular they barely recognized him, emerged from inside. He'd previously been part of the Black Iron Freight Corps's "cargo," and Mariela had saved him.

"This is urgent business. We would like to speak with Miss Mariela."

After leading the two of them to the tearoom corner of the shop, Sieg went to get Mariela.

"Welcome back, Captain Dick and Lieutenant Malraux. Glad you're both all right." Mariela, as easygoing as always, greeted them with a smile.

"Actually, Miss Mariela, we—"

"A basilisk put a petrification curse on General Leonhardt, and he's dying. Our need is urgent. Would you provide us with a curse-removal potion?" Dick cut straight to the heart of the matter before Malraux could explain the situation.

Mariela placed her forefinger on her chin and went "Mm…" as she pondered for a moment. "A high-grade specialized curse removal? Sure thing. Just give me a minute or two, okay? Hey, Sieg, I'll need some help." She withdrew to the inner part of the shop with Sieg close behind.

I cannot believe she would have even something like a curse-removal potion…

Malraux was flabbergasted. What kind of storage facility did this girl have?

Mariela was probably changing clothes before heading to her storage facility in the Fell Forest to retrieve a curse-removal potion. Even if she had a monster-warding potion, the sun had already set. That slave Siegmund would be an insufficient escort just on his own. If Malraux and Dick also accompanied her, they might learn the location of the storage facility.

Malraux surveyed the shop interior, slightly hopeful. It resembled neither an apothecary nor a teahouse. It seemed the pair had disappeared into some sort of living area.

She sure is slow. For someone who is merely changing clothes, she's taking entirely too much time. Unbelievable!

Malraux's mind spun with worry: Did she leave the two of them behind so they wouldn't find out where her storage facility was? Or could she have run away? Mariela had cheerfully received them just moments prior, but not only had they shown up in the middle of the night fully armed and armored, they'd urged her to hand over a rare potion without sufficient explanation. Perhaps she felt such boorish behavior wasn't fitting of a business deal and planned to hide out.

I have to stop her! If she doesn't give us that potion, General Leonhardt will...! He is indispensable to both the Labyrinth Suppression Forces and the Labyrinth City. We cannot lose him......!

In a panic, Lieutenant Malraux stood up with such force he knocked over his chair and rushed toward the back of the shop where Mariela had disappeared.

"H-hey, Malraux!" Captain Dick followed him.

When he opened the door at the back of the shop, which continued to the living area, he found a corridor with a door to the rear garden at the end, and stairs to the second floor to the left of it. He rushed up to the door to the yard and noticed signs of life coming from the second floor.

Am I too late?

Malraux muffled his footsteps as he hurried up the stairs.

He could hear voices coming from a room at the end of the corridor on the second floor.

General Leonhardt's life depends on her. We cannot afford to let her escape.

Driven by his sense of duty, Malraux forgot himself and threw open the door.

"**Anchor Essence, Enclose.** Aaand done!"

And taking place in that room was something that shouldn't have been possible in the Labyrinth City—potion transmutation.

"..............???! Whaaat?!" Malraux's mouth gaped as wide as the open door at this seemingly unfeasible spectacle.

"Whaaa—? Eeeek?! S-Sieg, hide it, hide it!"

Mariela was pretty flustered herself. She figured Malraux had deduced she was an alchemist Pact-Bearer, but it was still confidential information. She'd gone up to this room to make the potion in secret just as a precaution, so she couldn't help being flustered at the sudden intrusion.

What's more, the room was also in considerable disorder, and in her discombobulated state, Mariela couldn't decide which aspect was more embarrassing for him to see.

"Geez, Malraux! I said to wait, didn't I? The room's a mess, so please, don't just barge in here like you own the place!" Mariela chided, huffy and upset for all the wrong reasons.

Only Sieg—who was diligently tidying up changes of clothes Mariela had scattered across the floor along with abandoned cups and recently used gadgets left in place—shot a meaningful look at the man who'd entered without permission before promptly evicting him from the room.

05

Led by Siegmund, Malraux and Dick returned to the first-floor shop.

Malraux ruminated as he drank his tea. *I'd thought we'd been talking circles around each other back then, but...*

He'd first picked up that something was off when she'd suggested a discount. After that, she'd repeated the same kinds of self-effacing lines: "Even if the prices go down, I'm just happy I can help out." "Potions are consumable goods. If I need money, I can just sell a lot of them."

The Labyrinth City's only potions had been manufactured and stored over a hundred years ago, and their quantity was limited. That's why they were so rare and were valued as assets.

So if we take this to mean she can make as many as she likes...?

Malraux had thought Mariela owned a large quantity of potions in a storage facility somewhere in the Fell Forest. Turns out that hadn't been the case. Indeed, she'd also spoken of procuring housing and money as fixed assets rather than potions.

Because she could make potions.

It wasn't the potions that were rare and valuable, but rather Mariela herself. He could understand why she would go as far as offer a discount to ensure her personal safety and prevent her secret from getting out.

If she simply possessed potions, at worst she could just relinquish them. The potions themselves, not their owner, had value, so if she escaped, her personal safety would be assured.

However, if an alchemist who could make potions existed in the Labyrinth City...

Her value was immeasurable. If it ever came to light, she would be pursued relentlessly.

"You remember the details of the contract, yes?" Sieg, who'd seemed eager to say something ever since Malraux had trespassed on Mariela's workshop—no, ever since he'd requested the potion—spoke up.

"Yes, of course I remember."

The confidentiality was a given, and in the unlikely event information leaked and Mariela was exposed to danger, the Black Iron Freight Corps would take it upon themselves to resolve the problem and, depending on the circumstances, even aid her in escape.

Of course Malraux remembered their agreement.

My goodness. A condition like that isn't worth a mere 10 percent increase of the handling fee. Shouldn't we be introducing someone as extraordinary as an alchemist to General Leonhardt?

However, they were bound by a magical contract. They couldn't tell a soul that this girl was an alchemist. The Black Iron Freight Corps alone wouldn't be able to get her out of a fix should her secret get exposed. And even if they helped her escape, where could she go?

I suppose that means we've been utterly and completely duped...

Malraux drank the rest of his lukewarm tea and looked at Dick.

"Dick, she's—"

"Mm? Yeah, she was an alchemist after all."

"What? Had you noticed?"

"Well, that guy... Sieg, was it? If she weren't an alchemist, she couldn't have saved him, right?"

It was true. Sieg was a slave who'd been brought to the Labyrinth City to die before his fellow slave cargo, to serve as an example so that they wouldn't want to perish like he had. That was the agreement made with the slave trader, Reymond. Even the price negotiation in front of the other slaves had been nothing more than a part of the entire stunt.

Sieg's wounds had been too deep to be cured with cheap potions alone, and his body was so weak that healing magic would have proved ineffectual. Heaven knows how much the cost of treatment would be. Few people would go that far to heal a penal laborer. It would've been cheaper to just buy a new slave. If an alchemist hadn't taken a lot of time to carefully treat him, he wouldn't have recovered as well as he had.

Even Dick had noticed, yet I completely—

Mariela entered the shop carrying a small bundle.

"This white potion is a high-grade specialized potion for removing curses, and this one is a cure potion. It's high grade, so if he drinks it after the curse is nullified, then it should cure the petrification, too," she explained. "These here are high-grade Regen pills. Make sure he takes these if he's been petrified for a while; the lasting strain on his body will linger even after it's been cured. I'm giving you a three-day supply. They taste bitter, so tell him to swallow them whole." Once she finished explaining, she put the valuable potions in a paper bag and handed it over. "Be sure to get your money's worth! These are pretty valuable, you know."

As expected, she did not name a price.

I'll bet she wouldn't complain even if she got only a few gold coins out of the exchange, thought Malraux. *She's probably willing to sell us her potions just so long as we don't mark them up by a ridiculous margin. Mariela understands her own worth as well as the value her potions have in this town, yet she still wants to sell them at a normal price.*

Malraux glanced at Dick.

They really are the same. I suppose I ought to be pleased with this interesting turn of events.

In which case... Malraux thought it pointless to try to negotiate with Mariela, but he offered her a proposal despite being well aware that she was the kind of person who wasn't so satisfied with the way things "should" be.

"Miss Mariela, General Leonhardt wishes for potions."

"Which kinds and how many?"

"A large quantity, I'm quite sure."

"I wonder if I have enough materials..."

"If we arranged for the materials, could you make us as many as we wanted?"

"As many as my magical reserves will let me, sure. Ah, but I might not have enough potion vials."

"But the prices may be low. It's possible that you'll sell them at the same cost as potion in the imperial capital."

"Oh, that doesn't bother me."

"Miss Mariela," Malraux said calmly. He paused for a moment, then looked at her. "Would you work under General Leonhardt with us?"

Leonhardt, the most influential person in the Labyrinth City, would be the next margrave. There was no place safer than under his protection. However, Mariela considered for a little while and then replied.

"I want to live a nice, quiet life here in the city. I'd like it if we came up with a way for me to stay here while still supplying potions."

Not even a month had passed since she'd come to the Labyrinth City, but she'd made a lot of acquaintances. She had customers who came every day to enjoy tea and bask in the sunlight. She wanted to try gathering materials in the Labyrinth and the Fell Forest, too. The thousand-night flowers Ghark had showed her were beautiful. Finding unusual foods in the market to cook and eat with Sieg was fun as well.

If she were under General Leonhardt's protection, maybe she wouldn't need to hide the fact she was an alchemist anymore. She'd probably spend her days holed up all safe and secure in a cage making potions.

Mariela recalled her little cottage in the Fell Forest. She'd only lived alone there for a few years, but she'd made potions in a room all by herself in total silence. That in itself wasn't terrible; she'd always been the type to get completely absorbed in something.

But once in a blue moon, in that room that grew completely dark by the time she'd finished working, a certain thought would suddenly occur to Mariela: *Geez, I'm so alone!* Even when the room was a complete mess, nobody tidied it up for her, and nobody got mad at her for it, either. She'd spend her meals among the mess, shoveling food into her mouth before crawling into her disheveled bed. For some reason, she always felt so cold at bedtime and would sleep curled up in a ball.

Mariela imagined a life under General Leonhardt would be pretty similar.

She liked her life the way it was now.

In recent days, Sieg had become a tad strict. He would pick up stuff Mariela had tossed onto the floor and ask, "Is this burnable trash? Or trash for the slime tank? Which is it?" then insist she choose one or the other. But even this contributed to make every day pleasantly joyful and comfy.

After considering Mariela's reply for a short while, Malraux answered, "Understood. Let's come up with a proper strategy, then."

Ahh, I thought as much.

Malraux chuckled to himself—half exasperated, half sincere.

The future was almost certain to bring annoyances, tribulations, difficulties, and some interesting things, too.

CHAPTER 1

Peaceful Days

01

"Ugh, so cold…"

Mariela awoke as she always did: with every single blanket she'd piled on herself fallen onto the floor, save for one. Of course she was cold.

After getting dressed, she headed for the medicinal herb garden in the backyard. Sieg was already up and had just finished his morning training. The two of them picked herbs and watered the plants. It was said the stronger the magical elements, the easier it was for typical medicinal herbs to propagate. They could even grow outside of human domains, such as in the Fell Forest and the Labyrinth.

"Is it all right to pick this many?" Sieg asked. Mariela was freely harvesting herbs to the point where they were getting sparse.

"Yeah, it's fine. These varieties will grow back in a few days no matter the season. I'm grateful not to be short on materials, but if herbs grow this fast, the Labyrinth City really does feel like a region of monsters even with all the people living here."

She gave water infused with Drops of Life to the sacred tree. Of course, she'd prepared it inside and put it in a watering can so as not to catch anyone's attention. The tree seemed to love magical water; it dropped a ton of leaves for Mariela the first time she tried giving it some. At first, she'd panicked—"You'll wilt!

You're gonna go bald!"—but the trunk and leaves had somehow turned glossy, so ever since then she'd been preparing Drops of Life-infused water for the sacred tree and receiving leaves as thanks.

Once they'd finished tending the garden, Sieg and Mariela had breakfast. Afterward, the two of them divided up the cleaning, laundry, and shelf displays, then opened up the shop.

They sent items needed for urgent injuries and illnesses to healers and set aside emergency supplies such as salves and smoke bombs for the Adventurers Guild shop. Citizens seeking medicine, adventurers on their days off, and regulars wanting to bask in the sun visited Mariela's shop. Although the foot traffic in and out of the shop never really slowed down, time still passed at a leisurely, comfortable pace. Mariela spent the day affixing labels to salve tins and placing wrapped pills in bags while enjoying tea and chatting with her customers.

Incidentally, she'd received a tea set from Malraux as a gift celebrating the shop's opening. It included a card that read "My utmost apologies for intruding on your room." The set had an excessive number of cups for two people, leading Mariela to believe it was actually intended for her business.

I keep telling people it's not a café!

Mariela wanted to grill Malraux about the gift more than his barging into her workshop.

She drank tea with Merle of Merle's Spices and Amber from the Yagu Drawbridge Pavilion until just before noon. The spice shop had a dedicated delivery person—why had Merle herself shown up?

"Mariela, ever since you started serving my tea here, my sales have increased, too! Oh, this one's a new product. I decided to try using tea leaves that enhance beauty."

"Beauty?! Ela, I'd like to try it, too!" Amber exclaimed. With that, they formed a new ladies' group.

Merle seemed to be influential among the housewives in this neighborhood, and Mariela started gaining more customers through word of mouth. And since Mariela's apothecary was so popular, it didn't seem out of place when she received deliveries of medicinal herbs and alchemic materials from all over the place.

At lunchtime, Lynx came to visit.

Or rather, almost every day the shop was open, he would bring food he'd bought at the market and eat lunch at Mariela's shop, Sunlight's Canopy.

Not long after Mariela provided the high-grade petrification removal potion, the Black Iron Freight Corps had constructed a base in the Labyrinth City and stationed three of its members there. The base was located near the outer wall's west gate, an area not so popular with everyday citizens since it faced the Fell Forest—but the rent was cheap, and many novice adventurers lived nearby. Everyone in the Black Iron Freight Corps knew how to fight, so the location wasn't a problem for them, but since it wasn't a very safe area, Mariela had been told not to visit.

With the monster-warding potions Mariela supplied, the Corps could now lighten their carriages' armor, and they didn't need raptor-mounted guards. Of course, they lightened the armor in a discreet enough way so that no one could tell they were using potions, and their formation remained the same: two riders, three armored carriages. Since they were able to reduce their fighting power, the Corps also purchased three slaves who could drive carriages to replace the three members who remained in the Labyrinth City.

Those three Corps members alternated on a regular basis, and currently it was Lieutenant Malraux, Lynx, and the dual wielder Edgan. Dividing up the team meant the group staying behind could gather the cargo to be shipped next in their base's warehouse while the transport group was away, thus shortening the trip back and forth and increasing profits. At least, they were working under that pretense.

Mariela had signed a confidentiality agreement regarding potions with all members of the Black Iron Freight Corps, aside from the new slaves. Although the fact she was an alchemist hadn't been explicitly stated, Lynx appeared to have figured it out.

"This isn't a café! And no outside food, either. Excuse me, sir, you're disrupting business."

The "no outside food" rule sure made the place sound like a café, though.

"Don't be so stuffy, Mariela. Look, I bought some cockatrice egg galettes. Let's eat 'em together." Lynx handed a bundle containing souvenirs to Mariela, who was pouting.

"Guess I can't say no. Siiieg, we got galettes! Let's have an early lunch. Oh, Lynx, this is a new soap we just got. Take it with you."

"Want me to cook some sausages, too? Are you okay with fruit juice?"

"Ooh, yeah, sausages. Thanks, Sieg."

They obviously couldn't eat in the shop, where there were other customers, so the three of them sat and ate at a table in the adjoining kitchen. The fact that this area used to be a restaurant wasn't such a bad thing after all; this setup allowed Mariela to quickly tend to any customers who came by. Mariela threw the galette packaging into the slime tank. Slimes digested things like food scraps and paper with grease stuck to it without leaving any trace. They were very convenient.

"Oh right. Here's your souvenirs. There's been a lotta commotion since I got back, so I forgot to give 'em to ya," said Lynx as he fished something out of his pocket. "Gotcha an eye patch, Sieg. Kinda nifty, don'cha think? This's for you, Mariela. It's got a trick to it. Ya just do like so, and see, the locket opens."

Apparently, Lynx had brought them souvenirs from the imperial capital as a token of his gratitude for the cookies she'd made. He handed an eye patch to Sieg and a locket with an unusual contraption to Mariela.

"Huh? How'd you do that? I can't get it to open at all..."

The locket had been precisely crafted into the shape of a teardrop, designed to be opened by moving several parts like a three-dimensional puzzle. Opening it revealed the spherical hollow inside.

"I toldya, like this, and then do this. See? Open."

As Mariela went "Errm" and cocked her head in confusion, Lynx produced a pebble about the size of a fingertip.

"Here's a li'l bonus for ya. Real pretty, right?"

"A ley-line shard?! You can use these in special-grade potions!"

Lynx offered her the ley-line shard he'd obtained from the black death wolves the Black Iron Freight Corps had encountered on their way back to the Labyrinth City. It had been inside the largest wolf, which Lynx killed.

"Whoaaa, incredible!" Mariela exclaimed starry-eyed. A flicker of mischief crossed Lynx's mind.

"Ya put this ley-line shard into the locket, and ta-daa, it's sealed. Do your best to get it open."

"Hey, I didn't even get a good look at it yet! Urgh! It won't open! Lyyynx!!"

"Ha-ha. Well, good luck! Sieg, don't you dare help her!"

After hanging the drop-shaped trick locket around Mariela's neck, Lynx helped himself to the soap and chuckled happily as he went home.

From that point until closing time, Mariela ignored her customers as she struggled with the locket's trick. She'd wanted to take her sweet time inspecting the ley-line shard, but the locket just wouldn't open. At any rate, she couldn't make special-grade potions yet. The locket itself was pretty cute, so she decided to completely give up on prying it open and forget about its contents.

The shop closed after afternoon tea. Mariela and Sieg went to the Adventurers Guild to deliver goods and buy any necessary materials. They also stopped by the wholesale market to scope out any interesting bargains.

The Labyrinth Suppression Forces' expedition had ended about a week ago, but there were rare consumables and potion ingredients still to be found, so she couldn't let an opportunity pass her by.

The two of them returned home after buying ingredients for dinner, which Mariela cooked. All the recipes in the Library were extraordinary, certainly on par with what the owner of the Yagu Drawbridge Pavilion could make. When dinner was over, Mariela shut herself in her atelier to make medicine and potions while Sieg trained.

It would soon be time.

Mariela and Sieg headed to the cellar.

The cellar had three rooms linked sequentially. When they waited in the room at the very center, they could hear a faint noise coming from deep underground.

Bang, bang, bang.

It sounded like something striking a stone far away.

Clang, clang, clang-clang.

They hit the metal door with a fixed rhythm in return.

After a little while, a knock came from the door to the third room that ought to have been a dead end. They confirmed it was the beat they'd decided on ahead of time, and then Sieg unlocked the door to the third room.

"Hey Mariela, Sieg, good evening."

"Are these today's goods?"

Lynx and Lieutenant Malraux stood in the third room, which nobody should have been in.

"Man, they really widened this thing all right," said Lynx, sounding both impressed and surprised. The cellar wall originally filled in by the carpenter Gordon had been demolished again, and a path had been opened to the underground Aqueduct.

They'd devised this method of trade so no one would realize Mariela was the source of the potions.

Medicinal herbs were necessary for her to do her job. The kinds she could harvest in her garden were limited, and to make large quantities of potions, she had to buy the materials in bulk, including rare ones. She bought the items that wouldn't be strange for a chemist to want a little at a time from different merchants and had them delivered during the apothecary's business hours. Since the people delivering the goods usually enjoyed some tea before leaving, it was difficult for observers to figure out why they'd come.

The Black Iron Freight Corps bought up rare medicinal herbs

and materials and gathered them in their base's storehouse—nothing out of the ordinary for a transportation group. At night, they carried the materials into Sunlight's Canopy's cellar through the underground Aqueduct, and left with potions in exchange.

Any needed potions and materials were either discussed during a meeting in the cellar or written in a memo hidden in a paper bag containing Lynx's lunch. These memos were tossed into the slime tank and decomposed by the slime, leaving behind absolutely zero evidence. The "soap" Mariela gave to Lynx was the signal that the potions were ready to be traded. Though it resembled a package of soap, inside was a mid-grade monster-warding potion.

A large number of slimes had been appearing in the underground Aqueduct. Slimes were weak monsters, but since they had no sense of smell, low-grade monster-warding potions and incense had no effect on them. If there were only a few slimes, you could get through by trampling them underfoot, but since the slimes had been strangely multiplying, you would now have to wade through their acidic liquid. Without a mid-grade monster-warding potion to keep away high-ranking orcs and lizardmen, not to mention slimes, making it through the underground Aqueduct was almost impossible.

The ingredients for a mid-grade monster-warding potion were bromominthra, daigis, and the leaves of a sacred tree, all of which Mariela could obtain from her herb garden.

There was always somebody or other in Mariela's shop while it was open, and after it closed, she only walked through the town with Sieg. Late at night when the gates to the Labyrinth City were shut, neither of them left the house. People who thought the potions were brought from a storage facility somewhere probably turned their attention on the Black Iron Freight Corps, and even in the unlikely event they focused on the goods being brought to and from Mariela's house, there was nothing unusual about those items to tip them off. So, the odds of them suspecting Mariela and Sieg were low, and they would probably quickly lose interest in the two.

"These are the bones from a bone knight, as you requested. You can use these to make high-grade specialized potions for healing fractures, yes?"

Malraux set down a box packed with humanoid bones. They made a dry rattling sound as they bumped together.

"I can, but I don't recommend potions like that. If you use one incorrectly, the bone might heal in the wrong position." Mariela hid behind Sieg as she answered and looked at the bones.

Those things are freaky! What if they come back together and attack me?!

Lynx figured out what she was thinking and took a bone in one hand and imitated the monster from behind Malraux.

"That will not be a problem. The Labyrinth Suppression Forces are staffed with medical technicians."

Medical technicians—yet another new term. Sensing that providing Mariela with a full explanation would just add to her confusion, Malraux gave her a simple one.

"Since magic and potions are both finite resources, a medical team is responsible for managing the effective use of healing magic and potions. They have a thorough knowledge of the human body and perform treatments that use the minimum possible amount of these finite resources."

"I see," Mariela replied, ignoring Lynx, who was trying to scare her with his bone knight imitation. Malraux had a thorough knowledge of her, too, which is why he gave her the minimum possible explanation.

She handed over what they'd ordered—a hundred high-grade specialized potions for healing damaged muscles—then received the fee, empty potion vials, and materials she'd asked for.

"See ya tomorrow, Mariela, Sieg."

Lynx and Malraux picked up the box of potions and disappeared into the underground Aqueduct.

02

Finding the route through the underground Aqueduct had been somewhat of an accident.

It had been around ten days ago. Mariela went with Sieg to the Merchants Guild to let them know about the opening of her shop. Elmera, the chair of the Medicinal Herbs Division, was absent, so they were greeted by the vice chairman, Leandro.

"Goodness, that's quite a lovely shop by the sound of it. Ms. Elmera has been anxious to visit. Maybe I'll swing by some day, too. Ah, here's a letter of introduction for the Adventurers Guild shop. Ms. Elmera entrusted me with it."

When Mariela came with presents and an assortment of samples from her shop, she was given a letter of introduction for the Adventurers Guild shop on the spot.

I'm grateful and all, but isn't this coming together a little too fast? Is it really okay?

Mariela felt a little lost, so Leandro added, "You and Ms. Elmera can discuss medicinal herbs over tea when she comes to visit," to alleviate some of the awkwardness.

How did this whole café thing reach all the way to Leandro...? I mean, it's not a bad thing, but...

Sieg and Mariela departed the Merchants Guild and approached the wholesale market to find it extremely crowded. They discovered upon getting closer there was a Kraken Dissection Show going on. Countless giant mollusks as big as carriages were being unloaded, and men with huge knives prepped every last one of them, slicing them up and thrusting skewers through their bodies before finally cooking them. The cost—just one copper coin per skewer!

It was frighteningly cheap. At a price like that, Mariela just had to buy some. That settled tonight's dinner.

The marketplace bustled with throngs upon throngs of people: those who came to buy uncooked skewers, those who came to buy them cooked, and those who simply came to watch the show.

"Incredible! Where'd they find so many krakens?"

"I heard there were tons of 'em on the thirtieth stratum."

"I thought krakens lived around the fortieth?"

"Listen, we're in the middle of taking over the Labyrinth, and apparently adventurers are all gathered on the thirtieth stratum."

"So you're sayin' someone defeated these things? If this much meat, that's gotta mean there were a crazy number of 'em, yeah?"

"I hear the Lightning Empress showed up."

"Really? Aw, wish I coulda seen her!"

"Ha-ha-ha! I saw Lightning Empress Elsee! Only from a distance, though."

"Damn, I'm jealous. She as gorgeous as people say?"

"I said it was from a distance. Only thing I could see was the flash of light."

"What? Get outta here."

Mariela and Sieg listened to the conversations of people around them as they stood in line for the kraken skewers.

Lightning Empress Elsee appeared to be a young A-Rank adventurer within the Labyrinth City bestowed with powerful lightning magic under the protection of the god of thunder.

She wore a suit made of special material over her shapely body, and her long, pale, electrified hair seemed to billow out behind her. Along with the perfectly fitted suit and hair emitting a bright light, the tinted glasses she wore to protect her eyes meant no one could tell who she was. However, the red lipstick coloring her mouth that curved cheerfully upward was bewitching. The powerful electric shocks she sent out from her graceful limbs most certainly earned her the title of Lightning Empress. The fact she was rarely seen in public and nobody knew her identity only increased her appeal. "I want her to zap me with one of her electric shocks!" seemed to be a common sentiment among her fans.

A-Rank adventurers were greatly admired in the Labyrinth City; S-Rank adventurers were treated as legendary heroes.

"She sounds incredible, Sieg. I'd like to meet her, too!"

"This city's pretty small, so you just might."

All sorts of interesting things were taking place—just what you'd expect during an expedition period.

After buying their skewers, the two headed behind the dissection show. There was something Mariela wanted.

"Excuse meee, I'd like to purchase some kraken innards!"

"And just what're you gonna do with somethin' like that, young lady?" asked the shopkeeper with a quizzical look. "If it's fillets you're lookin' for, you can get some for cheap over there."

Mariela babbled an incoherent explanation. "Oh, uh, they have all sorts of different uses and stuff..."

"............Are they tasty?" the shopkeeper asked with a bewildered expression, to which Mariela dodged the question by giggling, "Heh-heh-heh," and he packaged up the intestines she needed. Mariela and Sieg took the bag full of the kraken innards and hurried home. Behind them, the shopkeeper picked up a piece of intestine, put it in his mouth, and violently spit it out.

"Mariela, those intestines aren't for eating, right?" Sieg fearfully asked after they'd gotten home. Mariela had just pulverized the organs, turning them into a muddy, viscous liquid.

"This here's the good stuff. Kraken entrails are hard to come by, let alone ones this fresh. Heh-heh-heh!"

Mariela divided the gooey liquid entrails into small bottles, putting on a show for Sieg. She purposefully placed the bottles down low and poured the liquid into them from high above, making the room smell a little briny. She meant to imitate a waiter in a fancy café, but clearly this wasn't the time or place for it.

After dividing the liquid entrails into ten or so small bottles, Mariela and Sieg headed to the innermost room of the cellar.

The two of them looked quite ridiculous in their getups.

They each wore two large creeper rubber sacks: one as pants, another over their heads with only a hole for their faces. A cord was tied around their waists, and they'd smeared lard over their exposed faces until they gleamed, then put goggles over their eyes and masks over their mouths. The goggles and masks were cheap items sold by the Adventurers Guild for novice adventurers, and their design emphasized functionality while completely disregarding appearance, so they only enhanced the pair's oddness.

"Well?" Sieg, clad in the same bizarre attire, pressing Mariela for a reasonable explanation. He held a pickax she'd given him.

"We're going to catch slimes in the underground Aqueduct. Now, destroy the wall, if you please."

Operation Slime-in-a-Vial—biosynthesis—had begun.

03

A Slime-in-a-Vial was a synthetic organism occasionally found in alchemy shops and the like.

The viscous liquid from a kraken was even higher quality than snapping clams and ghost clams, which were components of Regen medicine. It could be used in their place or in special-grade potions. The fluids had already been drained from the krakens in the wholesale market, and krakens themselves were quite rare, so the material was difficult to get ahold of.

Some alchemic materials were only formed inside monsters' bodies. Things like ghost clams and snapping clams were relatively easy to obtain, but it was difficult to get a steady supply of scarce materials that only came from rare and powerful monsters like krakens.

Slime synthesis was devised to solve this kind of problem.

Despite the complex-sounding name, transmuting these organisms didn't involve any advanced forms of sorcery. The method used a slime's own recovery abilities, and it was believed an alchemist invented it when she happened to witness a slime nucleus that had fallen into a puddle of blood absorb the blood around it to regenerate itself.

Making it was simple. After removing the nucleus from a slime and inscribing it with a Magic Circle of Subordination, you simply transferred it to viscous liquid made from the tissues of the monster in question.

Because the regenerated slime would have all the characteristics of the material and become stronger than the original, the Magic Circle of Subordination was indispensable to safely keep the creature. If you dripped your blood into the carved magic circle, the slime wouldn't attack you, recognizing you as its master. Also, the creature would weaken and die if not given magical power from its master for a few days, so there was little fear of it becoming a problem even in the unlikely event it escaped.

Taking care of the slime was simple, too. You kept it in a glass vial with a valve at the bottom to retrieve its secretions. The container was equipped with a three-legged platform inside so the secretions accumulated at the bottom. The slime sat on top of the platform, and the secretions were collected at the bottom of the vial from the gap between the platform and the container. Though a slime was gloopy, its internal nucleus was solid, which meant the creature couldn't pass through anything its nucleus couldn't. Since the outer shell was gummy, it was extremely vulnerable to magic absorption. So if you covered the area around the vial's lid and valve with a mesh cage woven from the ivy of the magic-absorbing daigis plant, the slime would quietly stay around the center of the vial.

Slimes themselves were widely used throughout town to decompose and purify things like wastewater and garbage, but there were also many uses for the acidic liquid they secreted. Giving them special feed to stabilize this liquid allowed it to have a wide range of applications. For example, it could be a means of attacking monsters, a component in the manufacturing process of a variety of goods, or a way of removing stains from clothes and tableware when diluted with water. Some merchants even specialized in breeding slimes, and containers for slime breeding were sold over the counter.

Of course, not just anyone could buy them, but when Mariela showed her chemist approval letter issued by the Merchants Guild, they were readily sold to her.

Although the population of slimes synthesized with the tissue of other monsters was small, in a big town they were handled similarly to regular slimes that produced acidic liquid. The Magic Circle of Subordination inscribed on the nucleus was simple, and since its difficulty was the same as magic circles inscribed on high-grade potion vials, it was not hard as a skill.

However, its success rate was extremely low.

Approximately 70 percent of slimes died when their nuclei were removed. When the Magic Circle of Subordination was carved into a removed nucleus that was still alive, there was an 80 percent chance that the slime would die. When the blood of the human who wanted to be the slime's master was dripped onto the carved nucleus, another half of the slimes had a negative reaction and died. Even if you skillfully transferred a slime nucleus with a magic circle into the viscous liquid of the creature you wanted it to fuse with, the odds of it being able to regenerate as a slime were less than 10 percent.

Collecting several hundred slimes was the most difficult part of making a Slime-in-a-Vial, but an ideal place for this existed underneath Mariela and Sieg's house.

The underground Aqueduct.

After breaking the previously repaired underground wall, Sieg and Mariela descended.

The border between the cellar and the sacred tree's roots was a gap large enough for one person to pass through, and it continued as a steep slope. They used the tree's roots and the soil between them as footholds as they went down. The masonry thought to be the ceiling of the underground Aqueduct had crumbled and a hole big enough for people to go through gaped open. The roots of the sacred tree extended into the water supply and the pair continued to use them as footholds on their way down. Illuminating the place with light magic revealed that this appeared to be a small stream—something too narrow to be called a giant waterway. They also saw a path built for people to travel along the canal, maybe for maintenance purposes. The footpath had crumbled in several places, and cracks had formed in the walls. They could tell the underground Aqueduct was an old structure.

Mariela and Sieg saw no trace of the sacred tree or slimes in the part of the underground Aqueduct directly below the house. Sediment that appeared to have fallen when it had caved in also seemed to have been cleaned up by the carpenter Gordon, as it had been collected against one of the walls, and the water current hadn't been clogged up from its debris.

The pair advanced downstream, and after traversing the approximate length of several houses, they saw an overabundance of slimes up ahead mushed together on one end of the stream as if a line had been drawn that they couldn't go past. Maybe the sacred tree's divine protection went no farther than that. The slimes had probably been attracted to the spot in reaction to the presence of Mariela and Sieg. They rapidly gathered not just on the floor, but also on the walls and ceiling, too, and even the canal. It was revolting.

Even though they were weak monsters that died if you stepped on their nuclei, there were too many of them. If you went into a place like this, slimes would cover your entire body in an instant and you'd suffocate or be crushed to death. Even if you wore protective clothing, they'd get into the gaps and dissolve your body until not even your bones remained.

Sieg took position at the very edge of the boundary so as not to leave the protection of the sacred tree, and then he seized a slime using bags made from creeper rubber as gloves. He then plunged his hand into the slime's soft body, pulled out the nucleus, and handed it to Mariela behind him.

Some of the slimes sprayed their acid at him, but his protective rubber clothing kept him safe, and as long as it was washed at regular intervals with water magic while he worked, there would be no problem. Any slime that leaped at a limb extending beyond the sacred tree's protection had its nucleus pulled out in midair, and Sieg then dropped its soft body onto the ground where it became food for its cohorts.

Sieg worked in silence as he tore nuclei from slimes.

What impressive dexterity! Sieg's practically a professional slime nucleus remover! He's like one of those guys in the kraken dissection show.

Mariela was deeply impressed as she checked the nuclei. Of course, there was no such thing as a slime-nucleus-removing pro.

CHAPTER 1: Peaceful Days

"Dead... This one's no good, either... Oh, this one's alive...or it was, until I broke it with the magic circle."

She flung dead nuclei in the direction of the slimes. Since there were so many of the creatures, even Mariela, who had no hand-eye coordination, could hit them, and it was kind of fun to see them spurt out acid in response.

By a stroke of luck, the Slime-in-a-Vial was successfully created on slime number 273. But rather than decreasing, the number of slimes gathered outside the protection of the sacred tree had only grown.

"Mariela, they may be slimes, but isn't this many a problem?"
"Ugh, definitely."

The underground Aqueduct must not have had much in the way of food as this accumulated a large number of slimes. Although they were small fry, it probably wasn't a good idea to let them be.

"Feels like a bit of a waste, but..." Mariela took several potion vials out of her bag and dumped the contents of one into the canal.

The entire body of water quivered, and the slimes lurking within died instantly before floating downstream.

"Whoa, mid-grade monster-warding potions are that effective on slimes?!"

When Sieg used wind magic to spray a mid-grade monster-warding potion, the slimes on the wall, floor, and ceiling squirted out liquid and shriveled up as if wilting, then dropped to the floor and died.

Mid-grade monster-warding potions keep orcs and lizardmen and the like away, so Sieg had sprayed one thinking it would scatter the slimes. But the creatures, with their mucous membranes, had seemingly absorbed it into their bodies, and this potion demonstrated its excellent effects on them. Even the survivors scattered and fled in an instant, leaving the Aqueduct clear once again.

Since so many slimes had been in one place, it would probably be best to wash the walls and floor, and they couldn't let the slime corpses clog the canal. After putting the successful Slime-in-a-Vial in a breeding container to keep in the cellar for the time being, Mariela and Sieg sprinkled a mid-grade monster-warding potion on themselves and went to inspect and clean the underground Aqueduct.

The waterway under the house was seemingly just a tributary after all. It traveled downstream for a while before branching off and connecting to a roaring canal worthy of the name "the underground Aqueduct." The sheer size of it was akin to that of a channel. There was no path for people to take; perhaps it had been washed away long ago.

More than half of the sewage and rainwater in the Labyrinth City must have flowed into this gigantic canal.

As for where the water was headed, it was beyond what the pair could see.

"Mariela, we can't go any farther." She had been leaning forward to try and get a better look, but Sieg held her back. He seemed to be saying this wasn't a good place to give in to curiosity.

"Guess you're right."

The two of them left the giant canal with its thunderous water and returned to the tributary junction. Most of the water running through it had been designed to flow into the canal. But the tributary itself continued downstream as if it was a channel that had been set up to prevent any flooding from heavy rain. Just to be on the safe side, they followed it downstream to check it out. Trench drains flowing from houses and forks running into the giant canal repeated at regular intervals in the tributary. Sometimes the channels from the tributary to the giant canal intersected, conveying a sense of the vastness of the underground Aqueduct.

Mariela and Sieg examined the tributary they were following, but no matter where they looked, nothing in terms of structure or deterioration seemed to have changed much, and no monsters approached them due to the mid-grade monster-warding potion they'd applied. Although a lot of slimes had appeared just a short while ago, there seemed to be no particular problems. Just as she thought about turning around, she saw a faint light ahead in the channel.

It was the exit.

"This used to be the edge of the Citadel City. Oh, and over there—isn't that the west gate to Labyrinth City?"

The channel stretched from the west gate of the Labyrinth City to a little way into the Fell Forest. The Fell Forest now engulfed the far reaches of where the Citadel City had once spread. The grating at the channel's exit was half rotted, and although it had a hole big enough for people to slip through, the daigis and bromominthra growing thickly there apparently prevented monsters from intruding.

The underground Aqueduct seemed to have drainage channels other than the tributary Mariela and Sieg had followed. Almost all the drainage flowed through the giant canal, but there were probably other channels that connected outside of the Labyrinth City.

The city faced the Fell Forest and had a Labyrinth at its center. A great waterway crawling with slimes flowed underfoot and even went into the Fell Forest.

The Labyrinth City's full of people, but maybe life in the Fell Forest isn't so different, Mariela thought.

04

After receiving the high-grade potions from Mariela, Malraux and Lynx followed the underground Aqueduct downstream. Thanks to the outstanding effects of the mid-grade monster-warding potion, they didn't even come across a single slime. The pathway was old and crumbling in several places, not to mention wet and slippery, but it didn't particularly bother them. They were only careful enough to make sure the potions they carried didn't break, and they hurried to the exit without stopping.

(Edgan, how are our surroundings?)

(No problems here, Lieutenant.)

Malraux and Lynx quickly slipped through the open west gate after checking in with Edgan. Nobody used this gate, which was adjacent to the Fell Forest. It was usually closed, and guards patrolled it at fixed intervals. As long as one avoided those patrols, it wasn't terribly difficult to go in and out. The Black Iron Freight Corps's base lay just beyond the gate.

Upon reaching the base, Malraux and Lynx transferred the potions, which had been sloppily packed along with a sorry excuse of cushioning material in the wooden box, into expensive and portable potion cases, then packed each case into the box. After loading the box onto a raptor newly purchased for transport within the Labyrinth City, they headed to the base of the Labyrinth Suppression Forces.

What a clever little trick we discovered.
Malraux thought back to the underground Aqueduct.

He had known about the Aqueduct itself, including how it was overrun with slimes. No one would think they would consume rare mid-grade potions to pass through, and even in the unlikely event they were followed, their pursuers couldn't go anywhere without one of those potions themselves. Although it was just a short distance from the underground Aqueduct to the Labyrinth City's west gate, it required going through the Fell Forest. Nowhere could they be easily followed without a monster-warding potion.

It probably didn't take long for others to figure out that the Black Iron Freight Corps possessed potions, but no one knew where they came from. Anyone who kept an eye on the iron carriages couldn't follow them through the Fell Forest. Even on the off chance the carriages were attacked, Dick rode in one of them. And he was not a man who could be defeated without a fight.

Their base's defenses were sparse, but even if it was raided, there were only ordinary goods to be found inside. The Black Iron Freight Corps delivered the potions to the Labyrinth Suppression Forces immediately upon receipt, and there were no documents to prove they carried potions in the first place. Any extraneous documentation was disposed of in slime tanks, so even if the base were searched end to end, it would appear no different from an ordinary distribution facility.

In any case, the potions were headed for the Labyrinth Suppression Forces. No fool would rob the Black Iron Freight Corps out in the open. Even if someone did manage to sneak in, the Corps was accustomed to skirmishes. After catching the perpetrator, they'd hand him over to the Labyrinth Suppression Forces, who would skillfully deal with the problem. As long as Mariela didn't get captured, there were all sorts of ways to handle any issues that arose.

Malraux and Lynx arrived at the Labyrinth Suppression Forces' base on the southeast side of the Labyrinth under the pretense of delivering goods brought from the imperial capital. People seemed to be buying their story that they were delivering small quantities of luxury items from their base to the Force's top brass. Malraux and Lynx had already delivered potions several times by now, and they were led in a familiar fashion to the underground storehouse.

"Been expecting you. Today's delivery is the high-grade specialized kind for muscular tissue, I believe."

A man around forty years old with black stubble and a sharp glint in his eye was waiting.

He had helped Malraux and Dick in the past, and to this very day, they still owed him a great debt.

"Medical Technician Jack Nierenberg. This is today's delivery. Please confirm the contents."

Malraux handed Nierenberg the box, and the man's subordinates inspected it nearby.

"With tomorrow's specialized potions for bone fractures, we'll be able to heal a great number of soldiers. And the timing couldn't be more perfect for a shipment this large," mumbled

Nierenberg. He seemed to imply they'd be able to heal those wounded in the expedition a few days prior.

When Leonhardt was hit with a petrification curse by a basilisk, the Labyrinth Suppression Forces teetered on the edge of annihilation. The front lines had been on the fifty-third stratum, a hellish place rife with S-Rank monsters. The Forces stormed the area with over a hundred units, but more than half the soldiers were B Rank and no match for these enemies. It was largely the effect of the Gold Lion General Leonhardt's inherent skill, Lion's Roar, that enabled the Labyrinth Suppression Forces to advance that far.

Lion's Roar boosts all the abilities of Leonhardt's forces by 50 percent, raising their powers to the equivalent of an A-Rank force and thus making it possible to advance in the stratum where S-Rank monsters lurked.

And then Leonhardt fell.

His body suddenly began to turn to stone before their eyes, and the army's abilities that his skill had raised decreased. Healing magic couldn't handle petrification of such speed. What saved Leonhardt were the high-grade cure potions that had been brought in just before the expedition. Applying one to petrified areas healed them, and drinking it slowed its progression. Petrification from a basilisk was in the form of a curse, so no matter how many times a potion removed the condition on the surface, it would start to advance again. Although they'd managed to defeat the basilisk that had inflicted the curse and thus weakened its progression, the curse was not removed.

They used healing magic to slow the progression of the petrification, and they used high-grade cure potions when it had progressed too far. Meanwhile, the army gradually retreated.

How many soldiers had fallen?

It was most likely thanks to Leonhardt's younger brother Weishardt's precise instructions and the soldiers' diligent daily training that the Forces were able to survive until the Adventurers Guild's guildmaster Haage's party came rushing in. Nierenberg's medical team continued their desperate treatment amid the melee. They couldn't let the soldiers die. Those who'd achieved B Rank and were skilled at coordinated fighting were valuable. Their legs may have been torn off, their arms may have been shredded, but if the limbs were picked up, they could be put back together later.

A healer's magic was required to remove Leonhardt's petrification. Only a little could be spared to heal the soldiers. The bare minimum healing needed for them to survive was achieved with potions. The new medicine provided by the Aguinas family was used liberally. The supposedly mid-grade red potions were weak, while the black ones, claimed to be high grade, varied wildly in their effectiveness.

The new medicine supplied by the Aguinas family wasn't nearly enough on its own. With the sixty potions Malraux and Lynx brought, the forces were just barely able to survive.

Those potions worked so well, it was astonishing. The high- and mid-grade ones had been exhausted, and they had relied on low-grade ones that had even saved soldiers' lives.

The low-grade monster-warding potions clearly weakened the monsters' pursuit. They really were incredibly effective—practically freshly made.

Nierenberg felt it was a miracle that with how much damage they'd sustained, only a small number of people died. Many had hands and feet torn off, bones broken, flesh gouged, and organs ruptured, but they'd managed to keep them alive. Their torn-off limbs were reattached just enough so they wouldn't rot.

And they'd even received the proper amount of potions needed for treatment.

If healing magic was used for bone fractures, it would consume a lot of magical power, and only a few patients per day could receive it before it ran out. However, if they received a delivery of high-grade specialized potions for bone fractures, this wouldn't be a problem. It would probably allow many people to be healed.

Now then, we've got the specialized muscular tissue potions. Time to begin treatment.

Medical Technician Nierenberg grinned.

We'll start with the one with the busted-open stomach. The damaged organs were treated with healing magic, but without enough stamina, the patient's flesh remained torn, and only the surface was closed up. If we reopen the wound and clean it out, then we can probably get away with using just a little bit of the specialized potion to heal it nicely. Many young healers balk at reopening wounds, so I'll need to show them precisely how it's done. We can't expect to have magical power for healing spells or potions in spades forever. If we don't prepare for future battles or gain experience, we'll be in serious trouble.

Medical Technician Nierenberg envisioned the various treatments he was about to perform and gave a low chuckle. He seemed to be enjoying this.

"We'll save a lot of soldiers thanks to the potions you two brought. They're truly invaluable. All the more reason for you to exercise sufficient caution." And with that, Nierenberg left to tend to patients.

*　　*　　*

"Hey, Lieutenant Malraux, I'm not sick or nothin', but I've kinda got a biiit of a stomachache."

"It's all right, Lynx. I do, too."

Nierenberg had "taken *thorough* care" of Malraux and Dick back in their military days.

They had him to thank for still having all their limbs and being healthy despite repeated injuries. However, the way he grinned while administering treatments was still the stuff of soldiers' nightmares. To this very day, they tensed up in his presence.

As for Dick, he would have been able to see Amber every day if he remained on their base in the Labyrinth City, but upon hearing he would also have to meet Medical Technician Nierenberg just as often, he immediately elected to accompany the transport group.

Nierenberg's subordinates nodded with "Uh-huhs" as if they agreed, and then they took the potions and followed him.

05

Someone watched Malraux and Lynx from a window as they departed the Labyrinth Suppression Forces' base.

It was the Gold Lion General Leonhardt and his younger brother, Weishardt.

"And you're fine with all this, Weis?" Leonhardt asked.

The day after he'd had an audience with Malraux and Dick,

the two visited him again with a high-grade curse-removal potion—and a high-grade cure potion to undo the petrification *and* high-grade Regen medicine, which wasn't readily available even in the imperial capital.

Malraux and Dick conveyed the following to Leonhardt, who had just barely escaped death. "We cannot return to the army. Our potion supplier is willing to cooperate with the Labyrinth Suppression Forces but wishes to provide potions behind closed doors. Because we are bound by a magical contract, we cannot disclose the identity of our supplier. However, we remain willing to serve as an intermediary between the dealer and the Labyrinth Suppression Forces."

Their expressions were steadfast, unwavering.

And yet, when Leonhardt asked what types and quantities of potions were available, the two answered that they had a vast number of potions high-grade and below. When he suggested all potions made by this cooperative supplier be brought into the city, they replied the dealer would need more potion vails to transfer them. When he requested them to be transported in storage tanks instead, the two retorted that it wouldn't be possible to bring them here.

Malraux's vague explanation didn't paint a complete picture; it made him sound evasive. Leonhardt had no desire to doubt the men who were still loyal despite having left the Labyrinth Suppression Forces. Still, they were capable of putting an end to the Forces' current crisis. Leonhardt's younger brother, Weishardt, had to calm him down as he shouted, "Do you understand how scarce potions are?!"

"That shouldn't matter. You owe this individual your life, Brother. Malraux, you said that your supplier is willing to give us potions, that if we just supply potion vials, we'll receive as many of the potions as possible. You're certain, correct?"

"I am," answered Malraux. Weishardt thought for a moment as he looked in the other man's eyes.

"Call on us if there is anything you need, be it soldiers or supplies. We won't hesitate to assist," he offered. "But please let us purchase the potions at the same price they sell for in the imperial capital. We will also pay the same amount for the Black Iron Freight Corps's transportation expenses and the fees for the supplier's protection. And let us know when your inventory is down to half."

Leonhardt hid his shock as he searched Malraux's and Dick's faces. The pair didn't appear surprised by the cheap price and simply replied, "Thank you for your understanding."

Starting with the day after Leonhardt's life was saved with the removal of the curse, Weishardt had the army gather empty potion vials they'd been keeping and ordered the head of the medic unit, Nierenberg, to draw up a list of potions needed to quickly heal the soldiers injured in the latest expedition. He was to appropriate only as much money as they'd need for it, disregarding availability and profit.

They had thousands of potion vials in storage. The Aguinas family stored their potions in tanks, so empty vials were required when the family supplied the potions. Potion vials were made using Drops of Life, so they couldn't be taken out of the region of the ley line they'd been created in. The vials themselves degraded extremely slowly, didn't require any special management, and could be remade by a glassmaker even if they broke. Needless to say, vials were highly valuable since only an alchemist could create the specialized glass they were made from. The army often used potions on the front lines and couldn't retrieve the vials from the battlefield, so their number had dropped significantly.

After Medical Technician Nierenberg submitted the potion list, Weishardt organized it in order of priority, rounded the quantities up to units of one hundred, and handed it over to Malraux and the others. He told them to bring as many as possible starting from the ones at the top.

Very few people knew of this transaction: Leonhardt, Weishardt, a trusted confidant in charge of the budget, Nierenberg, and his subordinates who administered treatment. Those under the budget manager were made to take an oath of confidentiality—a magic-bound oath, of course.

For each transaction, the person in charge of the budget paid the fee for the potions directly to the Black Iron Freight Corps. In accordance with the arrangement by Weishardt, the fee was calculated from the potions' selling price in the imperial capital, and the same amount was paid to the supplier and to the Corps. The total cost for such a large quantity of potions was not insignificant. If they continued to buy them at this pace, they would most likely also need to reconsider the army's expenditures.

However, as compensation for scarce potions, it wasn't an adequate price.

Weishardt had kept Leonhardt in check when he told him "You owe this individual your life," but wasn't it discourteous to this gracious individual to ask for so many potions at such a price?

But there was a reason for Leonhardt's question: *Any underground potion stores we locate should be managed by the army regardless of scarcity or strategy. Of course, we'd give the owner a proper reward. Paying the entire amount at once would probably*

be difficult, but they should be provided with social position and honor, as well as a pension for generations.

"Let's say, Brother, that the owner of these potions showed us where they're kept and offered us the entire stock. What would we do with them?" Weishardt asked.

"First, we'd treat our soldiers," the elder Schutzenwald replied. "They're accomplished warriors with whom we've shared many years of joys and sorrows. We can't afford to lose them."

"And once the soldiers were treated?"

"Fill our potion storage facilities, naturally. And provide some to our allied noble families. If we could afford to be more generous with our portion stores, we'd be even closer to taking control of the Labyrinth."

"Is that not exactly what we're doing right now?"

"That's not what I'm talking about," he replied. "I'm in no mood for this back-and-forth," Leonhardt's gaze seemed to tell Weishardt.

"Brother, we must defeat the Labyrinth to survive in this land. And only now do we have someone who can do it, the strongest person in the past one hundred years: you. However, we still cannot reach even the innermost depths of the Labyrinth. We're not in a position to be frugal with potions if we want to defeat the strata bosses. The situation is not one that can be overcome by begrudging the use of potions."

Weishardt had created the current structure of the Labyrinth Suppression Forces. The deeper they went into the Labyrinth, the stronger the monsters became and the casualties were without end. The offensive ability of the Labyrinth Suppression Forces would not increase simply because the monsters' did. It would only increase by surviving, continuing to fight, and not dying. A soldier who was killed or injured and withdrew from the battle-front must be replaced by two inexperienced soldiers. Naturally, offensive ability would decrease both individually and as a group.

To confront powerful monsters with limited fighting power, it was necessary to place importance on not letting soldiers die and continuing to fight for a long time. They had to guard against attacks from higher-ranked monsters and shave off their life force little by little. It was a long-term conflict with monsters that surpassed the soldiers' abilities. As casualties continued to pile up, healers' magical power wouldn't last if they're the only ones treating the wounded. In a long-term battle, soldiers' stamina also decreased, and healing magic might not be effective enough. Also, in this case it would be a disaster if the healers were injured.

Weishardt had solved these problems by organizing medical teams consisting of healers and "medical technicians." The medical technicians probed a person's body to assess the condition of injuries, then directed the healers to employ the most efficient treatment. Permission to use potions was given to the medical technicians, and after performing treatment that didn't use up magical power, medicine, potions, or healing magic was administered as needed.

By aiming for the optimization of healing magic, the length of time the Labyrinth Suppression Forces could fight and the depths they could reach in the Labyrinth increased.

However, it ended here. They'd reached the limit of this method.

As they were right now, they couldn't break through the fifty-third stratum.

They didn't have enough firepower, defensive capacity, or basically anything else, and none of these things were easily to obtain. They'd managed to get to this point by incorporating weapons and armor into the equation.

It's now or never. My brother's skill, Lion's Roar, is powerful. There's hardly a fault to be found in either his military prowess or his charisma. No one has seen a man as outstanding as Leonhardt within the past century—not even in the mighty Schutzenwald family. Our soldiers, too, are highly trained. We've nurtured them for many years.

A person's prime was short lived. Leonhardt might have escaped the petrification curse, but he could only maintain his current fighting power for another ten or twenty years.

If they didn't conquer the Labyrinth during that time, there would be a pervading fear of another Stampede from the Labyrinth or the Fell Forest, and they would continue to send soldiers into the Labyrinth to kill monsters or be killed.

"I thought our fates were sealed when I witnessed your defeat in the Labyrinth, Brother."

But salvation had been close at hand. The potions brought in just before the expedition had miraculously saved many lives and even removed the petrification curse. The Labyrinth City wasn't doomed.

"We are at a deadlock. Any potions at our disposal must be used to advance as far as we possibly can. We can reward the supplier for their meritorious contributions after we have conquered the Labyrinth."

"All the more reason we should take possession of them, yes?" replied Leonhardt.

He was talking about every last one of the buried potions—and their owner, too.

"Brother, do you recall how the seventh emperor protected the endangered unicorns?"

Unicorn horns were a rare, secret medicine that could be used in special-grade cure medicines. As a result, unicorns, whose numbers were already few, became overhunted and were in danger of extinction during the time of the seventh emperor.

"Mm... He walled in every forest they inhabited, didn't he?" Leonhardt appeared suspicious of his brother for suddenly changing the subject.

"Precisely."

Unicorns were such delicate creatures that only purehearted maidens could approach them. All the ones who were kept in enclosures for their protection had died.

No matter how large or elegant the enclosures were, they couldn't save the unicorns. So, the seventh emperor walled in the entirety of the forests in which they lived to protect them from poachers and monsters.

Conserving the unicorn population cost exorbitant amounts of money but proved to be worthwhile. Their numbers gradually increased little by little, and their horns eventually regrew to the point that there was enough to meet demand.

Alchemists who could create special-grade cure potions were always few and far between, even in the Empire. With a fixed amount of unicorn horns on the market, the scarcity of special-grade cure potions became due to the alchemists rather than the material itself—the horns. Even now, the killing of unicorns and the unlawful possession of their horns warranted a severe penalty. However, hardly anyone targeted these creatures now that they were no longer scarce, which therefore meant they were not worth the risk. These days, unicorns were said to live comfortably in their natural forest habitats.

"A metaphor that rare things require a suitable environment."

Weishardt's statement brought Leonhardt to a single conclusion. "You can't mean— No, impossible. But...thinking about it, I agree."

Even though Malraux's group hadn't said as much explicitly, Leonhard could understand why they might be able to deliver potions in large batches at prices as low as those in the imperial capital...if *a certain thing* were the case.

But, even if their guess was correct, would leaving things in the Corps's hands prove to be an issue?

As if sensing Leonhardt's misgivings, Weishardt answered him. "Malraux and Dick came to you with a curse-removal potion. Is that not your answer right there? They may have left the Forces, but they are still your soldiers."

"I suppose so," Leonhardt agreed.

"If we need a unicorn pen, if that's the price for life in this town, that is a road we must follow again."

If that were the case, they would have no choice but to meet Leonhardt's demands. After all, he was the one who governed the Labyrinth City.

06

"Sieg, Sieg, what do we do?!"

Mariela grew flustered upon peeking into the bag with the potion payment Malraux had given her.

"It's full of gold coins! Every day! Every day we're swimming in gold coins!"

Sieg looked at Mariela as if he wanted to say, "Geez, what am I gonna do with this girl?"

The payment for the curse removal set Mariela had given Malraux probably included a finder's fee, because it was way too much as compensation, but the contract had been reviewed since then and she was now getting the same amount for potions as they would sell for in the imperial capital. Considering how rare they were in the Labyrinth City, you could say this was highway robbery, but high-grade potions had never been cheap to begin with.

In the imperial capital's markets, a normal high-grade heal potion was one large silver coin, while a high-grade cure potion was one large silver coin and two silver coins. The price of specialized potions changed depending on the scarcity and cost of the materials, but it was two to three large silver coins. She made a hundred of those every day. Purchasing all the ingredients for the potions would cost about 30 percent of the total price. Mariela, however, used less than 30 percent for materials because she used inexpensive substitutes even though it took some time.

Under normal circumstances, distribution costs, shop and employee costs, taxes, and other fees were added in addition to material fees, but in the Labyrinth City, taxes were a fixed amount of the houses' rent, so a variety of expenses weren't necessary in this kind of transaction. Moreover, the Labyrinth Suppression Forces seemed to be paying the Black Iron Freight Corps's share separately, so the entirety of the potion payments went to Mariela.

Mariela was losing her mind at receiving the amount of gold a whole family could live on for one to two years every single day.

"Alchemy's a really big deal, huh?" she mused.

"You're saying that now?!"

Around ten days ago, when Malraux and Dick paid them a visit in the middle of the night, Sieg had a feeling this would prove to be a nuisance. Something as rare as a high-grade curse-removal potion doesn't just appear by coincidence. Furthermore, the receiving party was the general of the Labyrinth Suppression Forces. He probably already knew of Mariela's existence.

What's best for Mariela? How can I protect her? Sieg wondered.

His own personal strength was meaningless in the face of an entire army. They needed a lot of allies.

That's why he deliberately allowed Malraux, who hadn't known Mariela was an alchemist, into her workshop. He knew from their interactions up to that point that Malraux still hadn't realized.

I couldn't let them have potions and take them to the Labyrinth Suppression Forces the way things were. I had to make Malraux understand he's in a position to protect Mariela, an alchemist. They're bound by a magical contract. And he's an intermediary for the Labyrinth Suppression Forces and the general himself. Mariela doesn't dislike the act of making potions. And Malraux's not a fool—he surely has to realize there's some common ground there.

Sure enough, Siegmund's calculations bore fruit. Up to now, Mariela had been able to enjoy a carefree life while providing potions.

That in itself was good, but...

"Whoaaa, processing bone knight bones requires slime fluid. I've got money, so maybe I should just go all out and collect every kind of slime there is."

"You can't just take in every creature you find. Collect only the ones you need."

Mariela's tone was sarcastic as she glanced at him, so Sieg played along and replied like a parent would.

Wasn't she freaking out just moments ago? Sieg sighed in exasperation at Mariela's carefree demeanor.

"Mariela. If…if the Labyrinth Suppression Forces came to the shop and told you to come with them, what would you do?"

"Hmm? I'd go with 'em."

Sieg caught his breath at Mariela's lackadaisical reply. "…You wouldn't run away?"

"How? They're an army; no point in trying to run. Besides, I'm an alchemist, so I have to make potions. I hate the idea of being shut up in a dark room, constantly churning out potions for free, so I'm glad I've been able to make 'em here. And I get a ton of money for it. I dunno what Malraux and the others said about me, but I'm grateful."

If Mariela had said she'd run away, Sieg had thought he'd go with her anywhere she went. However, her response baffled him; she seemed to imply she would worry about it when the time came.

"It's okay, Sieg. You're plenty strong now. Plus you've got your own sword, so nothing awful's gonna happen to you like before," Mariela said with a smile in response to Sieg's troubled expression.

Did Mariela give me this sword because she knew the situation I was in? She knew what could happen to me, and she did this so I wouldn't find myself in dire straits if anything were to happen to her…

A lump formed in Sieg's throat.

"I am your sword, Mariela. I'll always be by your side," he finally answered, to which Mariela beamed and replied, "Thanks."

Then she added: "So, wanna smash some bone knight bones?"

"It's late. Let's do it tomorrow."

Mariela couldn't move the bones because they were too heavy. And since Sieg wasn't going to carry them for her, Mariela gave up for the day and withdrew to her bedroom.

07

"Haaaah!"

Mariela's gallant shout and the *whoosh* of the weapon in her hand cutting through the air echoed in the Labyrinth.

The girl who had lamented her own helplessness made great strides through the power of love, courage, hard work, and potions, and her sword attained the swiftness of a seasoned hero... Not.

The weapon in Mariela's hand was a thin stick, and since it was light and bent easily, the only splendid thing about it was the sound it made. It would've been a little better if the stick had at least caught an enemy, but it had merely been slicing through the air for a while now.

"Seriously, it takes real talent to not even land a single hit! Here, next target's a big one!"

Laughing, Lynx sent the next monster at Mariela. Sieg, too, laughed as he cheered her on: "Don't worry! If you watch their movements carefully, you'll hit them."

Mariela readied her stick, thinking this time for sure she'd finish off the monster.

Her approaching opponent toddled along—because it was just a mushroom. Yes, Mariela and the others were in the middle of gathering mushrooms.

The fifth stratum of the Labyrinth was a hazy forest called the Sleeping Wood.

This forest, covered in a thin mist, had trees and mushrooms so massive they made you feel like you'd shrunk. The inhabitants weren't giants the size of trees or the kinds of charming beings one might associate with the forest, but rather mushrooms as tall as a person's knees. The drifting mist was actually spores, many of which induced sleep, hence the name the Sleeping Wood. Anyone who inhaled the spores and fell asleep was doomed to become plant fodder and never wake up. Wearing a mask attracted the mushrooms to try and defeat you themselves; the fifth stratum was nothing more than a bonus floor for mushroom hunting.

Normally, defeated monsters in the Labyrinth disappeared. But in this stratum, the mushrooms had somehow transformed into monsters, so defeating them simply turned them back into giant mushrooms again. The poison ones were greater in number and variety than the edible ones, but there were a large number of the kinds used as alchemic ingredients, making the Sleeping Wood a much safer and more efficient location for collecting mushrooms than the Fell Forest.

"Yaaah!"

Mariela's stick whooshed through the air.

"Warrior Mariela! Once again you've sliced open an invisible enemy!"

Lynx guffawed annoyingly. One gutsy fungus had collided with Mariela's right knee and sent itself flying. Even though it was a monster, it was still a mushroom at the end of the day. It was so light and soft that it ended up killing itself, never mind Mariela injuring it. Maybe she would do better to just stand in place holding a pot lid rather than swinging a stick around.

Some of the more dangerous mushrooms were poisonous to

the touch; several had thorns or fangs; others had heavy, tough stumps. Sieg and Lynx eliminated those types without fail.

"Mariela, do you have all the mushrooms you need?"

"Yeah, but I wanna stay a little longer!"

On this day, they had come to gather mushrooms she was going to use as part of a substitute for treant fruit in high-grade potions. The substitute was made by blending thirteen different ingredients, but it required only two kinds of mushrooms, neither of which were rare, so she'd gathered more than enough. They'd all run into Mariela and killed themselves.

Mariela wanted to persevere until she had at least brought down one by herself, to which Lynx laughed, "Sheesh, fine," and held up her right arm.

"Mariela, you're overdoin' it. Just a light tap's good enough."

Lynx faced a mushroom that was rambling toward them, its cap shaking side to side. Together, he and Mariela raised the stick overhead.

"All right, now!"

"Hiii-ya!"

Pa-tup. With a feeble sound, Mariela's stick cleaved the mushroom's cap right in half.

"I... I beat it! I beat it, Lynx!"

"Wowww, that's *great*, reaaal *great*. Okay, let's head back. I'm starved."

Mariela clutched Lynx's hands in great delight. Observing this, Sieg suggested, "Mariela, let's defeat one more, you and me!" but Lynx spun Mariela around and pushed her toward the exit.

He'd come along because she said she wanted to go mushroom hunting, but he never imagined she'd be this clumsy. How many hours had they spent just on these mushrooms? It would've been way more efficient just to purchase them. Both Lynx and Sieg were strong enough to handle themselves in deeper strata, so it would have been more profitable if she'd pestered them into gathering more expensive materials.

"We got a lot of mushrooms, so I'll make a feast! Mushroom risotto, mushroom stew…"

"That ain't gonna cut it for my appetite. Add some meat to it."

"I'll cook meat, too! I'm gonna splurge."

Mariela was on cloud nine. Lynx wondered how she could be so happy about this.

"I know we got all these mushrooms, but you sure you won't you end up in the red if we add some meat?"

"Huh? We had fun, so why not treat ourselves?"

Only little kids unfettered by life's worries find having fun with good friends satisfying. An adventurer's work wasn't fun; their future was uncertain. In the Labyrinth City, meeting someone could be a once-in-a-lifetime occurrence, and everyone tended to be selfish about the unknown future.

Lynx realized what Mariela was trying to say—that being able to enjoy themselves in the moment should be carved into their memories and celebrated. *In this life where no one knows what the next day will bring, Mariela is cherishing the time we've spent together.*

"Then I'll take a huge helping!"

If that's the case, I'm glad, Lynx thought as he gazed at Mariela, who giggled merrily.

08

Bubble, bubble, bubble, bubble.

Mariela boiled apriore fruit in a large pot in the kitchen to remove its astringency. She could have done it with alchemic skills, but that would take a lot of time, so she processed it in the kitchen during Sunlight's Canopy's business hours.

Back in the shop itself, Mariela chatted with the regulars while sorting out apriore fruit. This had been harvested by children from the orphanage, so it was much cheaper than buying it in stores, but there was worm-eaten or rotten fruit mixed in with the good stuff. Mariela bought a heap of it, since the money was used to keep the orphanage in operation. Plus, sorting the fruit was a perfect way to pass the time when the shop wasn't busy.

Once its astringency was properly removed, apriore could be used as a potion ingredient, and kneading it into cookies gave them a delicious, crispy texture. Though it slightly increased the time it took to remove the astringency, she was coarsely crushing them before processing today in case she wanted to use it as an ingredient in sweets.

"Hello, Mariela." Elmera from the Merchants Guild visited the shop just after noon. The soap Mariela sold was Elmera's favorite, and every now and then, she came to buy some during a lull in her busy schedule. Today she had brought someone with her.

"Are you Mariela?"

It was a girl about the same age as Mariela who looked to be the picture of royalty. She had a dollish beauty with large, bright eyes that indicated a strong will, a shapely nose, and full lips. Mariela greeted her in kind as she wondered who this girl was.

"Nice to meet you, I'm Mariela. Um, Ms. Elmera, may I ask who this is?"

"She's a chemist like you. She doesn't have her own store, but she's quite talented. Her wares are top sellers in the Adventurers Guild shop. I brought her along thinking I might introduce you since the two of you are close in age."

Upon Elmera's introduction, the beautiful young lady performed a lovely curtsy and introduced herself. "My name is Caroline Aguinas. Pleased to make your acquaintance."

How did it come to this...?

"Such a cozy little shop, isn't it? It's quite pleasant."

"My, tea that enhances beauty? A new product from Merle's Spices? I should buy some to take home!"

Caroline and Elmera sat in the tea corner and grinned as they sipped their tea. The more women in the shop, the more glamorous than usual it became. The old men who gathered had their own charm, but they didn't hold a candle to the likes of pretty ladies.

Wait, no. She's not just a "pretty lady"—she's an Aguinas! That's not a name you hear every day. She's not from a different Aguinas family, right? It's the same Aguinas family in charge of the Labyrinth City's potions, right? What's an esteemed young woman like her doing drinking tea in my shop? Did she come here to do some sort of on-site enemy reconnaissance? I don't get it.

Caroline addressed the confused Mariela. "Are these apriore? There seems to be bad fruit mixed in."

"Oh, the kids from the orphanage collected those. It takes time to sort through them all, but the money goes toward supporting the orphanage, so I just thought I'd use these wherever I could."

"My, that's wonderful. I see you have an interest in charity work. Speaking of which, Ms. Elmera's father's enterprise, the Seele Company, supports the employment of women in their genea cream manufacturing. I would like for my own family to do something similar, but when it comes to my elder brother..." Caroline's willowy fingers gently pinched a worm-eaten apriore as if it were a fancy pastry and nonchalantly tossed it into the trash can.

"The Aguinas family has been researching potions for generations. Isn't that a wonderful thing in itself?"

Elmera also began to pick up the apriore all while leaving her gloves on. "This one's fine," she remarked as she placed them in the container with the others that had passed inspection.

"But we have nothing to show for it. I think developing better medicine without fussing over potions would prove far more beneficial for the Labyrinth City."

With a sigh, she sipped her tea and stretched her hand toward another pastry, no, another apriore. She skillfully chucked fruit into the container, then the trash, then the container again.

"That's why you work so hard to produce medicines, isn't it, Lady Caroline?"

Toss-toss-toss-toss-toss, toss, toss, toss-toss. Elmera was incredibly fast at sorting.

"Indeed. However, I have reached the limits of what I can do alone. When I heard a lady chemist close to my age had opened an apothecary, I felt I must speak with her."

Caroline turned her beautiful face toward Mariela, who was listening to the conversation as the apriore continued to go *plunk, plunk.*

Crap, I'm in a fix here! Sieg, help meeee!

For his part, Sieg had gone completely unnoticed as he added more apriores to the decreasing unsorted pile, changed out the trash and container, and then quietly disappeared into the kitchen.

Oh, yeah, right. Sieg is my sword, but he's not my shield. I mean, here I was not paying attention, and he somehow added more apriores and even emptied the sorting container! That's using both his strength training and magic, right? He's making full use of the techniques he learned from Haage, right?

No help would come.

"Um, I'll speak for as long as you want, if you'll have me?" she responded in defeat.

"I am so glad. I'm certain we'll become fast friends!" said Caroline, smiling.

"Oh, this salve is mixed after extracting components from the medicinal herbs, correct?"

"That's right. Lady Caroline. Because some parts of medicinal herbs inhibit healing."

"Please call me Carol. And the 'lady' part is quite unnecessary. We are friends, after all."

"But still…"

After a bit of back-and-forth, they settled on an odd mishmash of title and nickname: Lady Carol. They also decided Mariela didn't need to speak so formally if there were no other nobles around.

Is this really okay? It feels really wrong so I'm gonna speak as

politely as I can. I'm not that good at it, but I feel like I should at least be decent enough to get by.

At first, Mariela was worried whether a young female aristocrat was even allowed to enter a commoner's shop alone and eat there, but an escort seemed to be waiting for her outside. No wonder customers weren't coming in. Mariela asked her to have her escort join her inside whenever she visited in the future.

"Gosh, just look at the time!"

Once they'd finished their tea, Elmera and Carol reluctantly went home.

Mariela had thought they'd come to probe about potions, but all they'd talked about was medicine.

It wasn't as if she didn't wonder why someone from the Aguinas family had visited, but she'd enjoyed chatting with Carol and felt sad to see her go.

"Please come back anytime!" Mariela said, to which Carol replied with a smile, "Yes, I certainly will!"

Thus Sunlight's Canopy acquired another regular customer.

And not that it mattered much, but she'd made incredible progress in the apriore sorting.

CHAPTER 2
The Deluge

01

That day, Elmera, the chairwoman of the Merchants Guild's Medicinal Herbs Division, was extremely angry.

"Honestly, I never imagined anyone in the world would accuse me of something as absurd as 'trying to pick a fight.'"

Because of Elmera's bad mood, Gordon and the other two dwarves gave up the sunniest seats for her, and Merle chose her very best tea leaves to soothe her temper. Sieg quietly changed the sign out front to CLOSED.

Once the other customers got the hint and excused themselves, Mariela and Carol, who was now a regular customer through and through, sat down with a pot of herbal tea and listened to what Elmera had to say.

Elmera let the tea cool enough to drain it in big gulps, then began to talk.

Just after noon, a man named Kindel, who was in charge of the Construction Division, had waltzed into Elmera's office with no appointment. His business was the imminent delivery of a large quantity of processed medicinal herbs to the City Defense Squad.

"As I explained, the amount of goods delivered to the City Defense Squad has already exceeded the promised quantity," she had told him.

"Thith is a perthonal request from the Squad's leader, Colonel Teluther."

"Why would the chairman of the Merchants Guild's Construction Division bring us a request from the City Defense Squad?"

"Me and Colonel Teluther go way back. We were clathmates at the same academy."

"We have already responded to the City Defense Squad's official request."

"You tryin' to pick a fight with me, lady?!"

"Don't you find it strange for the chairman of the Construction Division to bring a request from another organization?"

"I'm a busy man! Buzz off!"

Such was how the conversation had unfolded. After wasting the busy Elmera's time, Kindel, the chairman of the Construction Division, apparently had ranted and raved before he finally returned home.

Um, uhhh... There's so much I could say here that I don't even know where to begin. Mariela felt she needed to say something, so she opened her mouth. Unable to find the right words, however, she instead drank her tea and closed it again.

Even Carol seemed to be at a loss, for all she could add was "Goodness." The people serving as Carol's escorts had melted into the background, their facial expressions indicating that they didn't hear anything.

For the time being, Mariela offered her cookies made with the apriores they'd sorted together. She hadn't kneaded any magical power into them, so they were pretty average cookies. Elmera crunched away at them like a squirrel, while Leandro, her vice chairman who'd come to pick her up, offered a detailed explanation.

The City Defense Squad was responsible for protecting the Labyrinth City and the region's breadbasket, as well as developing the Fell Forest and expanding that granary. Since their duties were far less risky than those of the Labyrinth Suppression Forces, many of the Squad's members came from good families and had less combat training. No one exemplified this better than the commanding officer, Colonel Bose Teluther.

Ever since he began leading the City Defense Squad, no more land in the Fell Forest had been cleared, and the region's breadbasket hadn't been expanded. Most of the Labyrinth City's wood was harvested from the Fell Forest, so the cost of construction would rise if reclamation stagnated.

The person balancing this situation was Kindel, the chairman of the Construction Division mentioned earlier by Elmera. Kindel was a man of ill repute who had been passed around from post to post within the Merchants Guild until he'd reached the age of fifty. A row of jagged teeth always peeked out from his open mouth, and his figure lacked muscles, thin and bony to the point that he was a rare sight in the Labyrinth City.

He spoke with a slight lisp and had a tendency to rattle on at length about his own business. People whispered he'd been appointed to his current position because, as he said himself, "Me and Colonel Teluther go way back. We were clathmates at the same academy."

Unlike Kindel, Teluther had an ample belly. Well, he *did* belong to the City Defense Squad, so no one looking at him would necessarily think he was too fat. However, he was short, so he appeared excessively rotund. The size of his belly suggested he ate a feast every day, and the top of his head shone like it was oozing grease. Not knowing when to let go, he'd used the remaining hair at his temples to forcefully cover other parts of his head.

Although he kept a firm grip on his own purse strings, he was famous for lavishing the Squad's supplies. The present issue was probably the result of haphazard use of rope made from monster-warding incense and daigis. It was almost the beginning of the sugar turnip harvest, which meant orcs would come after the turnips in large numbers, but this man had the gall to order supplementary supplies because they didn't have enough stockpiled.

Bromominthra and daigis, inexpensive medicinal herbs used in monster-warding incense, grew everywhere in the Labyrinth City, but the available hands to harvest and process them were limited. Since the incense was cheap, it was difficult to maintain the human resources necessary for these tasks.

The quantity delivered to the City Defense Squad was contracted annually. The Merchants Guild allocated the amount to the manufacturer to request production and delivered more products than planned. They had already exceeded the scope of the contract, and now it would probably be difficult to secure even if they made requests here and there during the medicinal herb harvest season.

The guild had notified the City Defense Squad of the situation when the contracted amount had been exceeded. If it had been managed properly, a sufficient additional quantity could have been delivered.

"Which is why the head of the Construction Division came barging in, whining for help," Leandro drawled. Was it really okay for them to divulge internal affairs? "Anywaaay, Mariela, about how much monster-warding incense and rope you think you could make in one week?" There was an unexpected shrewdness in Leandro's languid tone.

Mariela had a lot of powdered bromominthra stockpiled in

her cellar since it grew wild in her backyard. Making the incense was simple. As for the daigis, she couldn't make rope, but she could supply the herb in dried form.

"Oh, that'd be a huuuge help. Even if it's beyond the scope of the contract, we can't afford to be unprepared during orc raids. We'll have someone come get the daigis tomorrow. However much you can make of the incense is fine. Now, Ms. Elmera, our work is piling up. Let's be on our way, shall we?"

Elmera, who'd calmed down thanks to the tea and sweets, returned to the Merchants Guild with Leandro. Mariela gave her plenty of the apriore cookies to take with her.

You can do it, Ms. Elmera!

Mariela wished her well as she saw her off.

02

When Elmera returned to her office in the Medicinal Herbs Division, more work came in unexpectedly as if it had been waiting for her.

"We have a request from the Bandel Company. They would like us to hurry with preparations because there isn't enough treant fruit for the next yagu caravan to transport."

"Understood. Let's settle it straightaway. We'll get this done promptly this time around."

Elmera's usual vigor came back in spades as she munched on

her cookies and added, "Right, let's do our best." At that exact moment, Construction Division Chairman Kindel arrived with Colonel Teluther, head of the City Defense Squad, in tow.

"You'll have to excuthe me, Colonel Teluther. That bullheaded lady wouldn't lithen to your request one bit."

"She's been a thorn in my side, too. As you saw, she's smart and nitpicky, qualities that suit her position as chairwoman. So, Chairman Kindel, the question is—what should we do? We probably can't withstand orc raids with our current stockpile. I imagine there are alternatives, yes?"

"Y-yeth, sir. What would you say to asking the Adventurers Guild?"

"The Adventurers Guild? A fine idea. I'd love to invite Mr. Haage the Limit Breaker and hear his many tales of heroism."

Teluther hadn't bothered to hide his displeasure as he bad-mouthed Elmera, but as soon as Haage was brought up, he leaned forward in interest and his mood improved. Past his mid-fifties, this man had age-appropriate thinning hair and an age-inappropriate fondness of adventurers. Probably due to a yearning born of his own weakness, he was an enthusiast who loved high-ranking adventurers regardless of age or gender, and he knew the name of every single B-Rank to S-Rank adventurer in the empire who had a pseudonym.

He wasn't so irrational that he'd summon an adventurer for no reason, but if he had one, he would go to meet one with great delight. Although he was normally a miser, the strings of his coin purse loosened just for adventurers.

Incidentally, Lightning Empress Elsee was his very favorite, the A-Rank mystery woman. He yearned to meet her once before he died.

"Th-that…would be a rather *dazzling* conversation…," Kindel responded as he glanced repeatedly at Teluther's cranium. Not that there was much hair to speak of on his own shiny pate.

"…What were you looking at just now?"

"U-um, no, I was jutht dazed from imagining your combined auras, is all."

As it so happens, this dazzling conversation never came to be.

When Chairman Kindel brought the matter to their attention, the vice guildmaster, who was Haage's underling, said, "This price, this quantity, on this day? Impossible." Haage himself also gave a snappy refusal: "Sounds impossible to me!"

Kindel gnashed his teeth in obvious outrage.

At thith rate, I'm jutht gonna get told off again.

The likes of procuring supplies for the City Defense Squad wasn't his job in the first place, though.

Continuing to abandon his own actual work, Kindel prowled around and around his office while trying to come up with a good idea.

03

The wind was strong that day.

It blew gusts of chilly air through the Labyrinth City, signaling winter's imminent arrival. People walking along the road were starting to wear thick clothing made of yagu fur.

Even on days like these, Mariela's shop, Sunlight's Canopy, was nice and warm, and it bustled with regular customers seeking medicine and comfort.

Sieg and Lynx were having a late lunch in the kitchen. Mariela, who'd already finished her meal, tended the shop while making oral medicine from lynus wheat with Caroline.

"Mariela, lynus wheat heightens the effect of your oral medicine, yes? Which reminds me, my elder brother purchased lynus wheat to perform some sort of research with it."

Mariela's oral medicine was prepared by shelling, cooking, and then crushing lynus wheat into a paste, then kneading medicinal components extracted from powdered and non-powdered medicinal herbs into it. The Drops of Life incorporated into lynus wheat increased the effects of the herbs.

So the person who'd bought it all up the first time I went to the wholesale market was Lady Carol's brother.

Mariela stopped what she was doing as she listened to Carol. Incidentally, the stuff she was using now had been recently harvested. The merchant had expected the Aguinas family to replenish their stock in mass quantities, they apparently hadn't come to buy any this time, which is why the seller seemed to be troubled by the overstock and welcomed Mariela's bulk purchase.

She'd tried making it a lot of different ways, like crushing raw lynus wheat into powder and then mixing it, using just the wheat germs, which had a lot of Drops of Life in them, steaming it, cooking it, and boiling it. She'd also experimented with a range of temperatures, but the most normal cooking methods turned out to be the most effective.

From there, after crushing the lynus wheat, she had to diligently knead the other medicinal herb components into it. She understood the Drops of Life wouldn't incorporate just from normal mixing, but did she really have to knead-knead-knead it that much?

Whenever Mariela made the medicine afterhours, she'd kneaded with alchemic skills. Recently, however, she'd been making it at the counter with Carol. She had to use a mortar and pestle on those occasions. It was overwhelming work that reminded her of the time she'd relentlessly kneaded orc and orc king lard together to make general oil.

"What am I gonna do if I knead-knead-knead too much and my arms get all big and muscly?"

As Mariela flexed her biceps in indignation, Lynx suddenly peeked out from the kitchen, pinched both her arms, then chuckled before ducking back into the kitchen.

"Hey, Lynx! What was that for?"

As Mariela pouted, Sieg pinched her arm, too. "Heh…"

"You laughed, didn't you? Sieg, you laughed just now, didn't you?" She glared after Sieg, who disappeared back into the kitchen. Even Carol gave her a pinch from behind, too.

"Hee-hee."

"Gah, a pretty lady's smile! So cute!"

Mariela and the three dwarves basking in the sun were soothed by Lady Carol's gorgeous smile when Merle of Merle's Spices rushed in.

"Mariela, your laundry just went flying all over the place! I think the clothesline came apart. A whole bunch of it's scattered!" Merle said before handing none other than Mariela's underwear to her.

"Erk! S-S-S-Sieg, bad news! Hurry! It's an emergency!"

Mariela and Sieg scrambled off to pick up the strewn laundry.

Merle had rescued Mariela's underwear, but Sieg's was still unaccounted for.

Caroline watched the pair as they sped away.

"Those two live together, yes? Are they...boyfriend and girlfriend?" Caroline murmured to herself. Merle seized the opportunity; as an influential figure among the wives in the neighborhood, she possessed a gossip sensor that was by no means ordinary. Her area of expertise lay beyond the medicinal herbs and tea she offered at Merle's Spices.

"Actually, I heard they're childhood friends from the same village. After Sieg became an adventurer and left the village, he turned into a bit of a rascal. He ended up getting sent here to the Labyrinth City, and Mariela went after him and saved him."

"My." Caroline gracefully lifted her hand to her mouth. Merle's vague explanation had aroused her imagination.

"Mariela said they were childhood friends, but with that age difference? And how could she have followed him all the way here? Besides, this house may be a commoner's place to you, but it's not that easy for someone to afford. Mariela doesn't seem to have any family, so she must have put everything she inherited from her parents into the place to live like this."

"Goodness!" Although she was highborn, Caroline was also a young lady. She loved this sort of thing.

Sieg was always ready to guard Mariela at a moment's notice, and at first Caroline had thought he was her bodyguard. Caroline herself had had one ever since she was small. But when she saw the way he looked at Mariela, she realized Sieg was no mere escort. It's only natural for a bodyguard to keep an eye on the one he's escorting, but Caroline felt the passion in his gaze was different from that of her own.

From Caroline's point of view, Mariela acted very naturally around Sieg, like he was family. On the other hand, seeing how well Lynx got along with her made Caroline curious about the relationship between the three.

Surely, the two were more than friends but not lovers. There might even be room for Lynx to step in between them. Just imagining the scenario made Caroline giddy.

Caroline had a fiancé, an alchemist, in the imperial capital. They'd never met; he was apparently twenty years her senior. Though he was a lot older than she was, she'd heard he was a high-ranking alchemist who could make high-grade potions and even had several apprentices.

The Aguinas family has been researching potions for generations. Since it wasn't possible to connect to the ley line in the Labyrinth City, they couldn't make potions the same way alchemists could. To develop highly effective magic medicine without using Drops of Life, they needed medicinal herb-processing methods and potion-creating procedures passed down to alchemists via the Library, as well as particular information on magic medicine hidden by families and schools.

Since ages past, the Aguinas family had made their illegitimate children apprentice under alchemists in the imperial capital to obtain this information and knowledge and used marriage as a way to build alliances.

Caroline's engagement, too, was a part of that plan. This would be her first marriage, and she was certainly the appropriate age, but the second for her older husband-to-be. She'd heard his first wife had passed away and he had no children, but what kind of person was he? Caroline was also the daughter of a noble family. Political marriages were accepted as a matter of course, but it was unusual to see an age gap so large it made the couple look like father and daughter. As it was, she'd grown up in the Labyrinth City, physically separated from the imperial capital by a mountain range and the Fell Forest. She already felt uneasy about marrying into a family in the imperial capital, and the age difference only exacerbated things. Caroline's heart wavered with anxiety like the leaves of a tree dancing in the wind.

It wasn't just because the Labyrinth City was an insular location where Caroline could sell goods to the Adventurers Guild as a chemist, or spend time with the commoner Mariela every day. She probably only had the freedom to live as she wanted while she was in the Labyrinth City as her final self-indulgence before married life.

I wonder if I'll be able to live that happily with my future husband...

Caroline gazed at Mariela and Sieg, who were drawing nearer with their laundry in tow and chatting in relief, "Thank goodness we found it all!"

She didn't know their ages, but she assumed they were around ten years apart. The gentle atmosphere between the two of them made Caroline hope for a happy future for herself and her fiancé as well.

"If you ask me, Mariela's the kind of girl who lets Sieg barge in on everything."

The gossip had only just begun, but they didn't have enough fuel for the fire.

Merle shot a look at the three dwarves as if to ask, "You three, do you have any dirt on them? You're the ones who fixed up this shop, aren't you?" It was a scary look, the way a monster might look at its prey.

"Okay then, shall we get back to it?"

"I've gotta get this new idea sketched out."

"I just remembered—I've got a window repair job to do."

The three dwarves had grown uncomfortable. They rose to their feet, said their good-byes to Mariela and Sieg in front of the shop, and took their leave. As always, they each bought one salve tin. It was probably their way of tipping, and they bought medicine day after day, giving it to people in the slums they'd hired who were taking time off from adventuring due to injury.

"Hang in there."

"Best of luck to you."

"Keep at it."

Each of the three gave Sieg their well-wishes as they passed by him.

Puzzled by the dwarves' enigmatic encouragement, Mariela and Sieg entered the shop, where they flinched at Merle's piercing gaze.

"Anyways, guess I should head home, too," said Lynx as he exited the kitchen. "Mariela, I won't be back for another two or three days, so you'll hafta eat lunch by yourself. Later, Sieg. Keep at it."

He ruffled Mariela's hair before going home.

"Yeah, yeah, I get it already. I can eat by myself, y'know," Mariela replied, pouting. She couldn't protect her head with her hands full of laundry. She couldn't see his face either, but his gaze caught Sieg and seemed directed toward Caroline and her escort. Sieg realized Lynx's "Keep at it" carried a different meaning from that of the three dwarves.

"Yeah, take care," Sieg replied, and he and Mariela returned inside the shop.

Doesn't look like the Aguinas lady or her bodyguard did any funny stuff while Mariela and Sieg were out of the shop, thought Lynx as he gazed at Mariela's apothecary from a distance.

The daughter of the Aguinas house appeared at Sunlight's Canopy at the same time Mariela began supplying potions in large quantities. These potions were being used to heal the wounded soldiers of the Labyrinth Suppression Forces as well as replenish their stores, so they hadn't yet gone to other noble families.

Information about the subjugation of the Labyrinth had been kept secret for many years; not just about the deepest stratum that had been reached, but even the nature of Leonhardt's injury and the devastation of the Labyrinth Suppression Forces had a spin put on them. Details like the Labyrinth having more than fifty strata wasn't something to be conveyed to civilians. People watched the gallant march of the Labyrinth Suppression Forces led by Leonhardt as they headed out on the expedition, brimming with excitement at the increasing activity of adventurers and the variety of materials brought from the Labyrinth that came with it. However, the people weren't informed of when the soldiers had returned.

The Aguinas house was a family of alchemists that'd been managing potions for two hundred years. Some were aware of how obsessively devoted the family was to the production of potions over a period of generations. However, all of that energy was poured into alchemy, and no one had heard that they had access to especially high intelligence or powerful military strength.

So, Lynx believed it was too soon for them to learn of Mariela's existence.

Hey, even the most unexpected can happen.

He hadn't noticed anything suspicious in the vicinity of Mariela's shop even after Caroline showed up. Of course, he hadn't seen Caroline or her guard do anything suspicious, either.

Maybe I'll probe a li'l deeper.

Lynx's shadow disappeared into a back alley.

It lived in the underground Aqueduct.

No one knew when It had come into being.

Because It had nothing akin to intellect but was a fleeting thing that prowled around on instinct.

None of the drains flowing into the underground Aqueduct had nutrients. Its brethren didn't get very big, but arose and vanished, and arose again, and in this way their numbers slowly increased. It was only by pure chance that It had grown large.

It had a treasured feeding ground within its territory.

Wastewater flowing from the wholesale market was processed in and ejected from a slime tank. However, when a large amount of edible materials were brought in, such as during the time of the Labyrinth Suppression Forces' expedition, it was too much for the slime tank to process, and the wastewater would pour into the underground Aqueduct untreated.

The remains of monsters, infused with plenty of magical power, were a feast for It.

Feasts didn't always come pouring in. If they didn't, It would move to a different feeding ground.

It happened as soon as the current feast was over.

It slowly began to move to the next feeding area as it instinctually roamed for food.

05

"Colonel Teluther, sir, I've got a good idea!"

Construction Division Chairman Kindel was neglecting his own work again to pay his respects to Colonel Teluther, head of the City Defense Squad. He spoke with so much fervor, almost bounding with so much excitement, it seemed like he was about to polish Teluther from his shoes to the top of his head with his leftover energy.

"Is it a better idea than meeting with Mr. Haage the Limit Breaker?"

Teluther the adventurer enthusiast had really hoped to get together with the man. With a frown, he stared intensely at Kindel. He'd completely forgotten his original purpose.

There were many adventurers who went by aliases, but you

could say Teluther's obsession with a sultry middle-aged man made him particularly commendable among adventurer enthusiasts. Of course, Lightning Empress Elsee was his very favorite, so it wasn't as if he was biased toward male adventurers. This was crucial. Take note, because it might be on the next exam.

"Er, um, that is... I was thinkin' maybe it'd be better to meet Mr. Haage on leth formal terms, you see."

"Well said. Make an appointment," Teluther replied to Kindel's stopgap excuse. He was on board.

"Now, as for the medicinal herbth..." Kindel mopped away sweat as he returned to the subject at hand. "We should mobilize those slum residenth to harvest the herbth in that area."

"That certainly doesn't sound appealing." Teluther disapproved of Kindel's proposal. Perhaps you could say he wasn't in charge of the City Defense Squad for nothing, as he seemed to possess the minimum amount of common sense.

"Now, how can that be? Ithn't the Labyrinth City protected by a great iron wall? With its sturdy facade, the surrounding monster-warding herbth, and above all our City Defense Squad led by you, Colonel Teluther, it's surely invinthible. As impregnable as that legendary S-Rank adventurer, the Isolated Hollow, don't you think?"

"I-Isolated Hollow?"

"Yeth, yeth. It'd be no exaggeration to say the guardian of a place as vast as the Labyrinth City would be jutht as good—no, better than the Isolated Hollow. With you at the helm, it wouldn't be an issue if a few plants were taken from the slums here and there."

"Is that so? Now that you mention it, I feel the same way."

"That's right. Yeth indeed."

"I guess you're right. Quite so. Ha-ha-ha."

"Indeed! Wah-ha-ha-ha!"

The adventurer-loving Teluther's nominal good sense had quickly broken down in the face of the suggestion he was greater than an S-Rank adventurer. Both men roared with laughter as if something had struck them as funny.

"Then, to proceed with the plan, I'd like to borrow a soldier, sir."

"Make it happen. But I'll be the one giving orders."

Although it appeared as if nothing concrete had been settled, they'd somehow come to an agreement in their conversation. A tacit understanding? What on earth was the chain of command or the system of approval?

With all sensible evaluation criteria completely disregarded, the medicinal herb harvesting operation in the slums began the following day.

"This mobilization is under the authority of the great City Defense Squad!" Chairman Kindel shouted in the streets of the slums.

Colonel Teluther and several of his subordinates stood around behind him.

Why was Kindel shouting? Teluther's participating subordinates might also have had that question, but even if they had doubts, they couldn't escape. None of them were good at getting things done, and they all stood around staring vacantly into space with seemingly no motivation.

"What's all this?"

Three men gazed icily at the group.

They were the adventurers who'd helped remodel Mariela's house. As Mariela directed, they had applied ointment to themselves every day, and even after their wounds closed, they never failed to massage it in. Perhaps thanks to this, they were completely healed and able to become adventurers again. Currently they were working in shallower strata than before, but soon their instincts would get back to normal, and they would be able to return to the strata they'd reached previously.

"Medicinal herb harvesting? You could take all the bromominthra and daigis, but it won't get you much money."

The mobilization of slum inhabitants wasn't uncommon. A lot of has-been adventurers who'd been injured in the Labyrinth and forced to quit adventuring had ended up here. Enough food was rationed to them at regular intervals so they wouldn't die.

Employment of slum inhabitants was endorsed, and they were frequently hired in both the public and private sectors for daywork they could do even if their hands or feet were in bad shape. The wages they received were low, and it wasn't easy to leave the slums once they'd lived here for a while, but the arrangement allowed them to make ends meet, at least in the slums.

Kindel explained in a screeching voice that they'd pay one copper coin per armful of medicinal herbs, and one copper coin to dry and pulverize it. This was about a tenth of the normal price. Furthermore, he was recruiting people to make the herbs into monster-warding incense and rope for the same price.

Bromominthra and daigis grew everywhere in the Labyrinth City. Bromominthra's purplish-red leaves thickly covered places where flowers might be found in other towns, and daigis ivy crept along every building and outer wall in the Labyrinth City. There were no exceptions; not in the slums nor even where nobles lived. Kindel's idea was that surely contractors could be found who'd simply harvest and bring the medicinal herbs that grew everywhere.

The planting of bromominthra and daigis wasn't specified in the laws of the Labyrinth City. However, it was done at every house without exception. They were easy to grow, and if they grew too much, they could be processed and sold for pocket change. But that wasn't the reason to raise these hideous plants. The people of the Labyrinth City grew them for one reason only.

They were afraid.

The perimeter of the Labyrinth City was surrounded by tall walls as high as one could see and nearly as thick. Even the imperial capital didn't have walls like this.

However, two hundred years ago, the monsters from the Fell Forest tore through this wall and brought the Kingdom of Endalsia to ruins.

The Labyrinth in the center of the Labyrinth City had continued to grow for two hundred years.

The Labyrinth Suppression Forces regularly went on expeditions and massacred the monsters of the Labyrinth to weaken its power, but there had been no shortage of tales since long ago of villages and towns that had failed to control their labyrinths and been destroyed by monsters surging from them.

The Labyrinth on the inside, and the Fell Forest on the outside.

They really were living in a den of monsters.

It was said that people once lived in the Fell Forest to avoid the City. Apparently, they'd managed some peace and quiet by covering their homes with daigis ivy and surrounding it with bromominthra to prevent monsters from breaking in.

The Labyrinth City was built to imitate this method. If the medicinal herbs that monsters hated could be grown there, people made sure they grew in abundance. The fact that herbs that didn't grow in human regions thrived here made it clear this was the monsters' domain.

The Labyrinth City had endured for two hundred years despite all sorts of issues. But the people were still frightened. They built walls around their houses; some gates were small so large monsters couldn't get in, and large gates for carriages were located in rear yards overflowing with medicinal herbs. The buildings themselves were made of stone and the windows had iron frames. It was mandated that a cellar be in each home for barricading oneself in, so that in the unthinkable case that monsters entered the Labyrinth City, people would still be okay.

Outward appearance, exposure to the sun, and functional aspects such as ventilation were secondary. The ability to withstand a monster invasion came first and foremost in this town.

No one objected to such a rule. Even if it hadn't been established, people would have cultivated the gloomy-looking herbs in their own homes. At their core, humans and monsters were different. They couldn't coexist. And this instinctive fear of monsters was grounded in the Labyrinth City.

"Both bromominthra and daigis grow round there, right?! All you gotta do is pick 'em and bring 'em here!"

The three adventurers gazed coolly as Kindel ranted and raved.

"Let's go."

Today would be another day of hard work in the Labyrinth. The medicine they'd received would soon run out, and they wanted to buy more with their own earnings. They had no time to listen to the likes of this man. They spoke to each other as if they hadn't heard him, and even after they left, Kindel continued to shout. However, no one could be expected to want to devastate their homes for a little pocket change, and the slum residents simply threw suspicious looks at this annoying intruder from the shadows of buildings.

Even Teluther and his subordinates remembered they had *urgent business* to attend to and left.

"Arghhh! Lithen to me, will ya?!" Kindel stamped his feet. "Damn squatters, buncha worthless— Eh? Squatters?"

It would have been better if he'd contributed a productive idea to his own work, yet Kindel had apparently hit upon another superfluous plan.

A slimy, disgusting smile appeared on his face, and he returned to the Merchants Guild. His destination wasn't his own office, but rather the Residential Affairs Division.

The division that managed houses and residents in the Labyrinth City.

06

"Morning, Slaken."

Mariela woke up as she always did.

As of late, she had something to greet in the morning before Sieg. "Slaken" was the Slime-in-a-Vial she'd made from a slime core and kraken intestines.

Though it was a man-made organism derived from kraken

parts, Slaken had no intelligence. It didn't understand anything Mariela said, and she even doubted if it recognized her as its master.

The squishy creature wriggling within the vial wasn't cute, but Mariela was fond of Slaken. When it came time for bed, she would move Slaken's vial from her workshop to the desk in her bedroom.

Although she'd carved a mark of subordination into its core, at the end of the day, it was still a slime. They instinctively crawled around in search of food, so she couldn't interact and communicate with it like a pet. Even Mariela knew this, so she hadn't taken it out of the vial she was raising it in, but she was very partial to the little guy.

After returning Slaken to a shelf in her workshop, she headed for her medicinal herb garden as always. Since she'd sold a large quantity of dried daigis and bromominthra to the Merchants Guild, she needed to harvest a larger amount than usual for her reserves.

Sieg watered the sacred tree instead of Mariela, who spent all her energy on the herb garden. She'd prepared the water, infused with Drops of Life, in a watering can. The tree seemed to like Sieg, as it dropped many more leaves for him than it did when Mariela watered it.

Argh, there's nothing to be annoyed about. I've got Slaken!

Mariela brimmed with a strange sense of hostility. She and Sieg finished tending the garden, then carried the large quantity of daigis and bromominthra to the cellar where she dried them with *Dehydrate*. Next came breakfast; they were later than usual today because she'd harvested so much.

The pair rattled around as they finished up housework and preparations to open the shop.

Around the time the shop opened, children arrived carrying large sacks.

"Good morniiing! We brought the apriore!"

"Morning! You guys picked a lot again today, huh? Thank you. You're not hurt, are you?"

They were children from the orphanage. Apriores grew in the shallow strata of the Labyrinth where only slimes appeared, as well as in the ordinary forest outside the Labyrinth City, both places where even children could harvest them relatively safely. The older children served as escorts while they picked the fruit and then brought it here. Because they were picked by children, worm-eaten and rotten apriores were mixed in with the bunch, and it took time to separate them. Even though the apriore were cheap as a result, many shops refused to purchase them, since they would prefer not to do this extra step. Mariela, however, made sure to buy from the children.

"We're fiiine! Not even slimes today."

"We got lots more than usual 'cause we picked 'em early in the morning."

Mariela prepared a bundle of apriore cookies for the giggling children. They were normal cookies made from cheap, coarse sugar and yagu butter, and they had no special effects. However, they brought great delight to the children since sweets weren't cheap—a rare treat.

"Thank youuu! You're the best, lady!"

The gleeful children flocked around her.

Mariela was well-liked. She rode this wave of popularity without complaint.

"There's enough for everyone, so don't push. Here you are."

CHAPTER 2: The Deluge

Upon receiving the cookies, the ecstatic children unanimously expressed their thanks and left for the orphanage.

Mariela's wave of popularity was short-lived. It wasn't until after she saw off the children, who disappeared like foam, that she realized something.

"They completely forgot their payment for the apriores..."

Lynx wasn't coming to the shop today, so she would temporarily close up at noon and go with Sieg to the orphanage to deliver the payment. It would be great to have lunch at the Yagu Drawbridge Pavilion for the first time in a long while, too. Or maybe they could buy and eat food on the go at the wholesale market.

Mariela and Sieg discussed the day's plans as they set the apriores down on a kitchen table and set to work like they always did.

07

"Sorry for the wait. Let's begin treatment," Medical Technician Nierenberg said to his patient, a soldier, with a slight chuckle.

The soldier would have wanted to respond, "No, not at all! I wasn't waiting," but his leg had been twisted and stitched back together at an unusual angle, and the "seam" was also noticeably crooked. It looked as if it had been bitten off and forcibly reconnected to his body. If he stayed in this condition, he wouldn't be able to walk for the rest of his life.

"W-w-w...wait a second, Doc. Are you gonna use that red and black stuff?" the soldier asked before Nierenberg began his dreaded treatment.

"Mm, are you talking about the new medicine? What's wrong with it?"

There were two types of potions called "new medicine" supplied by the Aguinas family. The red ones were mid-grade, while the black ones were high-grade.

"Well, I've...only ever been treated with the red stuff, but, uh, I hated it. I know it's valuable and expensive, but how do I put it... It felt kinda cold. If anything, the pain from my wound feels more...hot, I guess. But, like, when that stuff was used on me, I felt chilled right down to my bones. So cold I couldn't stand it. And even when the flesh itself was healing up, I felt a sort of shiver, like something totally different from my own flesh was regenerating..."

"Hmm..." Nierenberg listened with deep interest as the soldier continued.

"As for the black stuff, well, this is just what I heard, but they say it's like having a weird dream. It's high-grade, right? The guys treated with it are usually unconscious at the time, but they have dreams like they're floating underwater. Their bodies don't feel anything while they're in this water, like it's neither hot nor cold, and they can't even move a single finger. Their eyes are covered with something, but they can see their bodies through a gap in the cover. And they see their bodies slowly crumbling all over. Their blood spreads through the water like 'whoosh.' And not just from one spot—it's all over, everywhere. Even though they shouldn't feel pain and stuff, in this dream they just get colder and colder, and their view gets hazier, and they think, *Ahh, I'm dying!* Lots of guys have had this same horrible dream. And they all think the same thing when they wake up—*I'm back in my own body.*"

The man rambled on and on, perhaps afraid of Nierenberg's treatment. "Don't worry, I won't use the new medicine," Nierenberg assured him and drew back the surgical curtain to hide the soldier's chest.

If a patient thrashed around from the pain of surgery, his hand might slip. So, when he performed painful treatment on someone at the Labyrinth Suppression Forces' base, he blocked their pain receptors. However, even without the pain, it wasn't good for anyone to watch their own body be sliced up or see their blood splatter, not even a soldier used to combat.

Ever since the previous expedition, Nierenberg had started using cloth to partition off the part of the body he worked on during large-scale treatments so the soldier in question couldn't see the wound or the procedure. Moreover, until now, he'd only blocked pain in the affected area, and patients were conscious while he worked on them, so they knew what he was doing. But now he would even use a sleep spell during the procedure. It was a measure to prevent them from knowing about the abundant use of potions, but the only ones who knew the truth were Nierenberg and the others who administered treatment.

But to the soldiers who didn't know what spurred this change, it shook them to their very cores to think Neirenberg was actually getting nicer.

"Probe Organism."

Nierenberg invoked a skill to confirm the soldier was asleep.

This soldier's leg had been torn off by a monster. The monster had been felled and the leg retrieved, reattached so it wouldn't rot, but the length of the flesh and bone wasn't quite as long as the original leg had been. The wound was so deep that it couldn't be fixed with healing magic alone. Nierenberg's subordinates opened the potion storage box containing several types of specialized high-grade potions. Truthfully, the wound warranted a special-grade potion, but it was possible to restore it with a cocktail of specialized high-grade potions and skilled healers.

"Let's begin treatment," Nierenberg announced, to which the healers under him nodded and began operating on the soldier.

Soon after the treatment finished and he was transferred to a different room, the soldier woke up.

He didn't feel discomfort. He'd had no terrible dreams, either. When he looked at the lower half of his body, he saw his own familiar leg in the correct position, and it felt fine, not out of place at all.

"I'm going to check for feeling in the leg. Tell me if you feel any pain." Nierenberg reached his hand toward the soldier's leg and pressed the knuckle of his forefinger into the sole of the man's foot.

"Yeeeooooooooowww!!" screamed the soldier.

"I see, it hurts. Good, that means it's healing properly. But, say—haven't you been drinking a bit too much? You should seize this opportunity to reflect," Nierenberg said with a grin. Somehow, he looked like he was really enjoying himself.

The whole thing about Nierenberg getting nicer was clearly a lie. The soldier could barely stand the pain. In any case, his leg had been healed. He could walk again.

"Wish you'd made my legs a bit longer while you were at it!" joked the soldier after thanking the medical technician. He had no idea that his leg had been broken and stretched during treatment.

"We'll discuss it if both your legs are torn off." Nierenberg took him seriously. His subordinates, who knew the details of the operation, turned a little pale.

"Mr. Nierenberg, your daughter is here to see you. I'll show her to your room," said one subordinate as Nierenberg got up to leave the treatment room.

"I see," he answered, and headed to his office.

"Ooh, little Sherry's here!" cooed the soldier as he got out of bed with some effort. "The fact that she's Nierenberg's daughter is a bigger mystery than the Labyrinth itself." Now to gently acclimate himself to his body. He left behind the treatment room he'd spent so long in.

"Papaaa, I brought you your lunch since you forgot."

A twelve-year-old girl was sitting in Medical Technician Jack Nierenberg's office.

She was his daughter, Sherry.

The girl had large, bright eyes, completely unlike Nierenberg's unpleasant gaze. She was so lovely that, other than her black hair, you would have never guessed they were parent and child. She would almost certainly grow up to be a beautiful woman. One could catch a glimpse of her future as a popular girl, even if she didn't give out cookies like a certain chemist.

No, even now she showed hints of that.

It couldn't be a coincidence that every time Sherry came, the number of soldiers loitering around in the corridor connecting Nierenberg's room to the Labyrinth Suppression Forces' base gate increased. It was a worrisome situation for Sherry, but it was also worrisome for the soldiers who gathered to see a twelve-year-old girl. Even Nierenberg's medical treatments seemed to get better when she was around.

Sherry's mother had passed away some years back, so Sherry took care of the home for her busy father. Of course, he'd employed a maid as well, but Nierenberg felt Sherry was an excellent cook for someone her age.

"I thought we could eat together, so I brought my lunch, too."

Nierenberg was delighted to share a meal with his beloved daughter.

For some reason, Sherry's homemade meals tasted like her mother's. And even her adorable features were steadily growing to resemble his wife. He couldn't help wishing for a bright and blissful future for his dear daughter.

Just another reason we have to defeat the Labyrinth.

After they finished lunch, Sherry returned home.

Nierenberg went as far as the base's gate to see her off.

"The slums are dangerous. Go around through the town's north side to get home."

"Papa, you're such a worrywart! It's still noon, I'll be fine!"

Thanks to Nierenberg's murderous glare, no one approached Sherry while she was on the base of the Labyrinth Suppression Forces. However, outside the base, who knew what could happen? Maybe he doted on her too much, but he emphasized his point that she should be taking the safest road possible.

"Anyway, come home soon, okay?" she said, her father's words rolling off her like water off a duck's back. She kissed his cheek, waved, and departed for home.

Disregarding Nierenberg's instructions, she took the shortcut through the slums.

08

The southwest part of the Labyrinth City was known as the slums.

None of the houses lining this place had permanent residents.

The homeless who couldn't afford a stay at an inn gathered here and settled in the abandoned buildings that still had roofs.

Naturally, some of the houses didn't properly treat wastewater, which flowed out of the houses where people living hand to mouth and contained little magical power. It was hard to call this water a bounty, but It had no taste buds to tell the difference between delicious and disgusting.

It wandered in search of food, absorbing and digesting. Nothing else.

Many of Its kin split apart after growing to a certain size, but It continued to get bigger without dividing.

Perhaps this was due to the evolution It attained in order to monopolize feeding grounds and survive.

It migrated from Its treasured feeding spot and slowly began to feast.

09

"No dawdlin'! Hey, you oughta be grateful for the copper coins you're gettin' for thith!"

Construction Division Chairman Kindel's screeching voice echoed in the slums.

"What do you think, Colonel Teluther?"

"Ho-ho, quite the harvest."

"I'm much more useful than that stubborn lady, aren't I? She's all talk and no action."

"Indeed. Unlike a certain someone, you're a fine chairman."

A small mountain of daigis and bromominthra collected from the slums was growing in front of Teluther. Several slum residents and withered elderly people dried the plants with *Dehydrate*. As if their magical reserves had long since dried up, they tottered unsteadily on their feet. Whenever they took breaks to recover their magic, which was often, Kindel shouted at them to get on with it.

The slum residents hauling in the herbs looked perturbed, but they carried them without complaint and returned home after receiving their copper coins.

"Hey, what's with that look? You got thomethin' to say? If you got a problem, come here and say it to my face! Don't think I'll forget it!" Kindel waved a sheaf of papers at them, and the slum residents turned their faces away, silently deposited the herbs, and left.

The papers in his hand were a list of vacant slum houses he'd semi-forcefully borrowed from the Residential Affairs Division. Teluther had allowed him to take two members of the City Defense Squad with him as guards, and since morning, he'd been going around to each house in the slums and saying the following:

"Thith house should be empty. Listen up, squatters! If you don't want to be evicted, collect the herbth on the property and bring 'em to the main road!"

Unlike other homes in the Labyrinth City, many houses in the slums had no outer walls. And the walls that remained from the ruins of the Kingdom of Endalsia were reinforced with only scrap lumber and cloth, making them structurally unsound. Even though these homes needed more herbs to protect them from monsters than any others in the Labyrinth City, Kindel shouted at the residents to harvest and gather all of them up: "Thith ain't your house anyway!"

Most of the slum residents were former adventurers forced to quit work due to injury. Only a handful of them had earned enough money to be successful in a different business afterward or non-combat abilities that landed them a new job. Many who'd suffered serious injuries with no prospects of recovery had lost everything and ended up in the slums.

Nobody wanted to live there.

Because they were aware of this, the Residential Affairs Division did not investigate anyone who settled in the slums without permission, and the Schutzenwald family tacitly allowed them to stay there. Moreover, they regularly distributed food and encouraged the hiring of people from the slums.

What kind of authority did this man Kindel have to display such reckless behavior?

The two soldiers staying behind Kindel watched him under a cold gaze. Their task was to guard him. They stood in silence, holding their tongues through this extremely unpleasant assignment.

They'd both grown up in the orphanage without any sort of family. Neither of them had enough combat prowess to join the Labyrinth Suppression Forces, nor enough intellect to become civil servants, let alone the ambition to be adventurers. However, they reliably carried out their duties for the sake of a stable life. The City Defense Squad, which attracted people with subpar combat skills and intelligence from well-to-do families, needed *useful* human resources like them. They kept their emotions in check and only did what they were told to do. That was how it had always been.

The two guards gritted their teeth while keeping their expressions neutral. It would have been easy for them to speak up and give a piece of their minds—if they were prepared to lose their jobs, of course. However, they both had families to look after.

If I can just put up with this, maybe I can give my children a better life, they thought.

Standing behind Kindel was enough to keep him safe. Although there were former adventurers among the slum residents, they were underfed, in poor health, and lacking in sufficient weapons or armor. As such, they were in no position to lash out in anger at the trained armed guards.

Thus, as Kindel predicted, the residents brought the slum's herbs to him one after another.

"You've got more daigis left over there." Kindel pointed to a corner on the main road, holding back the people who'd dropped off the herbs and were about to leave.

"There's a storm drain in that corner. Rumors say it connects to the underground Aqueduct," one of the slum residents answered.

These lowlifes dared to comment. They weren't following his orders. It enraged Kindel.

"Wh-who do you think you're talking to?! Did you not hear my orders?!" Kindel raved, his face bright red.

However, the residents had finished their own work, so they ignored him and receded into the slums' depths.

"G-g-g-g-graaahhh!! Damn it! Damn it! Damn you people!"

Kindel furiously uprooted the daigis around the storm drain.

He didn't have the faintest idea.

Kindel had no clue the slum residents had left the roots intact during the harvest so that the plants would naturally grow back in a few days, and the herbs themselves had been harvested so only a sparse amount remained.

He didn't realize the residents had harvested only the young and vibrant springs of ivy because they knew even wilted daigis ivy and roots were effective.

He didn't know that no one had so much as touched the daigis around the storm drain connected to the underground. The people had taken pains to leave it so it would provide the minimum amount of protection against monsters.

Completely ignorant of these facts, unaware of what lurked in the underground Aqueduct, Kindel continued to yank out the daigis near the storm drain by its roots until none remained.

10

—All of a sudden, a hole gaped open from the ground above.

It had noticed something above had changed as It lurked beneath the surface.

Its food was living creatures and the magic residing in their corpses. It dissolved a variety of things in the process of absorbing magic, but this was nothing more than a means to ingest nutrients.

Its body was soft and indiscernible, so if It touched the ivy or roots of daigis, the herb would easily absorb its magical power. It instinctively feared the sensation of its magic slowly draining away.

It carried acid that had accumulated over many years. Physical obstacles such as rocks and soil were inconsequential. If Its core couldn't pass through, It could simply dissolve the obstacles and move on.

However, the roots and ivy of daigis had stretched overhead like the mesh of a net, blocking It from going up to the surface.

But a hole had now opened in that entanglement.

Beyond the hole lay plenty of food. Exquisite food the likes of which It had never tasted before.

Schwip.

It attached to the ceiling of the underground Aqueduct so It could slither through the hole.

The water pipe running through the hole was so small that Its core couldn't pass through.

Fshhh, fshhh. It spit out acid. The water pipe dissolved and the exit widened.

A new feeding ground lay just beyond.

Kindel was toiling away at the plants, red-faced and short of breath, when the ground around the storm drain collapsed, and an enormous slime seeped out before his eyes.

"HAWHAAA—?!"

Its sudden appearance left Kindel frozen in terror.

A slime's nucleus was typically about the size of an egg yolk and its entire mass roughly as big as two palms put together. However, the nucleus alone of the one before Kindel was gigantic—around the size of a human head.

The ground near the storm drain had caved in, and a soft mass sent up smoke as it slithered out from the hole. In its gloopy body, which grew taller than eye-level, was its nucleus, which had the appearance of a giant eyeball. It really looked like an entirely different creature than a slime, evoking an overwhelming feeling of unease in anyone who saw it.

When most of its body had oozed up out of the hole like some sort of viscous liquid, the giant slime, about the size of a carriage, slowly rose up, ready to feast on its prey. It made to attack Kindel and a nearby slum resident as if trying to enfold them in its body.

The Alchemist Who Survived Now Dreams of a Quiet City Life, Vol. 2

"Look out!" shouted one of the soldiers from the City Defense Squad who'd been escorting Kindel around the slums since that morning. His name was Kyte. He promptly used his Shield skill and readied his own shield to block the giant slime's path.

Kyte's Shield skill temporarily strengthened any equipped shield. Wooden shields, for instance, were vulnerable to fire, while those made of metal could be dissolved by acid. Kyte's skill supplemented the weaknesses of such materials and prevented attacks beyond the surface of the shield for a brief period. That said, it couldn't protect against powerful attacks. It was a weak ability, no match for the shield knights in the Labyrinth Suppression Forces.

However, he rushed in.

No matter how gigantic this thing is, it's still a slime. Even my skill should be able to defend against its acid discharge!

Kyte employed a shield bash that repelled the slime, which was about to swallow its prey whole, and even blocked the acidic liquid it sprayed.

"Are you all right? Hurry, get out of here while you still can!"

"Th-thank you!" The slum resident Kyte had saved dashed off.

Kyte had put up with a lot since that morning. He'd continued to watch the persecution of the people of the slums, whose lives were already difficult, and even still he hadn't been able to do anything. He'd been annoyed, frustrated, miserable.

"I'm glad I managed to save at least one person."

Kyte shifted his grip on his shield, turned toward his comrade, and called to him to help evacuate the residents. Then he ran over to rejoin the City Defense Squad.

"Nuh, nooooo, ah, aghghgh, help, huuuulpghl—"

Kyte had protected a slum resident. The most he could do with his skill was protect a single person.

He'd done everything he could.

There was nothing he could do about Kindel, just a little farther away, being swallowed whole by the enormous slime.

It was beyond his control. It could only be lamented as a great tragedy.

Because he'd really done everything he could.

Watching Kindel dissolve before their eyes inside the giant slime in an instant, people on the main road of the slums fell into a panic and scattered in all directions. They were former adventurers. They had a much better sense of danger than the members of the City Defense Squad, who spent their time safe and sound at their posts. That thing was massive, but it was still a slime. It had no eyes, ears, or nose. It simply sensed the magical power of its prey and attacked. The people concealed their magic so it wouldn't be detected and scattered to prevent gathering in a single location.

Their judgment was exactly right. From the giant slime's point of view, although it had finally emerged into a place with a wealth of food, its prey had dispersed as soon as it arrived. If its prey ran away, the monster's instinct was to attack to try to catch it. The slime spurted out acidic liquid in all directions. Only those who'd immediately hid in buildings, as well as the few soldiers who possessed the Shield skill, avoided it, and the main road of the slums was engulfed in agonizing screams.

"Eeeeeeee!"

"Gyaaaaah!"

"Ahhh, it's hot, it's hoooot!"

People cried out at the white-hot burning sensation from their flesh dissolving. The acidic liquid had a long range, and even those on the circular road near the Labyrinth, far away from the uproar, suffered injury.

"Water, rinse it off with lots of water! Hurry!" shouted Kyte. Colonel Teluther, whose very job was to take command of the field, stood uselessly in mute amazement. Kyte's comrades, too, simply awaited orders in confusion.

"Pull yourselves together! It's just a slime! We're not the City Defense Squad for nothing, are we?!"

As Kyte's voice rang out, the soldiers remembered what they were supposed to do and mobilized.

"Evacuate the residents! Prioritize the wounded!"

"All communication personnel, send a request for aid to the Labyrinth Suppression Forces! Their treatment center isn't far. Take the heavily wounded there."

"Those of you with shields, block its acid! The rest of you, make a barricade with the gathered daigis. The slime won't come near it. Anyone with offensive magic, fire it at the slime to create a diversion!"

The City Defense Squad troops began calling out to each other.

If the slime were capable of thought, it would probably be thinking something along the lines of, *I climbed all the way up here only for my prey to flee out from under me. Even the food that's still left has gotten so much more difficult to eat.*

However, the enormous creature didn't stop. Food with a suitable amount of magical power stood defenseless nearby.

The giant slime began to attack Teluther, who was still dumbfounded.

"H-how? Why— Hooow?!"

Gasping for air, Teluther fled. The slime slithered after him, dissolving the ground as it went.

The enormous creature was leaving the main road, which had turned into a hazard zone, with many injured people.

What should we do? A mood of uncertainty swept through the City Defense Squad.

"Colonel Teluther is distracting the slime for us! In the meantime, hurry, help the injured and evacuate the residents!"

Once again, it was the shield user Kyte who called out.

"That's our Colonel Teluther, looking out for his men! We won't forget your bravery, sir!" Regardless of whether or not the soldiers actually thought this, the vast majority went to help the injured, while a small group of highborn people who always stayed close to Teluther slowly followed him, possibly to offer help.

"Sieg, something's making a huge racket. I wonder if there's a festival?"

After finishing lunch and delivering the payment for the apriores to the orphanage, Mariela and Sieg had headed to the slum entrance on the Labyrinth side. The orphanage was located on the west side of the Labyrinth City at the border between the slums and the residential district. The wall surrounding the Labyrinth had two entrances: the northeastern side with the Adventurers Guild, and the southwestern side with the slums. So it was fastest to cut across the area around the Labyrinth to go from the orphanage to the wholesale market. Since they were already out, they planned to buy dinner before returning home.

They had to cut through the slums just a little bit, but the area near the Labyrinth wasn't particularly unsafe. Even children could roam around there at this time of day. Not to mention, the pair were unlikely to run into any shady characters since they were concealing their presence and magical power.

Mariela wondered aloud about the noise as she and Sieg passed through a slum alleyway. Just then, Teluther came rushing by with a gigantic slime hot on his heels.

"H-help meeee...!"

"Whaaaaaa—?!" Mariela shrieked in a panic. Sieg, immediately grasping the situation at hand, hoisted her over his shoulder and broke into a run.

"W-w-w-waaaait...!" Teluther cried, somehow keeping pace with Sieg. The colonel was surprisingly fast.

Sieg held Mariela, her hands and feet dangling wildly in the air, slung over his shoulder, grasping her legs in his left arm as he sprinted away from the clamor. If weren't for Teluther and the giant slime chasing after them, it would look like a kidnapping.

A thick layer of viscous liquid blocked the slime's nucleus—its weak point. A sword wouldn't be able to get through it. In fact, the slime's acid would probably melt the blade. And if Sieg faced it head-on, Mariela would be dragged into the fight. Sieg doubted Mariela would be able to avoid the spewing acidic liquid.

They zigzagged through the narrow alleys of the slum.

Carrying Mariela, Sieg dashed while dodging the liquid the giant slime occasionally spewed. Even though Sieg was switching directions at random, Teluther followed him as if the whole thing had been planned out in advance.

"I think we'd actually be better off splitting up..."

Sieg and Mariela could have dealt with being hounded by a massive slime with a monster-warding potion so long as no one was looking. Even better if the slime just chased after Teluther alone. For Sieg, Mariela's personal safety outweighed everything else.

"M-my skill...*Synchronize*...activated...on its own!"

Synchronize made another person's thoughts vaguely conform

to work advantageously for the user. It wasn't very useful in battle, but it was extremely effective in everyday situations.

Teluther awakened this skill more than ten years ago, back when he was still a soldier in the field. The orc raid that year had been much larger than usual, and the Labyrinth Suppression Forces and City Defense Squad had combined to take them all down.

The Gold Lion General Leonhardt had already distinguished himself as the head of the Labyrinth Suppression Forces. Teluther's heart was sent aflutter not only by Leonhardt's personal strength, but also by his battle cry, which increased his troops' morale instantly, and the way he cut through the vanguard mowing down orcs.

When Teluther finally managed to earn a seat at the same table as the general during a war council, he loitered around, wondering if there was a particular spot where he could catch Leonhardt's eye even just a little.

However, Leonhardt was already a capable general and the margrave's successor. He was surrounded by throngs of people, so Teluther couldn't even get close. Still, he was happy just to be in the same room. His eyes sparkled as he gazed at the general—and that was when Teluther's chance finally came.

"What is the count of our current supplies?" Leonhardt asked him. Supply management was Teluther's domain.

I have to be precise!

In a panic, Teluther produced a notebook from his chest pocket and informed Leonhardt of the quantity. It was at that moment...

Tap, tap.

...a colleague named Sequoias had artfully taken up position next to Leonhardt and tapped his own forehead, seeming to indicate Teluther's helmet.

I-is my helmet dirty?

The flustered Teluther quickly removed his helmet and industriously began polishing it with a handkerchief.

"Oh, Teluther, you're mistaken. Your helmet isn't dirty. I meant surely you could've memorized that little bit of information," Sequoias said with a big grin. The entire war council burst into laughter. Teluther's face flushed a deep scarlet from being made the butt of a joke in front of Leonhardt.

"Enough foolishness, Sequoias. Good work, Teluther," said Leonhardt to smooth things over. However, Teluther was forever scarred from being humiliated in front of the general he so admired.

Sequoias had shrewdly taken a seat near Leonhardt and scorned Teluther. Sequois and Teluther were fairly similar in lineage, military prowess, and intelligence, but Sequoias used his cunning to inflict shame on the other man.

Mortifying. Horrible. Agonizing.

Those feelings sprang Teluther's skill Synchronize into being.

Afterward, that skill caused Sequoias to lose his position, while Teluther ascended to the rank of colonel.

Even now, with the giant slime chasing him, Teluther Synchronized with Sieg's split-second escape decisions to perform feats far beyond his own physical abilities: dodging the slime's flying acid, leaping over obstacles at his feet, and following sharp turns. Sieg and Mariela had suppressed their own magic, so if Teluther separated from them, the giant slime would probably follow him. It wouldn't have been a sure thing for him to escape this far with just his own physical abilities.

However, the dramatic escape met an abrupt finish.

"A-a dead end……"

Just ahead of the three of them was the end of an alley.

It wouldn't be long before the enormous slime caught up with them. The creature would probably soon turn the last corner and show itself.

Teluther looked up at the wall towering before him. It seemed extremely high; he probably wouldn't be able to reach the top even if he stretched his arms.

Is this the end…?

"I shouldn't have dragged you into this. I'll buy you some time—get out of here if you can," Teluther said to the man who'd fled all this way protecting the girl.

Perhaps he'd Synchronized with Sieg's desire to protect Mariela, as Teluther turned his back to the him and charged his right hand with fire magic, ready to launch at the incoming giant slime.

Teluther took a stance with his fire magic to strike back at the approaching slime, bringing to mind the gallant figure of Leonhardt he'd witnessed during an orc raid.

General Leonhardt had faced the repulsive monsters that seemed to completely cover the earth as they swarmed out of the forest. He extended his right hand and shot fire magic.

"Firestorm."

The flames bursting forth in a spiral from his right hand swept over the horde like a tempest. Teluther was recalling the events with the number of monsters and the spell's power were ten times more than reality, but Leonhardt's spell did indeed overwhelm the orcs.

"Ahh, all that edible orc meat…"

Weishardt's lament signaled Leonhardt to draw his sword. Perhaps one should say the god of war who protected him inhabited that sword, as a one-sided sweep of the enemy unfolded before Teluther's eyes.

Now, just like the general that day, Teluther extended his right hand.

He faced the giant slime that rounded the corner and closed in on him like an avalanche and chanted a fire spell.

"Fireball."

Teluther couldn't use *Firestorm*, but he focused the entirety of his magical power into the ball of fire he created. It burst into a huge flame of a size that could even rival the giant slime's nucleus.

"Take thiiiiis!"

Teluther's flaming sphere catapulted forward, aiming for the nucleus...

Fshhhh.

...and vanished completely as soon as it made impact.

Whaaaaa—?!

Sieg reacted quickly and covered Mariela's mouth, muffling her shout. *Mumble, mumble.*

"This way!" Sieg extended a hand to the dumbfounded Teluther.

While Teluther had been chanting *Fireball*, Sieg had deftly scaled the wall and perched at the top, carrying Mariela.

The wall that seemed so daunting to Teluther apparently hadn't posed much of a problem to Sieg.

"Wait for meeee!" cried Teluther, jumping up and down.

Teluther may have looked absolutely comical, but the giant slime was advancing on him like a massive tidal wave, ready to swallow the man at any moment.

Seeing this, Mariela decided to make a monster-warding potion.

She had all the materials; she'd torn off bromominthra and daigis while Sieg carried her as they fled from the slime and she also had the day's sacred tree leaves on hand. They hadn't been dried—it had been a very busy morning—so she'd just been carrying them unprocessed.

This might out me as an alchemist, but this guy jumped in front of that giant slime and told us to run. I can't let him die like this.

Mariela had made up her mind.

"Form Tra-"

"Thunderbolt."

Krrboooooom.

Just as Mariela was about to use an alchemic skill, a bolt of lightning shot from the heavens.

Though a single strike, it delivered a crushing blow.

That bolt alone burned through the slime's nucleus, and the slippery mass collapsed, transforming into acidic liquid and sending up clouds of smoke with a sizzle as it melted the earth beneath it. A lone woman swooped down in front of it.

Her electrified brown hair billowing out behind her emitted sparks of gold and silver.

The woman's special monster leather bodysuit flashed on and off from the electrical current surging through her body. She wore tinted glasses to protect her eyes, and her only makeup was lipstick.

This was no doubt—

"L…L-L-L-L-Lightning Empress?!" Teluther shouted, incredulous. He couldn't believe his eyes—it really was Lightning Empress Elsee, the A-Rank adventurer. He'd only dreamed of ever getting so much as a glimpse of her.

Lightning Empress Elsee spoke. "I'm glad more than anything

that you're safe, Mariela. But what is Colonel Teluther doing here as well?"

"M-Ms. Elmera?!"

Lightning Empress Elsee—real name **El**mera **See**le.

The one who'd obliterated the enormous slime in a single blow was Elmera Seele, chairwoman of the Merchants Guild's Medicinal Herbs Division.

Sieg carried Mariela down the wall. When her feet finally touched the ground, she stood frozen with her mouth hanging open, ignoring Teluther as she listened to Elmera with Sieg.

Using simple water magic, Elmera washed away the acidic liquid that had melted the surrounding area, and then began to explain.

"The medicinal herbs brought in by adventurers is always too much or too little, so it's the job of the Medicinal Herbs Division to collect the herbs we're short on. That's why I registered as an adventurer specializing in herb collection. But since I was born with the protection of the God of Thunder, I ended up becoming a bit famous."

Mariela pointed out the huge difference between Elmera's usual outfit and her current getup.

"Hmm? My usual outfit? Due to the God of Thunder's influence, I generate a bunch of static electricity. Just touching my skin will *zap* you. Hence, why I need to wear clothing over my entire body, even gloves. And it makes my hair stand up. But ever since I began using your hair soap, Mariela, it's become a lot more manageable. Hmm? Why do I have my hair down? If I used lightning magic with my hair tied up, it would burn to a crisp. Also, my eyesight has grown worse due to the light from lightning attacks.

During battle, I can adjust my eyesight with magic, but if I did so all the time, I would become electrified and make *zap* sounds even through my clothes. It's a real bother."

Um, uhhh…there are so many weird things about this that I don't really get it even after listening to her.

Mariela opened her mouth to say something, but the words wouldn't come out, so for the moment she smiled vaguely and closed her mouth again.

Teluther, who'd finally come back to reality, shouted "Ms. Eeeeeelseeeeeee?!" and rushed over to her on all fours in a frenzy.

"I-I can't believe it! The genius of the Merchants Guild, Chairwoman Elmera, is that famous lightning beauty!"

What happened to her being all talk and no action? Incompetent? A thorn in his side? Hardheaded?

Teluther edged up to Elmera, his eyes absolutely sparkling. She shot him an icy glare.

"My identity as 'Lightning Empress Elsee' is strictly confidential. If my workload were to increase, I would have to stay at the office even later. Which is why anyone who's just a bit too loose-lipped is subject to a bout of memory loss." Elmera made an L shape with the thumb and forefinger of her right hand, brought it very close to Teluther, and created a discharge with a loud crackle in front of his eyes.

"Have I made myself sufficiently clear, Colonel Teluther?" said Elmera—no, Lightning Empress Elsee, smiling. Teluther violently shook his head up and down to the point where it almost tore from his neck.

"The guildmaster of the Merchants Guild instructed me to come here concerning the list of vacant houses that Construction Division Chairman Kindel forcibly took from the Residential

Affairs Division. It seems the Labyrinth Suppression Forces are on their way due to the slime. I imagine you would be happy to offer a thorough explanation as to the meaning of all this to his lordship, General Leonhardt?"

Elmera headed to the base of the Labyrinth Suppression Forces with Teluther in tow, who was so exhausted from the dramatic escape he looked like a defeated soldier. He hung his head as he left, and it almost looked like there was a dark cloud hanging over his back.

Mariela and Sieg were simply bystanders who had gotten caught up in everything and, in fact, wanted an explanation themselves, but it seemed they were free to go home.

"Ask me about it another day," Elmera had said.

Incidentally, Mariela asked her why she wore a skintight leather suit.

"This is thunder dragon leather. My husband gave it to me before we were married. It is a very durable material that has a high affinity for lightning attacks. He said, 'I don't want to see you get even a scratch.' Hee-hee!" She pressed both hands against her cheeks and shook her head back and forth.

"So that's your husband's preference, then? You two must be very close. Thanks for that."

Mariela had received a generous helping of sappy mushy talk. She was sure Elmera had a lot more where that came from and hoped she'd share the next time they saw each other.

That was a close one, Mariela thought.

It had happened right after lunch. A giant slime suddenly appeared, and Sieg had run around the slums carrying her.

She was still shaking. It really had been dangerous.

She was glad she hadn't ended up as food for the slime scattered around the slums. Her name had almost been changed from "Mariela" to "Marinara." Blech.

"Let's have something refreshing for dinner."

As they talked, they went shopping in the wholesale market for sure this time, then Mariela and Sieg departed for home.

12

Along with several subordinates, Medical Technician Nierenberg was treating people on the main road of the slums. Since those with serious injuries had been carried to the clinic of the Labyrinth Suppression Forces, only half of his subordinates and his top healer were left.

He'd arrived at the scene immediately after being contacted for his combat prowess. When healers had been gathered to form a medical team, Nierenberg had been chosen to lead them not just because of his abundant knowledge and his Probe Organism skill. He possessed top B-Rank combat skills in place of the ability to use healing magic.

He also had the task of protecting healers who had limited combat skills. His skills wouldn't have been effective against the enormous slime, but that didn't mean he couldn't bring down something like it.

It would be easy enough for him to treat the injured while

buying time until the soldiers dispatched from the Labyrinth Suppression Forces got there.

However, when Nierenberg arrived at the main road of the slums, the giant slime had already disappeared, and the only thing left was a large number of injured people.

Apparently, Colonel Teluther of the City Defense Squad had used himself as a decoy to lure the slime to a more deserted area.

Although there were many injuries, word was that only one had died. The slime's acid was being washed away with copious amounts of water, and the first aid measures taken had been good, so magic and regular medicine were sufficient to heal the injuries.

If flesh came in contact with the acid, burn scars would be left after treatment. Because healing magic was used to draw out the human body's ability to heal and repair the wound in a short time, scars would remain even if the wound was healed with magic.

However, the slum residents they treated all thanked Nierenberg and the other members of the medical team who'd immediately rushed in to help them, even though they must have had things they'd wanted to say to the members of the City Defense Squad.

This line of work isn't bad. Nierenberg grinned.

Apparently, the Lightning Empress dispatched from the Merchants Guild defeated the giant slime. She had seemingly headed for General Leonhardt with Colonel Teluther and several members of the City Defense Squad. They were probably investigating the incident right about now. The soldiers from the Labyrinth Suppression Forces were restoring the slums along with the remaining soldiers from the City Defense Squad.

After finishing treating the injured, Nierenberg returned to the clinic with his subordinates.

*　　*　　*

"Mr. Nierenberg."

One of Nierenberg's subordinates who had been administering treatment in the clinic hastened over to him.

"Your daughter..."

Nierenberg rushed to the sickroom his subordinate indicated.

"Papa... I'm sorry..."

There he found his beloved daughter Sherry, her face wrapped in bandages.

CHAPTER 3

The Meat Festival

01

"Whoa, you serious?"

Back at the Yagu Drawbridge Pavilion, Mariela and Sieg told Lynx the entire story of the giant slime.

They kept Lightning Empress Elsee's identity under wraps since neither of them wanted to have their memories erased.

Elmera had claimed to make a *zap* sound whenever she touched something, which was the same sound she used to describe everything from static electricity to lightning attacks. That made it all the more terrifying. Plus, it was really more of a *crackle*.

If I got hit by that, I'd lose other important things besides my memory!

Mariela's lips were properly sealed, and she would let nothing slip from them.

According to Elmera, Construction Division Chairman Kindel abused his authority for personal gain. And it all culminated in Kindel letting a giant slime that had been living in the underground waterway into the slums. The man had been swallowed and killed by the slime, but all the assets he'd left behind were seized and set aside to help with the disaster recovery.

"I feel bad for Chairman Kindel's family," said Mariela, to which Merle of Merle's Spices, who was listening to the story, told her the following while acting it out with Elmera.

"His wife said, 'Oh, poor me. Please come with me to my parents'

home in the imperial capitaaal,' while nestling up to a young servant all happy. Like this."

Elmera squealed "Madam" in delight as she grabbed Merle's corpulent, orc-like body.

Just as one would expect from an A-Rank adventurer. Not even Merle daunted her.

More importantly, how did Merle know something like that? That network of wives was truly something else.

Elmera told Mariela with a wink that Kindel's seized assets would be used to repair houses in the slums so they would be more comfortable to live in.

As for Colonel Teluther, he was in charge of the City Defense Squad and caused the inadequate management of their medicinal herbs, which were necessary materials for strategy, and he bore heavy responsibility for Kindel's crimes. However, taking into consideration how he'd put his life on the line to protect the slum residents after the appearance of the giant slime, he was stripped of his position but remained with the City Defense Squad as an adviser.

His successor apparently originated from the administrative side of things, but Elmera hadn't heard details. He was completely inconspicuous and had unflaggingly worked in Teluther's shadow. He apparently said he would continue to work hard from here on out.

A commoner soldier named Kyte, who had worked hard to bring the situation under control, was promoted to captain. According to Elmera, he was "a serious but very interesting person." Adviser Teluther's job was not to offer advice to the new colonel or Captain Kyte, but rather to have a "discussion" with troops who abused their social standing and wouldn't listen to orders.

They all had dinner as they talked about these things.

The Black Iron Freight Corps returned to the Labyrinth City today, and since the Yagu Drawbridge Pavilion had held a celebration of their safe return, the food was extravagant. Every member of the Corps gathered there, and as always, Captain Dick made a pass at Amber and was skillfully rebuffed, then resorted to snuggling a pillow while calling her name over and over.

The three newly recruited slaves also ate in a corner of the restaurant, and when Mariela greeted them, they bobbed their heads to her.

"Mariela, isn't it about time for the kids to go to bed?" Lynx butted in before she could even ask the newcomers' names.

"Geez, I'm not a kid! Besides, aren't you basically the same age as me?" Mariela grumbled.

"I think it's about time to feed Slaken," Sieg whispered to her.

Oh, so it was. Mariela's mood lightened in an instant, and she left the restaurant with Sieg.

"Anyway, the newcomers sure are quiet, huh?" Mariela asked Lynx, who'd come with them to the front of the shop to see them off.

"Yeah," Lynx answered simply, then said, "Well, see ya," and waved. "It's 'cause their vocal cords were crushed," he continued, but Mariela was too far away to hear him.

The Black Iron Freight Corps had many secrets regarding their work of handling potions. They couldn't treat the slaves they'd bought the same as the comrades they'd risked their lives with over a long period of time. They were also concerned that the slaves' Orders would be forced out of them and their secrets exposed. To protect Mariela and Sieg's secrets, the slaves' vocal cords had been crushed so they couldn't talk.

Even such an act could be carried out on lifelong slaves and penal laborers.

*   *   *

(Our next shipment will be more slaves...?)

Lieutenant Malraux was speaking with Captain Dick telepathically. Ostensibly, Malraux was quietly throwing back his drink, while Dick had buried his face in a pillow, moaning Amber's name over and over as he rubbed it.

Their previous two cargos had been slaves requested by the slave trader, Reymond.

The Labyrinth subjugation expedition and the sowing of wheat were over. Winter would soon arrive. Seasons made no difference within the Labyrinth, but subjugations would become smaller in scale for a while. No one needed the extra hands during the winter. In the first place, it was common for yagu merchant caravans to carry people and goods into the Labyrinth City. The Black Iron Freight Corps's job was to carry expensive goods that were too much for the periodic yagu services to transport. What had happened to cause a shortage of only slaves?

(Lynx, how are things looking near Mariela?)

Having finished his communication with Dick, Malraux exchanged information with Lynx. Even after his conversation was over, Dick continued to massage the cushion, which meant he just wanted to squish it, rather than use it as a cover as they exchanged messages. It was a pitiful sight.

(Everything's normal. And the Aguinas girl's in the clear. The Aguinas family and the other nobles don't seem to know about Mariela. Come to think of it, I actually saw Reymond coming and going from the Aguinas house.)

Were the slaves headed toward the Aguinas house? What would a family of alchemists who managed and researched potions use slaves for?

(Suspicious.)

Malraux emptied his glass and disappeared into the night.

"Right, Newie, Nick, Jay, once you're done eating, return to the base," Lynx said to the three slaves.

Upon hearing Lynx's voice, Newie gulped down his remaining food and rushed over in a mad hurry. His full name was Newel.

The hunchback man following him was Nicolai, called Nick.

Quietly following at a reasonable distance, only his eyes restlessly glancing around at his surroundings, was Jacob. Jay for short.

Although the Black Iron Freight Corps had transported slaves last time, when they went to buy some several days after delivering them to Reymond, all the good ones had already been sold. These three seemed like they'd just barely manage to be drivers; only Jay was in his mid-twenties, while the other two were past thirty. These penal laborers with little magic and no decent combat skills were small, dishonest cowards who had repeatedly targeted the weak in robberies and other crimes.

The three of them followed Lynx as they headed to the base of the Black Iron Freight Corps.

Self-important whelp. The name's Jacob. Don't go around givin' me nicknames.

Without letting his thoughts show on his face, Jay, the last in line, mentally cursed Lynx.

All he does is chase floozies. I bet he'll have plenty of fun after he returns us to the base. Sonuva bitch, why him? And also, where've I seen that girl before? Ohhh, maybe the destitute girl who bought that old guy? This one had a real buff fella with her, but... Nah. No way that slave's still alive. He was about to keel over. You know what? I bet he's an adventurer in the Labyrinth City who fell for her. She must come from some reaaal good stock, that girl. And the guy with her had a nice weapon on him. Man, if I had that kinda loot, I could kill people a lot easier.

Jay had first seen Mariela inside the animal enclosures provided for guests at Reymond's place of business. It was after she'd woken up and gone with the Black Iron Freight Corps to the slave trader. Jay was a shrewd man, and he'd introduced himself as the caretaker of the animals there. He felt it shameful to eat for free before he was bought.

He didn't necessarily like animals or have a knack for taking care of them, nor did he possess an admirable attitude. A lot of the customers who came to the slave trading company came by carriage. Normally, those who did wanted slaves for dangerous heavy labor such as working in the mines, carrying luggage for the Labyrinth Suppression Forces during their usual serfs' off period, or fighting in the army.

There's no way I was gonna do that stuff. Even though I was gettin' fed up with the easy work doin' odd jobs, I'd rather stay unsold at the slave trader's.

If he took care of the animals, he'd make the customers think he belonged to the slave trading company, and he'd be able to stay out of the merchant room during business discussions. If the customers didn't think he was merchandise, he could cleverly remain unsold.

That was how Jay had been able to stay at Reymond's business for an exceptionally long time.

The Black Iron Freight Corps bought him because there was nobody else who seemed capable of driving. As Nick and Newie weren't enough, it took the Corps asking Reymond the slave trader whether there was really nobody else for him to remember at last. "Now that you mention it, there is one other."

The fact he was bought by the Black Iron Freight Corps, who

made trips through the Fell Forest, was bad enough, but then they immediately crushed his vocal cords after buying him. He never thought healing magic could be used like that.

It's that healer, Franz, I hate the most.

The loss of his vocal cords had been painless, but now Jay could no longer even make sounds like *ah* or *uh*.

From a penal laborer's point of view, by no means did the Black Iron Freight Corps treat him poorly. He had enough clothing, food, and shelter, and sometimes he even got to have delicious food and a little alcohol, like today. He could say with certainty that he was much safer than the members of the Corps who traveled through the Fell Forest and confronted monsters. He could even say his circumstances were too good for someone who'd attacked the vulnerable like girls and the elderly, stolen money, violated women, and sometimes killed people.

However, Jay's heart was filled with discontent.

Those assholes get to have their fill of booze, meat, and women, while I lie in bed under a thin blanket.

Jay seethed with envy.

But having no voice, that discontent never reached his mouth.

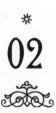

02

"Do you carry this salve?"

"I'd like to buy smoke bombs in bulk."

"Is this the apothecary of the girl and the pretty girl?"

The shop's been kinda busy lately, Mariela thought while attending to customers.

"And, as for you, didn't you leave off another 'pretty'?" she grumbled, to which Lynx, who was helping himself to some lunch in the kitchen, replied, "Huh? Itty-bitty?"

Hey, hey! Lynx, Sieg, wanna tell me why your eyes went straight to my chest?

The customer who'd said "girl and pretty girl" mumbled, "Itty-bitty girl and pretty girl... That's deep." The increase in weirdo regulars troubled Mariela.

Speaking of regulars.

The dwarven trio came as they did every day, took a break with some tea, and bought salves. As long as they bought the stuff occasionally, it would have been fine if they came just to drink tea, too, but apparently, they gave the salves to adventurers who'd been injured and were squatting in the slums.

The three slum inhabitants who'd helped with the renovation of Sunlight's Canopy seemed to have completely recovered from their injuries and returned to being adventurers. Recently, they'd come to the shop to buy salves. They said it was because they were able to afford it with the money they'd earned as adventurers. Mariela had been so happy that she'd thrown in smoke balls created from monster-warding and sleeping herbs as freebies. Their efficacy spread widely via word of mouth, causing her to receive a large number of orders. They weren't even potions, yet somehow the effects of these normal items changed with a little fine-tuning.

Merle's influence was quite astounding, too.

Mariela's shop offered several types of soap. These, too, were regular items, but *Essential Alchemic Products to Make Your Life*

Easier registered in Mariela's Library had recipes for powdered soap for laundry, liquid soap for dishwashing, soap for personal hygiene such as a liquid for hair, a solid for the body, and a creamy soap for the face. They had two effects: softening and cleansing. She also offered all kinds of scented soap.

In truth, there were many more recipes with names like "Refreshing" and "The Works," but she only sold the types she could make by combining lifestyle magic like *Dehydrate* and *Pulverize* without using alchemic skills at all. Considering the average in other shops, her soap cost a little more than the market price in the Labyrinth City, but the pack of housewives came in turns to buy it from her.

Amber, in typical Amber fashion, told her while laughing, "Ela, your medicine works so well! I recommended it to other ladies in the business. Oh, and I also recommended your salves to my customers. It does wonders and heals scratch marks in one night, so I think some of the customers were disappointed. Hee-hee-hee." Mariela wasn't sure she should ask for more details about the scratch marks.

She was certainly grateful she'd been getting more customers, thanks to word of mouth from her regulars, but…

"Hey, hey, hey, you quack chemist! Lookit how much my arm swelled up when I used your medicine! What're you gonna do about it, eh?!"

"Yeah, that's right! We're adventurers, ya know! What if we can't go into the Labyrinth no more?!"

Recently, she'd also been experiencing an influx in customers with ridiculous complaints about her goods: customers who said there were bugs in their medicine so big she wanted to ask them how they'd gotten them in there in the first place; customers who said their stomach hurt after taking the medicine even though they were shouting energetically at the top of their lungs; customers who pasted a Sunlight's Canopy label on a tin of ointment from another shop and then said the stuff inside was different than advertised.

They were all people who'd never been to her shop before and who really looked like thugs. Today's bunch, too, were obvious delinquents who cowed at first under the sharp stare of the regulars whose refined teatime was being disturbed before flying into a rage. Just as they were about to get violent, Sieg held them down and wrapped them up with rope he had ready on the corner of the counter. He could have taken them to the City Defense Squad's office, but just in case, Mariela and Carol examined the supposedly swollen area on one of the perpetrators.

"Ahh, this is daidara snail mucus," observed Mariela as she looked at the red rash on the restrained man's arm. He'd probably smeared it on himself just a short while ago, as some of the shiny stuff remained on his irritated skin.

A daidara snail was a huge snail that lived in the clammy strata of the Labyrinth, and its shell alone was about the size of two adult fists. It was not a monster, so if you killed one, you could recover its entire body. It was covered with sticky mucus that left a red, itchy rash if you touched it with your bare hands, but if you rinsed the rash with clean water and didn't scratch it, it would completely heal by the following morning.

Incidentally, the creature was edible. A large quantity had made the rounds at the wholesale market yesterday, so he'd probably used those to inflict this on himself.

Mariela had bought some, too, and put the leftovers in her magical tool for food storage.

"I said this happened 'cause of your medicine, twerp!"

Ignoring the delinquent's repeated false accusations, Mariela abruptly took out the daidara snail.

As if it were the first time Carol had seen it, she said "Oh my" with an expression of both surprise and great interest. Because it was cheap, gross looking, and only somewhat tasty, it was more of a commoner's food, so it had probably never crossed the dining table of the aristocratic Aguinas family. Too bad—daidara snails made a great soup stock, and the flesh was firm and mild. Because it went well with vegetables, it had a wide range of uses as an ingredient in stir-fries or soup.

"And here we have a daidara snail. The surface mucus poses no danger if immediately soaked and rinsed with water. However..."

With a clunk, Mariela used a hammer to split the daidara snail's shell.

She removed a pea-green sack from the intestines that spilled out, put it on a plate, cut it open, and removed the yellow fluid inside it. She then scooped the fluid with a spoon and held it up for all to see.

"...you seeee, if you add this venom to the daidara snail's mucus *like this*..."

Without any regard for the delinquent shouting, "Hey, what're you doing?! Cut it out!" Mariela smeared the yellow liquid onto the rash on his arm.

Then a tightly packed cluster of tiny, round spots swelled up on the affected area, a colorful variety of green, yellow, white, and blue from the roots to the tips. From above, it looked like fish eyes had sprouted from the man's skin.

"Eek!" The faces of the two delinquents turned white in an instant, and they were speechless.

Although Carol uttered "How revolting…," she stared fixedly at the spots without blinking.

Yeah. It's super-gross, but you just can't help but stare, right? I totally get it.

This unladylike side to Carol was probably why the two got along so well.

"So it was a daidara snail after all. Gee, if you'd only said so from the start, then I wouldn't have done something this risky. Now look what happened. It's really bad. It's turned all sorts of funky colors…… Would you like me to heal it?" Mariela threatened. Her little speech had been in a monotone. She wouldn't win an award for best actress, but it seemed to be enough for the delinquent who was overwhelmed by the sheer impact of the boils.

He nodded his head up and down in response.

The rest was simple. Looking like he might cry at any moment, the man truthfully answered Sieg's questions.

By the way, the fluid from a daidara snail's intestines isn't poisonous. Mariela had simply said so as a threat. It was surprisingly not well-known, but a daidara snail secreted this fluid in the mucus on the surface of its body to produce colorful spots for luring prey. Since they were just bubbles with nothing inside them, they weren't harmful at all and quickly came off if you rinsed them with water.

If you applied the fluid to the itchy rash, it would be cured faster than just rinsing it with water.

It's been a long time since I've seen spots like these.

Mariela remembered a long time ago, when she could just about make mid-grade cure potions, her master's face and neck had been covered in these spots. Her master had put on a convincing performance, crying, "M-Marielaaa, help meee, hurry and make a cure potion—not a low-grade one, mid-grade!"

Completely taken in, Mariela thought her master was going to die, and she cried as she desperately concocted a cure potion.

Incidentally, mid-grade cure potions didn't get rid of the spots. The spots were neither poison nor a disease but rather simply stuck to the skin, so there was no reason a potion would do anything.

"Th-they're not going awaaay!" Mariela sobbed as she made countless cure potions. Thanks to this, she'd mastered how to make them, but she would never forget her master's face or laughter as she was told "Just kidding!"

For the next three days, she'd only made food with daidara snails for her master as punishment.

The memory had gotten a rise out of Mariela, who used a needle to pop the delinquent's spots one by one to take out her anger. They were just bubbles, so they shouldn't have hurt. However, the two delinquents believed they were boils and apologized profusely through their tears: "I'm shorry, thank you sho mutch."

They were completely convinced it was a dangerous poison. Their tears inspired a bit of mischief in Mariela, who put water in a porcelain pitcher and colored it slightly with yagu milk, then used the lifestyle magic Light to illuminate the contents.

"Since you told me the truth, I'll use my special medicine to treat you," she said, pouring the water from up high so they wouldn't notice the light inside. Because Light illuminated the pitcher's interior, the cloudy white water looked like it was shining. Neither potions nor Drops of Life shone like that, but this was an amusing little trick.

The ordinary shining water rinsed away the colorful spots, which came off in large chunks. The two delinquents, who believed it was an incredible medicine, prostrated themselves in front of

Mariela and apologized, and then the guards Merle had summoned took them away.

"Another rival apothecary?" Mariela sighed. Her medicine had a reputation of being very effective, and she'd been getting more and more customers through word of mouth. What's more, even the most popular maker of medicine sold at the Adventurers Guild shop, Carol, came to her shop, and now the two girls made medicine together. It hadn't been long since the shop opened, but sales were through the roof to the point where any mention of medicine immediately brought Sunlight's Canopy to mind.

But the more their medicine sold, the worse the harassment became from other chemists whose own sales had taken a hit. At first, it had only been reputation damage, but Merle's network of housewives stamped that out...or rather, they beat the harassers at their own game.

Housewives are scary. What are they, masters of intelligence wars? Some sorta spy organization?!

If the harassers had given up there, Mariela would have simply shuddered at the might of the housewife intelligence agency, but her competitors seemed to have resorted to violence by hiring thugs. Mariela and Sieg's polite little "explanations" managed to coax the thugs into spilling whom they worked for, but things just couldn't go on like this forever.

What a fix.

When she turned toward Carol to discuss countermeasures, she found her absorbed in playing around with the daidara snail's mucus and yellow secretion, mixing them together to produce colorful bubbles. She was way too curious.

Upon noticing Mariela's gaze, Carol looked at her with sparkling eyes. "Mariela, how did you make that shiny water from before?"

She was in such high spirits that any further discussion would be pointless.

After Mariela explained the trick, Carol gleefully began pouring shining liquid into pitchers and teapots. One by one, she poured sparkly water or tea for the regular customers and the shoppers who'd been watching the whole thing.

Incidentally, this made its rounds as an extremely popular parlor trick—where the pourer struck a cool pose while pouring the shiny magic water. In fact, many children and fathers received a good scolding from their mothers and wives for making a big mess as they tried it for themselves. These stories dominated the conversation for weeks.

Even at Sunlight's Canopy, a self-service tea station was set up in one corner in response to zealous demand from the regulars. It offered several kinds of tea leaves, a tea set, and a magical tabletop burner you could put a kettle on. Because cleaning tools had been placed nearby, people tended to mop up their own spills.

Perhaps as a consequence, people posed with their shiny tea every day, making it harder and harder to determine exactly what kind of shop Mariela was running.

It wasn't until a few days later that Mariela could finally talk with Carol about the harassment from owners of other apothecaries.

Carol didn't seem aware of it at all. Befuddled, she simply replied, "My... If only the other chemists could make medicine as good as yours, Mariela."

"Well, yeah, exactly. The way they make it, for instance... Ooh, that's it! I've got it!"

She'd hit on a bit of an idea. She closed the shop earlier than usual that day, then went with Sieg to see Elmera.

03

"You would be willing to teach how to make medicine?" parroted Elmera, chairwoman of the Merchants Guild's Medicinal Herbs Division. Her vice chair, Leandro, looked just as stunned as she did.

"Yes. Not every kind, of course, but my best sellers, like salves, painkillers, and smoke bombs. Oh, and Lady Carol's on board, too."

Mariela and Sieg had visited Elmera at the Merchants Guild for advice about the harassment from owners of other apothecaries.

"But all of them are your smash hits."

"That's right, but they're all simple to make. Isn't it a bad look to have a huge discrepancy in sales for something as basic as salves?"

Mariela's question about the pharmaceutical situation in the Labyrinth City was on point. The standards for chemists in this place were low, and many people didn't even have the basics down to a satisfactory degree. Thanks to the high quality of materials from the Labyrinth, medicines managed to have passable effects only. In truth, medicinal problems had cropped up here and there, and trying to raise the chemists' skill levels was quite the headache for Elmera.

The Medicinal Herbs Division published all kinds of books on how to make basic medicine, including the enormous *Encyclopedia*

of Medicinal Herbs and Their Effects that consolidated information on herb effects and processing methods. They were also steadily working on a certification system by way of seminars. But Chairwoman Elmera's expectations and the reality of these chemists were way too different, which was why she hadn't been able to get the results she wanted.

Not every chemist made medicine in a half-baked way. Information in *The Encyclopedia of Medicinal Herbs and Their Effects* and other publications related to medicine was proof of their research. That meant the reason the pharmaceutical situation in the Labyrinth City hadn't improved was because of how low their alchemic skills were.

Not only could Mariela make high-grade potions, she had a firm grasp on the basics, such as processing materials. That's why she could identify and discern the condition of materials and partially processed goods just by looking at them. As a skilled chef can tell just by tasting a dish how the ingredients were processed and what spices were used, alchemic skills can easily tell a person information beyond the five senses.

Although alchemists from the imperial capital employed by the Aguinas family could probably do the same thing, they didn't show up in town. It would be nice if alchemists from the Empire and its neighboring countries paid them a visit, but people with that sort of knowledge and skill could make a living in the region where they'd formed a pact with the ley line. They would never go out of their way to a place like the Labyrinth City where alchemy couldn't be used.

Ghark, who ran a medicinal herbs shop, possessed the Material Appraisal skill from a young age. Now his skill level was high. Even in a batch of combined materials like medicine, he could use specialized magical tools along with Appraisal to glean information.

But those who had increased their Appraisal skill, which was excruciatingly difficult to master, were few and far between, and skill users generally concealed it to avoid nuisances. Few people knew Ghark possessed it, and the degraded, second-rate products lined up at the front of his shop served to disguise the place as an ordinary medicinal herbs shop.

In other words, hardly anyone in the Labyrinth City could accurately grasp the condition of medicinal herbs and the workmanship of medicine.

Chemists didn't clearly understand the quality of the materials they used or the medicine they made. Even in the case of new products, they had to perform several tests to understand their effects. This whole thing might have been different with the support of the public, but compared to magic that could heal wounds instantly even in battle and potions that could make up for its shortcomings, medicine was seen as inferior, and people were forced to study it on an individual basis.

It was when Elmera became chairwoman that the Merchants Guild's Medicinal Herbs Division began to focus on medicine quality improvement. The division, originally in charge of the regulation of medicinal herb shipments from the Labyrinth City, was responsible for the optimization of processing expensive medicinal herbs to preserve their value. In the Labyrinth City, where efforts had to be focused on subjugating the Labyrinth and there was no spare energy for other things, the advancement of medicine was inevitably slow.

These were the circumstances Mariela was under when she suggested she could teach others how to make medicine—which combined techniques left in the Library by senior apprentices with material processing techniques. It was way higher than the quality of medicine in the city. Although salves were basic medicine, it would be incorrect to say the know-how of making them was also not advanced. Teaching your competitors on how you make your livelihood wasn't something that was usually done.

It was understandable for Elmera to be perplexed by Mariela proposing to disclose this information.

However, neither Mariela nor Carol had any reason to be worried about teaching how to make medicine. Orders had been on the up-and-up by large quantities, and Mariela couldn't make them all in time. Besides, even if she stopped selling salves, painkillers, and smoke bombs, Carol could focus her efforts on medicine that alleviated the aftereffects of a disease while Mariela made a variety of other medicines.

Incidentally, Mariela had been working hard with the desire to make medicine that was sweet tasting and easy to take, but it hadn't been going well at all.

Although neither of them put it in words, they weren't really making their living from medicine sales. And their problems would increase if they hired people. Mariela and Carol knew it would be too much for anyone to wrangle in the sixteen- and seventeen-year-old girls who had too much knowledge in one field and knew nothing else.

Not to mention Mariela had her secret of being an alchemist. She couldn't afford to be hassled by her unskilled adversaries. It would be better to provide some amount of information and be hidden in a sea of chemists than to scale up and monopolize.

"Mm, you could get a onetime payment as an informational fee at the time of contract, and then receive a portion of the sales while maintaining the rights to the manufacturing process. What do you think?"

"The patent system used in the imperial capital? A 'medicine' category does not exist."

Leandro's suggestion baffled Elmera. Of course she knew the system. The Labyrinth City was part of the Empire, so the system applied here, too.

Although the Empire's patent system protected new technology, the categories were limited. The most popular one was "magical tools." On the other hand, categories for alchemic goods like potions didn't exist. Alchemists had the Library, and only those permitted by their masters could learn the information, so protecting it with a patent would actually be a hindrance.

Smithing techniques weren't covered, either. The production of ordinary iron increased in scale with advancements in technology, but magical metals such as mythril and adamantite couldn't be manufactured unless the blacksmith's skill level was sufficient, whether for smelting or forging. Conservative theory remained steadfast regarding the acquisition of rights for products that only skilled people could create.

On the other hand, magical tools technology, which was growing rapidly due to development in the Labyrinth City, didn't require a particular skill, and disclosing information about it would be very likely to harm the interests of its developers. It wouldn't be an exaggeration to say the Empire's patent system developed due to the advancement of magical tools.

The only area within the Empire where potions couldn't be made was the Labyrinth City's region, so even though the city had medicine, it was the only location without a "medicine" category in the patent system. Therefore, if you wanted to apply for a medicine patent, you would have to request the creation of a category for it, but considering the market scale for medicines, Elmera felt it wasn't likely to work.

"A category application, hmm...?" she mumbled, to which Leandro offered a suggestion.

"Ms. Elmeraaa, I bet you're thinking it won't go through even if we apply for a 'medicine' category, yes? You're right; we'd be lucky if it did go through! It could take years to see results. So for now, why not accept a 'seminar fee' and draw up a contract for royalty payments as well?"

Ever the adaptable one, that Leandro.

"Aha. A fine idea. We shall make participation compulsory for the chemists who have been causing trouble at Mariela's apothecary."

"In that case, I'll locate some staff with extra time on their hands and have them draw up a plan based on the patent system. Ms. Elmera, if you would, please speak to the guildmaster. Mariela, we'd be happy to have you as a lecturer." Leandro gave a wave of his hand, then went to find available subordinates to delegate the entire job. Although it had been his proposal, it didn't appear he would be writing it himself.

"I've got some reeeally fun work for you all. How about you collaborate? Fear not, I'll supervise, only for a little while," they heard him say, skillfully manipulating his subordinates.

"Mariela, I'll serve on the staff as well. Any insubordinate chemists will be getting a *zap* from me, don't you worry. Ah, with this, the Labyrinth City's chemists will improve by leaps and bounds!" Elmera gushed. Wasn't her identity as the Lightning Empress a secret?

And what good would it do to give them a *zap*? Mariela felt like it might make them forget whatever she taught them, which would just defeat the entire purpose.

After Leandro delegated every last task, the staff worked on a plan all night, and Elmera got permission from the guildmaster of the Merchants Guild the following day. The chemists received an explanation of the contract and usage fees, and a seminar was held after the roughly two-week-long notification period.

Incidentally, the contract and usage fees differed depending on the information provided. For the first installment, the planned contract fee for salves, painkillers, and smoke bombs was one large silver coin each. This would be the seminar fee. The usage fee would be 2 percent of sales, paid yearly. These terms were signed in a magical contract before the seminar, so no one could provide a false report at the time of payment. If someone made a significant improvement to a product based on the methods they learned and obtained clearly superior or different effects, it would be considered a different product and thus outside the scope of the contract.

Once Mariela held the seminar, the harassment at her shop immediately ceased.

That was because other chemists in the apothecary trade were improving their skills instead of wasting their time giving Mariela grief. Those individuals attended the seminar to beat the rest at their own game. That was why the seminar was a great success, and Mariela wound up holding it at the same time every week.

The chemists who'd been caught pestering Mariela listened silently in a corner. They even participated the following week, too. The seminar fee served as the contract fee, meaning they were paying double to attend twice. They looked uncomfortable when she asked them why.

"I tried to make it like you said, but it just never turned out well."

Apparently, they'd used the entirety of the dried curique—even the veins and stems.

It hadn't occurred to Mariela and Elmera that there were people who didn't know which components of medicinal herbs to use. It seemed so obvious to the two of them that they never thought to mention which parts. Once they realized this this, they tried incorporating practical exercises into the seminars and held regular study groups for the participants.

As she continued to interact with the chemists, Mariela was able to learn things from them, such as how to choose medicine based on a patient's condition, shops that stocked quality herbs, and little-known spots that were easy to gather herbs from, even for chemists.

Through this seminar, Mariela finally managed to fit in with the Labyrinth City chemists.

04

It was time for the annual Orc Festival.

When the sugar turnip–harvesting season arrived, orcs would come out of the Fell Forest in droves to loot the crops. A large amount of meat from the slaughtered orcs would appear on the market at low prices, which benefitted the winter food situation in the Labyrinth City. Thus, people in the City didn't call it a "raid" or a "subjugation," but rather a "festival," and they looked forward to it.

Orcs, minotaurs, sahuagins, and other bipedal monsters weren't considered food at the imperial capital, but they were important sources of meat in the Labyrinth City, where the food security was a real problem. Most of the farmland was located outside the City walls, and monsters constantly went after crops other than sugar turnips, including wheat, potatoes, and other vegetables. Some of the city's produce was even brought in by yagu caravans, so there were very few spare resources for raising livestock. Only aristocrats ate such meat.

This year, the stock of monster-warding incense and daigis rope ran out under then-Colonel Teluther, causing the slime uproar in the slums. However, the needed materials were somehow collected, thanks to the medicinal herbs provided by Mariela and some kind members of the Merchants Guild following her lead, as well as those scraped together during the uproar.

A huge number of adventurers participated in the Orc Festival. If you submitted tails from orcs you'd defeated, you'd receive a share of orc meat in proportion to the number of tails. Even if you couldn't obtain these, submitting a certificate of participation would let you join the orc-roasting party at the end of the weeklong subjugation period.

Although the Orc Festival was a yearly custom, it was not without its dangers. They were subjugating monsters, after all. However, orc hunting was much more efficient in a group than alone. In the unlikely event a mid-grade monster like an orc king appeared, the participating senior adventurers would defeat it, so even young adventurers and older people who'd already retired from adventuring participated in these events.

Orcs were a highly fertile race consisting of only males who violated females of other species in order to bear children. Although they birthed males and females in equal number, some scholars said the race was male because they killed young females before they reached adulthood, but it wasn't known for certain.

In any case, since women were at high risk of being targeted, they could only participate if they were C-Rank adventurers or higher. Instead, they were free to join the orc meat–roasting party after the subjugation period. Because it was also a place for young men and women to meet, single women would doll themselves up and put all their energy into cheering for others from quite a distance away, rather than participate in the subjugation itself.

Unless they had the Eagle Eye skill, these cheerleaders wouldn't be able to really see the single male adventurers and members of the City Defense Squad, who still tried their utmost to show off their strong suits. And few female adventurers eligible to participate actually did, since it was much more fun to spectate from a distance and chat with the other girls than to hunt repulsive orcs.

In other words, the Orc Festival was the most masculine celebration of all in the Labyrinth City.

The curtain now opened on the festival of meat, where muscles and orcs meet.

"Sieg! Lynx! You can do it!" Mariela cheered them on while watching with unprecedented passion.

This wasn't a harem situation developing here. The only

"meat" that caught her eye was the kind just beyond her scope of vision. Oh, maybe it was "king meat." It was said that orc kings were very likely to appear during the festival.

Mariela and Elmera observed together. Elmera's husband wasn't participating, but several young employees from the Medicinal Herbs Division had joined the event. Although it was a guild for merchants, there were times when they had needed to gather herbs to bolster their scanty supply, which meant a suitable amount of fighting power was necessary. Elmera had been saying things like, "I wonder what sort of battles will unfold this year?" in excitement for a while now, so maybe the young employees had been compelled to participate for her to observe.

Since Mariela would be safe next to the A-Rank adventurer Elmera, Sieg and Lynx had given into her pressuring—"I wanna eat orc king meat!"—and were participating in the Orc Festival.

The festival this year spotlighted the City Defense Squad's newly appointed commander, Captain Kyte. People believed he was eager to do something exemplary.

He began to address the crowd: "Adventurers gathered here today, my name is Kyte and I will be leading the charge in this year's event. I met my wife at the Orc Festival, but it wasn't until my fifth time participating that things started going well for me. I suffered minor injuries during my first two festivals, so my comrades hauled me away to the clinic for treatment, and I couldn't join in the festivities. I ended up covered in blood during my third festival and had to change clothes, which made me late to the celebrations afterward. The fourth time, I was determined; however, I managed to lose all my tails, the proof of my participation, to a certain lovely lady. The competition during my fifth festival remained fierce, but I was able to win over my wife's heart. Do you understand what I'm saying here? The orcs are merely a preliminary encounter. A warm-up. The orc tails are like the flowers you offer to a woman. The true battle will begin after this. Pace yourselves, and don't take things too far—let's get to hunting orcs as planned and earn ourselves the most magnificent bundles of their tails!" he concluded.

It didn't at all sound like a pre-battle speech, but hearing it from someone with the experience to back it up made it weightier. Everyone nodded in agreement when Kyte finished speaking. Some shouted "Idiot, this is my seventh time!" but they listened earnestly to the strategy. As this was the festival with the highest number of foolish injuries in the Labyrinth City, he seemed to have skillfully controlled the enthusiasm of the bachelors who were already inattentively daydreaming about the meat-roasting party.

The strategy was simple. Boil sugar turnip skins and other scraps at the border of the Fell Forest near the turnip fields. After the sweet smell wafted toward the forest with wind magic, the orcs who came near the Labyrinth City in search of food before the winter would snort and sniff as they emerged from the forest.

To prevent the fields from being damaged, rope mixed with daigis zigzagged across palisades to make a simple fence at the border of the Fell Forest, save for the place where they planned to stage the battle. Since they burned monster-warding incense and blew the scent toward the forest with wind magic, they could make the orcs appear in the approximate area of the planned battlefield.

If an orc king was leading them, the orcs moved in a controlled fashion, but in most cases, they appeared as several groups, in which case adventurers lined up to fell them in order.

The strategy was the same every year, but it was a wonder they could catch so many orcs without a problem. Did the monsters never learn? Having said that, even Kyte had been unsuccessful in the Orc Festival his first four times, so maybe the monsters were no different.

Lured by the smell of sugar turnips, three orcs immediately appeared. A team of young adventurers who had lined up early in the morning with their first lances in hand charged forward with a mighty battle cry. They were overdoing it. The adventurers following the youths heckled them.

"Lure them farther. It's a huge pain to carry 'em!"

"No lady wants a man who can't keep his cool!"

"Shut yer trap! Jealousy ain't a look good on an old fart like you!"

As they returned the taunts with their own, the youths cut off the tails that were proof of the orcs' subjugation. Then they rounded up serfs and escorted them as they carried the orcs to the back of the ranks before lining up again.

"The back of the line is this waaay. Don't be impatient, now, the orcs will keep coming out."

Because some of the people holding these placards and controlling the crowd were members of the City Defense Squad, the adventurers obeyed—foulmouthed but well mannered.

Incidentally, a line had been drawn at the midway point between the forest border and the ranks of fighters, so that when an orc crossed it, the next adventurer in line could bring it down. This strategy enabled adventurers fighting near the line who had no confidence in winning to retreat and ask for help.

The adventurers defeated the orcs in order as they appeared in

CHAPTER 3: The Meat Festival

a string of ceaseless clusters. The felled orcs were placed in wagons prepared in advance near the ranks and transported to the Labyrinth City, where they were drained, dismantled, and frozen with ice magic by Adventurers Guild dismantlers and butchers from the wholesale market.

The yagus hauling the wagons were all male, and they raised their splendid horns high while triumphantly pulling the wagons as if affected by the battle atmosphere. Among the yagus was the one that had helped Mariela and Sieg in the past. Their hooves clacked on the ground as they transported the bloody orcs.

Yagus are herbivores, right? They're way too into this..., Mariela thought as she absentmindedly observed the spectacle. Then it was Sieg and Lynx's turn.

The pair assumed natural poses near the centerline.

"Hey, hey, heeey, ya plan to run away from the very beginning?"

"Without a tail, you won't be popular at the party!"

Right as the adventurers were ridiculing them, four orcs approached.

Sieg rushed out just before the orcs reached the centerline, and Lynx took a step forward and threw knives with a *whoosh*. Lynx's knives pierced the eye sockets of two orcs all the way to their brains, and they came crashing down to the ground. Sieg was faster than the clubs the orcs swung at him. He slit the first one's throat, dodged the second one's blow by a hairsbreadth, then closed in and pierced it through the heart. He settled his side of the fight in the blink of an eye, too.

Along with the commotion, the adventurers' booing reached a head.

"We don't need your kind here! You're high-ranking adventurers who can attract ladies just by existing!"

"I pray you guys get eaten alive by malicious women!"

The only person who squealed in a high-pitched voice was Teluther.

"That's the guy from back then! Who are those guys?! What's their rank? They must have aliases!"

He was extremely giddy. Released from the heavy responsibility of being colonel, Teluther freely enjoyed the adventurers' activities and now shined the brightest. He ignored the gaze of the soldiers who seemed to be telling him to get to work.

Incidentally, since it isn't required to register your name or anything when participating, there was no reason for Teluther to ever know Sieg's or Lynx's name. Please rest assured this isn't the start of another kind of story.

Sieg and Lynx raised a hand to ward off the adventurers' booing in style as they returned to the back of the line like they were hot stuff. Their gallant figures, including when they were battling, were too far away for Mariela to see.

At the support corner set up far away in front of the Labyrinth City, Elmera seemed to be enjoying covering the events as they happened.

"Goodness, Mariela, those friends of yours are doing quite well. They got two orcs each. You'll have no shortage of meat come winter. You ought to take some as sausages. They are delicious in a pot-au-feu." She was definitely using magic to sharpen her eyesight. For a while now, every time her hands were about to touch, static electricity went flying with a *zap*, and it hurt.

Mariela, who'd seen the pair off, was honestly a bit tired of it.

The battlefield was so far away that she couldn't see what they were doing, but she could hear the carnivorous conversations of the young ladies in the vicinity.

"No real standouts among this year's newbies, huh?"

"Say, would it be bothersome to get just a tail from someone you don't care for?"

"That guy? I think she broke up with him. But I hear he still follows her around."

Mariela was also a carnivorous girl acting on animal instincts in her food preferences alone, and her prey today was orc king meat, so she had no interest in any of the conversations she overheard.

As Mariela absentmindedly wished from the bottom of her heart she'd brought along *The Encyclopedia of Medicinal Herbs and Their Effects*, one of the women called out to her.

"Hey, you run an apothecary, right?"

"Yes, I do," Mariela answered as she looked in her direction. The woman was around twenty years old and wearing town girl–style clothes, but she had a toned figure packed with muscles and little in the way of flab. Probably an adventurer.

"I was wondering if you had something that might heal this burn mark." She rolled up a sleeve to show Mariela the terrible burn scar underneath it. "My healer took care of the burn itself, but there's still a scar. It doesn't really bother me, but my companion looks so upset whenever he sees it."

Apparently, she'd received the injury from protecting one of her party members—the companion she spoke of. Maybe he was her boyfriend; she was gazing at the Orc Festival grounds with a gentle look on her face.

Mariela's words caught in her throat at the woman's question.

"I'm so sorry. It might fade a bit with some whitening cream, but…"

Mariela didn't sell any medicine that could cure a burn scar. This wound could have been easily cured by a high-grade potion.

Mariela looked down, but the female adventurer smiled happily at her.

"I see. Whitening cream, right? Do you sell any at your shop?"

When Mariela replied she'd make it for her, the female adventurer promised she'd definitely come to buy it and then departed.

By the way, Elmera heard the skin-brightening cream conversation and placed her own order, too. The other women in the vicinity also apparently overheard, and Mariela ended up with a whole slew of orders.

Being busy was a good thing. As she was thinking this, an air of chaos suddenly came from the direction of the Orc Festival grounds.

It seemed they'd suddenly gotten busy over there, too.

"Here come the orc kiiiings!"

The men at the Orc Festival grounds were fired up.

Orc kings come with several orc generals and hundreds of orcs. Back when General Leonhardt had participated in the subjugation, not only did he not have adventurers assigned to him, but seven orc kings had attacked at once. This time, though, there were only two, accompanied by five generals and around five hundred orcs. Since this was right after the start of the Orc Festival, one could say it was a reasonable appearance rate.

The strength of a single orc king was below C Rank, and a C-Rank adventurer could beat it in a one-on-one fight. If you converted the level of a soldier in the City Defense Squad to an adventurer's level, a D Rank became an E Rank. Those with C Rank and higher military strength were assigned to the Labyrinth Suppression Forces, which meant the City Defense Squad only had mid- to low-grade fighting power. However, as long as there was a chain of command, it was possible for them to subjugate a group of orcs led by one or two orc kings. Not only that, adventurers had gathered now, too.

This might be off-topic, but the deployment of adventurers had been a plan devised by Teluther's successor, the current colonel, and pushed forward by Teluther. Well, this was before Teluther had been promoted to colonel.

"We can observe the adventurers' activity from nearby and mingle with them at the party after the subjugation," Teluther had suggested, and demonstrated tenacity like never before to push the plan through a number of obstacles. In fact, this might have been the first and last time he used his skill Synchronize so effectively.

The result was a big hit. Besides guaranteeing inexpensive fighting power and the coinciding increase in safety, it produced a variety of secondary effects: providing entertainment to the public, promoting interactions between the public and private sectors, and improving the reputation of the City Defense Squad. This series of events had promoted Teluther to colonel. If you gave him the benefit of the doubt, you might say his interest in adventurers had saved him. Or you could say he's been just plain lucky.

As with the City Defense Squad, many of the adventurers participating in the Orc Festival were below D Rank, but among them were some senior adventurers who had been badgered by their wives to participate for the meat.

If you were a senior adventurer, you had enough money to buy orc king meat at the market, but more than a few husbands had been forced to participate in the Orc Festival, which did not go undetected under their wives' radars, signaling things like "bargain," "cheap," and "the husband next door is participating, too."

Thus the curtain opened on the great struggle for orc king meat.

"Sieg, the B-Rankers are after that king over there. Let's get this one!"

"Got it!"

Lynx and Sieg shot off, running at the speed of a gale. Naturally, the adventurers around them broke from formation all at once and began to sprint, too.

The appearance of the orc kings was a cue for the melee to start.

They mowed down the approaching orcs as they ran for their target, an orc king. Hordes of adventurers seemed to be targeting the other one. One moment, several ice lances floated in midair, and the next, they aimed to pierce the monster. A blade of wind swept them away.

"Hey, asshole! Get outta my way!"

"Shaddap! This one's mine! You stay out of it!"

The B-Rankers began an ugly squabble among themselves to mass produce "foolish injuries." A long sword user rushed out, thinking this was his chance, but an earth magic user lurking somewhere literally swept him off his feet, causing him to somersault and fall flat. He collided with several orcs and sent them to the next world.

It was a free-for-all. At the distant cheering grounds, Elmera provided live updates with great excitement. Every time she gestured as she talked, static electricity came flying out with a *zap*, which was super-painful. Did she really care about hiding her Lightning Empress identity? When Mariela asked her, she responded with a smile, "I'm just a lightning magic user." When she winked, sparks scattered with a *zap* from the tips of her eyelashes, so all Mariela could say in reply was "I guess so."

Sieg and Lynx made a dash for the orc king while dodging the spells flying toward their feet in an attempt to butt in.

At that moment, a man from the crowd covered head to toe in a cloak leaped high into the sky with inhuman jumping power and landed in front of the pair.

His presence overpowered the battlefield. The orcs near his landing spot became frightened and shrank back.

The top of the cloak fluttered in the breeze like the wings of a magical bird and revealed the face hidden within.

"I'll be taking that king!" the mystery man declared snappily, looking as dazzling as always.

Why are you here, Haage? Aren't you obviously way too powerful for this...?

Before the adventurers could express their thoughts aloud as they got ready to give up, an invisible net lightly spread out from his landing spot and caught him.

"Whoa there, that's not enough to bring me down!" Haage swung his arms, trying to tear off the net. But before he could get away, several shadows appeared from who knows where and surrounded him in the blink of an eye.

"Guildmaster, we're leaving. You're bothering everyone."

"Please go back to work. You've been goofing off too much lately."

"You're too predictable, so it was easy to set a trap."

"L-let go of me! Can't we talk this over?! If I don't get the king and bring it home, my wife, my wife will...!"

In their office clothes, the top brass of the Adventurers Guild wrapped the struggling Haage in a bamboo mat and lifted him high as they hauled him off. Although no one could see their attacks, one could understand their strength by the way they cut through the orcs blocking their path. However, Haage's rank was higher than theirs. One could say he showed all the young adventurers that even a higher-ranked opponent could be brought down with strategy and teamwork.

"Wh-whooooooaaaaa! That's Team Haage, isn't it?! Incredible, absolutely incredible!" Teluther cried in great excitement. The soldiers around him watched over him halfheartedly with facial expressions that could only be described as saying "Good for you."

By the way, "Team Haage" was not the official name. It was a popular nickname. The leaders that Haage personally trained substituted for one another according to the situation. It wasn't like they said "I hate being on the guildmaster's team" and refused to introduce themselves as team members. Maybe, just maybe, they liked him.

Now that the greatest threat, Haage, had been eliminated, Sieg and several adventurers seized the opportunity to close in on an orc king.

"GROOOOOOOOOOOOOH!"

The orc king let out a war cry. It was taller than a large man and probably heavier than several put together. From a body worthy of the title "king," the incredibly intimidating roar echoed like tremors to terrorize the adventurers. However, it couldn't stop the warriors who'd made it this far.

The orc king swung a gigantic club the size of an adult human's torso that generated enough wind pressure to launch the surrounding orcs into the air. However, one person absorbed it into

their sword and sent it flying back at the king's throat, and another used the club as a foothold to spring at the king's head. Sieg, too, ducked under the club and used his Achilles tendon to fly like a bullet and pierced the king's heart with his mythril sword.

With its head, throat, and heart attacked at the same time, the orc king was helpless as it fell.

They'd done it. They'd defeated the orc king. But who? Who attacked at the same time? Who would get the meat?

"Nice work, Sieg. Okay, let's get goin'! Party at the Yagu Drawbridge Pavilion!" Lynx had appeared unnoticed next to Sieg and addressed him. Sieg silently made a fist and bumped it against his comrade's.

Lynx held a splendid tail in his fist, one that was clearly different from a normal orc's.

"Maaan, I never woulda thought Haage would show up."

At the Yagu Drawbridge Pavilion, Lynx recounted the entire story of the battle in an amusing way as he sunk his teeth into the meat of a king orc. He talked of a scene that few people would ever experience: how he circled behind the orc king to cut off its tail while Sieg drew the attention of the adventurers as he challenged the monster. However, Mariela and the beautiful girl who worked at the inn, Emily, were both engrossed with the orc king meat and not really listening.

Thirty pounds of the orc king meat were distributed to Lynx, who'd brought back the tail, and twenty pounds to each of the three people who finished off the king, including Sieg. Meat from the orc kings, orc generals, and other high-grade monsters was divided among those who had contributed to killing the monster even if they didn't bring back the tail. Because of this, members of the City Defense Squad in charge of high-grade meat painstakingly kept track of the battle situation. In any case, senior adventurers had gathered with the goal of obtaining this kind of meat. The Squad could not allow mistakes in the distribution no matter what. Food grudges were a scary thing.

Ten of the fifty pounds of orc king meat were brought to the Yagu Drawbridge Pavilion and cooked for the after-party. Twenty pounds went to Mariela, and the inn kept the other twenty for the Black Iron Freight Corps.

Although they called it an after-party, the only participants were Lynx, Sieg, Mariela, and Emily of the Yagu Drawbridge Pavilion. Aside from them, the owner and Amber took turns sitting in an empty seat to snack on meat in between serving customers.

Elmera had been invited as well, but she'd turned them down, saying she was going to have dinner with her family. Always one for a big party, Captain Dick was currently visiting the imperial capital, and Lieutenant Malraux, who was stationed in the Labyrinth City, had work to do and couldn't make it to the inn right after sunset.

"I'll bet Captain Dick would've joined in the festival if he were around!" said Mariela.

"Yeah, for sure. That's why I didn't tell him about it," Lynx replied. This time, the clueless guildmaster had intruded, but if Captain Dick had been there, he would have participated to get orc king meat for Amber, no question. Amber sat next to Mariela, stuffing her face with orc king meat with delight.

"So gooood…"

"It just melts in your mouth!"

"Ish really good. Daddy should hurry up and eat shome. *Nom, nom.*"

"Mmm..."

Although it looked like Sieg and Lynx were surrounded by a harem and could have their pick from a young girl, an older girl, and a beautiful woman, it was painfully obvious that the two younger girls were ruining the whole thing. They blissfully stuffed their faces with orc king meat and their full cheeks jiggled as they chewed.

Sieg and Lynx exchanged glances, laughed, and chomped into their own helpings.

About half of the meat obtained in the Orc Festival was distributed to the participants, and if they didn't need it, they could get money instead. Any remaining edible potions were sold to civilians at a cheap price through the wholesale market. All the butchers who received orc king and orc general meat had booming businesses, and there, too, fierce battles among the housewives unfolded. It was fortunate to be able to get orc and orc king meat at the start of the winter season, because it would have been impossible for Mariela to make it through an intense battlefield for discounted meat.

When adding in the dissection costs, the costs for setting up the battlefield and the party venue, and all kinds of other fees, there was a slight deficit, but the original purpose for this event was the subjugation of the orcs who went after the sugar turnips. And this was more cost-effective than the City Defense Squad going after the orcs on their own.

The Orc Festival lasted until the sugar turnip harvest was over, so about a week.

At night, monster-warding incense was burned and the City Defense Squad patrolled around the battlefield, making adjustments so the orcs would smoothly converge in the daytime. Lynx and Sieg's battle ended when they'd obtained the orc king meat, but the battle of the remaining sad men wouldn't be over until the meat-roasting party on the final day.

No one knew for sure if the day ever came when orc king meat graced the dining table of the Adventurers Guild guildmaster, Haage.

CHAPTER 4
The Path Toward Reclamation

Black armored carriages covered in a layer of iron traveled through the Fell Forest.

They followed the leading cavalrymen at a steady pace.

As planned, they were on schedule to arrive at the Labyrinth City in the evening again, and Donnino, the male guard riding the raptor, felt relieved about the journey's progress. Donnino was in charge of maintaining the iron carriages. Although he had enough knowledge of battle to escort the carriages in this way, tinkering with armored carriages suited him much better than fighting monsters.

He had traveled this road many times in both directions, but making any progress while shaking off the constant monster attacks was difficult. Although they were goblins, forest wolves, and other weak ones, their numbers were nothing to sneeze at. The wolves in particular were a nuisance, and they would continue to attack the carriages no matter how many times he tore them off.

What about this? Why not use several low-grade monster-warding potions so they'll run away instead of attacking? If we do that, we might be able to lighten the carriages' armor and restructure them for more speed.

After the Corps's base had been established in the Labyrinth City, the members who stayed behind prepared goods to be

The Alchemist Who Survived Now Dreams of a Quiet City Life, Vol. 2

transported to the imperial capital. So, after arriving in the Labyrinth City, the group could immediately leave for the capital again after they'd finished resting and performing maintenance.

As before, they had established a four-day stay in the Labyrinth City, so there was a lot of time for maintenance checks. By setting up a base, it was now also possible to install large-scale tools for servicing the carriages.

Up to now, the armored carriages had been nothing but sturdy boxes that were expected to take attacks. They were uncomfortable to ride in, and they weren't very fast. When they endured attacks and somehow made it out of the Fell Forest, the carriages' own weight caused the axles to rattle. It was a difficult situation, but even if they went through large-scale remodeling, it didn't seem like it would be a problem.

Donnino kept a vigilant eye on the road while ruminating on remodeling the armored carriages.

The male slave named Jay gazed at Donnino's back while grasping the reins on one of the carriages. Jay had worked under the slave trader Reymond in the Labyrinth City taking care of the animals and other things, and the Black Iron Freight Corps had bought him a little over a month ago.

This was his second round trip through the Fell Forest.

For Jay, the forest was a terrible place. He'd been brought to the Labyrinth City by yagu caravan, so he'd never been through the forest before the Corps had bought him. However, he knew from the stories of slaves who had traveled through it that it wasn't a place where people could just come and go.

As magically Ordered, he held the reins while trembling in fear. When they'd appointed him as the nighttime driver, he was so frightened he'd vomited inside the coach box. Then he was literally kicked out of there with a "Gross, wash up and come back," whereupon he disgracefully cried and screamed that the monsters would eat him while clinging half-crazed to the foot that booted him out.

However, Jay—no, the Black Iron Freight Corps hadn't been attacked by monsters, let alone lost their lives. Even if they encountered monsters, and the monsters happened to be blocking their way forward, it seemed the creatures were completely warded off. Pedestals with burning monster-warding incense had been set up at the top of the iron carriages, but was this really something that would have that much of an effect?

I don't get it...

Jay stared vigilantly as he observed his surroundings. His vocal cords had been crushed. Since he could neither read nor write, he could only learn things with his own ears and eyes. Without standing out or being noticed, he continued to search for information.

Afterward, they encountered just a few unexpected goblins along the road before the armored carriages finally arrived on schedule in the Labyrinth City.

"We have been expecting you." The slave trader Reymond welcomed the Black Iron Freight Corps upon its arrival at his business.

The cargo was, once again, slaves.

The "baggage" was unloaded from the armored carriages and inspected, as usual.

However, something was a little off. People with one eye, people without all their fingers, and even people missing arms and legs were mixed in with the others. Among those with no physical defects were people who seemed to be felons, as they were hauled off bound and gagged.

The only slaves sent to the Labyrinth City were penal laborers and lifelong slaves for labor. People tended to avoid slaves with physical defects who couldn't work satisfactorily and felons who weren't usable because they didn't get along with other slaves, even if they were offered at a cheap price. The Black Iron Freight Corps did not choose these slaves. The slave trader Reymond requested them.

"I have confirmed receipt of the goods. Here is the payment, as always."

Reymond's true motives couldn't be read from his facial expression. The business of buying and selling people had been his livelihood for many years. Just like usual, he completed the transaction without much emotion, as if he were dealing in live-stock. No, with even less emotion than usual. The Black Iron Freight Corps's livelihood, too, was the delivery of "baggage." They never openly pried into their customers' orders.

After the transaction was finished and he saw off the Black Iron Freight Corps, Reymond stopped one of his subordinates who was taking the slaves to the cells.

"We have a lot of orc meat. Please treat today's group. Tomorrow they will be shipped out. If that happens, then..." Reymond trailed off. The subordinate bowed in silence and then disappeared into the building along with the slaves.

"Sheesh, this is exactly why I don't want to grow old. Sentimentality has no purpose. Well then, time to notify them of this arriving." Muttering this to no one in particular, Reymond headed into the estate.

02

The estate of the Aguinas family was located a small distance from the aristocratic quarter's center in the southeastern part of the Labyrinth City, near the outer wall. The site, which had been passed down since the time of the Kingdom of Endalsia, was as grand as the Labyrinth City itself. It was surrounded by high walls, so no one could see in from the outside.

It was said that when the monsters flooded out of the Fell Forest two hundred years ago, the head of the Aguinas family left the region to escape the danger. Afterward, they hastened back to the ruined country with soldiers, secured a safe zone with liberal use of monster-warding potions and medicinal herbs, and gathered the surviving alchemists to help with reconstruction. They distributed the potions they'd made to the surviving citizens and to the imperial soldiers who'd rushed to the rescue, and the Labyrinth City was built as a place for people to live.

As a result of their deeds, the Aguinas family was appointed in the Labyrinth City to manage the large quantity of potions left behind by the alchemists. The potions supplied by the family had continued to contribute to the subjugation of the Labyrinth over these long two hundred years.

The current head of the family, Robert Aguinas, descended a concealed staircase in his estate's building annex down into a cellar.

He was in his early twenties, praised as a prodigy from an early age. His mother had passed away when his younger sister, Caroline, was still a child, and when his father had become bedridden due to a failed experiment a few years ago, Robert succeeded him as the head of the family.

The Aguinas family annex was an old structure from the time when this town was restored as the Labyrinth City, and the main building, constructed decades ago, was on the same plot of land, a little removed from the annex.

Even after the main building was newly constructed, the annex was used as a potion research facility, and only a very limited number of collaborators could go in and out apart from the head of the family and his successors.

Even his sister Caroline had never set foot in there.

The building had a vast cellar that stored a large quantity of potions meant for supporting the capture of the Labyrinth. Robert was descending into a hidden passage that only generations of Aguinas family heads knew about, separate from the staircase that continued into the potion storehouse.

He headed to the back of the dim corridor. Beyond the door that only the head of the family possessed the key to was a room resembling a graveyard.

A number of old-looking coffins lined both sides of the room. There were more than ten, and even someone looking in from the room's entrance could see all their lids were open and no one was inside them. The very back of the room was raised, and a single glass coffin lay there.

Several magical tools for illumination had been installed around the glass coffin, lighting it up brightly. A cloth cover with delicate rose embroidery hung over its lower half, and the way it spread from the top of the coffin to the floor made one feel like they were inside a rose garden.

Considering the scarcity of goods in the Labyrinth City, this cloth with its ample embroidery was an expensive luxury item that wasn't used in such unseen places. It seemed to clearly express the gift giver's feelings toward the person the coffin belonged to.

Robert approached the glass coffin.

A girl slept inside it.

She was an incredibly, incredibly beautiful person.

Shining silver hair flowed around her in loose waves, framing her small face, which was as white as snow and looked just like porcelain. Along with her lovely and shapely nose, she had small red lips that curved in a smile like she was dreaming. A soft rose-colored dress covered her slender body and enhanced her beauty.

Her eyelids with its long lashes seemed like they'd flutter open at any moment.

What color could her eyes be?

Her lips were glossy, looking as if they were touched with nectar. He wondered if they would call his name with a bell-like voice when they moved.

"Oh, my fair Estalia. Our First Alchemist."

Robert Aguinas knelt before the coffin.

He had met the sleeping girl when he was ten years old and had been formally established as the family heir. The impact of seeing her for the first time was still etched in his mind.

She was the most beautiful person Robert knew.

She had been sleeping for two hundred years, the last alchemist of the Kingdom of Endalsia.

"Estalia, you will become the First Alchemist of this Labyrinth City. Until that day comes, I won't let anyone disturb your slumber."

When the Labyrinth was conquered and this region returned to the hands of people, alchemists would be able to connect to the region's ley line via a Nexus once more. However, making a pact with the land required an alchemist. Only alchemists who were able to take on apprentices knew this, and even then, many did not. This is why the master-apprentice relationship was considered more important than anything else, because an alchemist could access the Library and gain new alchemic knowledge even if their master was absent.

Those with no master could not become alchemists.

After an apprentice dived down into the ley line with the help of the spirits and connected a Nexus to it, their master used a technique to bring them back to the world. Therefore, Estalia was essential to reviving alchemists in the Labyrinth City.

She will be the master to all the alchemists in the Labyrinth City, and her name will live on for eternity.

Robert gazed at the sleeping Estalia in the coffin.

What dwelled in that gaze? Love? Adoration? Madness?

"Rest easy, Estalia— Until the moment the Labyrinth is destroyed and a new dawn breaks over this land, when you'll awaken as was promised in the days of old. Until then, my new medicine will aid in the Labyrinth's destruction," Robert promised her. Countless times he'd repeated those words, that determination.

After pulling the rose-embroidered cloth just a little to the upper half of the coffin, he stroked the coffin as if soothing her, then left the cellar.

03

"The subjugation of the fifty-third stratum's boss, the King of Cursed Serpents, begins now. We'll have our revenge!"

"Sir!"

More than a hundred elites handpicked from the Labyrinth Suppression Forces responded to the Gold Lion General Leonhardt.

The fifty-third stratum of the Labyrinth was now the forefront of the subjugation. Because Leonhardt had received the curse of petrification from the basilisk during the previous expedition and been forced to retreat, he had a personal vendetta against this stratum.

As they defeated ordinary basilisks and advanced to the back of the corridor, they emerged into a huge open room lined with pillars that looked man-made. That was where the King of Cursed Serpents, the king basilisk, lived.

A basilisk was a monster with a head and tail like a snake's and a wide torso like a lizard's, with four short legs sprouting from it. It was said to have evil eyes of petrification that cursed anyone they stared at, and this curse couldn't be completely healed by cure potions. However, the odds of curse symptoms occurring weren't very high. Even if it did activate, the protective spell *Holy Talisman*, which prevented curses and repelled the undead, could protect you from it.

It was also possible to reflect a curse of petrification with a mirror, so a basilisk's curse could be reliably prevented by carrying a shield that'd been polished like a mirror. Incidentally, a basilisk was immune to its own curse.

Basilisks had petrification poison on their fangs, claws, and tails, and it was horribly strong. If you got poisoned, petrification would always activate. However, since it was not a curse, it could be removed with cure magic or a cure potion.

They were powerful S-Rank monsters that attacked with their long tails and heads, but people in Leonhardt's Labyrinth Suppression Forces could defeat them.

The problem was the King of Cursed Serpents raising its head in the center of the spacious room.

Its body was several times the length of a normal basilisk, and its mouth was large enough to swallow a person whole. Several horned protrusions grew crookedly from the top of its head like a crown. It was as if the ribs of the prey it had devoured were piercing its skull.

Covered in verdigris-colored moss, its body had rusty-looking sediment floating around it. The pieces of sediment wriggled like a cocoon right before hatching and occasionally burst open and melted into the atmosphere before merging with the sediment in the Labyrinth to form a new basilisk.

The king basilisk had eight legs, double the number a normal basilisk possessed. Its large torso prevented it from moving to the edges of the room where pillars crowded together or from entering the corridor. However, once the battle began, it would probably create several normal basilisks, inundate the entire room with the petrification curse, and swallow those who had turned into stone.

Even Leonhardt hadn't been able to escape this. The birth of several basilisks all at once had thrown the battle into chaos, forcing a retreat. The basilisk, identifying Leonhardt as the general, incessantly showered him with the curse. Though *Holy Talisman* was chanted numerous times, the curse had found its way through a gap in the effect and reached Leonhardt.

However, they had no reason to fear this time.

"The holy water."

In accordance with Weishardt's command, all the soldiers dowsed themselves in holy water. This was followed up with *Holy Talisman*. Holy water had the same curse protection effect as *Holy Talisman*. Moreover, it increased resistance against basilisks' petrification poison. *Holy Talisman* couldn't overlap with itself, but it could overlap with holy water. The water would protect them in the interval between when Holy Talisman wore off and when it was cast again.

"Purify your weapons, including ammunition."

This time, they poured holy water on their weapons. This would increase their attack power against the serpent king, which was covered in the curse.

The mages began to chant, using the holy water as a core to create lances of ice.

The archers poured holy water into thin metal molds and inserted shafts, and those who could use ice magic quickly cooled the water to make arrowheads.

They were about to confront a mighty foe they'd challenged many, many times and had never defeated. How many comrades had become its victims? However, the soldiers showed no trepidation at facing this powerful enemy.

With this strategy, they couldn't lose. They believed in Lieutenant General Weishardt.

Because the holy water had been prepared "by the barrel," they had about eight hundred potion vials of it.

It takes a formidable alchemist to be able to prepare not only a hundred high-class vials every day, but this much holy water in less than two weeks.

Weishardt and the soldiers impatiently awaited the Gold Lion General Leonhardt's command.

"Now is the time we'll have vengeance for that day."

At Leonhardt's order, the curtain opened on the King of Cursed Serpents' subjugation.

"Holy Shield!"

The shield knights assigned to teams of roughly six people each activated the spell in succession. By using it in conjunction with a shield polished like a mirror that could bounce back curses, they could ward off the basilisk's petrification curse without difficulty.

The teams of six, consisting of shield knights, vanguards, enchanters who could use *Holy Talisman*, and healers, skillfully dodged and pinned down the normal basilisks created by the King of Cursed Serpents.

They mustn't defeat the normal ones just yet.

If they reduced their numbers, the King of Cursed Serpents would make new basilisk servants. Because no one could predict where the new servants would appear, the battlefront would become disorganized in an instant if the basilisks targeted those challenging the king.

For that reason, eight teams had been given the task of holding down the basilisk servants.

While the pests were pinned down, the main force move forward to confront the King of Cursed Serpents.

"Ready your arrows! Fire!"

At Weishardt's signal, the archers fired their arrows of frozen holy water. The arrowheads had an aerodynamic shape and were more than ten times the size of normal ones. These were created to be a size that could just barely reach the King of Cursed Serpents by taking air resistance and the relative density of iron into account, which meant, of course, that they were no faster than normal arrows and couldn't be expected to have penetrative power.

The arrows arced through the air and rained down on the King of Cursed Serpents in a barrage. The arrowheads weren't frozen solid on the inside and crumbled away upon impact with the monster's scales.

The holy water inside the arrowheads spread across the king's body.

"HISSSSSSSSSS!"

The basilisk thrashed its disproportionately long tail and head to shake off the ice arrows. The archers' arrows weren't meant to injure the King of Cursed Serpents. Rather, the holy water purified the rust-like cursed miasma covering the monster's scales then and there, and its body quivered in displeasure.

Now.

"All soldiers, attack!" Leonhardt shouted, and the soldiers followed him at once.

Countering Leonhardt's attack, the King of Cursed Serpents raised its head and jerked its jaws wide open as if to swallow him. The mages hurled frozen holy water in the shape of lances at its head.

The ice lances slammed into the king's head, damaging its tough scales and piercing its wide-open mouth. Holy water was like poison to the curse-clad basilisk. As it crunched the lances with its teeth, Leonhardt and the other soldiers drew their swords and attacked its closed mouth.

Did this monster have the emotional capacity to think they were annoying? From the perspective of the King of Cursed Serpents, Leonhardt and the others were probably tiny, fragile creatures. The creature glared with its evil, petrifying eyes, hoping to turn the crew into stone to devour them, but Holy Talisman stood in the way and prevented the curse from reaching Leonhardt. No matter how many times it tried to break through its protection, the mages standing at the ready in back cast it again and again, and even in the slight moments between each spell, the holy water served as a second barrier without fail.

As if to trample them, the King of Cursed Serpents stomped its eight gigantic feet and came forth to challenge the humans.

"Scatter!"

With a single command, the Labyrinth Suppression Forces moved into battle formations all around it. Aiming for the small opening this movement created, the basilisk's long snake tail stretched crookedly and cracked like a whip. It blew away soldiers, slamming them into the stone pillars as the shock waves from the high-speed swing ripped off soldiers' limbs.

It was a powerful attack that could cause fatal wounds in just a single blow, but the healers assigned to the front lines wasted no time in sending out healing magic to prevent instant death.

This strategy experimented with putting the healers on the front lines. Up until now, preserving their magical power to endure a drawn-out battle had been their top priority. By putting them on the front lines and minimizing the number of shield knights there, Leonhardt and the vanguards could switch to an attack-focused strategy even against the King of Cursed Serpents.

Those with wounds difficult to instantly treat with healing magic were immediately removed from the battlefront and carried to the medical team led by Nierenberg. There were only a few healers who weren't fit for the front lines, and they remained with the medical team. Up to now, that wouldn't have been enough people to administer treatment in time. However...

"Don't be frugal with potions. Use the red and black ones first. The effects of the black ones vary wildly. If they're not enough, use mid- and high-grade potions. The soldiers' physical strength takes priority, so don't waste it with healing magic." Nierenberg barked out instructions to his team.

It was the same one that had healed the latest round of wounded people with Nierenberg. Even if the soldiers' organs were about to rupture, even if their limbs were bent in strange directions—or gone altogether—they wouldn't be shaken this time.

"If we slice it cleanly off, it'll be easier to heal!"

"Next time, please go find and collect your own limbs!"

They even had the capacity to say that kind of stuff.

The healed soldiers immediately returned to the battlefront. Back into the very middle of the war of attrition that would whittle away at their bodies and minds.

04

Two weeks prior.

"Whaaat? That's impossible. A hundred high-grade specialized curse-removal potions? I don't have enough moss. Why can't you harvest planada moss in the Labyrinth, anyway? And Mr. Ghark doesn't sell it either. I can't do it."

A rare sight. Mariela gave a decisive refusal to a potion request.

She'd used up her planada moss back when she made the potion vials, and the amount she had on hand now was nowhere near enough for a hundred potions. And there wasn't a way for her to buy more. Even Ghark had told her "I dunno." The moss wasn't mentioned in *The Encyclopedia of Medicinal Herbs and Their Effects*, which Medicinal Herbs Division Chairwoman Elmera had boasted included every medicinal herb found in the Labyrinth, so they ought to understand its rarity.

"Besides, if you're up against curses, wouldn't you be better off using holy water?"

Mariela had no idea at the time the words that casually slipped from her mouth would have a big effect on the subjugation operation for the King of Cursed Serpents, or that she'd get stuck with waking up at the crack of dawn every morning.

When they'd put in the order of holy water in units of Mariela-sized barrels, she asked the request to be repeated several times.

"Good morning, Mariela. Time to get up."

Sieg had gotten up early today, too. The fact he seemed to be fine on little sleep made her extremely jealous. As Mariela rubbed her sleepy eyes, she somehow managed to crawl out of bed. It was still dark outside, and the morning sun hadn't yet risen. This was all because some general or lieutenant general had made an incomprehensible order: one barrel of holy water. The equivalent of eight hundred potion vials. As far as rank went, they were mid-grade and not difficult, but gathering the materials was really taxing.

"Ugh, it's cooold. I know this was my idea, but this is waaay too much overtime. I'm gonna tack on a surcharge..."

It was on the verge of winter. It was very cold before sunrise, and her hands and feet grew numb. Being forced to water plants at this hour was some kind of cruel joke.

She stored water infused with Drops of Life in the can and bucket Sieg had prepared for her, and the two of them ascended to the rooftop. Since a sacred tree grew right next to Mariela's house, the top of the tree could be reached from the roof. The tip of its branches was still higher than Mariela even when she stood on the roof, but it was fine.

She poured the water in the watering can from the top of the roof toward the tree. Sieg used wind magic to lightly blow the water droplets so they would reach all the leaves, and in this way, the two of them uniformly and thoroughly watered the tree.

Once in a while, a mischievous gust of wind would blow the flowing water in Mariela's direction, and it was as cold as could be, but since they had to finish this task before dawn, she silently endured it.

When this was done, they descended to the first floor and

placed every last object from all over the house that could hold water under the tree—from washbasins to buckets, from pots to dishes. The excess water on the tree dripped down from its branches, and the water was still cold. When it landed on her neck, she shrieked, "Eeyah!"

After they finished placing the containers, all that remained was to wait for sunrise.

Sacred tree dew was an ingredient in holy water. The blessing of the sacred tree melted into the dew that was bathed in morning light, and the drops of water contained holy power to drive away evil. The important components were the morning sun and the tree's blessing, which meant it didn't have to be condensation—it could be rainwater, irrigation water, or anything else. It was said that using water mixed with Drops of Life would enhance the effect all the more, so that was why they'd prepared it without delay before the sun rose. They placed the containers after excess water droplets had fallen to not dilute the morning dew, and the droplets were chilly as they fell on the pair, but this was a collection method unique to residents in a house with a sacred tree.

They waited for sunrise in front of the fireplace while drinking steaming cups cocoa with plenty of sugar. They had planned on gathering furniture at the winter Furniture Market, so there was none in the living room with the wonderful fireplace, save for a white, soft fur rug spread on the floor. It was apparently the pelt of a snow monkey called a yeti.

Since the Labyrinth City lacked artisans, it was difficult to obtain woolen products, but monster fur appeared on the market at a regular frequency. This rug, with its long, white, warm fur, was one of them. It was a popular item for household use; each individual hair was firmer than it looked, they didn't clump together even if bread crumbs and such were spilled on them, and it could even be washed at home.

How luxurious it was to relax on a soft, fluffy pelt in front of a fireplace in the morning.

Due to the lack of furniture, the room smacked of poverty with a wooden box used in place of a table, but Mariela actually found she could unwind better.

"It'd be nice if they sold a table that's better than this box."

"Do they even sell tables that are worse?"

As she and Sieg chatted like they always did, the sun came up.

The sacred tree sparkled in the morning sun. The abundant drops of water covering the leaves absorbed the light, and when the two components came together, the water seemed somehow divine. Seeing the tree like this really did make it feel like it was special.

When Sieg lightly rustled the branches with wind magic, the water droplets fell like light rain into the prepared containers.

Plink, plink-plink, tink, tink-tink.

If spirits lived in this place, they must have been dancing to the rhythm of the falling water. Enjoying the timbre of the sounds, Mariela and Sieg collected the morning dew in a barrel.

They continued this work day after day, and in about two weeks, they'd finally collected one barrel's worth of morning dew.

The remaining ingredients were salt purified by a spirit's flames and the hair of a maiden.

For the salt, Mariela summoned the salamander for the first time in a long while to heat it for her. Though the term was *purified*, it was more correct to say, "melted and hardened."

The last ingredient, the hair of a maiden, meant the hair from a pure girl. Mariela just needed a small snip. Apparently, the younger the girl, the greater the effect. That said, it wasn't like a baby would do the trick. It seemed the subject had to be conscious of their own gender.

As though it was perfectly timed, the poster girl of the Yagu Drawbridge Pavilion, Emily, came crying, "Daddy cut my hair all jagged!" and Mariela straightened out her bangs for her, so she was able to use the hair she got from that. Emily was ten, and she had such a kind heart that she'd once decided to give her father her own share of the cookies. Mariela figured her hair would be staggeringly effective.

If this strategy worked well, the secret top contributor might be the owner of the Yagu Drawbridge Pavilion, the one who had cut Emily's hair poorly in the first place.

Thus, from this barrel of holy water that Mariela had made, the curtain opened on the subjugation of the King of Cursed Serpents.

One could object and say the materials other than the salt were free. But Mariela's blissful sleep and Emily's hair were priceless.

05

It was just a few hours before Leonhardt and the Labyrinth Suppression Forces challenged the King of Cursed Serpents when the carriage of Reymond the slave trader entered the Aguinas estate.

"I have come with the delivery of the 'merchandise' at your request."

The Aguinas family steward cordially handed over a bag containing the payment.

"...Safely received."

After taking the payment, Reymond expressed his thanks and left the estate. He didn't say anything else, even to ask about the next order. Reymond was a slave trader. When he received an order, he fulfilled it. He wasn't picky about his customers, and he never pried into or leaked their secrets. He didn't interpose his personal feelings into business transactions. That was one of the "restrictions" imposed on slave traders.

However, this customer *went through their goods too quickly.*

Slave trading engaged in the buying and selling of people, and it was avoided as an occupation by most of society. But the job called for them to act as prison guards and law enforcement, and it was an occupational category protected and monitored by the country. Reymond and other slave traders possessed the skill of Contract of Servitude, which could be extremely dangerous depending on how it was used. It could even forcefully enslave innocent people.

Skills that few people possessed were highly valued by the country and classified as "Other" on appraisal paper, which didn't even provide any details on it.

People who possessed "Other" skills were gathered by exclusive organizations and evaluated with particular appraisal paper. These abilities were selected and promoted by the country. Those with the Contract of Servitude skill also received specialty thought training from a young age, and after undergoing a great number of restrictions, they found success as slave traders.

The repeated act of buying and selling people might have chipped away at Reymond's heart until it stopped protesting, but he used to be a fair person who could distinguish right from wrong. He'd been raised that way ever since it was discovered he had the Contract of Servitude skill.

Reymond knew there wasn't enough spare time, energy, or money in this world to rehabilitate someone for committing a crime, other than to make them a penal laborer. That said, he also understood that they weren't a "thing" that could so easily be "used up."

So every time he met this kind of customer, he couldn't help thinking the slaves were being used as "parts" or something similar. However, because he was bound by so many restrictions, he couldn't stop being a slave trader. Even if he knew the "goods" were being "used up," he wasn't able to choose whom he would or wouldn't sell to.

Reymond believed it was better to feel nothing, as if the slaves really were parts—even though his heart seldom stirred.

The two carriages that had transported the slaves returned to his business first, while Reymond ordered his coachman to drive slowly through the town on their way back. He absentmindedly watched the scenery of the town passing by: a mother soothing a child who'd fallen, children chasing each other around, a high-spirited shopkeeper selling a mound of ingredients for dinner.

Reymond liked gazing at mundane sights.

A young man and woman suddenly appeared in his field of vision.

"How come you and Lynx didn't take me to the Orc Festival barbecueee?"

"What, were you in the market for a boyfriend?"

"N-n-n-no! The meat, I was in it for the meat! It was a rare chance to get free meat! What a waste! ...And I wasn't looking for a boyfriend, sheesh!"

"Ha-ha-ha. Well, even if you had gone, you'd be stuck eating meat by yourself since Lynx and I were extremely popular."

"Grr, no I wouldn't! I'd be sooo popular, I wouldn't even have the time for any meat!"

"So what's the problem, then? You wouldn't have been able to eat the meat anyway. Since we're here, why don't we have minotaur today? I bet you're tired of eating nothing but orc."

"Ooh, mino meat! Hamburg steaks would be good. I'll knead 'em into big patties!"

"...Mariela, you *really* like kneading things, don't you?"

I remember that girl. She's the one who bought that dying slave. And that man next to her... Don't tell me.

When Reymond sharpened his sensitivity, he could sense the remnants of his own Contract of Servitude in the man.

That's him, all right. So he lived, huh?

The slave who had once been on the verge of death was standing next to the girl and smiling gently. His expression was very natural and calm. But Reymond could tell he was paying close attention to his surroundings to protect her.

Good, he thought. He was very glad the man had met a good master.

He would not pry into how that dying slave had been saved. It was enough for him to know one of his "products" had been blessed with good fortune.

He never cherry-picked his customers, pried into their affairs, or divulged their secrets. Because these were restrictions placed on slave traders.

Reymond's carriage passed by the pair and slowly made its way through the town and back to the slave company.

06

There's somethin' strange goin' on.

The thought crossed the mind of one of the slaves who'd been brought to the Aguinas house as he looked at the warm soup placed in front of him.

Even though he was a branded slave, his legs were chained and his hands were shackled in front of him.

He'd been a member of a famous group of thieves in the imperial capital and a felon who'd murdered many people. The location of their hideout had been leaked, leading to his boss and comrades getting killed for resisting. Perhaps he should say he was lucky; he had been beaten unconscious with a blunt weapon and captured along with one of his friends who was like a brother to him. After they were done interrogating him, he'd become a penal laborer.

Not much time had passed since he'd become a slave, but he hadn't eaten anything decent. All the bread he'd been given was old and on the verge of being thrown out—or dry, hard, and rotting, with a sour smell and packed mold inside.

When he'd arrived at the slave trading company yesterday, he was given orc meat for dinner. There was only a small quantity of it, thinly sliced and seasoned with just a smidgen of salt, but it was the first piece of meat he'd had in a long time.

To make sure their "marketability" wasn't lowered from fighting behind the guards' backs, the slaves who appeared to be obedient were put in a large room together, while the felons were put in a private room in the dungeon. The wall facing the corridor had iron bars, and the other cells were clearly visible, perhaps so they would be easier to monitor.

After the guards left, the thieves talked in loud voices while eating their meat.

"Looks like we were sold to da same place, so let's all get along. Right, li'l bro?"

"Yeah, big bro. I'm lookin' forward to gettin' to know all of ya reeeeal well."

"Anyhow, I'm staaarved, this piddlin' hunk o' meat ain't nearly enough." Saying this, he thoroughly scowled at each one of the slaves in the other cells.

Now that they all knew they were sold to the same place, they couldn't afford to become his target.

Unable to bear it, one of the slaves offered his own meat, and others around him piled theirs on the same plate until the thieves had more than they could finish. Thanks to this, the thieves had eaten their fill of meat even in the morning.

So, they weren't hungry. The other slaves who'd given up their meat gulped down the soup with meat scraps provided by the Aguinas family, but the two thieves ate only the meat in theirs, then poured the soup into the other slaves' bowls while the guards weren't looking.

There's somethin' strange goin' on. Aren't we bein' treated too nice?

They'd been given meat upon arrival to the company and warm soup with more meat where they'd been purchased.

Thieves knew better than to hold on to optimistic ideas that they were being welcomed. They knew they weren't first-rate slaves.

The man held his empty soup bowl and carefully examined his surroundings.

All the people in this mansion were gangly men. If their slave brands hadn't been activated, these men could easily be felled, even if the thieves had their hands and feet in shackles. No "master" had been there when they'd been branded. The contract had been sealed with blood from a bottle, so he didn't know who could Order any of them.

Who could it be...?

If there was no master, maybe they could escape.

"Urgh..."

With a clang, a slave next to them who they'd given their soup to tipped over his bowl and collapsed. Perhaps there had been too much for him to finish, as soup splashed from the container onto the thief.

He tried to say "Nastyyy," but the thief realized he couldn't move his mouth very well.

Poison... No—anesthetic?

There was no point in killing slaves they'd just purchased. At once, he glanced around and saw that all the other slaves who'd been brought here had collapsed. He quickly exchanged looks with his friend to silently say, "Let's follow their lead." His friend had eaten some of the medicine, too, but it seemed like he hadn't lost consciousness.

There are usually opportunities in these types of situations. We'd be idiots to be reckless.

The same thing had been true when their den had been attacked. The thief had enough sense to wait for his chance.

Whatever the ones who bought us are plannin', it ain't good, but those gangly beansprout-lookin' guys probably can't put up much of a fight.

But this group had robbed the slaves of any free movement with shackles on their hands and feet and even poisoned them despite their slave brands. He was certain they did this because they would be in a bad spot if the slaves grew violent. Fortunately, he hadn't eaten much of the soup. He'd pretend to be unconscious and then escape when the numbness had worn off, before anyone could give him an Order. If he knew who his "master" was, the chance of success would go up significantly. The master was bound to show himself if the thief pretended to be unconscious.

Well whaddaya know, I remember the way. This is a dungeon in an old mansion. It'll be a straight shot, no way we'll get lost.

The thief pretended to pass out and motionlessly peeked at his surroundings. After all the slaves finally stopped moving, the back door opened, and several men came through, rolling a cart with wheels big enough to carry a person to take the unconscious slaves one by one to the back room.

One of the men inspected each slave put on the cart and gave directions, something along the lines of "That one goes to the red space. This one to the preparation room." Apparently, those with physical defects were sent to the "red" room, and those without went to the "preparation room."

Not good. Li'l bro lost one of his arms when we were captured. At this rate, we'll go to separate rooms. Better to have someone to watch your back even when you're runnin' away. That self-important bastard goin' "red room" and "preparation room" is prolly the master, but doesn't look like he's gonna leave anytime soon.

One after another, they took the slaves away. The thieves'

turns were imminent. He gradually grew impatient. His friend probably felt the same way. The younger man had been sending restless glances his way for a while now.

The numbness in his hands and feet had gotten a lot better, too. Soon it would be sink or swim.

Just when the thief's patience was about to reach its limit, something happened in the back room. The man appearing to be the master, the one giving directions, withdrew inside.

Now! He made an eye signal to his friend, and the pair leaped to their feet and started toward the door they'd come from.

That's when it happened.

"**Don't move.** Such a shame. You can't escape this place."

When and where did he come from? The thieves heard the voice from behind them.

He sounded like a young man. They couldn't see his face, because they'd been Ordered to stay in place.

"Take the cart over here. And don't forget the restraints. They were clever enough to avoid the drugs, so be on your guard."

A Contract of Servitude's Order consumes magic. Its effect varies with the magical power of the one issuing the Order, the substance of the Order itself, and the recipient's awareness. How long would the effect have lasted if the Order they were given was "We're going to kill you, so don't take a single step"?

The thieves were tied to the cart before the effects wore off, which wasn't long. They were carefully gagged as well, so they couldn't rant and rave. If they could have thrashed around and shouted, the other slaves under the effects of the medicine might have woken up, which would allow them to get lost in the chaos.

Son of a bitch, rotten luck...

The thief tied to the cart was taken to the "preparation room," and his friend incomprehensibly moaning "Mm-mm" was taken to the "red space."

"Finish moving and restraining the others. The medicine will wear off soon."

His eyes were no longer even looking at the thieves who'd attempted the desperate escape. No, they hadn't seen the slaves as individuals from the very beginning.

"Those two seem to have some physical strength. I hope they last a long time."

After ascertaining the transfer of the remaining slaves, Robert, the man who'd Ordered the thieves, headed for the back room holding the slaves.

There seemed to be some sort of disturbance in the red space a little while ago. Probably a slave who somehow woke up and went berserk. The manager was headed that way, so I imagine he has the situation under control.

About a month and a half had passed since the last expedition. It was time for the potion orders to start rolling in, which meant they needed to hasten production. The new medicine that Robert created was groundbreaking. It didn't have as strong of an effect as an alchemist's potion, but it wouldn't too off base to call it "magic medicine." It would certainly assist in the subjugation of the Labyrinth as a substitute for potions.

The Aguinas family had been making progress along the same path for two hundred long years. Apart from the alchemists' extinction, why should their progress be halted?

No matter what it takes, we will at last reach our destination. And I'll take Estalia with me...to the promised land, when the Labyrinth is no more.

Once again, Robert repeated his long-held desire.

As if to tell himself, as if to bind himself.

And once more, Robert stepped forward with no hesitation—to not halt their progress.

07

"Seriously though, Mariela's medicine is nothing but kneading," said a chemist while rolling his shoulder in pain.

The Merchants Guild's conference room was still bustling even after the seminar on how to make medicine had finished.

Each person could only attend the seminar once since the informational fee was also included in the price, but participants could attend the post-seminar study groups as many times as they liked. The participation fee was inexpensive, about the price of the materials plus a cup of tea, so many chemists attended every study session to use it as a place of information exchange even if they'd learned the skills already. Today, they were reviewing how to make painkillers, and about twenty chemists were using mortar and pestles to knead-knead-knead lynus wheat.

Walking around the chemists who were knead-kneading, Carol gave advice like, "Just a little more, you can do it." Carol was a young lady from the Aguinas family. At first, she'd been asked to refrain from involving herself in these burdensome affairs, but all the participating chemists were diligent and not in the least suspicious, so she joined in as an assistant like she'd wanted to do all along.

Because there had been people who had gone to great lengths to hire people to pester her store in the past, it was anticlimactic that nothing more troublesome happened. Well, it was a good thing that everyone was super cooperative. After all, if someone said something harsh to Mariela's face, even she would get sad. When this was discussed with Leandro during a break in the study session, he smiled and divulged a secret.

"That's becaaaause you're providing such valuable information. Ms. Elmera and I had a 'talk' with the participants. That's part of the Merchants Guild's responsibilities, you know."

Apparently, Mariela owed the conflict-free study sessions to Elmera and the others working behind the scenes. She should be grateful. Incidentally, none of the participants' hair had gone frizzy, so the "talk" must have been verbal only. Above everything else, she was glad those had gone by without a hitch, too.

"If you don't knead it, the Drops of Life contained in the lynus wheat won't mix with its medicinal components," Mariela replied to the chemist while knead-kneading. Wasn't there some decent method out there that would let her move on from this kneading-and-mixing hell? If so, she wanted to be the first to know.

"I think we've all wondered if it'd be better to use something with a high concentration of Drops of Life to increase the efficacy, since we can't draw up Drops of Life ourselves. It must have been tough work to find a way to blend it well."

The medicine-making methods Mariela taught were effective in a variety of applications. The ideas themselves were valuable, since she'd had to go through dozens of rounds of trial and error to test them out, and they had to pass numerous inspections. In truth, the gathered chemists also had their own ideas, but none could establish methods to make the medicine themselves.

The chemists were grateful that Mariela was willing to teach them these valuable techniques, even at a cost, especially after they'd harassed her for taking away their sales. And it wasn't just because Elmera's "talk" had caused them to have a change of heart—though there was no doubt it had been super effective. Thanks to the recipes from the Library and her own alchemic skills, Mariela had found relatively easy ways to make medicine. She continued to talk leisurely to the other chemists without realizing their unspoken gratitude.

"Oh, it makes sense that you'd try to figure it out."

Knead, knead, knead. Mariela kneeeaded and kneeeaded to stretch out the lynus wheat. It was pretty obvious she was getting sick of knead-kneading.

"Hey, how come we're not using magic to mix it? Wait, would that be bad?"

"Hmm? Sure, you can use magic. That'll make it a bit more effective, too."

There were several methods for kneading and mixing that didn't use alchemic skills. Mariela simply didn't know any other than kneading by hand, but apparently the chemists thought there was some meaning to doing it that way. Upon hearing Mariela's answer, the man looked surprised and responded with a question.

"Magic increases the effects?!"

The room quieted down in response to this question, and all eyes settled on Mariela.

"It does. But the magical power will fade in a week."

Kneeead, kneeead. Playing with the stickiness of the lynus wheat, Mariela answered readily without noticing their collective gaze.

The cookies with magical power kneaded into them that Mariela had once given to Lynx and the other members of the Black Iron Freight Corps had reverted to normal cookies in a week. She suspected that might be the case, which was why she was more surprised Sieg had held on to his like treasure for a week than she was about the magical power fading from them.

Sieg seemed to have a habit of squirreling away trivial items. Maybe it was a reaction to the long period of time he lived as a slave without any personal possessions, but among other things, he'd secretly tucked away shopping lists Mariela had given him, and he tore off the labels from the bottles of wine they'd drunk together.

Yet when Mariela left her room a mess, he mercilessly made her throw things away.

She formed the lynus wheat she kneeeaded and kneeeaded into a ball and poked it. Every time she did, it bounced and jiggled. This was fun.

The way it jiggles makes it look kinda tasty. I wonder what we should do for dinner?

This time, it was Carol who interrupted Mariela as she toyed with the ball of lynus wheat.

"A potion's efficacy is enhanced with Drops of Life, yes? You can increase its effect even at the extraction stage with Drops of Life. For mid-grade and higher potions, I heard that by mixing together apriore and lunamagia, which can contain Drops of Life, the effect is heightened even further."

"We've made medicine with apriore and lunamagia before, but even though these are 'vessels' for Drops of Life they don't actually contain much of it," replied one of the chemists. "So even when we used them, the effect didn't increase. It would be more effective to use natural plants like lynus wheat and genea cream containing a lot of Drops of Life. Don't you think?"

"Yes, I agree."

At the sign that Carol and the chemists were serious, Mariela finally stopped playing with the lynus wheat and looked up to find them having a discussion with intent expressions.

"Drops of Life can't be drawn from this region. But, if the effect of the medicine can be increased with just magical power, wouldn't it be better to do it that way?"

"Won't the material determine the amount of magical power that can be put in? If you use a material as a 'vessel' like how you use Drops of Life, wouldn't that maintain the effects for a reasonable period?"

"What's a 'vessel' for magical power?"

"…Magical gems?"

"That's inadvisable. In the past, research was apparently done in the imperial capital in which magical gems were placed into test subjects' bodies. Their magical power temporarily increased, but every one of the test subjects was consumed and killed by the gems."

The discussion between the chemists and Carol continued to unfold. Mariela, who'd stopped playing with the lynus wheat, found no opening to jump in. Since she couldn't do anything about it, she sought water to stretch out the kneaded wheat and resumed knead-kneading.

"Is there no other medium to store magical power in…?"

In response to that question, one of the chemists voiced an answer that perhaps everyone else was thinking.

"What about…blood?"

08

"As I thought, blood is the only way," Robert Aguinas mumbled in a room called the "red space" in the cellar of the Aguinas family annex.

What lengths had he gone for research up to this point?

He'd concentrated the small amount of Drops of Life found in well water, used plants like lynus wheat and lunamagia that contained a lot of Drops of Life, and charged potion ingredients like apriore fruit and lunamagia with Drops of Life extracted from nature. None of these methods had gone well.

The more he researched, the more he thought Drops of Life was the stuff left behind by people.

It was said that the Nexus that connected an alchemist to a ley line wasn't a pipe that Drops of Life was drawn up from but something that bound part of their own spirit to the ley line. The right and power to handle the energy from Drops of Life was obtained this way. In other words, it was thought potions were created using the power of the ley line.

If so, what was the energy people could control?

Robert focused on the manufacturing of magic medicine through magical power.

It could contain, or carry, ample amounts of magical power, and it was compatible with people.

An obvious medium for magical power was human blood,

which achieved a more powerful effect than other substitutes developed at the same time.

Healing magic improved the subject's ability to recover. In other words, they got help from the healing magic to cure their injuries with their own physical strength. And potions borrowed the massive power of the ley line. On the other hand, it was hard to accept something so repulsive as healing an injury by using someone else's lifeblood. But Robert didn't hesitate even for a moment.

"Prep the slaves for blood collection."

If he were collecting blood in good faith, it might have brought about a different effect in the people who used the magic medicine and a different future for Robert.

Use human beings as materials. That command had been a turning point in the life of the man named Robert Aguinas.

And on this day, too…

"Ughhh, ooooh, gaaah…!"

Biting his gag, the younger thief writhed in place. His eyes were bloodshot, and he thrashed around to try and tear off the restraints.

Including his, many carts were lined up in the red space he'd been brought to. All the people sleeping in the carts were restrained with their legs and heads elevated so their bodies were in a slight V shape, and thin tubes stretched from their noses, arms, and what looked like their lower half. The tubes going into their noses most likely went down to their stomachs. Each of these tubes was connected to a bag above the cart that fed nutrients blended with medicine that dripped into their nostrils. If this assumption was correct, the lower tube was probably for urine. There was no need to say what was in the red tubes that stretched from the people's arms.

How long had they been tied there? The muscles of the people in carts in the back of the room had weakened, and their fingers and toes had curled up and stiffened.

The men of this estate who came and went between the carts occasionally checked the magical tools connected to the red tubes and scribbled something down in their notebooks.

"Lord Robert, number twenty-eight has not met the minimum required magical power value for three days."

"Increase the magical gems to seventy."

"But—"

"He's reached the end of his life span. When his magical power value exceeds the minimum, extract all of it."

The man who Robert had ordered to execute this task approached the cart of the man called "number twenty-eight" and replaced the bag connected to his nasal tube with a different one. Number twenty-eight was nothing but skin and bones, and as the liquid from the new bag flowed into him, his emaciated body began to shake.

"G... Guh..."

Number twenty-eight's neck bent backward, his mouth opened wide, and his tongue thrust out.

His convulsions continued as he took shallow breaths. After being restrained for so long, his muscles had probably wasted away and his joints stiffened. Number twenty-eight didn't have much strength left, so his final spasms were so weak they could hardly be called struggling. But it was that very reason that made the onlookers feel terror.

"Magical power has reached the minimum required value. Initiating suction."

"Do it."

Under Robert's direction, the man activated the magical device.

A human being was withering and dying in front of the thief's eyes. How long had they been squeezing his blood, magical power, life, and everything in his body out of him? And even at the end of his life, would they take and take until nothing was left?

Will this be me? Am I gonna go through the same thing for who knows how long...?!

The younger thief twisted and turned and struggled with all his strength to break free of his restraints. His eyes were bloodshot and full of fear, and saliva bubbled and spilled from the corners of his gagged mouth.

"Sleep."

Robert gave an Order to the thief. *Sleep. Sleep. Sleep.*

No, no, if I sleep I'll never wake up again. Help me, big bro!

Was this the price he paid for mocking the people who'd begged him to spare their lives before he cut them down? Was this retribution? In response to Robert's Order, the younger thief finally released his hold on consciousness.

"What about...blood?" repeated one of the chemists in the conference room of the Merchants Guild's Medicinal Herbs Division.

What about blood as a medium for increasing the efficacy of medicine with magical power? This was probably the solution everyone gathered there had thought of.

"Blood, huh? I mean, sure, blood's used in contract rites. It has a lot of magical power, and you can add things to it... But, y'know..."

"It's bad news."

"Yeah. That's no way to heal people."

All the chemists breathed a sigh in response to their conclusion.

Such a repulsive thing surely couldn't be called medicine. The chemists fell into silence, interrupted only by the *sproooing, sproooing* sounds of the lynus wheat Mariela was kneading and stretching. It was super-stretched out now. A new record. Too bad the medicine's efficacy would remain the same.

"Just think, 'Pain, pain, go away' as you put magic into it. It'll lose that magic before long, but at least the feelings won't go anywhere."

The chemists smiled wryly at Mariela, who was industriously kneading away. Mariela's medicine seemed to work well. Not just for physical pain, but for healing hearts, too.

"Well, magical power aside—Mariela, would this not work if we used a mixer?"

"Huh? A mixer? What's that?"

Silence fell over the room for a second time.

"Mariela...," Sieg whispered from behind. "We're from a really rural village, remember? We hardly had any magical tools. There's a tool that can mix these kinds of things. And confectionery shops use it to knead dough."

Their handy "childhood friends" cover story to hide Mariela's two-hundred-year time lag had sprung a leak.

"Huhwhaaaaaaat?! Something that useful exists?!"

"...And here I thought you just liked kneading, Mariela."

"I think kneading a wish for the pain to go away is a lovely idea, myself."

Mariela felt her biceps, worn out from all the excessive mixing, swell from the sympathy of Carol and the other chemists.

After that, specialized mixers for making medicine, with mixing and kneading patterns and stirring blades, were manufactured through the cooperation of the chemists and a magical researcher. The very first machine was donated to Mariela's shop, Sunlight's Canopy.

The mixer that freed Mariela from kneading-and-mixing hell was equipped with a bowl and stirrers for making sweets, and she used the machine not only to make medicine, but also a mountain of cookies. Thanks to this, Sunlight's Canopy became more and more confusing as to what type of shop it was, but this was inconsequential compared to the high quality of medicine that had become the norm in the Labyrinth City.

10

"Raaaaaah!"

The shout of the man known as the Gold Lion General inspired the hearts of the battle-worn soldiers. No matter how many times he was knocked down, Leonhardt got back up.

A lone queen escaped the Kingdom of Endalsia's destruction two hundred years ago. It was said that the queen carried a little princess inside her. The Margrave Schutzenwald of the time loaned soldiers to the head alchemist of the Aguinas family, who had saved the queen, and endeavored to restore the Labyrinth City.

The princess born to the queen married into the Schutzenwald family, giving them the right to govern the Labyrinth City. Her blood flowed in Leonhardt, who was the next in line to be head of the family, and he had proper qualifications to be the city's king.

Of course, this didn't mean he wanted to rebel against the Empire. The Empire recognized to a certain extent the control and autonomy of the land by the ruined country's descendants, and the Emperor had conveyed this to the head of the Schutzenwalds: "Schutzenwald, take back thy land with thine own two hands."

Yes. The Labyrinth City was the Schutzenwald family's domain. It wasn't a place for monsters to rule.

"May we defeat the Labyrinth and make this land ours once more."

This wish, the dearest one of the Schutzenwald family, bound Leonhardt like a curse.

Fight, fight, fight, and die.

And then, he'd be succeeded by someone from his bloodline lucky enough to survive.

How many of Leonhardt's brethren had died under his banner for the sake of the Schutzenwalds' deepest desire?

No matter how wounded and crushed he became, he could not stop.

He must not fall.

Because Leonhardt's life was not yet at its end.

Leonhardt slashed at the King of Cursed Serpents. His kin followed behind him.

The main force attacked with their swords, then withdrew while bows and magic covered them. Soldiers who were sent flying and suffered serious injury were immediately healed and returned to the battlefront.

How long did they repeat these actions in this battle?

The King of Cursed Serpents, who'd petrified and consumed so many of Leonhardt's comrades, let loose with a horrible cry as if to curse all living things and finally collapsed to the ground.

"Huuuoooooooooh!" Leonhardt thrust his fist holding his sword upward. The soldiers followed suit.

The King of Cursed Serpents, which had defeated his army countless times, had finally been slain.

Watching Leonhardt, who was overcome with emotion and giving a great shout of triumph, Medical Technician Nierenberg breathed a sigh of relief. He couldn't suppress the feeling that they'd won by the skin of their teeth. His own reserves, as well as those of his medical team, were on the verge of running out. It was probably the case for everyone else, too. Considering they hadn't been able to win until now and their magical power and materials had run dry, there was no denying it was a worthwhile victory. He never realized possessing large quantities of potions could influence war efforts.

"Give me the number of potions used. Just the high-grade ones."

"Yes, sir. Three hundred seventy-eight."

It was more than ten times the number used in regular expeditions. Moreover, eight hundred potion vials' worth of holy water, equivalent to mid-grade potions, had been prepared. The team had been ordered in no uncertain terms to use these freely, and all the soldiers chosen this time had been made to sign a stronger magical covenant than usual so no information from the expedition would leak out.

Even so, this strategy involved a drastic use of potions... But, we probably had no other way, thought Nierenberg.

It was as if a chess piece had fallen from the heavens just when the opponent was about to declare checkmate. Nierenberg felt this changed the state of the board as a critical turning point.

"You have my congratulations, Brother," Weishardt said to his wounded sibling. Weishardt himself was also on the verge of running out of magic. Even standing was difficult.

"You fought well, Weis. Everyone did. This victory is momentous. Now, what about the stairs to the next stratum?"

"Yes, we've confirmed its location. A unit of scouts has been sent to investigate. We should know more any moment. However, you look exhausted. Please return to the base first."

"Don't worry, Weis. We've made it this far. Do you really think I'm going to head back now before we've even heard the initial report?"

Now that they'd broken through the Labyrinth's fifty-third stratum, the way to the fifty-fourth lay open. No one knew how far down the Labyrinth went. Maybe, just maybe, the fifty-fourth stratum was the last.

It was said that the labyrinth boss resided in the deepest part. Apparently, this monster was completely different from the other stratum bosses. Not its shape, but its very being. Legend held that anyone who had participated in subjugating a labyrinth could tell with just a glance that it was the labyrinth's boss.

So, maybe the scouts would return with the news they'd reached the final stratum.

Everyone here probably thought the same thing. So, worn and battered, Leonhardt sat on the ground in the safe zone at the boundary of the stratum and waited for the scouts' return.

The news he waited impatiently for came earlier than expected.

Leonhardt could tell the situation just from the scout's bewildered look. It wasn't the final stratum.

However, the report she brought further betrayed his thoughts.

"Reporting in, General. The fifty-fourth stratum…is underwater."

The scout reported an endless ocean lay in the fifty-fourth stratum.

Though Leonhardt had vomited blood and been on the verge of death many times to finally reach this point, yet another obstacle awaited him.

Nierenberg returned home in the afternoon the day after the King of Cursed Serpents had been defeated.

After transferring from the Teleportation Circle they'd placed in the fiftieth stratum to the one in the second stratum, the

Labyrinth Suppression Forces returned to their base through an underground corridor.

A Teleportation Circle was an expensive magical tool that allowed instant movement between places with the same latitude and longitude. In other words, the transfer could only happen vertically. Plus, it required two Teleportation Circles being magically connected.

The Labyrinth was an area controlled by a labyrinth boss and constructed from its magical power, which the Teleportation Circles made use of when they were established, but they'd cease functioning if the boss fell. In short, you could say they created an artificial bypass route that used the magical power of a living labyrinth.

Teleportation Circles had been set up every ten strata starting from the twentieth. The ones that transferred to the twentieth, thirtieth, and fortieth strata had been installed on the first stratum and were open to the public, so although one had to prepare enough magical power or gems to activate them, anyone could technically use them.

The fact that the Labyrinth was a den of evil that went beyond fifty strata was hidden from everyone not authorized to know. So, the Teleportation Circle connecting to the fiftieth stratum had been installed in a secret chamber on the second stratum, and the general public wasn't aware of it. The second stratum was a damp, humid cavern inhabited only by monsters like slimes, and since the slimes ate moss, medicinal herbs, and other vegetation, it had no resources to gather. The Labyrinth Suppression Forces protected one corner of it, ostensibly as a Labyrinth garrison.

In truth, the section maintained as a garrison contained a

Teleportation Circle connected to the fiftieth stratum, and farther back, it connected to the underground Aqueduct. A large number of slimes had been multiplying in the underground Aqueduct, so normally it couldn't be used as a passage. Over many years, the Labyrinth Suppression Forces had lined the water supply connecting the second stratum of the Labyrinth to their base with magic-absorbing daigis fibers to quarantine the slimes and establish it as a direct route to the Labyrinth.

The Labyrinth Suppression Forces put on their heroic parade and marched en masse to the Labyrinth only during the regular expedition periods. In reality, they performed far more subjugations than what the public saw.

Even when Leonhardt received the petrification curse, he was transported via this route, which was precisely why the public never knew of his injury or the Labyrinth Suppression Forces' crushing defeat.

He was now on his way back from felling the King of Cursed Serpents and completing his revenge, but Leonhardt walked with heavy feet.

They'd said the spiral staircase leading to the fifty-fourth stratum was partially flooded with seawater. All they could see from there was endless sea and sky. A horizon a full 360 degrees around them. The only other thing visible was the unnatural-looking hole at the top of the stairs leading to the fifty-third stratum.

They hadn't identified any land in this world of blue sea and blue sky. A single point off in the distance looked like a pillar. The scout unit was probably exploring the stratum right about now with a focus on that structure.

Everyone involved in the King of Cursed Serpents' subjugation was covered in wounds. Even the medical team had run out of magic, so they couldn't provide enough healing within the Labyrinth. They needed to return to the base, where they could get enough healing and rest. Leonhardt didn't show his discouragement on his face, but rather thanked his soldiers and dedicated the victory to their fallen brethren. From behind him, the soldiers gazed at Leonhardt, who kept moving, and started forward again themselves.

Nierenberg treated soldiers after returning to the base. By the time he finally arrived home, it was already past noon.

"Welcome home, Papa."

"It's good to be back, Sherry."

Although it was midday, the curtains in Sherry's room had been drawn closed and the lights were off, making the room dim. Nierenberg hugged his beloved daughter tight and gently stroked her bandaged head.

Sherry's face was still covered in bandages even now.

It wasn't as if the wound she'd received from the enormous slime hadn't gotten better. Healing magic had taken care of that.

A terrible burn scar remained where her skin had been dissolved.

How could he even be happy about the small mercy that her eyes had been spared?

The left half of his dear Sherry's face had melted due to the slime's acidic liquid that struck her temple. Her eyelid was stuck half-closed. The skin that had been regenerated with healing magic was dark red and bumpy, and the hair roots at her temple had limited function and grew only a little hair.

The white skin, fine features, and glossy black hair coloring the untouched right half of her face only served to make the left half stand out all the more. That's why she wore the bandages. She was far more beautiful wearing them.

It had already been three weeks since the incident. Sherry hadn't taken a single step outside her home. She spent all day and all night locked up in her room, with the curtains drawn to block the light.

"Papa, did you already have lunch?"

"Come to think of it, I haven't eaten anything since yesterday."

"Good. I made bean and orc meat tomato stew." Sherry showed him her smile as she always did.

The two of them sat at the dining table talking about how the housekeeper had bought huge chunks of orc meat that she'd prepared herself.

What wrongdoing had the girl committed? Nierenberg stifled the hollow feeling in his stomach and smiled at Sherry.

Of course, he'd told her not to go through the slums. But that was more in hopes she wouldn't meet an unsavory boyfriend, and there was no inherent danger in something like walking along the main road near the Labyrinth, especially in the middle of the day. How could anyone blame Sherry for taking a shortcut that children all over town used?

He wanted to tear the fool limb from limb who'd led the giant slime into town, but the monster had dissolved and swallowed him. Not even his bones remained. The indirect cause of the incident, Teluther from the City Defense Squad, offered no excuses for his negligence in managing supplies and allowing Kindel's reckless behavior, nor for his meritorious deed of leading the giant slime away from the main road himself. Instead, he had bowed deeply and accepted his punishment.

Nierenberg had no one to direct his anger at, and his heart was filled with grief.

And if he had just a single high-grade potion, Sherry's wound could be healed.

Even if she just went to the imperial capital, Sherry could be cured. That was the most certain way, which also presented a problem that quickly dashed his hopes. He had no relatives. Ever since his wife had died, he'd lived alone with Sherry. Although responsible, she was still just twelve years old. Even if she traveled with a yagu merchant caravan, there was no way she could make it to the imperial capital alone on such a harsh journey. If Sherry were to be cured in the imperial capital, her father would probably have to accompany her. However, he had responsibilities in the Labyrinth Suppression Forces. He managed the medical team, and few people had a clue how to manage potions. He didn't think it would be peacefully accepted if he applied for time off or a discharge.

How long would Sherry spend in this gloomy house until Nierenberg could take her to the imperial capital, or until she became able to go to the capital by herself?

How much time as a young girl full of hopes and dreams would she lose?

Nierenberg couldn't say for certain he'd be able to cure her someday.

Three hundred and seventy-eight.

The number of high-grade potions used to bring down the King of Cursed Serpents.

They'd all belonged to the Labyrinth Suppression Forces. It was a serious crime to steal the army's potions or use them for personal reasons.

Though Nierenberg had the authority to use them, he wasn't allowed to give even one to his beloved daughter, no matter how many he administered to the soldiers.

"Papa, what's wrong? You look angry." Sherry gazed at her brooding father.

"I'm just a little tired. It's nothing to worry about," Nierenberg answered and downed the last of his stew.

12

"Are these the only requests for potions this month?" Robert Aguinas asked the elderly steward.

"Yes, Lord Robert. When they asked for a price reduction yesterday, I requested a transaction at the usual price as you directed, and they responded with this amount. There appears to have been some sort of budget cut."

According to the elderly steward's explanation, the Labyrinth Suppression Forces had requested was no more than half of potions they'd requested up to now.

"How strange. The last expedition should have seen a staggering number of casualties for the Labyrinth Suppression Forces. They couldn't possibly have surplus potions."

The Aguinas family prioritized potion management and research, but that didn't mean they had no sources of information. They acquired intelligence on the large number of casualties

in the Labyrinth Suppression Forces. They even had ways of fig-
uring out how many high-grade potions supplied by the Aguinas
family the Forces had left. At any rate, they seemed to have had
a difficult struggle during the previous expedition. The Aguinas
family confirmed that a month and a half afterward, the Forces
had finished treating their wounded and begun their usual subjugation. They had to have used up most of the potions made a few
days ago, so Robert assumed they would make a large order.

"Are they contriving to withhold buying more to entice a price
reduction? It's a little late to start haggling. The suppression ought
to have resumed by now," Robert mused.

The steward responded to Robert's question.

"According to our sources, there was a discovery of buried
potion stores."

"That's *impossible*. Even an old man would know that. However, if new potions have been discovered..."

It couldn't be. Robert mulled over the situation.

There was no way anyone could find a stash of buried potions.

Even the Aguinas family's best potion storage facilities could
only preserve Drops of Life's effects for about a hundred years.

After the Stampede two centuries ago, the development of
potion storage facilities rapidly improved magical tool technology. The storage facilities invented by scholars boasting the
highest intellect in the imperial capital convected the source of
potions' magical effects, Drops of Life, within the potions and
continuously provided an effect similar to the alchemic skill used
at the final step of making a potion, *Anchor Essence*. In this way,
they succeeded in suppressing potion deterioration.

In theory, the effect would last two hundred years.

Storage facilities that allowed the preservation of potions for just a hundred years should be commended, even if the deterioration of their potions began sooner than current facilities.

But that was only a hundred years. No potions made immediately after the Stampede should remain. Of course, this information was concealed. The potions kept in the storage facilities of each family, including the Labyrinth Suppression Forces and Margrave Schutzenwald, were being replaced by the ones supplied regularly by the Aguinas family, so even they shouldn't have realized the truth. The Aguinas family's secrets, including the number of years storage facilities could preserve potions, continued to be a secret.

So, if new potions appeared in the world, it meant the *same type of person* as the one sleeping in the Aguinas family's cellar had awakened.

It wasn't impossible. He couldn't say with certainty that no one else had taken the same measures.

However, it was unbelievable for this to have happened all of a sudden. The post-Stampede circumstances had been passed down through the generations in detail, and the Aguinas family knew of every single alchemist who had been involved in the Labyrinth City's restoration.

Who in the world could it be?

Robert gave an order to the steward.

"Find this person. If they're an alchemist, we must bring them here to our estate."

The steward bowed deeply and left the room. He, too, was connected to the Aguinas family. He would appoint trustworthy subordinates.

"Contact our informants. Bring to light the conveyer of the

potions. Do not forget to thoroughly search where the conveyer goes to and from," the steward told them.

"I will now make my report."

The report on the investigation of the fifty-fourth stratum arrived from the scouts under Leonhardt's command.

According to the details of the investigation, the water that spread throughout the stratum was almost the same as real sea-water, and its depth was unknown. The stairs connecting to the lower floor continued at least two hundred yards, but the scouts hadn't been able to confirm any lower because it exceeded the limits of their diving abilities. The depth of the water exceeded a half mile, the limit of their sonar depth detection.

"In short, we were unable to see the bottom with our limitations, and there's a possibility it's endless."

"The fifty-fourth stratum itself may manipulate space. Now, tell me about the monsters."

"Yes, sir. We couldn't identify anything airborne. We also couldn't detect any underwater within our sonar's limits. The only magic we could sense was from the aforementioned pillar."

At the scout's report, Leonhardt and Weishardt looked at each other.

A single pillar standing alone in a vast sea.

It was unlikely anyone would think this wasn't suspicious.

"And what about the pillar?"

Prompted by Weishardt, the scout reported the status of its investigation.

The portion of the pillar above water was higher than a three-story building and thicker than a spire on a castle wall. Four head-like structures sat at the top of the pillar, each one at a right angle to those next to it so they all looked in different directions with no blind spots. They were shaped like dragon heads, but they each had three eyes, one on the forehead and two in the usual spots, and they all jutted out in a bizarre way. Instead of jaws that opened and closed, the mouths had something cylindrical protruding from them. The scouts didn't have the slightest idea how deep underwater the pillar went, but sometimes it bobbed up and down slightly with the waves, so it was highly likely it was floating.

Their insect summoners had sent magical insects toward the spire, and they were about a half mile from it when the cylinders protruding from the dragon heads fired beams of light, vaporizing every single insect. The scouts' inspection of the beam's launch conditions showed that its range was a sphere with a radius of a half mile centered at the top of the spire, and they said a beam of light would be shot at anything from the air to sea level that invaded its space. The time between beam shots was less than five minutes. Even if they were on land, it would be difficult to approach the pillar while the cylinders were on cooldown, but the scouts said the cylinders shot high-pressure water attacks during those intervals. But the insect summoners couldn't determine if these attacks occurred in rapid succession or how many, as their resources had been relentlessly consumed.

Insect summoners could manipulate special magical insects hatched from eggs and experience their senses to safely obtain information from a distance. They were essential for investigating new strata in the Labyrinth where no one knew what kind of dangers lurked. However, when the insects were killed, the summoners received a feedback response, so considering the scarcity of the skill, it needed to be used with caution. This time, they seemed to have finished the inspection of the area above water through brute force, despite many insects being killed.

After communicating to the insect summoners to get sufficient rest, Leonhardt asked about the long-range attacks in the report.

"A type of light magic, huh? Can we reflect it with a mirror shield?"

"We sent mirror shields fixed to rafts into the range of fire, but the light beams vaporized every one of them."

The beams the tower shot appeared to be one-hit kill magic. The water attacks were powerful as well, causing serious damage to the rafts and sending the mirror shields flying with dents in them. It would be difficult to launch a frontal attack by sea.

"Next, the report about the underwater area. We floated a raft to just beyond the range of the beams and used water magic to fire a harpoon beneath the surface. We confirmed the beams do not fire at depths greater than ten yards. These are the results of the current stage of our investigation."

Once again, Leonhardt and Weishardt looked at each other in response to the scout's report.

Weishardt spoke up after the scout left. "Shall we dive in, Brother?"

"Going a half mile without breathing?"

"Should we prepare bags of air weighted with stones? Would a long air pipe be better?"

"Even if we got close that way, how would we destroy the spire?"

"Indeed. Let's wait for more detailed results from the investigation and have them inquire as to whether potions exist that allow underwater activity."

"Potions, huh? Come to think of it, the effect of that holy water was magnificent."

"It is said that its effectiveness differs greatly depending on the materials used, so I'm guessing it was quite good."

"Material? What was it?"

"The hair of a maiden, apparently. The younger and purer the young girl, the more powerful the effects."

"What?!" Leonhardt stood up with a jerk. The hair of a maiden. Although it was for the subjugation of the Labyrinth, had a young girl behind the scenes cut off her hair?

Leonhardt imagined a young, beautiful maiden like Caroline lopping off her own long hair with a single stroke. In reality, it was just the hair of the Yagu Drawbridge Pavilion's ten-year-old poster girl, Emily, and only a little bit had been used.

We'll defeat the Labyrinth for sure to repay her devotion.

Leonhardt was filled with fresh determination. Upon hearing of the maiden's hair, he seemed ready to dive underwater straight for the pillar, whether he did so while carrying a bag of air or holding the end of a long air pipe in his mouth.

14

"Maaariii, look, look! Daddy said he was sorry for how he cut my hair and got me this suuuper-pretty ribbon!"

Emily, a key player in the slaying of the King of Cursed Serpents, had come to visit Sunlight's Canopy with her new ribbon from the Yagu Drawbridge Pavilion's owner tied in her hair. The hair on the left and right was at different heights, and the ribbon was tied in a granny knot like usual, as if she'd done her hair herself.

Mariela and Caroline neatly retied it, and then they all had a snack together. A peaceful sight, as always.

Emily's ribbon was made from fabric that had been delivered along with the payment for the holy water. Lieutenant Malraux had explained, "We received this from General Leonhardt as thanks for the material in the holy water." It was a splendid fabric that wasn't readily available in the Labyrinth City. Mariela wasn't sure how much General Leonhardt knew, but it was probably a present for Emily, so she had Malraux give it to the owner of the Yagu Drawbridge Pavilion.

Since it was an expensive item, she was worried about their reasoning for giving it to him, but Malraux had said "the fabric got wet and we can't sell it" and "this is for all the trouble the Black Iron Freight Corps has caused you" when he handed it to the owner. Apparently, the owner had gazed fixedly at it, then said things like "For Emily's wedding dress..." in a serious tone. It was a bit early for that.

In the end, the only thing he could immediately give Emily was only a ribbon made from the edge of the fabric, but it had made her elated.

Additionally, Mariela never received any bonus payment for all the precious sleep she'd missed out on. She felt miffed. Sieg put three marshmallows in her cocoa when she broke the news to him.

Winter would soon arrive in the Labyrinth City. The chilly nights spent cozied up by the fireplace drinking hot cocoa and relaxing with Sieg were priceless to Mariela.

CHAPTER 5
The Beautiful Blue Sea

01

"Um...but it's already winter?" Mariela responded to Lieutenant Malraux of the Black Iron Freight Corps. She eyed him like he'd said something completely ridiculous. What could have made Mariela, who normally was happy-go-lucky, make such a face?

Malraux took a deep breath and, after regaining his composure, asked Mariela again. "So, is there a potion that would allow a person to move around underwater?"

Mariela muttered "But it's so cold..." among other things before tapping her forefinger to her chin and murmuring "Mm..." as she considered his question.

"I think you could do it with a merfolk polymorph potion, but could we even get the ingredients? Aurora ice fruit, mermaid's tears... Even if those are out of the question, things like merfolk gill gems are really, really valuable."

Polymorph potions were also called "morph potions." It was a sort of wonder drug that everyone wanted to try once in their life.

If you could perfectly transform into a specific person, you'd probably be able to do all sorts of things, from organized crime to personal mischief.

Unfortunately, polymorph medicine wasn't so convenient. It used your body as a base to transform a piece of yourself into an organ of another species.

For example, in the case of the merfolk type, a high-grade

polymorph potion would transform your respiratory system. You developed gills for breathing underwater, and webbing between your fingers and toes. Your eyelids disappeared, and your eyeballs changed into fish eyes. If the potion was well-made, part of your body hair would change into scales, and you'd look even more like a merperson.

However, your physique wouldn't change just from a high-grade potion, so your skin and the hair on your head would remain the same. You wouldn't look perfectly like a merfolk monster, but rather you'd change into a mix of merfolk and human that was neither of those things. If you wanted to transform completely, you'd need a special-grade polymorph potion, but this was distinguished from other special-grade potions by the difficulty of obtaining its materials, the difficulty of making it, and the time required to make it.

Many people who desired polymorph potions want to use the aviator type to soar through the air. With the high-grade version, your arms changed into wings like a harpy. However, the fact that humans couldn't fly even with wings due to their body weight and lack of sufficient muscular strength was spoken of even in fairy tales.

If you thought of it that way, you could say a merfolk potion was very practical among polymorph potions for allowing you to breathe underwater.

"Aurora ice fruit and merfolk gill gems, yes? Understood. We'll get those ready for you."

Malraux nodded in total seriousness. Following his lead, Mariela also flashed a grave look as she asked him, "Going for a wintertime swim?"

"No."

Seems they didn't hold any sort of "Labyrinth Suppression Forces Beefcake Polar Plunge" event. What a shame.

As usual, after returning from Sunlight's Canopy through the underground Aqueduct, Marlow and the others divided up the work at their base.

"Merfolk gill gems...? What're those for, Lieutenant?" asked the dual wielder, Edgan.

As the name suggested, merfolk gill gems were gems formed in the gills of merfolk, similar to pearls in that they started off as stones or other foreign objects caught in the gills and then were coated over a long period of time by gill secretions. They had a distorted shape and a color similar to pearls, but unlike their spherical counterparts, they had a slight elasticity to them. Because they circulated in the market more than natural pearls and they were made in the gills of merfolk, they were not considered as valuable as pearls by the nobility, so they were traded among commoners as the people's pearl. Even so, since they were not the kind of thing that could be cultivated, they were not so common that you could go to a jewelry shop and buy them whenever you wanted.

Mermaid's tears were even rarer. It wasn't merely a legend that tears from a mermaid become precious stones similar to pearls. Though the tears were pearlescent, they were faintly transparent and filled with a mysterious light that made them look like they were reflecting the moon from the bottom of the sea. Naturally, commoners had no opportunity to obtain or even look at one. They were fine items that royalty and nobility only had a few of.

Compared to those, merfolk gill gems were far less difficult to obtain.

"I'll look for aurora ice fruit, then."

"Oh, me too."

Lynx and Edgan offered to search for the aurora ice fruit, a seemingly even less difficult endeavor than attempting to track down merfolk gill gems.

"*Sigh*, very well. I trust you'll properly handle the task."

Thinking the two young men might not be suited to obtaining jewelry just yet, Malraux requested they get the aurora ice fruit.

Yahoo!

It wasn't until several days later that the pair regretted being happy about getting the easier task.

"Aurora ice fruit? Another rare item?"

Lynx and Edgan had visited Ghark's shop with the hopes that if anyone could help them in medicinal herb matters, it was the old man. However, he expressed disapproval. Apparently, he didn't have any in his shop.

"C'mon, ol' man Ghark, you gotta know where to find some, right? Get some for us, pleeease!" Lynx requested cheerfully.

"Quit pushin' us old folks around. Been doin' a lot of that lately, haven't ye? I'll tell ye the place, so go get it yerselves. It'll be easy-peasy fer two or three B-Rankers. This old man ain't up to the task."

Ghark shoved a roughly drawn map at Lynx and chased the two of them out of the shop. Though it was only just past noon, the old man closed the shop and left with a "So long." A sign reading FOR ANY INQUIRIES, VISIT SUNLIGHT'S CANOPY hung on the door of Ghark's Herbal Supplies.

"The ol' man even made a sign for that?"

"He practically lives there!"

After leaving the dumbfounded Lynx and Edgan, who were gawking at his sign, Ghark arrived at Sunlight's Canopy, handed over the herbs Mariela had ordered, made tea for himself at the self-serve corner as if it were his own home, and relaxed in a sunny seat.

"Ahh, now this's the life."

Next to him sat a chemist whom he'd recently become friendly with and who frequently visited the shop under the pretense of checking the condition of the mixer. Thanks to this, the mixer now had a bunch of optional parts unrelated to making medicine, such as the specialized cookie dough stirrer. In addition to bowls for making salves and for making internal medicine, there were several for making sweets. Mariela could make large batches of crisp cookies to enjoy with the tea at her store. Even Mariela herself, the owner, couldn't help but wonder what kind of shop Sunlight's Canopy actually was.

"Oh, Ghark, I wondered if ya might have lund petioles. No rush, though."

"Ah, I do. I'll bring 'em round here about this time tomorrow if that's all right with ye," Ghark answered the chemist. Recently he'd begun arranging product deliveries at Sunlight's Canopy. What was he, a peddler? The man owned a shop of his own.

"The cold gets more unbearable the older ya get. Leave that kinda thing to the young'uns."

Ghark get out a satisfied "Ahhh" as he finished his tea, and the chemist stylishly poured a second helping into his friend's cup.

In his warm sunny spot, Ghark stretched his limbs that had been tensed up from the cold with an "Mmm" and passed the time chatting merrily with the chemist.

02

Several days later, Lynx and Edgan, who'd been tasked with gathering the aurora ice fruit, dragged Sieg with them to the ice and snow stratum, number thirty-two.

"Gaaaah, s-so c-c-cooold!"

Clad in extremely fluffy winter clothes, the three men trudged through the snowy field. The way they cried "Brrrrr" and "Freeeeezing" made them sound just like yetis.

Mariela was at the seminar and study group at the Merchants Guild. Apparently, Elmera was spending the entire day at the guild, so Lynx asked her to look after Mariela.

As she sent Sieg off, Mariela herself had told him, "Sieg, you ought to take a breather every now and then. I'll wait for you in the Medicinal Herbs Division after the study group, so don't worry about me." As for Sieg, though, he fidgeted nervously and would much rather hurry up and go home.

Knowing Mariela, she might get hungry and go home if I'm not back by dinner. No, she might be lured away by a stranger with the promise of food...

What on earth kind of person did he think Mariela was? Even she wouldn't be that careless. Probably.

Ignoring Sieg's worries, Lynx complained about how absolutely freezing he was while also saying things all giddy like, "Hey Ed, look, look. **Water.** Awesome, it freezes instantly! I'm an ice wizard!"

Thanks to the party's use of low-grade monster-warding potions, beast-type monsters like snow wolves and snow bears didn't attack them, but yetis, frost trolls, and other monsters that looked like the living embodiment of the frigid air did occasionally.

"Wind Edge."

Sieg cut a frost troll to pieces with the blades of wind his mythril sword emitted, while Lynx let fly several ice daggers created from water magic at a yeti.

In this stratum, the cold was a more formidable foe than the monsters. The party's limbs grew numb, and their bodies wouldn't move as they wanted them to. Sometimes a powerful wind swept over them, kicking up ice and snow and stealing their body from its heat.

Howling wind began to blow again.

After a little bit of walking while enduring the wind, Edgan pointed to a cave that had come into view.

They decided to take a break there. After entering the cave, the three of them started a fire and warmed up. They nibbled on nuts coated in hardened honey and drank strong spirits to warm their bodies.

"Say, Sieg. You live with Mariela, right?" asked Edgan, his face a little red. "Sooo, how's it been goin'? How far've you two gone?"

"C'mon, Ed, you drunk already? You're such a lightweight, geez. Anyway, Sieg... He's got the wrong idea, right?" Lynx's narrow eyes widened and stared fixedly at Sieg.

"Uh, w-we...haven't yet—"

"Yet?! Did you say 'yet'?"

"The hell, Sieg?! How much younger than you do you think she is—?!"

"Chill out, Lynx. Well? Well? How's it gonna go? Maybe you'll get lucky one day and witness a 'wardrobe malfunction'? That could happen, right? Or maybe she'll be in the bath and you'll just happen to walk in! Like, 'Oops! It was an accident!' I mean, when two people live together, sooner or later that's gonna happen, yeah?!"

Edgan, twenty-four years old. Got weirdly hyped up when drunk. And he was on the market, ladies!

Edgan was convinced that guys who play it cool get all the ladies, so anywhere women were present (such as at the Yagu Drawbridge Pavilion), he would openly scoff at women to show his utter disinterest. In reality, though, he was a simple guy who loved dirty talk. He got along well with the younger Lynx, too.

Lynx quieted down Erotigan—no, Edgan—as if this wasn't the first time this had occurred, then asked Sieg a question of his own.

"Well? Did it happen? A 'happy accident'?" Lynx's normally narrow eyes were still open wide from before. It was seriously creepy.

"I've never barged in on her...on purpose," Sieg answered, intentionally averting Lynx's gaze.

"Wait, 'on purpose'? That's what you just said, right? So you've done it by accident, right?! S-spill it! Tell us, what was it like?" Edgan seized on Sieg's slip of the tongue. Lynx made no attempt to stop Edgan; maybe he was interested, too.

"No, it's just...um...Mariela fell asleep in the bath and nearly drowned... And a slave's brand stings when his master is in danger, so..."

With no other choice, Sieg explained. When the pain in his brand had informed him Mariela's life was in jeopardy, he'd burst into the bathroom in a panic and found her completely submerged in the bathtub. *Glug, glug.*

"...She...almost died taking a bath...?" Lynx said, incredulous.

"Sure sounds like her..."

"That was the first time I felt glad I'd been branded... If it weren't for that, Mariela would've..."

The three men hung their heads in exhaustion. Their slouching backs made them look like yetis. But even among his fellow yetis, Edgan wasn't discouraged.

"And? What was she like?" Eyes ablaze, he urged Sieg to go on.

Two piercing gazes demanded to know the rest of the story. There was no escaping them.

However, his master's dignity was at stake. Siegmund thought about it. He had to convey Mariela's goodness and magnificence without crossing over into lust. Making full use of his brain with its intelligence score of four, Sieg returned the two men's gazes and slowly spoke.

"She makes good use of her, um, ingredients?"

"*Ingredients?!* What, is she lightly seasoned?!"

"Was she tasty?! Refreshing? Or maybe more like mild?!"

Lynx and Edgan were in hysterics. It seemed Sieg had been able to protect Mariela's honor. Probably.

After warming their bodies and killing the yetis that had gathered upon hearing their laughter, the three men headed out to look for the aurora ice fruit once more. According to Ghark's map, they would arrive at the location soon.

The party headed through the snowfield in the gloomy polar night. The wind had largely died down, so it didn't take them long at all to reach their destination.

Just as Ghark had indicated, aurora herbs were growing at the top of a small hill.

More resembling moss than herbs, they were fleshy plants that crawled along the icy ground with small fruit bulging from at their tips. The fruit ranged from blue to purplish red and resembled an aurora. It grew during white nights and ripened and changed color under the ice during polar nights.

The three men smashed the thin ice covering the small fruit and picked it. Each piece of fruit was only the size of about half a bean, and even after gathering all of it, there was barely enough to fill two palms.

Their hands grew numb with cold, despite wearing gloves, and they knelt on the frozen earth to gather the fruit. By the time they finally finished, their bodies, which the alcohol had warmed, were completely chilled.

It made sense why Ghark didn't want to have anything to do with this.

"Well, shall we get outta here?"

What had happened to the enthusiasm from earlier? Their objective achieved, the three men trudged along as they left the stratum of ice and snow behind, but in a much friendlier manner than when they'd first arrived.

"Welcome back, guys! Whoa, your cheeks are bright red. Must've been freezing! Let's have some pot-au-feu."

Mariela, who'd obediently waited for the trio's return in the Merchants Guild, talked about dinner as she fluffed up Sieg's soft winter gear.

Since it was the beginning of winter, it was cold outside, but it felt warm to the three people who'd just come from the ice-and-snow stratum. They removed their cold weather clothing as they walked, and Mariela invited them to dinner to warm them up.

"Lynx, Edgan, you guys want some pot-au-feu, too? The ingredients give it a really robust and tasty flavor."

"Bwa-ha, the ingredients!"

"A mild, delectable soup!"

For some reason, Lynx and Edgan blurted this out, much to Mariela's confusion.

"All right! Let's eat, let's eat! I'm starved! C'mon, Mariela, let's get goin'!" Lynx took Mariela's hand and began to run, laughing.

"H-hey, wait! Lynx! You're going too faaast!"

Sieg and Edgan ran after Mariela as Lynx pulled her along.

03

"This gives us the aurora ice fruit and merfolk gill gems that we needed."

A few days after Lynx and the others gathered the aurora ice fruit, Lieutenant Malraux delivered the correct amount of merfolk gill gems to correspond with the fruit. Considering the gems were technically jewels, it was surprising he'd been able to obtain this many so easily.

"The merfolk gill gems are from mermen and sahuagins. They're quite easy to obtain if you think about where adventurers might take them."

He seemed to have gone to several bordellos. He said when he'd offered a higher price than the market value, the bordello ladies had scrambled to sell the merfolk gill gems their customers had given them.

"And since we acquired the aurora ice fruit so cheaply, I was able to allocate more of the budget to the merfolk gill gems," Malraux said with a laugh. Behind him, Lynx muttered, "Sooo not fair. It was suuuper cold out there."

As it so happens, a few days later, the dual wielder Edgan visited Sieg and grumbled to him in the least sunny corner of the shop, "You know Belisa, from the Yagu Drawbridge Pavilion? She's not wearing the merfolk gill gem pendant I gave her anymore... And she *always* wears it when I visit."

"She probably just lost it. Maybe she'll find it again soon," Sieg consoled Edgan, who was looking so dark and gloomy, it seemed like he could sprout mushrooms.

"You're a good dude, Sieg..."

Ever since they'd gone to pick the aurora ice fruit together, Sieg and Edgan were apparently getting along well.

A few more days later...

"Belisa was wearing the merfolk gill gem! She must've lost it after all," Edgan came to tell Sieg. "She must've broken the chain, 'cause she had a new one on. The gem seemed kinda different too, but those things are pretty soft, so their shape can apparently change."

"Uh... Y-yeah, that's right. They sometimes change color and shape and size," Sieg replied, offering an unnatural explanation.

"Mariela always wears the pendant I gave her!" interjected Lynx, completely unnecessarily, as he looked at Edgan and Sieg.

They've gotten super-tight ever since they gathered the aurora ice fruit together, thought Mariela as she casually observed the three men.

She now had gill gems, which had an element of merfolk in them, and aurora ice fruit, which incited the transformation. The kraken mucus that regulated the physical functions that accompanied the transformation was secreted by Mariela's pet, Slaken, every day. As for the potion's base material, she always had a large quantity of lunamagia, since it was needed for high-grade potions. Beyond that, all she needed was time-cheating nectar for the preservation of the transformation effect.

To obtain this, Mariela and Sieg went through the underground Aqueduct to the ruins of Mariela's old cottage in the Fell Forest.

"It *should* be buried around here."

Mariela industriously dug up the ground in a corner of the house's ruins, which had been completely covered with low-grade medicinal herbs.

"Ah, got it. A lot of it went bad, but with this much still left, I think we'll manage."

Inside the hole Mariela dug up was a large ceramic pot that could barely be held in two hands. Many small glass vials wrapped in cloth lay inside the pot. The pot was broken, and so were about 30 percent of the vials. The contents of the broken vials had spilled out, degraded completely, and been reabsorbed by the earth, but the plant seeds stored in the unbroken vials still maintained their shape after two hundred years.

Wearing rubber gloves, Mariela carefully took out the intact vials. She checked their contents one by one and transferred the usable ones into new vials. The broken or otherwise useless seeds she burned and disposed of in one go.

The seeds she'd stored here were all dangerous. They had powerful poison and couldn't be planted normally. Instead of falling to the ground and sprouting there, they grew either in corpses or living creatures that they turned into seedbeds. Burying them in the ground was a much safer storage method than keeping them in a storehouse because even if the vials broke and the seeds spilled out, they would be absorbed back into the earth after a long period of time.

These seeds lay dormant within a thick shell to survive for long periods of time until a suitable living creature with the potential of becoming a seedbed comes along. Still, the seeds that spilled out of broken vials seemingly couldn't withstand two hundred years of damp soil and microbe corrosion, rotting away over time, but among the ones still sealed in their vials, about 10 percent could germinate.

When Mariela found the seeds she was looking for among the ones that survived, she planted some in the corpse of a goblin Sieg had killed on the way.

Schhhwp.

The seeds absorbed the goblin's blood, and sinews resembling blood vessels rose to their surfaces. Roots split open its thick shell and stretched out from the seeds to instantly spread throughout the goblin's body.

About two hours passed as she transferred surplus seeds into new vials and harvested and dried overgrown low-grade herbs, and at that point, the time-cheating herbs sprouting from the goblin seedbed had reached her knees.

After plucking a number of leaves from the herbs, she crushed them between her fingers and formed them into two balls.

"Sieg, hold this between your back teeth. If you suddenly feel hungry, bite down hard on it. It'll act as an antidote."

Mariela also held one of the balls with her back teeth and covered her mouth with a cloth.

The time-cheating herbs had already started to bud.

She put water in the creeper rubber bags she'd brought, then covered each time-cheating herb bud with a bag and tied them closed. She fastened the ends of the cords, tying the bags to supports, so the weight of the water wouldn't break the stems.

Each time-cheating herb seedling had two or three buds. She couldn't afford to overlook a single one. After she'd put bags on all of them and checked several times to make sure she hadn't missed any, the buds bloomed.

The reddish-orange flowers with multiple petals, which didn't seem like they could have possibly bloomed within four hours of being planted, resembled ripe fruit.

The bags prevented the scattered pollen and the smell of the flowers from escaping. If she hadn't attached the bags, the irresistibly sweet scent of the petals would have attracted forest creatures, and anyone who inhaled the pollen would have experienced an unbearable hunger from its poison. Then, thinking the petals before them were sweet fruit, they would bite them and fall asleep from the nectar, and the mature seeds within the petals would be taken into their body.

Time-cheating herbs grew from the blood and magical power of living things. After breaking through the body of a sleeping creature, the flowers beautifully bloomed in a rich profusion. It was said that a creature who'd fallen asleep from the time-cheating nectar neither aged nor deteriorated until its blood and magical power had run dry, probably because the plant could reproduce longer if the seedbed was still alive.

This was also why the flower had gotten the "time-cheating" part of its name.

You could adjust the transformation time of polymorph

potions up to a maximum of one hour by mixing it with this nectar that'd had its sleeping poison removed.

When the flowers had sufficiently bloomed, Mariela shook the water bags covering them to dissolve the nectar in the water. After transferring the water mixed with nectar, pollen, and spilled seeds into an alchemic Transmutation Vessel, she was able to refine it into nonpoisonous nectar on the spot. She also took the opportunity to dry the collected seeds, seal them in vials, and bury them in the hole again along with the other seeds.

Mariela ended up with about a tablespoon of the time-cheating nectar. It was the bare minimum needed to mix with the other materials.

Time-cheating nectar sold at a high price, but looking at the shriveled goblin corpse with the blood sucked out of it didn't really make her want to make more than she absolutely needed. After Mariela and Sieg burned and buried both the time-cheating herbs and the goblin corpse, they returned to the house through the underground Aqueduct.

"My master told me once...," Mariela said to Sieg on their way home, "even though time-cheating nectar is valuable, you shouldn't make more than you need. Like how a hunter only hunts as much game as they need. And..."

Although her master had been irresponsible, Mariela had been properly taught how to handle dangerous plants with only knowledge from the Library. She'd never made polymorph potions, but she'd learned how to make time-cheating nectar, so it was a big help.

It may have been the first time Sieg had heard Mariela speak of her master's proper side. Mariela hesitated to go on, but Sieg looked at her and urged her to.

"And my master also said that if you make more than you need, time-cheating herbs will sprout from your belly button! I wonder if that's actually true?!"

"They could be sprouting right now!"

Sieg joined in the lie, almost relieved that her master was pulling the usual shenanigans.

Mariela tightly squeezed the area around her belly button with both hands. Even though she realized it was a lie, this kind of conversation made her feel like her stomach hurt.

She unthinkingly made bean soup for dinner that night and said, "Beans are a kind of seed, too," while chewing her food much more than usual.

Despite the fact nothing would sprout from her belly button even if she swallowed the beans whole.

"I'm going to bed early." Mariela quickly headed upstairs, holding her belly button until she disappeared into her bedroom.

04

"The Black Iron Freight Corps is transporting the potions?" Robert Aguinas had just finished listening to the elderly steward's report. "Are there any regular stops on their route that you feel are particularly suspicious?"

In response to Robert's question, the steward listed names and characteristics of places from the documents in his hand.

The Yagu Drawbridge Pavilion, which was the Black Iron Freight Corps's regular inn; the weapon shop that outfitted them; the companies where they replenished their stock to take to the imperial capital; and each member's favorite restaurant. The steward's report included not only a summary of each shop, but even the personal history of the shopkeepers.

"According to your report, wouldn't you say that 'Sunlight's Canopy' apothecary is the most suspicious? For one thing, the owner came to the Labyrinth City from abroad around the same time the Black Iron Freight Corps started dealing in potions..."

After hearing the steward's report from beginning to end, Robert bluntly stated his opinion about the new resident.

"As it so happens, Lord Robert...Lady Caroline has become good friends with the shop's owner..."

"Huh? Carol?" Robert closed his eyes for a short while in response to this unforeseen development, then gave an order to the steward. "I'll have a little chat with her. Please prepare some tea."

His sister Caroline arrived in the dining room around the time the tea had been prepared.

He used to have dinner with his family in this dining room, but ever since he became the family head, Robert had his food delivered to his own room or the laboratory. It had been a very long time since he'd sat down at a dining table with his sister, let alone had tea with her.

Caroline seemed to feel the same way.

"What a delight for us to be together like this, Brother," she said, smiling. "It's been quite some time since you last came to dinner."

"My research keeps me very busy, as you know. But I'm glad to see you're doing well. Come to think of it, isn't there a shop in town that's caught your eye as of late?"

"Goodness, Brother. Nothing gets past you." Completely ignorant of her brother's intentions, Caroline cheerfully told him about Mariela's shop.

"…and Mariela and I make medicine together. Mariela's medicine uses the effects of lynus wheat. Brother, I believe you used to focus on that as well. Moreover, she has been teaching the town's chemists how to make it, and now their medicine has improved by leaps and bounds," Caroline chatted in good spirits. Robert continued to listen to her with a smile as he thought.

She appears to be an excellent chemist. It wouldn't be a long shot to assume she's an alchemist as well. But the same age as Carol? That's too young…

According to the information given to him, Estalia, sleeping in the cellar, should have been the youngest alchemist.

"Carol, you seem to have made a very brilliant friend. However, she's from outside the Labyrinth City. It leads me to wonder if she has some kind of secret. Yes, I fully understand that you think she's a very good person. That said, until I've made her acquaintance, I can't be sure. You're a young lady who's soon to be wed; as your brother, I'm just worried."

Robert tried to discreetly squeeze information out of his sister without hurting her feelings.

"A secret…about…Mariela? …Oh, but there is! Brother! The hidden feelings and friendship of Sieg and Lynx, who both vie for her affection! Ah, but I cannot say any further, dear Brother. I cannot talk about such things, even to you. That would be improper! I am Mariela's friend, you know. I must consider her feelings first."

However, Caroline's thought process apparently veered far away from Robert's purpose.

She'd simply found a kindred spirit in Mariela. It was clear they had their similarities.

"Er... *Cough*. Carol? It seems they're all good people. I'm relieved. Speaking of which, I've heard some strange rumors lately; have you seen anything unusual at that shop?"

What an unnatural way to frame a question. Perhaps he was overwhelmed by the reckless behavior of his sister, whom he hadn't seen in a long while.

As for Caroline, rather than the forced nature of her brother's question, she seized on its substance.

"My, Brother. You're curious! Please rest assured. I have acquired this information. It has all the mystery and intrigue of a potion—shiny tea!"

Caroline rose up and grasped the teapot in her right hand. She pressed the lid with her thumb and held the handle with her middle and ring fingers. Her index and pinkie fingers stuck out straight, but she must have had quite a grip. She hadn't been knead-knead-kneading medicine with Mariela every day for nothing.

Holding both the saucer and the cup in her left hand, she lit the interior of the pot with light magic, then poured tea from it into the cup.

She lifted her right hand holding the teapot up high to show off the shining tea to Robert as she poured it into the cup. The tea really looked like a mysterious waterfall.

With a background in dance, Caroline's posture was excellent, and her pose was graceful. Full points to her.

Actually, Caroline was showing her potential of becoming an advanced tea pourer, seeing how she secretly used water magic to prevent the tea from spilling. But Robert knew nothing of "stylish tea parties." With his mouth agape, he stared at the tea infused with magic for aesthetic purposes and at Caroline, who proudly exclaimed, "Well? What do you think?!" His eyes darted back and forth between the tea and his sister.

"Now here you are, Brother."

Robert accepted the tea, which was now subtly cooled due to being poured from up high and easy to drink. He smiled at his sister and commented, "You seem to be enjoying yourself day after day."

The tea his sister poured was quite delicious.

After leaving his little tea party with Caroline, Robert pondered alone in his room.

Looks like Sunlight's Canopy is in the clear...

Mariela's obliviousness seemed to have deceived even the mind of Robert, who boasted an intelligence score of five. Unaware of this, Robert thought things over.

It was obvious when he thought about it calmly. For the girl to appear in the Labyrinth City at the same time the Black Iron Freight Corps began handling potions would be too bold. The Corps was a transportation group founded by former commanding officers of the Labyrinth Suppression Forces. They couldn't possibly be that foolish. It was reasonable to think they'd prepared her as a red herring.

The girl named Mariela was probably an alchemist summoned to the Labyrinth City from the outside. Thinking this, he was convinced.

A shop reminiscent of a teahouse would normally be conspicuous, thus reducing the danger of fools meddling with it who didn't realize she was put there by the Corps. By offering to share her manufacturing secrets, she could buy her safety,

Robert decided. The more acquaintances she made and the more important she became to the community, the harder it would be to half-heartedly make a move on her.

In the first place, it was irrational to think an alchemist of the Labyrinth City would still be out in the town. The Black Iron Freight Corps transporting potions might itself be a diversion to make people think "They're transporting goods that were buried in the ground." There was no doubt they'd secured a key alchemist a long time ago. Was the alchemist at the Labyrinth Suppression Forces' base? Or the estate of Margrave Schutzenwald?

Unbelievable that they would get their hands on an alchemist when we, House Aguinas, should be the ones safeguarding this person. We must take them back. We must extricate them—before it's too late. This much is necessary for the future of this region. But, how...?

Robert Aguinas ruminated.

How should they infiltrate the Labyrinth Suppression Forces or the house of Margrave Schutzenwald?

He needed information. Robert perused a file concerning recent affairs of the Labyrinth Suppression Forces, where he found a "Slum District Giant Slime Damage Report."

"What's this?"

"This is a report documenting the list of the victims from the recent giant slime hubbub. I had prepared it as a possible source of new 'materials,'" the elderly steward responded.

The most recent small expedition from about two weeks ago used the new black medicine almost offhandedly. Up to now, they had used one bottle from time to time, but now they were going through them like it was cheap medicine. Owing to this, most of it had been *used up*. The "materials" in Robert's possession were enough to cover the amount needed for next time, but though they were of low quality, they weren't cheap by any means.

So, the steward had seemingly searched for a way to acquire cheaper materials.

The victims of the giant slime incident were being treated by the Labyrinth Suppression Forces' medical team. However, the scars from the acidic liquid stiffened like deep burns and probably couldn't be cured with a single treatment like they normally would. Fortunately for Robert, most of the victims were slum residents, with no family or money for medicine, let alone for a healer. It would be easy to lure them with false promises of treatment.

"This is..."

A single name jumped out at Robert from the list of victims.

Sherry Nierenberg. Twelve years old. Female.

Nierenberg—wasn't that the name of the head of the Labyrinth Suppression Forces' medical team?

Sherry Nierenberg's injury was from the left side of her face to her temple. Robert could guess it had left an atrocious scar for a twelve-year-old girl.

"Heh, heh-heh-heh...," he laughed. He'd found a lead for the identity of the alchemist the Labyrinth Suppression Forces were hiding. With a large grin that twisted the corners of his mouth, he ordered the old steward to carry out his plan.

05

"Is this the merfolk polymorph potion?"

Leonhardt and Weishardt stared at the thirty vials of polymorph potion Malraux handed them. This was the first time they'd seen it, too.

"Yes. The length of the effect has been adjusted to the maximum time of one hour, as requested."

From the aurora ice fruit, Mariela had been able to make thirty vials this time. The white nights and polar nights in the thirty-second stratum alternated every hundred days, so if the Forces wanted more medicine than this, they'd have to wait another two hundred days.

Even in the treasure trove of materials that was the Labyrinth City, this was the maximum amount that could be made. That should have been enough for you to surmise the value of polymorph potions. They were so valuable that one vial would make even an aristocratic dilettante brag for a long time about how he'd enjoyed a stroll underwater. And there were thirty of those vials, no less.

More than a hundred soldiers had fought the king basilisk on the fifty-third stratum, but this time, the number of people had to be reduced even further. However, the information gained from three weeks of scouts surveying the fifty-fourth stratum, combined with the thirty vials, were enough for Leonhardt and Weishardt to predict that they might be able to win.

*　　*　　*

"The subjugation of the fifty-fourth stratum's boss, known as the 'Sea-Floating Pillar,' begins now! After you take the polymorph potion, enter the water!"

More than a half mile from the Sea-Floating Pillar, Weishardt issued instructions from a small boat atop the water in the fifty-fourth stratum. Though they were in an ocean with no end in sight, the waves were gentle to the point that even boats small enough to carry into the Labyrinth could get a half mile from the pillar.

Though it was winter outside the Labyrinth, the sky in the fifty-fourth stratum was blue, and the climate was warm, so no one hesitated to dive into the water. Perfect conditions for taking a dip in the ocean. Although the Labyrinth Suppression Forces had female members, none of them had met the conditions for today's mission, which meant, regrettably, that only men were present.

The "Beefcake Polar Plunge" mentioned by a certain alchemist had unexpectedly come to pass.

It would have been nice to at least have a spectator shriek, but the only ones watching the men getting wet were Nierenberg and the rest of his medical team with icy gazes. It was absolutely just a gross swim meet. No, wait, a stratum boss subjugation. (I almost mistook the enemy for something else before the battle even began. What a trap that was! Very dangerous.)

The member selection for this subjugation considered superiority in underwater combat. The focus was on spear users, but shield knights, sorcerers who could cast spells without chanting, healers, and sonar users who could detect the enemy underwater as well as act as messengers also participated. Every single one of them was an expert at swimming. They all wore hurriedly con-structed armor consisting of tight, low-resistance leather pants and basilisk leather on limited areas of their bodies: shins, arms, chest, and forehead. Even the shields carried by the shield knights weren't ordinary but had been replaced by equipment special-ized for underwater use that resembled aerodynamic, shortened spears.

Adjustments had also been made to the equipment of spear users. Some had tridents, while others carried harpoons suited for underwater combat. Among them was a single large man carrying a black spear.

"Thanks for coming, Dick," said Leonhardt.

Captain Dick nodded vigorously in response.

There was no better spear user than Dick in the entire Laby-rinth City. When Leonhardt had asked him to join the operation as a mercenary, he accepted without a moment's hesitation. He'd been warmly welcomed back into his old stomping grounds. Those who were friends with him said they were happy to fight alongside him again, while the younger people looked at him with inspired gazes.

Dick swallowed the polymorph potion he was given in a sin-gle gulp.

He was assaulted by a sensation like something in his chest moving. It resembled the feeling of your belly churning when you have an upset stomach, only it happened in the chest area. Although no pain accompanied it, he suddenly felt like he was choking and instinctively jumped into the sea, and cool water poured through gaps between his ribs into his body. When he put his hands to his ribs at the unexpected sensation, he found several notches there; he had acquired the gills of a fish.

He tried to see what was happening, but he had a hard time getting his eyes to focus. Instead, his field of vision had widened, and he could even see behind him, which was normally impossible. It was hard to see things in the distance, but his kinetic vision had improved. Was this merfolk vision?

Something felt out of place with his hands. When he raised them to look, he found webbing had formed between his fingers. Scales had sprouted on the backs of his hands, and he couldn't feel the cold of the water, as if his sense of touch had changed.

Every one of the soldiers who changed into merfolk dived lithely into the water and checked their movement. Just being immersed in the water didn't make them feel like they were suffocating at all, and they could freely move around as if they were on land. They seemed able to see better underwater than above.

"Neeeeeeyoooooooooooom."

Hearing the sonar users' sound wave tuning, the soldiers formed a line underwater to receive Leonhardt's orders.

Leonhardt stood underwater in front of the soldiers as if he were floating in space.

His hair trailed around him like a lion's mane.

His thick, sensual lips seemed even larger, his mouth, which emitted a well-projected voice, had extended sideways a good deal, and his eyeballs were bigger and pronounced, with no eyelids. The eyeballs seemed to protrude a little as if to ensure a wide field of vision.

Yup. Looks like a fish.

Dick and the other soldiers surveyed their surroundings with the eyesight they were now accustomed to.

He hadn't realized it before because he'd been so engrossed in how freely he could move underwater, but everyone had a fishlike face. Although Leonhardt was a fish, enough of his original face remained that Dick could recognize him, which was indescribably comical. If even the fine-featured and honorable Leonhardt looked unexceptional as a fish, the soldiers didn't even want to begin imagining their own faces. There were some soldiers who were impressed by Weishardt's thoughtfulness to not include women in this operation. It was sheer coincidence no women were participating, though.

At the very least, this medicine wasn't something they would want a girl they liked to take. They didn't want to see her with a fish face. The soldiers decided even if they became rich someday, they wouldn't use merfolk polymorph potion for an underwater date.

At any rate, they were in the middle of an operation.

The polymorph potion would last for one hour. They couldn't spare even a short time getting used to their transformed bodies. Thanks to their wide field of vision, the soldiers unfortunately had to look at the humorous faces of their transformed colleagues while directing their attention at Leonhardt by exhibiting powerful self-restraint.

The operation had already been drilled into their heads. All that remained was to await Leonhardt's command.

As he turned to survey his soldiers, Leonhardt gave a vigorous nod to all present and opened his mouth to deliver his final words of encouragement.

"Blub, blub."

Apparently, merfolk vocal cords were somehow different from a human's.

In response to Leonhardt's mouth repeatedly opening and closing like he was a fish being reeled in on a hook, air bubbles burst from the soldiers' gills.

*   *   *

"Commence the operation."

With the sonar user's announcement, the Labyrinth Suppression Forces began to swim toward the pillar.

They maintained a depth of twenty yards to avoid the beam.

When they were around a quarter of a mile from the pillar, the sonar users detected several objects rapidly rising from the ocean depths.

And here they come.

At Leonhardt's signal, the Labyrinth Suppression Forces prepared to intercept.

Compared to the impossibility of approaching the pillar above the water, the depth of ten yards or more underwater had been too safe. Of course, very few methods allowed activity that deep, and it was a plenty high hurdle considering the rarity of polymorph potions, but Weishardt and the others weren't foolish enough to think no obstacles existed, even ten yards underwater. None of the Labyrinth subjugation operations up to now had been easy.

As the Forces prepared to intercept the enemy from below, they became able to distinguish the enemies' forms.

From far away, all they could see was a blue glow.

As the enemies got closer, their silhouettes came into view.

Their dazzlingly beautiful blue hair hovered in the dim ocean. They had pale skin and the tail of a fish, which should have made them the species known as merfolk.

Their faces were covered by their hair and obscured, but the soldiers could discern large eyes and lips peeking out from gaps in their hair in the same place as human facades. Their ample chests gave the impression that the merfolk were female, and their arms stretching to the lower half of their bodies were clad in something that trailed behind them like dress sleeves fanning out toward their wrists.

The sleeves spreading through the water were probably pectoral fins, but they were the same beautiful blue metallic color as their hair. The creatures seemed to dance as they traveled through the water, resembling blue, gemlike butterflies that inhabited tropical regions.

The fish tails spread out and fluttered every time the creatures flicked them, and the blue glow changed to a variety of different colors. It really was as if the creatures were in the midst of a passionate dance in fluttering dresses, like beautiful maidens who drew all eyes to them at an evening party.

Were merfolk really this beautiful?

The beautiful merfolk swam toward the gross half-men, half-fish of the Labyrinth Suppression Forces as if to welcome them. There were more than twenty of the creatures. They all seemed to be smiling.

The soldiers' grips on their weapons weakened from what could be human instinct to see something beautiful up close. All the approaching merfolk had their hands down, carried no weapons, and didn't appear to be readying magic.

The merfolk had now intruded within reach of ranged attacks. Just when the soldiers were thinking they would try to interact with the creatures, who were similar to humans and hadn't taken fighting stances...

"Dragon Spear Attack!"

The attack that sallied forth from a lone black spear formed a vortex like a tornado and rushed at the leading merfolk.

Don't be fooled! Those are fake hooters!
Dick's shout was hindered by his fishy vocal cords and the

ocean water and, luckily or unluckily, didn't reach the soldiers of the Labyrinth Suppression Forces.

However, his attack did reach the leading merfolk, piercing it and spilling blood into the water. The other merfolk paid no heed to their cohort hit by the merciless assault, nor did they get angry about it, but calmly opened their mouths.

Gwap.

The merfolk's mouths looked as if they were splitting open from the place assumed to be the mouth all the way to the chest.

Their chests are jaws!

How many soldiers in the Labyrinth Suppression Forces thought the same thing?

To be exact, each merfolk's "chest" was actually bones protruding from its lower jaw joints, but it probably didn't make much of a difference since it wasn't a chest. Their giant mouths featured several layers of sharp teeth and were open wide enough to bite off a human torso. It had been incorrect to think the merfolk—no, giant fish—had no weapons. Their mouths were their weapons—already prepared to strike.

Only after allowing the creatures to get close enough to snap at them did the soldiers finally understand the full picture. The fish had dark scales on their necks, waists, and what had been mistaken for their cleavage. In fact, their bodies had no curves. The arms clad in sleeves were actually pectoral fins similar to those of flying fish, and bladelike bones were exposed where their hands might have been. What appeared to be strands of hair were actually distorted dorsal fins and a protuberance akin to those on deep sea fish to attract their bait.

Once they were close enough to grasp the complete picture,

the soldiers saw them as nothing more than grotesque fish in gaudy colors. Why had they thought these were beautiful merfolk?

No matter how similar their bodies were to fish from the polymorph potion, the soldiers couldn't beat the speed of a real fish underwater. They let loose with their spears at the looming giant fishes as they came closer with their equally giant mouths, and the shield knights thrust their shields into the mouths of the ones about to bite them to avoid a fatal wound. The tips of the bones sticking out from the pectoral fins inflicted deep gashes on the soldiers' chests and legs.

Did the blood drifting through the water belong to the soldiers or the giant fish?

In the midst of the melee, Leonhardt sent a signal to Weishardt.

With a nod from Weishardt, a guerilla group consisting of himself, Dick, the sonar users, and several sorcerers left the battlefront and began to swim at full speed toward the pillar.

Leonhardt fired a harpoon at the giant fish that was about to pursue Weishardt.

We're the ones you should be fighting!

The attacks from spear users and sorcerers that sallied forth one after another seemed to succeed at attracting the giant fishes' attention. They swam around and around Leonhardt and the rest of the Labyrinth Suppression Forces, and the curtain opened on a battle to the death with the fish that would take every opportunity to hound them.

Away from Leonhardt and the others in a do-or-die battle in an unfamiliar environment, Weishardt's guerilla group aimed for the pillar.

The Sea-Floating Pillar was a huge column with a diameter of about five yards that extended twenty yards above water and over a hundred yards below. Atop it were four heads resembling dragons that shot beams or water bullets, each at a right angle from its neighbor. The pillar's range extended a half mile around the dragon heads above the water, and there was no way to protect against the extremely high-power beams that caused even shields to disintegrate instantly.

Brutal water bullets fired in the intervals between beams, preventing enemies above the water from approaching. Above water, the power of the stratum's boss, the Sea-Floating Pillar, couldn't even be compared to that of the previous strata's bosses.

One other characteristic of this stratum was its overwhelming vastness. The horizon extended 360 degrees, and the water was more than a half mile deep. It would appear that space itself had been controlled by the boss to support the sheer magnitude of its attacks. From the power of its beams to its ability to make space yield to its desire, the boss possessed far too much magic than that of any other previous strata.

"Most of the magical power in this stratum is used for the beams and to control space."

This was the conclusion Weishardt drew based on the information from the scout unit.

In a normal stratum, the boss would generate monsters to protect itself, but nothing like that was visible here. Of course, the pillar fired at anyone, friend or foe, who came within range, so perhaps this was to prevent friendly fire, but it would make more sense to consider the possibility that no magic could be allocated to generating monsters.

Weishardt's prediction was that the underwater defenses had to be the weakest. Did the fact that no new giant fish appeared to chase them mean he was right? If so, he still had one more conjecture.

Weishardt's group hurried to the pillar.

The giant fish were most likely weaker than the basilisks. However, they couldn't easily be felled underwater. Every soldier in this operation had been given several high-grade potions. The openings of the glass vials had been secured with glue so that when a soldier went to drink one, they could bite through the glue. In this way, the glue should fulfill its function as vial stoppers even underwater, at least for the hour that the polymorph potion lasted. The healers treated wounds, but if that wasn't enough, they used potions at their own discretion.

How much time could they buy with this?

Weishardt's group finally reached the pillar. The sonar users felt the pillar and probed its internal structure, then told the others it was just as Weishardt had conjectured.

Weishardt's eyes gleamed, confident in victory.

A shield knight far from the pillar used all his strength to force the giant fish gnawing on his shield toward the water's surface. When it got within ten yards of the surface, the water evaporated with a sizzle, and a beam fired, disintegrating both the giant fish and the shield.

Gah, hot!

The heat from the beam evaporated the seawater, and a column of water erupted from the surface. The hot steam and water churned the area where the Labyrinth Suppression Forces and the giant fish were fighting, throwing them into disarray.

Although the shield knight used a shield skill to protect himself, he suffered deep burns all over his body, but he immediately downed a potion and healed the wounds.

The giant fish chomped at the disordered ranks of the Labyrinth Suppression Forces to try and drag them into the depths, but this was also expected. The soldiers provided backup for each other and reformed their ranks to prepare for a counterattack.

The pillar's beam was the cue.

Weishardt and the sorcerers followed the cue and poured magic into one spot in the pillar. Not flames, but heat. Hot enough to melt glass or iron. Although the temperature rose, it needed no oxygen. Few sorcerers could raise temperature correctly even underwater. Those limited few continued to heat the single point in the pillar.

Burble burble burble burble burble.

Bubbles rose up. They weren't coming only from the seawater. Wasn't the pillar itself emitting bubbles, too?

That was the instant when Weishardt's conjecture was proven correct.

It was necessary to know the pillar's structural design and materials to subjugate it.

The pillar's structure was easy to imagine. It was a single giant object floating vertically in the sea. The entire thing was probably buoyant, with a hollow interior and weight in its lower portion. It was thought that the stability of the entire pillar was secured by lowering the center of gravity.

And the material?

Was it a material that could withstand high-powered beams?

According to the scouts' report, the Sea-Floating Pillar fired a fixed number of water bullets after shooting a beam, even if its target wasn't in range. After a number of attempts, they were fortunate to be able to obtain water from the bullets. They secretly brought this along with seawater from the fifty-fourth stratum to Ghark's Herbal Supplies and were thus able to learn what the pillar was made of.

According to Ghark's appraisal, the water fired as bullets seemed to lack a certain component.

It was the component that created seashells, and seawater contained an abundance of it. The Sea-Floating Pillar was made of the same component as shells, so every time it fired a beam, it absorbed that component from the water and repaired the interior damage caused by the beam.

When shells were smelted at a high temperature, they emitted a gas and turned into the same composition as lum stones. When this happened, their volume changed. No matter how thick the pillar was, no matter how much it was reinforced with other components, if a powerful strike were to be inflicted on a single point where its volume had changed through thermal decomposition…

"Dragon Spear Attack!"

Dick's spear pierced the deformation in the pillar created by the sorcerers.

Snap.

The cracks created in the pillar quickly began to spread under the pressure of the water.

At Weishardt's signal, the guerilla group withdrew. After confirming the soldiers were a sufficient distance from it, Dick struck one final blow, then retreated as well.

The sonar users confirmed the interior of the pillar was hollow, just as anticipated. The cracks inflicted on it spread from the water pressure, and the enormous chamber filled with water.

Weishardt's guerilla group fell back to Leonhardt's location so they wouldn't be dragged into the churning water created by the sinking pillar. The Sea-Floating Pillar fired a final volley of water bullets to try and drag the Labyrinth Suppression Forces down with it, but the seawater hindered the bullets and weakened their effects so that they instead merely let Weishardt's group get away. The pillar's main weapon, the beam, had just been fired and didn't seem to be ready to fire again.

Leonhardt's group was obviously riddled with wounds, but nobody seemed to be missing any limbs. They'd reduced the giant fishes' numbers to about half. With the assistance of Weishardt and Dick, the Labyrinth Suppression Forces dominated the battle with the fish.

The Sea-Floating Pillar sank toward the bottom of the endless ocean even as the Labyrinth Suppression Forces fought the enormous fish.

Would the pillar completely collapse under the water pressure first, or would it perceive the bubbles and shards as enemies and fire its next beam first?

Bubbles floated up from around the sinking pillar with a burbling sound.

It had probably fired a beam. Did the pillar's dragon heads get blown off by the pressure caused by the beam, which superheated the seawater and turned it into steam? Or did the beam's energy, converted into heat, raise the water temperature around the dragon heads to an extreme, causing the heads to disintegrate from the heat and pressure? Leonhardt and the others had no way to know.

However, in that instant, the fifty-fourth stratum that had been so vast before suddenly shrank. After the Labyrinth Suppression Forces annihilated the giant fish in the more favorable environment, the stratum had changed to a normal stratum's size and now resembled a beach cavern.

The curtain closed on the subjugation of the fifty-fourth stratum's Sea-Floating Pillar, which had self-destructed from its own abilities.

The stairs between the strata were located on a sandy beach and confirmed to lead to the next stratum. Since scouts for exploring the new stratum hadn't accompanied the soldiers on this operation, exploration would start the following day.

When they pulled the defeated fish onto land, they couldn't find that beautiful blue color anywhere, but instead found grotesque fish with large mouths, purplish-red scales tinged just slightly blue, and brown skin. The visible areas around the neck and waist had red scales.

"It's because red seems to be difficult to see deep underwater."

Leonhardt listened to Weishardt's explanation with deep interest. To think these were the fish he'd mistaken for beautiful women.

"But this guy knew all along they weren't mermaids......," Leonhardt said to Dick in admiration.

Leonhardt had seen the giant fish as beautiful, amicable mermaids.

But he saw that Dick's eyes had been opened to enlightenment from one glance at the fish's lower jaws.

"It's because they didn't jiggle at all."

Dick didn't stare at Amber's chest just for show. He was a true connoisseur of chests. No, actually, he mainly squeezed cushions.

You could say the sad days he spent compelled to massage cushions had given him the ability to discern the truth.

"I...I see. At any rate, you performed a great service for us today... Having said that, it's probably best not to tell the others how you caught on."

Leonhardt's gaze turned to the young spear users surrounding him and Dick from a distance and watching them.

Leonhardt clapped Dick on the shoulder and walked in Weishardt's direction. He was giving the young spear users time to talk with Dick.

The distinguished A-Rank spear user who saw through the giant fishes' camouflage and sank the pillar. With eyes full of admiration, the young spear users ran up to Dick.

Incidentally, a lot of merfolk gill gems were harvested from the giant fish.

Even after paying the fee for the polymorph potion, there would be plenty left over. With this, maybe they could have the skin from the fifty-third stratum's King of Cursed Serpents added to their armor and develop new magical tools from the remains of the Sea-Floating Pillar.

Weishardt's heart filled with excitement at these prospects for the future.

The soldiers who participated in this operation felt relieved that no mermaid's tears came from the giant fish.

Those weren't mermaids. Beautiful mermaids were still out there somewhere.

As if light were shining in from somewhere, the fifty-fourth stratum, now a beach cavern, was filled with a blue glow reminiscent of the giant fish that had looked like ravishing mermaids.

CHAPTER 6
At the End of an Eternal Sleep

01

This... This is a monumental breakthrough!

That night, Mariela stood trembling before a magical tool in the kitchen.

"Mariela? What's wrong?" Sieg asked as he peered at it.

Mariela had flung open the door to a refrigeration device. It enabled long-term preservation of food items like orc meat by freezing them and was groundbreaking for Mariela. It was a huge refrigeration tool for business use that had been here before Mariela and Sieg moved in, so the interior was divided into several sections, which even had its own temperature control function. The existence of such a convenient thing made Mariela feel the incredible progress of the last two hundred years once again.

After all, the refrigeration tool had cultivated aurora ice fruit.

Aurora ice fruit was a medicinal herb that grew during a white night and bore fruit during a polar night. It was one of the ingredients in polymorph potion. There seemed to be a variety of theories on how it had gotten its name: because it was often found under auroras; because its transformation resembled the swaying appearance of an aurora; or because the fruit had aurora-like colors, among others.

The day Sieg and the others gathered the aurora ice fruit on the thirty-second stratum, Lynx had spoken fervently about how cold the stratum had been as he enjoyed freshly made pot-au-feu with everyone. Since they could gather aurora ice fruit there, he'd thought surely it would be a beautiful place where they'd be able to see an aurora, but apparently that wasn't the case.

"The sky in the Labyrinth might look like a real sky, but it's different, y'know?"

Mariela had gotten a flash of inspiration while listening to Lynx's complaint about not getting to see an aurora.

Was the growth of aurora ice fruit unrelated to real auroras?

She was easily able to find out about the sky in the thirty-second stratum by asking Ghark.

Apparently, rocks called luminous stones glow during a white night, and moonstones glow during a polar night.

Luminous stones shone with magical power and were used in general household magical lighting tools. Moonstones' brightness was low compared to the amount of magic they used, so they weren't sold for general household use, but they could be easily obtained because they were in demand by lunamagia farmers in the imperial capital, among others.

To prepare a suitable environment for cultivation, Mariela put luminous stones in the magical refrigerator she had set to the same temperature as the thirty-second stratum's white nights and put moonstones in the magical frozen storage unit set to the same temperature as the stratum's polar nights.

She'd sifted through the aurora ice fruit's seeds when she made the polymorph potion, so she sprinkled them on a tray with a thin layer of soil and placed the tray in the refrigeration tool.

They bore fruit in just five days. After that, she transferred the tray to the frozen storage unit for another five days. The aurora ice fruit completely matured and ripened in the frozen storage unit.

She'd so easily made high-grade materials for polymorph potions, worth two large silver coins each, at home.

Sieg was astonished to see the aurora ice fruit in Mariela's hand and Mariela going "oh crap" while shaking in front of the frozen storage unit.

"Sieg, I grew aurora ice fruit..."

"Which means I don't have to go collect it anymore."

Apparently, collecting the aurora ice fruit had been extremely rough. Sieg suddenly clenched his fists tightly, a rare sight.

Last time, I could only give them thirty vials of polymorph potion due to the limited materials. But maybe, just maybe, I'll get more orders for it. So I'm gonna grow a bunch of aurora ice fruit, just in case.

With her abundant resources, Mariela bought jumbo-size magical refrigerators and freezers and grew aurora ice fruit in large quantities in her cellar. Unfortunately, no additional orders for polymorph potion came, and the fruit remained in the frozen storage unit and turned into fertilizer. However, thanks to the high-capacity unit, Sunlight's Canopy could now offer cold drinks and frozen desserts in the summer, and more and more customers who came just for the tea filled the shop, so maybe this was a good thing.

Even so, magical tools are sure useful...

Mariela couldn't keep up with two hundred years' worth of advancement.

Even without magical tools, she could manage anything with old-fashioned methods and alchemic skills, so she never realized there was a convenient tool for a particular task until someone suggested, "Why not use a magical tool?"

Surely there were many useful tools for making medicine that Mariela didn't know about. Not just magical ones, for sure, but also techniques and implements that had been created over the past two hundred years.

One day, Mariela asked Carol a question while watching the mixer whip up skin-brightening cream.

"I grew up in a remote village, so I had no idea such convenient things like this existed. What other kinds of magical tools could there be?"

"Well, Mariela, if you're that curious, how would you like to visit my atelier?" Caroline suggested with a smile. "I have a full selection of all the necessary implements. I think that would be just splendid. Please do come and visit. It pains me to constantly impose upon you."

A certain something about her made it extremely hard to refuse.

If only Mariela hadn't vaguely responded "Next time, then" to Carol's pushy offer, maybe she would have continued to live as she had been, in blissful ignorance...

02

That day, a sudden downpour encouraged people walking in town to stop at nearby shops.

Beneath a cloudy winter sky, the people were pelted with a

frigid mixture of rain and sleet. Those with no umbrellas waited in shops with roofs for the rain to stop.

Mariela and Sieg were among those people. They'd headed to the Seele Company in the northeastern part of the Labyrinth City to buy genea cream in bulk.

By the time they'd dashed into the building, Mariela and Sieg were soaking wet from the rain and chilled to the bone. Although they dried their clothes with the lifestyle magic *Dehydrate*, they could hardly warm their cold bodies. Mariela placed her order and shivered as the two of them waited for the rain to dissipate. However, it kept growing more intense, and they didn't know when they'd be able to return home.

At that very moment, a lone carriage happened to pass by.

"Is that you, Mariela?"

Whether by divine providence, or just the usual path she took, Caroline happened to be passing through. She saw Mariela and stopped the carriage.

"Please, come inside."

Caroline took Mariela's hand to lead her to the carriage. Noticing her friend's hand was ice cold, she said, "Gosh, you're freezing to death! Any longer like this and you'll catch cold. My estate is not far from here. By all means, come over and get yourself warm," and invited her to the Aguinas estate.

The Aguinases were a noble family that managed potions in the Labyrinth City.

And Mariela was most likely the only alchemist in the Labyrinth City who could make potions.

She knew Caroline had no ill intentions, but she couldn't so readily visit a place that risky.

Mariela tried to refuse, saying she shouldn't intrude on Caroline so suddenly and she didn't know proper etiquette as a commoner.

"But you simply mustn't catch cold! And I promised I would invite you to my atelier. We can work together there, so please don't think you are being a bother."

A noblewoman and a commoner girl. Curious bystanders had started to stare at them as they talked, wondering what was going on. This, coupled with Mariela running out of excuses to refuse, led her to board Caroline's carriage with Sieg, and they were whisked off to the Aguinas family estate.

03

The rain grew worse and worse, soaking Jack Nierenberg's coat.

No one had been severely wounded in the subjugation of the Sea-Floating Pillar, so he'd been able to go home early these past few days.

The sky had looked like it would start pouring rain any moment, so Nierenberg had hurried along the road home even faster than usual, but it picked up before he'd reached his house.

Blasted rain...

He didn't like this kind of rain. It crept through the gaps in his clothes and stole his body heat, reminding him of his fellow men who didn't receive treatment in time and grew cold to the touch.

Nierenberg had no gift for healing magic. What he could do was probe the insides of living creatures and stitch them up. The only other thing he had was his training in martial arts, and those abilities of his were more suited to an assassin or one-on-one combat, but if he were to encounter a human-sized monster, he could probably find its weak point and hit that spot to defeat it in a single blow.

Nierenberg's hands were always stained with the blood of the enemies he'd defeated. He didn't know how many lives he'd mowed down with those hands. He'd given up on counting a long time ago.

However, after Weishardt discovered his abilities, he appointed Nierenberg as a medical technician, and the medic's hands became stained with the blood of his comrades. The more blood flowed into his hands, the more his comrades escaped death. He couldn't count how many lives those hands had saved.

One thing Nierenberg was aware of was that he no longer hesitated to touch his beloved daughter, Sherry.

When Sherry was born, he'd been reluctant to hold her. Would his bloodstained hands contaminate her? Would his own sinful deeds sully her?

Every time he stroked Sherry's head and she said, "Papa, your hands are so big and warm," Nierenberg felt grateful to Leonhardt and Weishardt for giving him work as a medical technician. Even when soldiers grew enraged with him or complained about his ruthless methods, the way his colleagues admired him as a medical professional reminded him that he was a fellow member of the Labyrinth Suppression Forces.

He fervently hoped they could reach the deepest part of the Labyrinth without losing a single person.

"Ah, such a despicable rain…," Jack Nierenberg muttered. He'd been having thoughts that were out of character for him. His clothes were thoroughly soaked, too. He had to get home right away and change.

He had to get home before the rain took away his body heat.

When he finally reached his house, not a soul was inside. His beloved daughter Sherry had been taken away.

The unceasing rain painted the stone walls of the Labyrinth City black.

Few people were out in the cold, sleety rain, and no one was suspicious of a lone man who paid a visit to the Aguinas family estate at the edge of the aristocratic quarter.

"Welcome, Jack Nierenberg, sir."

With a courteous bow, the steward of the Aguinas family led Nierenberg to their annex. The building had been constructed sometime after the Stampede two hundred years ago, and the wide entrance and the shape of its pillars and beams were characteristic of its age. However, it was well maintained from repeated reinforcement and repairs, and it could be used even now.

The current head of the family, Robert Aguinas, welcomed Nierenberg in a room at the back of the building.

"Tell me where Sherry is."

"She's sleeping in the back. What a lovely young lady. It's a great pity she has such a terrible scar. Surely you have the authority to use potions, Medical Technician Nierenberg. Don't you wish to use just one vial for your daughter?" Robert spoke to Nierenberg, who glared at him with murder in his eyes. "Meanwhile, the Labyrinth Suppression Forces have been doling out as many potions as they like."

Nierenberg scrutinized Robert, who'd spoken as if he knew the true state of things. How much information did the Aguinas family have?

"Potions are strategic materials. They can't be appropriated for personal gain. No exceptions."

"Such devotion! You would sacrifice everything to destroy the Labyrinth?"

"Of course. What's it to you?"

"If you mean it, if you yearn for the Labyrinth's defeat, then you must cooperate with the Aguinas family." Robert began to speak of the truth behind the Labyrinth City over the past two

hundred years. "Even our potion storage facilities can only pre-serve potions for about a hundred years. Do you understand what this means?"

"A hundred years? Then... No..."

"Precisely. For generations, the house of Aguinas has contin-ued to make potions—together with the alchemists who survived the Stampede."

Two hundred years ago, when monsters had flooded out of the Fell Forest and attacked the Citadel City, some people safely escaped to the mountain range. Others had left the Kingdom of Endalsia by chance and avoided the disaster. Around ten alche-mists survived the night of the Stampede.

"Are you familiar with the Magic Circle of Suspended Ani-mation?"

Nierenberg grimaced at the words he was unaccustomed to hearing from Robert's mouth. When they'd taken away Sherry and left a written invitation to this place, he'd had a rough idea of what the Aguinas family was after. They wanted to find the source of the potions that had been brought to the Labyrinth Sup-pression Forces for the past two months.

As if Nierenberg's reaction was just as he'd anticipated, Robert continued. "As its name implies, the Magic Circle of Suspended Animation puts its user into a deathlike sleep. A person in this state will wake up only when the conditions for their revival have been met."

Putting someone into this slumber was a complicated technique in itself. On top of that, how difficult was it to suspend biological functions while preserving the flesh for such a long period of time? How complicated must that single magic circle have to be to achieve that kind of power? Nierenberg, who led a medical team, understood the difficulty was off the charts.

"It's said that two hundred years ago, before the Stampede, the then-head of the Aguinas family, Robroy, was given the opportunity to borrow the original Magic Circle of Suspended Animation."

Robroy then supposedly had made an exact replica of it.

"As I mentioned before, the alchemists who assisted in the City's reconstruction were the ones to identify that the potion storage facilities would not last two hundred years. Lamenting that the Labyrinth subjugation would reach its limit due to the lack of potions, they reproduced the Magic Circle of Suspended Animation and fell into this sleep of their own accord."

The alchemists' worries had become reality, but it appeared that waking an alchemist and having them make potions anew every time the current potions ran dry or deteriorated would solve the situation.

"The biggest miscalculation was that the duplicated magic circle wasn't perfect."

Robert looked toward Nierenberg. However, his gaze wasn't on the older man, nor was it fixed in any one location; it was as if he were gazing at something far away.

"Half of the alchemists who went to sleep were never revived, turning to salt and crumbling away. Even those who did awaken had terribly short lives; one ran out of magical power and collapsed, never to wake up again, while another vomited blood and passed away less than a year later."

Although the alchemists who woke up knew their own fate, they continued to make potions until their final moments.

"Did you understand the nature of the potions your Forces used?" Robert asked Nierenberg with his hands calmly raised.

"Then what's this stuff you call 'new medicine'? If there's a surviving alchemist like you say, there's no need for any of that."

The corners of Robert's mouth lifted in a smile that made him look entirely like a lunatic as he answered Nierenberg's question.

"There is no longer anyone who can make potions. I don't know how precise the Magic Circle of Suspended Animation created by the alchemist that the Labyrinth Suppression Forces captured was, but even the Aguinas family could only borrow the original, not obtain it. It's not possible for that alchemist to have used the original. They may seem perfectly healthy, but don't let appearances fool you. The Magic Circle of Suspended Animation is complex. No matter how accurate he tried to make it, even my ancestor Robroy Aguinas's magic circle couldn't compare to the original. I'm sure you also know that a distorted magic circle produces distorted effects."

Robert was implying that the Labyrinth Suppression Forces' alchemist would soon die. He seemed confident in this speculation.

"Have your alchemist create as many potions as possible, but put them back to sleep while they still have life remaining. We must not use them up until the Labyrinth is destroyed. We must have alchemists at our disposal no matter what it takes. Given how long you've been treating the Labyrinth Suppression Forces, surely you ought to know—the value of potions, the necessity of potions. You *have* to know."

The same person who spoke of the tragedy of the alchemists from two hundred years ago also spoke of the alchemists as if they were tools.

"That's the very reason that I, that the Aguinas family has gone so far as to make this new medicine—for the sake of my brethren and the alchemists who perished before accomplishing their goal. Until the day the Labyrinth is destroyed, until the day this land is returned to the hands of mankind, I—*we*—must pre-serve potions."

Robert continued his incoherent speech as if everything he said were correct.

"For that reason—for that very reason—we must control the alchemists! You understand, yes? For us to continue to use potions, we have to make the alchemists create more and more, and then if those alchemists are still alive, if they have life remaining, we must put them back to sleep and pass them down to the next generation!"

In the midst of his perversion and madness, Robert Aguinas recalled the words of his father and grandfather, as well as the memory of an alchemist who'd vomited blood and melted into nothingness when Robert had still been a child.

Robert was facing Nierenberg, but his eyes weren't looking at him.

He was remembering those who'd reawakened and perished these past two hundred years as if they were right there in front of him, delivering tales of their regrets and desires.

04

…He couldn't allow her to wake up.

Every alchemist who had woken up from their suspended animation had expressed the same thing: "She is essential for the rebirth of alchemists in the new world."

That was the truth. However, Estalia was most likely chosen as the First Alchemist for her youth.

Estalia had become an alchemist right before the Stampede. It was said that she'd been just six years old at the time. The alchemist who was her master had taken her on the back of a yagu and escaped to the mountain range. What awaited her afterward was the harsh reality of reconstruction day after day.

She had neither sufficient food nor a warm bed. She spent her nights sensing the panting of monsters on the other side of a thin wooden wall and holding her own breath.

During the day, she gathered medicinal herbs while staying out of the monsters' sight and single-mindedly continued to make potions. Estalia was raised without being able to play like a child or even act like one, and she never laughed gleefully like a young girl.

It was said that the more beautiful Estalia grew, the more people became sympathetic upon hearing about the quality of her food, her clothing, and her miserable circumstances. That was how beautiful she was. If she'd been born in a different time—no, if she'd even been born in the imperial capital—what beautiful clothing she would have worn, and she would have had a wealthy, joyful life, surrounded by people who loved her.

But such a fortunate period of time did come to her. She fell in love. In the midst of a difficult life, people imagined a bright future for this young lady who smiled happily. If this girl were happy, surely the future of the Labyrinth City would be bright, too.

However, as if to mock this, Estalia's beloved was attacked by monsters and abruptly left this world.

Estalia sank into despair. But she didn't stop making potions. Day after day, she continued to make them until her magical reserves ran out.

So that people could reclaim this land.

All Estalia could do to fulfill the goals of the man she loved was to make potions.

Around ten years after the Stampede, the Labyrinth City had just barely returned to being a functional city. The most brilliant researchers in the imperial capital estimated that it would take two hundred years to subjugate the Labyrinth, which would reach fifty strata at most. And other researchers set forth a plan for storage facilities that could preserve potions for two hundred years.

They were unanimous: "It's theoretically possible."

In accordance with that theory, a huge storage facility was built in the Aguinas family cellar. The alchemists made as many potions as they could up to the limits of their magical power and filled the giant potion tank in the storage facility.

Small-scale storage facilities were also built in the houses of like-minded noble families who were determined to live in this land of monsters, including the Schutzenwalds, who had been selected to govern the Labyrinth City. All of the storage facilities were filled with potions.

However, this didn't eliminate the concerns of the alchemists, including the Aguinases.

What if the Labyrinth wasn't subjugated in two hundred years?

What if it exceeded fifty strata?

What if the potions ran out midway through?

What if the potion storage facilities couldn't last for two hundred years?

The glorious Kingdom of Endalsia, which people believed would last forever, had been destroyed in a single night.

No one was dim-witted enough to believe the word of those who said "theoretically" without ever taking a single step outside the imperial capital, even if the scholars were absolutely brilliant.

Above all else, an alchemist master was needed to perform the contractual rite for other alchemists to connect to the ley line with a Nexus. So, the surviving alchemists put all their faith in one magic circle in the Aguinas family's possession: the replica of the Magic Circle of Suspended Animation the Aguinas family had once borrowed.

The alchemists reproduced the Magic Circle of Suspended Animation. The magic circle was complex, and working on it was extremely difficult, but they reproduced and reproduced. They probably wouldn't achieve an effect as good as the original.

Even if they woke up, they didn't know if their original physical functions would be maintained, and they might not wake up at all.

But they took a gamble on the future.

All the potion storage facilities that had been built were full, and the alchemists couldn't do any more.

"Using the Magic Circle of Suspended Animation, we will slumber in a secret cellar separate from the Aguinas family's potion storage facilities. Should the magic circle function correctly and our coffins are sealed to cut off all oxygen, we most likely won't wake up until the day our coffins are opened."

Resolute in their decision, the alchemists exchanged last words in the Aguinas family's cellar on the day everything was ready.

"To return the region to mankind."

"So that alchemists can be reborn in the new land."

Estalia was among them.

The rose-colored dress she wore was a gift from the alchemists out of the kindness of their hearts.

Her face, beautifully made-up, was no less stunning than Her Majesty the Queen of Endalsia, famed for her beauty.

The first time she'd worn beautiful clothes, the first time she'd worn makeup, the first time she was dressed up was in that place, right before she went to sleep in the coffin under the Magic Circle of Suspended Animation.

As Estalia lay in the glass coffin, the alchemists told her:

"The next time you wake up, a new world will be waiting. A bright, joyful world worthy of your clothes and your beauty. We wish you nothing but happiness in the new world, Estalia."

Estalia was just like a daughter to the alchemists.

They couldn't even describe how much the sight of this young girl continuing to make potions under these harsh conditions had encouraged them—or how it had made their hearts ache.

"Our fair, piteous daughter—our potions are sure to last until the new world of mankind arrives. We wish for you the greatest happiness when you awaken."

Estalia replied, "Thank you, my fathers. I'm so glad…to have met you; to have been with him."

After they watched her fall asleep, the alchemists went to sleep in their own coffins as well.

The single remaining Aguinas followed in their footsteps. And so did his child, and his child's child.

Along with the alchemists who occasionally awoke, they continued to protect the coffins and the potions.

To deliver Estalia, the First Alchemist, to a new world.

At the moment when Robert Aguinas was giving his fervent speech in the midst of the madness that gripped his very soul, Mariela and Sieg were visiting the Aguinas family's main building.

"Th-this is—!"

"A pelletizer—it makes pills. It works by adding moderately damp material and rotating this disk."

"Oooh! You don't even have to roll 'em by hand. S-so, um, what's that?"

"That is a sieve shaker. If you set it with a specialized net and press this button, it will shake and sift for the designated length of time."

"O-oh my gosh, how convenient! My arms won't hurt anymore! Oh, and this thing here, what's this?!"

"A vacuum evaporator. You simply pour water in here, and it gets suctioned from over here. You can set the temperature of the hot water here to dry it at whatever temperature you like."

Caroline's atelier was packed with experimental equipment Mariela had never seen before.

With Mariela's alchemic skills, she didn't need a single piece of equipment, but this was something completely different. To her, such implements and devices were the stuff of dreams and fantasy.

The two girls went over the devices one by one and giggled happily.

For girls their age, they should have been holding flowers or baked goods or accessories, but instead they gripped bundles of dried medicinal herbs and glass tools. It was enough to make one wonder just what was so thrilling about these things.

Caroline's personal maid urged the giddy pair who kept oohing and aahing—"Wow!" "Incredible!"—to take a break. "You two must be thirsty. I've prepared some tea."

Of course, she poured the (naturally) shiny tea in a stylish pose. Was this really the proper etiquette for an aristocrat's maid?

The pair drank tea at a table set up at the edge of the atelier. Sieg seemed entirely devoted to guarding Mariela and remained behind her.

After the tea break, Caroline nervously asked Mariela a question.

"Mariela, I wanted to ask you about a rumor... Are you an Alchemist Pact-Bearer from the imperial capital? I was wondering if you might tell me what it was like to make a pact with a ley line."

Caroline, a young noble lady of the Aguinas family, had alchemic skills. But since it wasn't possible to connect to the Labyrinth City's ley line through a Nexus, she could neither become an alchemist nor improve her proficiency with alchemic skills.

However, the Aguinases had been a family of alchemists since long ago, and Caroline yearned to be one herself.

For generations, alchemists had been summoned from the imperial capital in return for marrying into the Aguinas family. However, they never ventured from the Aguinas estate's annex, so Caroline had only ever exchanged greetings with them. She'd never had a chance to hear stories about alchemy until now.

"One usually makes a pact at a young age. It may be late in my case, but after I marry in the imperial capital, I would very much like to make a pact myself if possible. I'm just so curious..."

Caroline was uneasy yet ever hopeful. Mariela told her the story of when she made her own pact while keeping the details vague.

Mariela had been eight years old, not long after being taken in by her master.

Before the Stampede two hundred years ago, Sunlight's Canopy was the site of a place called the Spirit Sanctuary where many sacred trees grew.

Even now, Mariela clearly remembered the time she entered the sanctuary, led by her master.

It was a whimsical, wondrous place; flitting about in the air were what looked like fluffy clumps of snow that shone faintly. When she got a closer look, they resembled butterflies, or birds, or people with wings. They came in all different sizes and each one seemed to be playing, whether they were sprawled on flower petals, shaking tree branches, or appearing and disappearing.

"Mariela, I'll be waiting here, so you go play. If you make a friend, bring 'em back with you," her master had said, then sprawled out on a bench at the edge of the sanctuary and took a nap.

Mariela had helped out at the orphanage and looked after the younger children for as long as she could remember, so she didn't know what to do even after being told to go play. She roamed around the sanctuary and saw other children who appeared to be fledgling alchemists. Led by their masters, they were saying something to the shining puffs of snow.

This seemed to be something that masters normally helped with. But Mariela's was off in dreamland, out like a light.

Feeling somewhat uncomfortable, Mariela headed toward the back of the sanctuary.

Mariela followed one snow puff that lightly brushed the side of her face before flying away, then pushed aside branches as long as she was tall and came upon a child around the same age as herself. The child was alone, with no adult resembling a master in sight, and seemed to be searching for something in the clearing, crouching and using both hands to check plants one by one.

"...H-hello. Are you looking for something?" Mariela asked timidly.

"I'm looking for a seven-petaled flower."

The child had green hair and green eyes with large pupils, and appeared to be glowing faintly. *What a weirdo*, Mariela thought, but since she had nothing else in particular to do, she told the child "I'll help" and began to search, too.

"Fooour... Fiiive... Siiix... Nope, not this one."

Mariela was just about to pluck the flower that had the wrong number of petals when the child said, "No, don't. You only take what you need. Poor flower..."

The kid seemed sweet. Mariela really liked the child, and she did her absolute best to find a flower with seven petals.

"I found one! Look, it's got seven petals, see!"

"Wow, thank you!"

"What do you do with it?"

"You use it to drink water." The child cupped the flower in both hands and slowly lifted it.

Mysteriously, the child lifted the flower, which snapped at the roots and changed into a porcelainlike bowl.

"I bet you're thirsty. Here, have some."

The seven-petaled cup the child offered was filled to the brim with faintly shining water.

Come to think of it, Mariela was thirsty.

"Thanks."

Mariela accepted the seven-petaled cup and gulped down all the shining water. It tasted slightly sweet and had a gentle flavor that seemed to spread throughout her body.

"It's yummy! **Water!** Here you go."

With the sole lifestyle magic spell she could use, Mariela filled the seven-petaled cup with water and handed it to the child. The child gulped down Mariela's water in turn and said "Yum!" with a smile.

"Marielaaa...," came her master's voice from far away. Come to think of it, her master told her to bring back a friend, right?

"I'm Mariela. Wanna be friends?"

"Sure! I'm ❋❋❋❋❋❋❋❋❋❋."

What had the child said? Mariela should have remembered, but she couldn't recall it. Mariela took the child's hand and ran back to her master.

Perhaps the other fledgling alchemists had already made their pacts and gone home, because the sanctuary was deserted. Only Mariela's master sat on the bench from before and greeted her. "Welcome back."

"Master! Master! I brought a friend!"

Looking at her friend, Mariela's master uttered, "Wow!" and then added, "All right, let's make that pact!" and smiled at Mariela like always.

"You show Mariela down to that real deep place for me," Mariela's master told her new friend.

"You sure?" asked the child, to which Mariela's master replied, "Yeah" with a laugh.

"Mariela."

When Mariela turned in response to her name, her master hugged her tightly.

"Masterrr, that tickles! And you're really warm!"

Mariela writhed around in her master's tight embrace. She had almost no recollection of anyone ever hugging her. It was somehow really embarrassing, and warm.

"Okay, Mariela. Remember—this is where you belong. So, when I call you, make sure to come right back."

"Yes, Master."

She didn't really understand, but she remembered something her master had said to her in their little cottage in the forest after taking her in:

"Starting today, this is your house. Welcome home."

Despite being an incredible person who knew everything, her master couldn't clean, do laundry, or cook, and the house was a mess. Mariela was shocked at how useless this person was for an adult. But every day she came back to that house, her master always greeted her with "Welcome home," so if her master, a truly incredible person, said this was where she belonged, then it had to be true.

"Mariela, let's go." The child clasped both of Mariela's hands.

"Okay!" Mariela replied. She didn't know where they were going, but she turned to her master, waved, and said, "See you later."

Plip.

Although they ought to have been standing on the ground, Mariela and the child were somewhere dark and dim. It somewhat resembled underwater, but it wasn't hard to breathe at all.

When she looked up, she saw her master standing on the earth's surface. This place appeared to be below the ground.

The child held on firmly to Mariela's hands and smiled as if to say "It's okay." Mariela finally realized—this child was a spirit. Although they were in such a strange place, Mariela wasn't scared at all. She thought it must have been because she could see a gentle light far below her feet.

To Mariela, the light looked just like a river of stars floating in the night sky. But it continued on and on and looked like a large river. Many lines of light softly floated up from it and disappeared, and sometimes particles of light smoothly streamed into it from above.

So pretty, thought Mariela.

Led by the child, she descended toward the river of light. From above, it really did look like shining water, but as she got closer, it seemed more like small beads of light.

Although she'd already entered the river of light, there was no feeling of a boundary like when one enters water. Her feet were just incredibly bright and warm, and the light grew weaker the farther up she looked. Pulled along by the child, Mariela ventured deeper and deeper. And as she did so, her surroundings both above and below were illuminated, and she was no longer even sure of the boundary where her own body ended and the light began. Still, the child clasped her hand tight, and she thoroughly understood that she and the child and the light were all separate beings. She understood, too, that the light was a very "huge being."

"Mariela, this is the heart of the ley line. Tell it your True Name. Once you do that, the ley line will tell you its True Name, too. Then you can connect to it." The child spoke with just a hint of worry on her face. But this was probably what Mariela's master told her about "connecting to the ley line with a Nexus." Mariela faced the light and gave her True Name.

"I'm Mariela. Who're you?"

'✳ ✳ ✳ ✳ ✳ ✳ ✳ ✳ ✳ ✳.'

Was that someone's voice? In that moment, Mariela connected to the ley line.

It was so, so very warm. Mariela felt like all her wants and needs had been filled.

Up to that point, she'd always been alone. Mariela didn't have any exceptional talents, incredible intellect, or an abundance of skills. Plenty of people had alchemic skills, and many more children had other useful abilities as well.

Cute little girls, children blessed with talents and skills, and boys who could handle physical labor with ease quickly found someone to take them in and left the orphanage. Mariela was never chosen. Her young mind knew she was a child with no value. So, she became a good kid.

She helped out a lot. She did her utmost to look after the younger kids, too.

The teachers at the orphanage always told her "Such a good girl," "You're a big help," "Thank you."

But nobody came for Mariela.

Loneliness and isolation were Mariela's constant companions from the time she was old enough to recognize them. But the moment she connected to the ley line, those feelings melted away.

No, actually, this loneliness, this isolation, was something she'd felt for much longer than that, since the moment she'd been born into this world. It had been healed. She instinctually sensed she'd come home. This ley line was the source of all life. She had been born from it and returned to it. She was finally one with it again.

It's so warm.

In a carefree daze, she felt like she was melting into and blending with the ley line.

"Marielaaa……"

I can hear someone far away. Who…is calling me?

"Marielaaa……"

That's…my master's voice.

Mariela's master had chosen her, the "good girl" whom no one else would take. And not because she was the only option; despite there being plenty of other children with alchemic skills, her master chose her, no one else. Her master had squeezed her tight.

The ley line was a source of life, a place to return to. A place where she could be released from the constraints of her physical form, be healed and fulfilled, and become one with once again.

But she was still "Mariela." She could feel the alchemic skills that had taken root in her soul. Mariela understood those skills connected her to her master.

"Are you leaving?" the child asked. She'd held hands with Mariela this whole time. The warmth of those hands, their very existence had told Mariela the whole way that it wasn't yet time for her to return to the ley line.

"Yeah. My master's calling me, so I gotta go home. My master can't do anything alone, y'know. If I'm not there, our room'll be a huge wreck!" Mariela laughed. This place was very cozy, but her home was somewhere else.

"Okay. Bye-bye," said the child.

"Let's play again sometime," Mariela replied. The child grinned, said, "See you!" and waved.

She had to get home. Curiously, with this thought, Mariela began to rise steadily. As she got closer to the earth's surface, she sensed that something was flowing into her. It felt as if something were pulling her upward. Once she realized her master's experience was flowing into her alchemic skills, Mariela was back in her own body. The child who'd held her hand from the beginning was gone, and instead, Mariela's master was holding her hand.

Although she had felt amorphous and so fulfilled that it was as if she'd merged into the world, she felt completely cut off from everything after returning to her own body. She'd become a separate entity again. But she remembered that place. She understood in the depths of her heart that she was connected to it. Her alchemic skills had connected her to the ley line.

After returning, Mariela had come to understand that she was part of the world.

"Geez, how deep did you go? I was worried sick you'd never come back! You practically ran off with all my alchemic experience."

With a look of both anger and relief, her master had one thing left to say.

"Welcome home, Mariela."

"I'm home, Master."

07

"And that's what it felt like when I formed a Nexus with a ley line."

Even if she subtracted her two-hundred-year slumber, it had been a very long time ago. And yet, she vividly remembered the brilliance of the ley line and the warmth of her master.

"With a spirit's guidance, an alchemist leaves their physical body and takes a spiritual form to pass through the ley line. There, a Nexus is formed by exchanging True Names with the ley line. The act of connecting to the ley line without a physical form is actually very dangerous. It feels pleasant, comfortable. The ley line is a large current that acts as the source of life in this region, and the joy of returning to it makes you want to cast off all the loneliness you've ever felt in your life. Unless you're very emotionally attached to your own world, you can't shake off that feeling or return to your physical body by yourself, so that's why you need a master there. The master sacrifices a part of their alchemic experience to guide their apprentice back. You're told you have a physical place to return to, a place where you belong. Apparently, alchemists form pacts when they're young because children are full of hopes and thus more likely to return rather than stay with the ley line."

Apprentices who passed through a ley line with a spirit's guidance returned to the world with their master's guidance. The process was similar to rebirth. That was the reason masters and apprentices had a deep bond.

The master's experience used in this ritual was transferred to the apprentice, and it became possible for the pupil to draw up Drops of Life from the ley line with the experience inherited from their master. It was said that the Library was shared with the apprentice through the bond created by the master-apprentice experience transfer.

"That's what forming a Nexus Pact with a ley line is like. The bond between a master and apprentice alchemist is said to be thicker than blood. But as long as you make a Nexus, you have access to a Library, which means you can still get by through self-study. I lived with my master for about five years, not knowing if I was being taken care of, or if I was just being made to help out. But then my stupid master suddenly disappeared somewhere and is no longer—"

Mariela thoroughly bad-mouthed her master. However, Caroline was gazing at her with her large eyes brimming with tears.

"Oh, Mariela!"

All at once Carol hugged her tightly.

"That was so very moving. I am here with you, too, Mariela. You're not alone anymore."

Mm, she's warm. And soft, too.

You could say the same thing about Mariela's arms and belly, though. Squishy, squishy.

It's really warm in here, thought Mariela as she looked between Carol and Sieg, who for some reason had started to beckon her closer with his hands.

Outside the mansion, it had gotten very cold, and the rain had turned to snow.

08

"There is one, isn't there? Surely you've noticed—the Labyrinth Suppression Forces have obtained an alchemist!" Robert Aguinas declared to Jack Nierenberg. Robert believed without a shred of doubt that he was the alchemists' keeper, and his speech and conduct was already close to that of a madman.

"We need to help them. Bring them back to the Aguinas family, for the sake of this ley line's new world! What good has it done you to be part of the Labyrinth Suppression Forces? They won't give a single potion to help you who has pledged your loyalty, nor to help your innocent daughter! But I, *I* can help you! Help your daughter! Let us go toward this new world together! We still have a Magic Circle of Suspended Animation!"

As if trying to grab something, Robert spread his fingers as wide as he could and extended the palm of his hand toward Nierenberg.

"We must put them to sleep, again and again and again! As many times as it takes! We can't use that alchemist up just once! You understand, don't you? You ought to understand—how many potions we need to conquer the Labyrinth! How many soldiers our new medicine has saved up to this point! You should know! You who have saved countless soldiers—you should know!"

"We're done here. Give Sherry back," Nierenberg spit out coldly.

"Why? Why, why, why?! You need it, don't you? It's indispensable, right? That's why you used it up until now! My new medicine! The red and black magic medicine! You! Used them! Which makes you my accomplice! You and I must work together!"

Robert widened his eyes and raised his voice in his lunacy. As if fed up with the whole thing, Nierenberg moved to restrain the other man.

That's when it happened.

"Whoa now, stop right there."

A low, gruff voice caused Nierenberg to halt.

"Don'cha care what happens to your daughter? Wouldn't ya rather at least half her face still be pretty?"

A man who looked to be the very picture of a bandit came out of the back room pointing a cutlass at a black-haired girl whose face was wrapped in bandages.

"Papaaa…"

There was no mistaking that face.

"Sherry…"

Nierenberg stopped in his tracks.

"You have no choice but to work with us," said Robert, extending his hand toward Nierenberg as if inviting him. A black something trickled down from his palm, which appeared to be empty. The room grew dim, and it felt as if the temperature dropped several degrees.

A black stain burbled and rose from the carpet at Nierenberg's feet. Like bloody pus that oozed from a wound no matter how many times its bandages were changed, the stain polluted the carpet as if boiling up from underneath, and sediment resembling rust lurked above the short pile carpet.

Nierenberg had seen this sediment before. It was the curse that had floated around the king basilisk's body. No special skills were required to use this black magic. And, because of its characteristics, not only the use, but even the research of it was prohibited by imperial law.

The curse gushing up around Nierenberg wriggled and squirmed as if it were alive.

"Don't…don't move, or who knows what'll happen ta yer daughter…!" The bandit kept his cutlass pointed at Sherry, but his voice shook as if something had frightened him, and his eyes darted to and from Robert.

"There's no reason to be afraid. I'm just making a little *connection*. The same kind as with the people who work in this building."

Laughing darkly, Robert refined the curse.

The curse's sediment wriggled like a cut-off lizard's tail, or like the limbs of an insect crushed to death, and narrowed in a circle around Nierenberg.

"Confirmed illicit use of black magic. And a forced-coercion type with no slave merchant or contractor qualifications, at that. Abduction, blackmail, and breach of faith with the Labyrinth Suppression Forces— This all oughta be enough, right, Papaaa?"

"You may have Sherry's face, but the languid, creepy way you call my name is nothing like her."

The bandit holding the beautiful girl hostage suddenly tried to use his right hand to cut off her head, and then he noticed there was nothing left of the hand that had been holding the cutlass from the wrist upward.

"A-ahhhhhhhgh, my hand, my hand's…!"

Realizing his right hand had been severed without the least

bit of pain, the bandit uttered a pathetic scream. The cutlass he should have been holding was instead in the bandaged girl's hand.

"Hup!" The girl shoved the handle of the cutlass into the bandit's stomach. The bandit, still holding his right wrist, fell forward with a groan and lost consciousness.

"Wha—? What?!"

She dispelled the curse enshrouding Nierenberg with nimble kicks. Cutlass in hand, the bandaged "girl" landed next to Nierenberg.

"Sheesh, aristocrats are a real pain in the butt. But hey, this evidence should suffice."

The "girl" rummaged around in her pocket and pulled out a magical tool for recording. It could record not only conversations, but also magic that had been activated, down to its very technique.

Realizing what was going on, Robert began to edge toward the door to the inner room from where the bandit had come.

"Give it up. This estate is already surrounded," Nierenberg stated coldly.

"No... Not like this..."

Robert violently gnashed his teeth, then put the entirety of his magical power into a shout at the bandit, who was lying facedown and holding his right wrist.

"Get up, and kill them!"

In an instant, the bandit's eyes snapped wide open, and he leaped on all fours like an animal at Nierenberg and the "girl" from his position on the floor.

"Aaaaaaaaah!"

A single kick from Nierenberg threw the wide-eyed, beast-like bandit back to the floor. Looking at the man who had finally stopped moving this time and who had bloody foam dripping from his mouth, the "girl" spoke.

"What a cruel way to use a slave brand. I hope he's back to normal once he wakes up."

Robert's Order had forced the man to get up and move in ways that surpassed the limits of his body's abilities, even though he'd been struck down in a way that should have knocked him unconscious. Now, as he lay on the floor with his mouth dripping bloody foam, his limbs convulsed occasionally. Would the bandit still be able to function normally when he came to?

Robert seemed to have escaped to the annex's inner room while the bandit was making his last attack.

"The lieutenant general's waiting outside. I'm gonna report back to him and then go home. Any more than this is outside the scope of my contract."

"Right, thanks for the help... How long do you intend to look like Sherry, anyway?"

"Hee-hee... See ya, Papaaa."

Smoothly avoiding Nierenberg's fixed gaze, the bandaged "girl" walked toward the annex entrance.

The Labyrinth Suppression Forces already had the building surrounded, and apparently the Aguinas family steward had also been taken into custody. Weishardt was on standby near the entrance. When the "girl" handed him the magical tool for recording, she reported something to him, and then left the Aguinas estate behind.

Snow fell on the Aguinas family's expansive yard as the "girl" walked through it, unraveling her bandages. Although terrible scars remained on the face under them, they vanished completely when she passed through a gap in the trees. Her features were now completely different. When she reached the massive gate, she removed the long dress and stored it in a bag, revealing a young boy wearing trousers.

When he showed a sign to the guard protecting the gate and left the estate, the boy returned to the commercial district.

The boy hurrying to the commercial district on the snowy night road was probably a delivery person for a shop somewhere.

No one was suspicious of him. He returned to his own shop.

"I'm back, Auntie. I made the 'delivery.'"

The boy said what he always did, and the shop owner responded in the usual way as well.

"I told you to call me Merle here in the shop, didn't I? So, how'd it go?"

"You like gossip as well as coarse sugar, huh, Auntie? You're as insatiable as an orc."

"You don't get to be sassy with me if you're a rookie who can only change his face!"

No potion existed that let you completely transform into a specific person, but there was a skill that did this. It was not hard to imagine what kind of work people who possessed this extremely rare ability were hired to do.

The kindly owner of the spices shop, who dealt in everything from luxury items like rare spices favored by nobles and wealthy merchants to tea leaves and coarse sugar affordable to the general public, was influential among housewives, and she was a member of Margrave Schutzenwald's personal intelligence organization.

A helpless young girl from abroad wouldn't find it easy to settle into the Labyrinth City while paying exorbitant remodeling fees for a large house, unlike a high-ranking adventurer raking in easy money. It was Merle's job to monitor and investigate such unique cases. Subsequently, Merle and the other housewives managed to spread inoffensive rumors about Mariela and Sieg, the kinds often heard in gossip circles ("an alchemist from the imperial capital," "came here to help her childhood friend"). That gossip helped the pair to blend into the neighborhood as average, everyday residents. Of course, this spin on things came at the orders of Weishardt himself.

Merle would probably pay a visit to Weishardt tomorrow as well—to settle his "bill" and deliver new tea leaves, along with the information she'd just obtained today.

09

Hi, everyone, Mariela here.

Right now I'm in Lady Carol's drawing room. Could you even consider this a drawing room, though? I mean, it's huge. It's got all these elegant couches and sculptures and a table that practically sparkles. Even the mantel for the fireplace is fancy. Also, the walls are decorated with paintings. Many of them have flowers or landscapes, but one features fruit. I wonder what kinds of fruit those are. I've never seen them before. They look delicious, though.

The carpeting is exquisite, too. For something made of fabric, it has all sorts of complex patterns. I bet it's expensive. Is it bad that I walked over it with my shoes on? Everyone else is wearing shoes, though.

I'm sitting in a chair brought out for me in a corner of the room, and boy, this chair is fluffy. The cushions are incredible. Sieg was standing behind me when I started bouncing up and down on it, and he put a hand on my shoulder and chided me to "Quiet down." Sorry.

Lady Carol is in the middle of the room talking to a blond-haired, blue-eyed man who looks just like a prince. They're both so gorgeous that they look straight out of a painting, like I'm watching a love story between two royals unfold. The prince-like guy is smiling as he talks, but Lady Carol's face is pretty grim. That alone makes it seem a bit like they're in some sort of dramatic lover's quarrel. But it's no wonder Carol looks so severe.

That's because this room is full of armed soldiers.

With too much time on her hands, Mariela narrated this stream-of-consciousness commentary in her head while dangling her legs from a chair in a corner of the room. Her escort, Sieg, stood at the ready behind her, and behind Caroline stood her personal maid and escort as well, but many of the Labyrinth Suppression Forces' elite gathered around them, so it was simply a ceremonial act of "allowing their personal escorts to be there."

They'd just moved to the drawing room. Mariela and Caroline had noticed a racket from outside the room as they'd been enjoying a chat in Caroline's atelier. One of the maids came to bring news to Caroline in an extremely flustered state, and after hearing the details, Caroline explained it to Mariela with a bewildered look on her face.

"It appears Lord Weishardt of Margrave Schutzenwald's house has arrived, apparently to investigate something... He has ordered everyone who does not wish to rebel against the margrave—family, guests, servants—to assemble."

When Mariela followed Caroline out of the room, the blond-haired, blue-eyed man resembling a prince was standing by the entrance accompanied by numerous guards.

That person was probably Weishardt.

For some reason, a soldier questioned Mariela, who had followed Caroline to the entrance. "Are you a family member? Or a merchant? You go over here," he said and tried to take her to a different room.

"She is my guest. I don't know what business you have here, but she has nothing to do with it," Caroline explained, covering for Mariela. "I will not tolerate such roughness." Weishardt shot a puzzled look at Mariela and said, "Your guest?"

It was inevitable. Mariela's clothes and general appearance practically screamed "commoner," so she didn't look at all like a guest of the Aguinas family. Even a servant might wear finer clothes as a work uniform. There's no doubt Weishardt would have believed it if someone told him Mariela was a delivery girl who had come with medicinal herbs.

One of the soldiers standing next to Weishardt whispered something in his ear. Weishardt furrowed his brows just a little, then asked, "Lady Caroline, is this the girl you've befriended from the apothecary?"

"That's correct. Mariela is a chemist authorized by the Merchants Guild's Medicinal Herbs Division. My family, as well as Chairwoman Elmera, can vouch for her authenticity."

A commoner's rights were fragile things in the face of the

Labyrinth Suppression Forces, not to mention Margrave Schutz-enwald. Caroline was desperately trying to protect Mariela.

"If she is a friend of yours, we will not treat her poorly. All of you, mind your manners. Insolence will not be tolerated."

Weishardt directed the soldiers to treat Mariela with respect in response to Caroline's wish. Agitation showed in his eyes, but he didn't express his inner thoughts in his words or actions, and no one noticed.

Apparently, the other family members had gathered in a different room, but Weishardt kept incomprehensibly insisting, "This is Lady Caroline's guest," Mariela quietly sat in a chair placed in the corner of the drawing room. Since her escort, Sieg, had been allowed to stay with her and even keep his sword, it may have been a case of special treatment. They were surrounded by the Labyrinth Suppression Forces' very best, though, so Sieg and Caroline's escort would be subjugated immediately if they lashed out.

Some sort of obstruction spell prevented Caroline and Weishardt's conversation from being audible. Mariela might have been able to eavesdrop with Wind's Whispers, but even she wasn't clueless enough to do something like that.

Time passed without her learning any more about the situation, and Mariela grew hungry. It was already dinnertime. If she didn't make today's potions soon, she wouldn't be able to fulfill tonight's delivery. Come to think of it, would she even be able to get home before the delivery time? Lynx and the others might worry.

Guuurgle.

Mariela's stomach made a noise. Although Caroline and Weishardt's conversation wasn't audible, apparently Mariela's stomach was, because a nearby soldier rummaged around in his pocket, produced what looked like a huge cookie, and gave it to Mariela. She was going to give part of it to Sieg, but apparently he didn't need it. For some reason, he gave a slight nod to the soldier as if to say "Please excuse this child."

The cookie contained nuts, dried fruit, and a huge dollop of honey, so it was delicious, but it was a bit hard and dried out. It could have been emergency rations. Mariela held it in both hands, munching away in her corner. Caroline saw this from where she stood in the middle of the room, and her face softened from its previous grim expression as she giggled. "Hee-hee…"

"This reminds me, shall we have tea as well?"

Caroline had regained a bit of her composure, and smiling like a young lady, she instructed the maid in waiting behind her to make tea.

Unfortunately, though, news was delivered to Weishardt before the tea was brought out.

"We discovered the atelier for making new medicine in the annex cellar, but the current head of the family, Robert Aguinas, is nowhere to be found. There's no evidence he escaped from the estate."

"Lady Caroline, are there any secret passages or hiding places in this estate?" Weishardt asked upon hearing the news. Caroline thought briefly before answering.

"I've heard of a secret cellar, but only the family heirs have any knowledge of its location."

"Hrm, then does the previous family head know?"

"My father, Royce…? I can't say whether he is in a condition to speak…"

"Could we possibly meet with him?"

"…By all means."

Caroline and Weishardt left their seats. By the time they returned, Mariela had finished eating the giant cookie. Thanks to the cookie, her stomach bulged, but the preserved food had been dry, and now her mouth was parched.

After coming back, Carol's eyes were slightly red, as if she'd been crying. Weishardt had a look of bafflement and wandered aimlessly around the drawing room with his left hand stroking his chin.

Thinking something probably happened, Mariela gazed at the two of them and accidentally met Weishardt's eyes. Weishardt gazed intently at her.

Wait, did she have cookie crumbs on her? As Mariela scrubbed at her mouth, Weishardt approached.

"You must be Mariela. Since you're a friend of Lady Caroline's, I had a bit of investigation done on you. I hear you are an alchemist from the imperial capital and an excellent chemist. I'd like to pick your brain just a bit."

To a plebian like Mariela, Weishardt's sparkling, noble aura was almost enough to give her a heart attack.

"Y-y-y-yes, sir. I'm Mariela. Um, er…"

She sprung up from her seat, tightly gripped the hem of her tunic, and bowed clumsily. Was she trying to curtsy?

"No need to be so nervous. Please don't worry. It appears there's something wrong with Lady Caroline's father's psyche. I wondered if you might know a way to cure him."

Lady Carol's father… So that's why her eyes were red…

Caroline was her friend. She'd fervently stuck up for Mariela. Mariela didn't know if she could cure something psychological, but if there was something she could do, she wanted to do it.

"I don't know if I can help, but…," Mariela answered with no self-confidence. Accompanied by her and Sieg, Weishardt headed for Caroline's father's bedroom again.

The room was dim. Thick curtains had been drawn across the window, and there was no light, not even from the moon, other than a small lamp on a bedside table. A man lay in a large canopy bed.

The old man standing with guards just outside the room must have been the family's steward.

When Mariela entered the room, Caroline's father, Royce, lying on the bed, opened his mouth.

"The…li…light…" "It…hur…huuurts…"

Royce writhed around, seeming to both reach for the light shining from the corridor and shrink away from it. His thin arms, like withered branches, moved in different directions separately from each other in the air. Although it was hard to tell in the dim light of the room, each side of Royce's face looked like an entirely different person.

It was the same face, yet it was as if the left and right sides were two entirely different lives.

Mariela stood stock-still at the entrance to the room as she gaped at Royce. Her face was frozen in shock.

"Why…are there two people?" Mariela muttered without thinking.

Royce's face lifted with a jerk and stared at her with a different expression on either side of it.

The dryness of her mouth wasn't the fault of the cookie she had earlier.

Remembering her thirst, Mariela swallowed her saliva.

*   *   *

"Two people? Did you figure something out?" Weishardt responded to Mariela's reflexive comment. As she stood motionless in the doorway, Sieg gently placed a hand on her shoulder as if he was worried about her. Mariela placed her own hand on his, took a small breath, and addressed Weishardt.

"Can I use a sleep spell on him?"

After receiving Weishardt's permission, Mariela asked Sieg to cast *Sleep* on Caroline's father, Royce Aguinas.

"H…he…lp…me…" "This…body…is mine…!"

"It's okay, just go to sleep for a little bit," said Mariela as she approached Royce's bed with Sieg. Which face was she talking to? After looking at her, Royce nodded slightly and closed his eyes, then opened them again.

From the side, it was like watching a very leisurely blink.

"…The sleep spell didn't seem to work," said Weishardt.

"No, it's working. Who…who are you?"

Lying in bed, Royce answered Mariela's question.

"I aaam…Ruiz. Ruiz Aguinas. The…head of…this family."

"Ruiz?"

"This man is the previous head's elder brother," answered the elderly steward standing just outside the room with the guards. "It's been a long time since our last meeting, Lord Ruiz."

"G…good…to see…you," answered the individual calling himself Ruiz. However, only in that moment did he appear to be sane. The next instant, that eye stared into space, and he started shouting nonsense.

"Any time nooow! Not much…longerrr… It huuurts… The Sacrificial body…is stiiill……"

Watching Ruiz writhe around complaining of pain, the elderly steward's face darkened as if it were his own pain, and he began to speak quietly.

"The previous heads of the Aguinas family were twins—Ruiz, the elder twin, and Royce, the younger. The Sacrificials adopted Lord Ruiz as a child."

"The Sacrificials?" Weishardt asked, frowning. The Sacrificials. He'd heard the rumors.

And according to those rumors, the Sacrificials were a group of human offerings meant to protect the emperor.

Many people approached high-ranking figures like the emperor with malicious intent. It wasn't a reflection of the emperor as a person. Consciously or not, some people were steadfast in their convictions by simplistically directing their resentment, envy, hatred, and scorn at those at the top. Numerous as ants crawling on the ground, they blamed those in power for their misfortunes.

They could illegalize black magic all they wanted, but if thousands of those with malicious intent and magic came together, these feelings could fester into a curse that reached the emperor. And not just an amorphous manifestation of malice—there existed people with clear hostility who would turn to acts of violence against the emperor as a result.

People from the Sacrificials were said to absorb all such acts of ill will, be they material or spiritual, in the emperor's stead.

"I have heard rumors, but…," muttered Weishardt, to which the elderly steward continued.

"Because the Aguinases create magic medicine in place of potions, they place children who won't inherit the family leadership under the jurisdiction of alchemists or healing mages in the

Empire. Originally, Lord Ruiz was the chosen Aguinas family heir while Lord Royce was to become part of the Sacrificials."

The wise and brilliant older brother Ruiz, whom Robert resembled, and the kind younger brother Royce, who resembled Caroline. The two had been very close, and apparently Ruiz, who loathed to be parted from his brother, had accompanied him to the imperial capital. There fate showed its cruel sense of humor. Discovering Ruiz was extremely suitable as a sacrifice, the Sacrificials wanted to take him in, not Royce.

In exchange for as much knowledge as he could ask for, Ruiz was adopted into the Sacrificials.

"None of us ever found out if something had happened to Lord Ruiz after becoming part of the Sacrificials. However, we received correspondence from him a few years ago."

The correspondence from Ruiz was apparently mixed among the unicorn horns the Aguinas family had coincidentally ordered for research purposes. It was a scrap of paper confirmed to be addressed to his brother Royce and wrapped around a vial. The vial was about the size of a pinkie finger and contained a liquid of a mysterious, dark red color shining with a dim light.

The scrap of paper stated Royce could drink the mysterious liquid to gain the knowledge Ruiz had acquired from the Sacrificials. There were many cases around that time where items sent to the Aguinas family had been lost. Ruiz had sent this liquid to Royce in a number of different ways, and all but this one vial had been prevented from reaching their destination.

Royce, who missed his brother dearly, ignored all attempts to stop him from the people around him and downed the liquid.

"That's when it happened. Lord Ruiz merged with Lord Royce."

At first, it had only been for a short length of time when Royce was sleeping. To not waste the short time Ruiz was there, he shut himself away with Robert in the annex's atelier and told Robert the secret art of the Sacrificials.

However, as time passed, Ruiz began to complain of pain, and he started to appear for longer and longer lengths of time as if he were trying to escape from his suffering. Eventually, Ruiz appeared even when Royce was awake, and the two mingled together as if they were in chaos. They remained separate people, like water and oil that didn't blend together no matter how much you mixed it, but their consciousness and thoughts came apart in minute pieces and recombined.

"Please, I beg you, put Lord Ruiz and Lord Royce at peace," the elderly steward entreated Weishardt.

This wasn't an illness. Everyone present could understand that.

"Is there any way to help them? Perhaps a curse-removal potion...?" said Weishardt, but Mariela shook her head.

Surely this body was the "closest" for Ruiz. Even more so than his real body now.

Mariela was an alchemist. If your alchemic skill was high, you could use it to discern the condition of materials. You could sense the state of the Drops of Life that dwelled in plants, animals, and every living thing.

That's why she knew. Two kinds of Drops of Life existed in Ruiz's body. It was very unnatural for two people to inhabit one body, so that's probably why they'd lost their sanity.

However, their respective Drops of Life weren't tainted like they'd been possessed by an evil spirit. Two different beings from the same source had entangled and intermingled, but existed as individuals in one body. In an absolutely distorted way, both conformed to this body. That's how it felt to Mariela.

Ruiz, who hadn't been affected by the sleep spell, was certainly not the owner of this body.

"You can't return to your own body?" Mariela asked.

"This is...my body... Ahh... It huuurts...... This...is aaaaaaaah mine... S-soon, I'll be released...from this pain... Aaaaaaaaagh!"

"If it's not a curse, could it be some sort of evil spirit? Have you brought in a priest or an exorcist?" asked Weishardt.

"We most certainly have, but..."

The steward explained that Ruiz could not be exorcised like a demon, and Weishardt frowned, saying, "Is there nothing that can be done?" As a Schutzenwald, he didn't want to ignore someone who was suffering, but he also had a duty as the lieutenant general of the Labyrinth Suppression Forces to capture Robert, who was hiding in the cellar of the annex even now. However, they couldn't get information about the secret cellar's entrance from the previous family head, Royce, in this state.

Just when Weishardt was wondering if it would be better to demolish the annex, Mariela timidly spoke up.

"Um, would it be okay if I talked privately with him for just a little bit?"

"Very well."

Weishardt indicated the door to the steward, who had a puzzled look on his face, and left with him.

"Sieg, you too. I'll be fine." Sieg was the last to leave, and at last, Mariela quietly closed the door.

With the light from the corridor blocked, the room, now lit by only the small lamp next to the bed, was extremely dim. The oppressive atmosphere of the room that had long had its curtains closed reminded her of the inside of a deep cave.

"Gaaah... It huuurts... Ahhh..."

Mariela asked the complaining, writhing Ruiz a question. "Your real body is in pain, isn't it?"

"Aaah... That's...no longer...my..."

"You can't go back to it, can you? Even if you wanted to, you're not connected to it anymore."

Mariela looked in Ruiz's eye. It was clouded over with pain, but it didn't look to Mariela like the eye of a madman.

"But this body isn't yours. Even if Royce weren't in there, even if you had this body to yourself, you would still be in pain."

Watching someone in such agony would be heartbreaking for anybody. All the more true if the person suffering was their father.

How extremely sad must Caroline have been every time she looked at her father, who'd lost his sanity?

Mariela wanted to help everyone: this suffering man in front of her, Royce who was suffering along with him, and the elderly steward who couldn't do anything but watch over them. She felt the steward's words, "Please, put them at peace," weren't something he said lightly.

"H...elp...," Ruiz begged in Royce's body. He wanted to be saved, to be released from this suffering.

"If you can't return to your own body, there's only one place you can go."

Mariela activated her alchemy and enclosed Royce's body within a Transmutation Vessel.

"Drops of Life."

Those drops were an overwhelming sight.

Water shining with white light filled the space around Ruiz

like a spring gushing forth. Within the dim room, it looked like he was floating in a river of stars.

"Oh... Oh... Oh..."

The Drops of Life that were emitting a warm and gentle light lost their form and vanished as soon as they touched Royce's body.

It was so very frustrating. Even though this person was so hungry and thirsty, even with this water enveloping his body, he still couldn't touch it or feel it?

Even though he was so cold.

Even though he was in such pain.

Even though this was so cruel and sad and lonely.

Even though he wanted to return to oneness...

As if seeking the Drops of Life, to hold it, Ruiz's hand searched for the light.

"Drops of Life flow into a ley line—a place where you...no, *everyone* returns to," Mariela told him. *It's not a scary place. It's a place where you can be released from everything, even the form known as your "self."*

Mariela didn't even know this herself, but her Nexus that formed the pact with the ley line deep in the earth was thicker and stronger than anyone else's. The reason she didn't lose her "self" in such a deep place was because the warmth of her master's tight embrace had permeated the depths of her heart. And because the spirit who became her friend firmly grasped her hand and desperately protected her.

Mariela continued to draw up Drops of Life from the Nexus that was stronger than anyone else's, calling forward an incredible amount of magic without any reservation. No matter how much she drew up, the Drops of Life that touched Royce's body came undone and vanished, as if she was pouring it into a bottomless bucket. Even as she remembered her dizziness from consuming a large amount of magic when she made the plate glass, Mariela didn't stop.

She didn't know how Ruiz had entered Royce's body. A spirit had been the one who'd taken Mariela out of her body when she connected to the ley line with a Nexus, so she didn't know how to take out Ruiz. All she could do was show him there was a place for him to return to after he left his physical form.

"Ah, ah, ah..."

Ruiz's hand swam in the light of Drops of Life as if seeking what he couldn't touch.

Somebody, please, show him the way...

Mariela didn't have much magic left. Would this man suffer through a life of pain again after she'd shown him a little glimpse of hope?

Anyone...

"...E......lia...?"

Had Ruiz spoken someone's name?

In that instant, Ruiz Aguinas melted into the light and returned to the ley line.

10

"Phewww...!"

Mariela breathed a weak sigh.

She'd used up too much magic. She didn't pass out this time, but the room was spinning. This hadn't happened since that time she'd had alcohol. Her body felt light, like she was floating. Had her diet been a success?

Mariela used the momentum of her stagger to collapse into a chair.

"Mariela! Are you all right?!"

She could hear Sieg's voice from just beyond the door.

"I'm fiiine. C'mon in!"

In response to Mariela's usual cheerful voice, the door burst open with a bang, and Sieg rushed over to her. After checking her face and body to make sure nothing was wrong, he let out a big sigh of relief at last.

"How did it go?"

Weishardt entered the room next and asked Mariela about the situation after confirming Royce was sleeping.

"What did you do?"

"Um, I talked to him about the ley line. I got the feeling he wanted to return to it. And it seemed like he did. Now Royce is alone."

"M...Master!"

The elderly steward rushed over to the bed and shook the sleeping Royce. Maybe he thought he had died. After all, when the two men were in one body, they'd probably stayed awake for countless years.

"Mm..." Shaken awake by the steward, Royce spoke with eyes that were tired but clear. "Ruiz...returned home..."

"Master! Ohhh...!"

The elderly steward broke down crying upon learning Royce was safe and Ruiz had passed on.

Wasn't this the kind of role a beauty like Carol was supposed to play? Something about this felt off to Mariela. With Sieg, she quietly left the room since they were merely bystanders. Weishardt seemed like he wanted to say something, but as his original purpose was to find the secret cellar, he approached Royce to ask about it.

"Father!"

"How I've worried you so, Carol."

Caroline ran up to Royce, who was being transported in a wheelchair. It was a real tearjerker of a scene. Definitely the kind that called for a pretty girl.

Yup, definitely. Sitting in her designated chair in a corner of the drawing room, Mariela nodded her approval.

It was a trivial thing, but when they descended the stairs, someone from the Labyrinth Suppression Forces had easily lifted the wheelchair from both sides. So powerful.

"Wow, so strong! Nothing less from the strongest soldiers in the Labyrinth Suppression Forces," Mariela said in admiration, whereupon Sieg went behind her chair and agilely lifted it for about ten seconds.

Mariela's eyes sparkled as if to say "Higher!" It was an incredible difference from Carol's eyes sparkling with tears. Perhaps this was what separated the itty-bitty girls from the pretty girls. Society could be so cruel and polarizing.

In contrast to Mariela, who was satisfied with a single lift of the chair, Royce, who had heard the general story from Weishardt, spoke seriously with him and Caroline in the middle of the drawing room.

"I'll guide you to the secret cellar," said Royce. "Carol, you come, too. As a member of the Aguinas family, you should know about this."

Caroline nodded, and Royce turned toward Mariela.

"Young lady, I'd like you to come as well. You're the one who released Ruiz."

"Huhwhat?"

Mariela, who'd been relaxing in the corner of the room thinking her work was finished, straightened up with an "Eek!" at Royce's absurd request. Weishardt, Caroline, and all the soldiers from the Labyrinth Suppression Forces turned to look at her.

This sure took a strange turn...

Even though the presence of soldiers from the Labyrinth Suppression Forces in the Aguinas family's drawing room meant it was an emergency, was it necessary for a mere chemist to be present for every single important detail? Or was she supposed to be a representative of the commoners? Were they inviting her as an adviser with an outsider's perspective?

No way any of that was true. At a loss, Mariela looked to Caroline for help. For her part, Caroline had a look of "What should I do?" when she was invited herself. Were she and Mariela in the same boat? No, this had much more to do with her than with Mariela.

Next to Caroline, Royce and Weishardt looked as if they knew exactly who Mariela was. That said, when she'd freed Ruiz, Royce had been asleep and Weishardt had been outside the room, so there was no reason for them to have known she used Drops of Life.

"Time is of the essence. Let's go!"

At Weishardt's command, Royce, Caroline, and several soldiers began to head toward the annex. Mariela just stood there flustered, so the soldier who'd given her the cookie urged her with a gesture to go with them. She briefly glanced up at Sieg, who nodded, seeming to say that she couldn't afford to say no. Reluctantly, Mariela followed the rest of them.

A number of soldiers were guarding the area around the annex, so alert that even a single kitten couldn't have gotten through.

A cold rain had been falling when Mariela and Sieg arrived at the Aguinas estate, but it had now turned into snow. If it continued to fall like this, it would really be piled up by the next morning. *Think I could just sprint through this huge yard to my heart's content? Nah, probably not*, Mariela thought as she obediently followed along behind the rest of the group.

"We'll go to the second-floor study first."

In accordance with Royce's directions, they all ascended to the second floor.

A stone staircase leading to the second floor lay at the back of the room where the confrontation between Robert and Nierenberg took place. The room beyond the stairs appeared to be a study. Many documents and books were lined up in a systematic fashion in this room, which Robert still used, and through this, one could infer Robert's methodical personality.

Royce stopped his wheelchair in front of an antique bookshelf, took a book from the left edge of the middle section, and placed it in the same spot one shelf above.

Clack.

They heard a very soft sound. There seemed to be some kind of switch. On a closer look, she noticed on the floor to the right of the bookshelf had scuff marks from something heavy being dragged across it. And those scratches were the exact same width as the bookshelf itself.

Whoa. I bet that's the entrance to the hideout in the story Lady Carol was telling me about!

The bookshelf's mechanism excited Mariela, who'd become completely used to the stuffy atmosphere of being surrounded by soldiers, and she glanced at Carol. Carol apparently had the same thoughts, as she looked at Mariela with slightly red cheeks.

The pair nodded to each other, walked up to the bookshelf, and heaved to push it to the right.

"Hrrrgh. Huh?"

"It's not moving?"

Although they'd built up a lot of strength from knead-kneading every day, the two of them couldn't get the bookshelf to budge even a little. Robert wasn't a warrior, either, so the girls' combined power should be at least as good if not better than his.

"Ah... Only the switch is in this room," Royce said apologetically.

"Then what are those scratches on the floor?"

"Everyone who sees the contraption for the first time has the same reaction. It was installed around two generations ago. In other words, it's a fake."

Mariela and Caroline exchanged confused glances.

"Then where is the entrance?" Weishardt asked calmly, and Royce answered, "Downstairs."

Mariela and Caroline continued to look at each other as they trotted behind Royce, who was carried in his wheelchair to the first floor.

"...We were tricked."

"Lady Carol, your ancestor was a mischievous one, huh?"

The group headed for the opposite side of the first-floor stairs in a somewhat calmer mood.

On the other side of the stairs, a large vase sat on a stand with a splendid lace tablecloth that ran all the way down to the floor.

Upon closer inspection of the wall near the stand, a single stone was protruding just a little.

Surely *this* was the entrance. Mariela was certain the wall behind the stairs opened like a door to reveal a passage to the secret cellar. Since the vase was there, the wall behind the stairs might slide open.

Thanks to the trick a short while ago, all the prudent adults surrounded the wall at a distance and tried to avoid eye contact. It was very similar to the reaction of the participants in Mariela's medicine-making seminars who didn't want to be called on to answer a question.

"Carol, and you, young lady, could you pull on that protrusion for me?"

Mariela and Caroline had been called on. When they pulled on the stone together, it smoothly moved forward just a bit, and they heard a *ka-chunk* like a latch had been opened.

Now for the wall. Should they pull, push, or shift it?

"It's under the flower stand."

When the soldiers flipped up the tablecloth per Royce's instructions, they found the floor under the vase had sunk about a fist's width.

THAT'S where it was...?! It had nothing to do with the wall?!

Everyone had the same thought.

After moving the flower stand aside, they could see the corners of the sunken stones were rounded from long use. The tablecloth had been used to skillfully hide this fact, as it was obvious from one glance in sufficient light that they looked very out of place. The drape of the tablecloth was beautiful lace, and some of it could be seen through.

Apparently, when the soldiers of the Labyrinth Suppression

Forces had lifted the tablecloth to check, there had been just the right amount of delicate shadows so that they didn't notice. You could say it was a clever disguise, but the fact this was the door the hidden switch in the bookshelf opened ruined the hideout feeling. The kindhearted Caroline looked disappointed as well.

"In any case, he must be extremely agile to have ascended to the second-floor study, opened the entrance, and then returned here to escape to the cellar in the short time before the soldiers broke in. Stay focused, everyone."

Weishardt called on the soldiers to brace themselves, but...

"Erm, most likely he left it open ahead of time..."

Royce's brief comment further ruined the atmosphere. What an inability to read the room. Maybe the time he spent blended with Ruiz was still having an effect on him after all.

The sunken floor slid open easily. So easily, neither the power of knead-kneading nor the power of friendship was required to open it.

There was a ladder on the vertical wall that went down about two yards before the wall became a gently sloping corridor. A soldier carried Royce, and the others formed a line and went down one by one.

The light escaping from the back of the corridor was about to tell the end of the alchemists' story that spanned the course of two hundred years.

11

"Estalia, Estalia, Estalia!"

After using the bandit to get away from Nierenberg, Robert had escaped to the cellar where Estalia slept.

He clung to her coffin.

Did he intend to betray the alchemists' wish that spanned two hundred years and open the glass coffin, awakening Estalia?

But Robert gripped the coffin, looking at her while calling her name over and over, but didn't try to open it.

There was only one entrance to this cellar.

This room was a dead end, the point of departure for the awakened alchemists, and the end of the line for Robert, who had given everything to Estalia.

"Estalia…"

All he did was call her name as he continued to gaze at her. How long had he been down here? It was as if time had stopped.

Robert slowly lifted his head at the sounds of the secret door to this room being flung open and the footsteps of several people coming down.

"Welcome to the graveyard of the ruined country's alchemists." Like a ghost, Robert stood and welcomed Weishardt and the others.

"Robert Aguinas. I trust you understand the gravity of your crimes. You'd best come with us," stated Weishardt.

"Robert…"

"Brother!"

"Carol… Father? Have you returned to your senses? But how…?"

Royce captured his attention. Robert understood his father's condition better than anyone. It wasn't possible for him to regain his sanity.

"I see… An alchemist! I knew it, one has awakened! Where?! Where are they?!" Robert shouted as if he'd lost his mind.

"Stop this now, Brother! If you properly explain yourself, Margrave Schutzenwald will understand!"

"Understand? Understand what? Explain? It's a little too late for that! All the margrave does is make demands! What does the margrave understand about the resolve of those individuals two hundred years ago, the hopes they had when they made those potions?! What does he understand?! He couldn't possibly understand! They didn't make those potions for his sake—they made them for Estalia! For Estalia's sake! If you say the margrave will understand, then hand over the alchemist! Estalia needs this alchemist to awaken her—to lead her to the new world!"

Robert stood between them and Estalia's coffin with his hands behind him as if to protect it. A black curse trickled from his body and formed a vortex, perhaps to shield the glass coffin.

However, Robert was no warrior. It didn't matter if his curse was powerful or if it was one of forced subordination, his specialty. In the face of the Labyrinth Suppression Forces' elite, this was child's play compared to the King of Cursed Serpents. At Weishardt's eye signal, a soldier leaped forth and dispelled the curse in a single blow, then twisted Robert's arms behind his back and brought him to the floor.

"Let go! Let me go! Let go, let go, let go!! Stop! Don't you dare lay a finger on herrrrrrr! She will awaken once more in the new world!! Just as they all hoped and dreamed of!!"

"She won't..." Mariela mumbled so softly that Robert could scarcely hear her.

Next to her, Weishardt asked, "What do you mean?"

Mariela was staring at Estalia with incredible melancholy.

"Because...she's already..."

The moment he caught on, Weishardt walked briskly toward the glass coffin and laid a hand on the delicately embroidered cloth covering.

"STOPPPPPPPPPP!!!" Robert's scream echoed through the cellar.

Beneath that cloth covering, the lower half of the sleeping Estalia's body had crumbled away in her glass coffin.

Salt gently spilled out from the hem of her long, rose-colored dress.

This room was a dead end.

The place where Estalia's story came to a close.

Mariela didn't know when Robert had realized Estalia had died. He probably understood that she'd long since "returned home" and would never come back no matter what kind of magic medicine or secret art he used.

Although he realized it, although he understood it, Mariela felt he hadn't been able to accept it. If he had, his plans would have come to a halt.

Several empty coffins lay in this cellar.

Looking at Estalia in eternal sleep in her glass coffin, Mariela wasn't foolish enough not to understand what had happened.

She knew the potential consequences of an imperfect Magic Circle of Suspended Animation.

Her master had gone through great lengths to Imprint simple magic circles again and again in Mariela's mind from a young age. It was all to build up her tolerance before burning the Magic Circle of Suspended Animation directly into her brain. This enabled Mariela to draw the three-foot magic circle precisely, down to the last speck. And all because her master knew the slightest distortion, gap, difference in a spot's size, or difference in a line's angle or length would lead to disastrous results.

The alchemists who'd slept in the coffins most likely knew their own fate.

It was all to lead Estalia to the new world.

There was no doubt Robert's words echoed the alchemists' hope.

She understood this just by looking at the glass coffin Estalia slept in. Glass deteriorates. The stuff in the ruins of the atelier where Mariela made the plate glass had turned white and shattered into pieces. Even in a cellar where the sunlight couldn't reach it, the glass coffin had endured exposure to artificial light for two hundred years, which meant it must have used the highest quality of ingredients and created by those with advanced skills.

They must have hoped to see her again.

Though they couldn't converse with the sleeping girl, it was as if they'd prayed they could see her again if she ever woke up, even if it was just a glimpse.

Hence the glass coffin.

The alchemists believed Estalia would find joy upon awakening in the new world. Not knowing how long they would live, those who sacrificed themselves passed their records down through successive heads of the Aguinas family.

Not a single one of the alchemists who were able to awaken lamented their fate, but continued to make potions until their last breath.

How had those hopes come to an end?

Lead Estalia to the new world. Even if they never woke up. The Aguinas family had spent two hundred years supported by that thought alone.

When they had no potions, they even involved themselves in forbidden activity.

All so they could bury the Labyrinth.

"Nevertheless, Robert, the hopes, the lives, of the alchemists who awoke were theirs. The same is true for those you sacrificed for your new medicine. They are not your playthings," Weishardt stated.

Robert's face twisted in a laugh.

His expression said it all. He'd already known this.

"But I suppose if you didn't have an alchemist, you would have continued to use the new medicine despite knowing its *ingredients*," Robert replied.

After the Labyrinth Suppression Forces hauled Robert away, a lone soldier asked Weishardt what should be done with the glass coffin.

"Leave it be. Keep it safe until the new world arrives."

Royce bowed his head deeply in response to Weishardt allowing him to bury her in the new world.

After hearing the details from Royce, Caroline silently gazed at Estalia in eternal slumber. Mariela tightly grasped Caroline's hand.

"Don't worry; she made it back to the ley line. And I'll bet she got to see the people important to her, too."

"Estalia"—Ruiz had said her name when he left Royce's body.

Mariela believed Estalia had heard the wishes of the Aguinas family and then came to take Ruiz home. She gritted her teeth tightly as she came to grips with the fact that she really was the only alchemist in the Labyrinth City who could make potions.

Caroline's hand, which returned Mariela's squeeze, was the only thing that brought her warmth in this cold cellar.

The snow blanketed the Labyrinth City and engulfed sound and scenery alike. It continued to fall silently and coat everything in its wake.

What Flows Through

01

A number of huge glass tanks stood in a row in a room in the Aguinas family annex that formerly served as a potion storehouse.

"Is this the black new medicine...?" muttered Nierenberg in distaste.

The Aguinas family's engineers involved in creating the new medicine had been arrested and held in a corner of the room. Their faces were characteristic of those who'd stifled their emotions for a long time, with sunken eyes and listless fatigue, but the little remaining emotion that could be read showed their relief at finally being free.

Royce Aguinas, the previous head of the family who had regained his sanity, cooperated with the Labyrinth Suppression Forces' investigation. Weishardt surmised from Royce's testimony that the case touched on classified information, so only he and a trusted confidant were involved in the questioning. Based on the testimony from Royce and the engineers, the written report on the black new medicine began as follows:

The black new medicine was made from black magic to transfer damage by using the secret arts of the Sacrificials.

The Sacrificials redirected atrocities set to befall the emperor and other preeminent individuals onto a substitute. From time immemorial, these curses or misfortune were instead transferred to human-shaped objects known as Proxies. These objects didn't need to be flesh and blood to absorb the bad luck that came with wicked thoughts or impurity, as long as it had yet to amount to an actual curse. Rather, as in ancient times, it was the job of the group known as the Sacrificials to transfer these misfortunes to objects they made from paper, wood, or soil, and subsequently purify them.

However, as the human world evolved and the small country developed into an empire, magic and technology advanced. Evil thoughts became more complex and numerous, and the clan's methods for dealing with them grew more effective and sinister in equal measure.

They began to use living humans as Proxies.

But that didn't mean it was okay to use just anyone as a Proxy. First, they had to be compatible with the person they were protecting, the Recipient. If it was a single incident or a limited number of successive atrocities, all they had to do was activate the Proxy with their technique for that period of time. However, there were victims who would eventually attract more malice, just like swamp air that's always stagnant and damp, in a way that threatened to change their future. In these cases that required a constant substitute, innate compatibility was necessary.

Since few people were capable of serving as Proxies, others in the clan searched for techniques to dispel the wicked thoughts the Proxies absorbed. Since there wasn't an abundance of people with an affinity for any given Recipient, it was imperative that the ones available lasted for as long as possible.

For generations, every emperor had visited the village of the Sacrificials and formed a Sacrificial Pact with the Proxies deemed most compatible. The Proxies who signed this contract bore all

EPILOGUE: What Flows Through

the hatred and atrocities focused on the emperor. It was said that sometimes, they even sacrificed themselves to the daggers of assassins who plotted to overthrow the emperor. The Sacrificials had aided the emperor and the Empire from the shadows by healing and protecting the Proxies tormented by others' ill will and purifying them from malice.

A select few high-ranking aristocrats, such as Weishardt, had heard this much. There had been talk of allocating someone from the Sacrificials to Leonhardt back when his skills had become clear. The reason he didn't sign a Sacrificial Pact was because he would take a lot of physical damage in the course of subjugating the Labyrinth, and he had poor compatibility with the Proxies who specialized in curses, so it was highly unlikely a Proxy would be able to withstand it. Also, the man himself was strongly opposed to it based on the Schutzenwald family doctrine: "The next generation shall inherit our dying wish."

The repulsive truth behind the secret art of the Sacrificials was the Proxies themselves.

The bodies of children chosen as Proxies were restructured from an early age with medicine and magic to increase their affinity with their Recipients. Completely replacing their blood was only the start; their bodies were opened up countless times to engrave black magic crests directly onto their bones.

They might get their right arm dissected one time and their left leg the next, followed by their flesh, skin, fat, and nerves—all immersed in a special magical liquid to transform them before healing magic was used to restructure their original form. Apparently, even the tissue of those who had poor affinity with their Recipient was replaced with artificially cultivated tissue.

It was said that a body remade in this way was highly efficient at absorbing atrocities aimed at the Recipient. However, it wasn't possible to have a normal life in a body remade with such dark arts. The body didn't move how its owner wanted it to, and even light and air caused pain. Those who'd had their flesh replaced with artificial tissue couldn't even stand to leave their liquid medicine bath.

But none of that posed a problem for the Sacrificials.

The body of the Proxy didn't belong to that person but rather was a second body for the Recipient. The Proxy was solely intended to transfer the Recipient's misfortune onto themselves. And their pain and suffering never reached the Recipient. No matter how much the Proxy writhed in pain, it was only temporary—until they became a completed Proxy.

Ruiz had learned the secret art of the Sacrificials that bound Recipient and Proxy together. As promised, the Sacrificials divulged everything to him when they welcomed him into the fold. Ruiz had devoted his entire soul to deciphering the secret art and developing practical uses for it.

Because he knew what would happen to him once he became a complete Proxy.

Since ancient times, the role of Proxy had been assigned to human-shaped dolls with no will of their own.

A Proxy was their Recipient's second body. There was no reason for them to have a will.

Ruiz was fortunate enough to complete his research just a short while before his body was fully restructured into a Proxy. He used every method he could think of to send the black magic medicine he'd created to his younger brother, Royce Aguinas.

Ruiz had anticipated the Sacrificials might interfere. They never intended for their secret art to be revealed to the outside world. They'd disclosed it to him because they knew he wouldn't be able to do anything about it once he became a Proxy. Ruiz was on the verge of his full transformation into a Proxy and couldn't leave the village. No matter how much he'd mastered their secret art, it would remain secret as long as they inspected his letters and packages.

He didn't record the secret art in writing. Such an unwieldy, conspicuous method would never reach Royce. It would be a success if even just one vial of the magic medicine out of more than a hundred sent to Royce reached him and he got to drink it. Ruiz and Royce were identical twins. There was no higher possible compatibility between individuals. Even if he didn't use any kind of technical means, Ruiz had bet that this drug would *work* on Royce.

In the end, Ruiz's gamble succeeded. Just before his "self" was destroyed in the Proxy completion ritual, he began to inhabit Royce's body. Ruiz's magic medicine, charged with his essence in a vial the size of a pinkie finger, made use of the Proxy contract. Instead of unilaterally sending misfortune from a Recipient to a Proxy, the soul of Ruiz the Proxy was transferred to the Recipient, Royce, by activating a technique that used the medicine as an intermediary. Ruiz appeared when Royce wasn't conscious and imparted the clan's secret art to Robert.

Ruiz's sole miscalculation was the fact he continued to feel the pain inflicted on his original body despite being robbed of it. The hatred and malice toward the emperor horribly tormented Ruiz's body and continued to inflict pain and suffering on him even as he inhabited Royce's body.

Every time he tried to escape from the pain, Ruiz encroached further on Royce. Royce's body was temporary for Ruiz. If Royce strongly rejected Ruiz, he might have been able to stop the appropriation of his body.

However, Royce didn't. He had been the one originally meant to be taken into the clan. He should have been the one to endure the pain and suffering Ruiz was experiencing. Royce chose to accept Ruiz, and together they suffered and lost their sanity bit by bit.

The black new medicine was a magic drug based on the secret art Ruiz had imparted.

This cursed medicine transferred the damage suffered by whoever ingested the drug onto a Proxy.

There were three requirements to be a Proxy:

First, a person's disposition.

It was possible to mitigate a Proxy's compatibility if they weren't constantly redirecting calamities to themselves—as long as they weren't expected to handle more than a generic Proxy in a fully-matured body.

Second, the pact that bound Recipient and Proxy together.

This was achieved through Ruiz's applied research. Pact conditions could be temporarily created by the Recipient ingesting part of the Proxy's flesh. In the case of Ruiz and Royce, who were extremely compatible, they stayed bound together. But a connection with a generic Proxy restructured from an adult's body would be severed shortly after it absorbed any damage. It was quite convenient for Robert's purposes as it required a constant supply of potions.

And finally, the third condition—a *flesh puppet* incapable of sentient thought.

02

"Y-yaaaaaagh! What…what the hell are those?! No, please, help me! I'll do anything, anything at all! Please!"

At exactly the time the Labyrinth Suppression Forces were subjugating the King of Cursed Serpents, the thief Robert had Ordered to sleep woke up, saw the Proxies sleeping in the tanks, and screamed bloody murder. He was one of the ones who'd been brought to the Aguinas estate.

The same bandit who had flown at Nierenberg under Robert's orders.

"Anything? Now that I think about it, my family lacks sufficient human resources suitable for fighting. Should everything go as planned, I won't have you used for ingredients," Robert proposed.

The bandit clung to him as if he'd been sent from heaven itself to help him.

Humans—no, flesh puppets with patterns drawn all over their bodies and tube after tube protruding from them floated in the giant tanks lined in up the black room. The tops of their heads were open with their brains exposed. Probably to remove their craniums. Their scalps had been peeled like the skin of fruits and dangled in front of their eyes as if to hide their faces.

The bandit, who'd murdered countless people, had seen the inside of a human head before. So he knew. The flesh puppets with no craniums floating in the water tanks had had part of their brains removed.

With a burble, the flesh puppets in the tanks spit up blood bubbles and shuddered.

In the next moment, their stomachs ripped open, and their limbs burst into pieces with audible cracks, even though they didn't appear to be struck by any outward attacks.

The black room suddenly became very busy as people who appeared to be healing mages treated the puppets, while the engineers operated a nearby magical device to send something through the tubes into their bodies and to adjust the liquid medicine in the water tanks.

"No, this is far too rough. They won't survive," muttered Robert. The engineers' efforts appeared to be in vain, as in the next instant, the bodies of the flesh puppets turned black and fell apart like pieces of rotten meat.

03

After hearing Weishardt's report, Leonhardt breathed a deep sigh.

"So that was the nature of the new medicine we were using…?"

Heresy to the most reprehensible degree—but that didn't change the fact they would never have made it to the fifty-third stratum without it.

"And what of the people who were designated as materials?" asked Leonhardt.

"Only half of the 'red' ones woke up."

The remaining half had passed away when their tubes were removed. They must have been forcibly kept alive, barely managing to stitch together their remaining life force with the medicine that had completely replaced the blood in their bloodstream.

"Even among the ones who woke up, those who received high dosages of magical gems will continue to have some sort of impairment. All of them were identified as either penal laborers or lifelong slaves. It seems those with physical disabilities became their preferred materials for the 'red' medicine, while those without have been difficult to handle after a little bit of healing."

The Labyrinth City always had labor shortages, but there weren't many jobs for slaves and others with disabilities or physical impairments. This might become a burden that would consume the assets of the Aguinas family, who'd lost its source of income, the sale of new medicine.

"And the 'black' ones?" asked Leonhardt.

Weishardt quietly shook his head.

"Medical Technician Nierenberg has seen to them."

"I see... Yet another nasty job we've thrust upon him..."

One could say the turmoil surrounding the Aguinas family progressed as Weishardt had predicted and ended without any losses. However, the truth that had come to light left a lingering discomfort in the hearts of the Schutzenwald brothers.

Because they couldn't refute Robert's parting words: "I suppose if you didn't have an alchemist, you would have continued to use the new medicine despite knowing its *ingredients*."

04

The fresh snow crunched underfoot as Nierenberg hurried home.

By the time he'd finished most of his work and given directions to his subordinates who'd arrived at the Aguinas estate, the night was over. The city, dyed completely white from the snow that had covered it before he knew it, looked like a wholly unfamiliar place.

When he got close to his house, a single snowball came flying at him.

He knew who the offender was. He'd gotten a fleeting glimpse of black hair when they quickly hid behind a corner of a stone wall. Rather than dodging the snowball, he lightly caught it in his hand.

"Welcome home, Papa! You were late, so I made all these snowmen!"

When he rounded the corner toward his house, he saw Sherry wearing a wool hat low over her eyes and pointing to a line of snowmen in front of the house.

The skin on both sides of her face was as white and beautiful as snow. Not the faintest hint of the gruesome scar remained on her face that broke into a lovely smile. Her black hair hadn't completely grown in yet, but since the season just happened to be winter, she could sufficiently cover it with a hat. Her hair would soon grow full and frame her sweet face.

The piles of snow sparkled in the morning light, indicating to Nierenberg that it was time to begin anew.

05

Weishardt had been troubled since the incident with the Aguinas family.

He'd long wondered whether they had alchemists. It started when he stumbled across a preliminary calculation report of the potion storage facilities in the estate's library. Weishardt was no expert in magical tools, but it was easy to see from these calculations that this situation was very different from the conditions two hundred years ago, even if he accounted for other factors.

These potions couldn't last for two hundred years.

When he reached that conclusion, he understood how relatively fresh potions had been supplied at fixed intervals over the past two hundred years to each family who owned a storage facility. The Aguinas family explained the freshness was a result of new tanks being unsealed, but what if there had been an alchemist at those times?

So, when the Black Iron Freight Corps began bringing in potions, he realized an alchemist who'd made a pact with the region's ley line had appeared, and he predicted how the Aguinas family would react upon learning of the alchemist's existence. You could say formulating a plan to ensure the safety of Mariela, the alchemist, was a matter of course.

Weishardt cut the quantity of potions they purchased in half and observed the reaction of the Aguinas family. The Aguinas family may have concealed the existence of an alchemist and demanded a high price for the potions, but they were to cover the costs to manufacture and store the potions, on top of research and development—not for selfish gain. The fact that the family had continued to provide potions for two hundred years to compensate for the shortcomings of potion storage facilities built by the Empire and the margrave's family should be appreciated.

And if they had been forthcoming that this was humane and necessary for the Labyrinth subjugation efforts, he would have given them more leeway.

It was an accident that Nierenberg's daughter was a victim of the slime incident, but it was a convenient one. For one, she was the most suitable decoy for the Aguinas family, but more than that, Nierenberg was loyal to his professional duties, which was why he drew the line at special treatment and refused to take a potion for himself. He apparently intended to entrust Sherry to the Black Iron Freight Corps so she could be taken to the imperial capital and treated there. But hundreds of potions became available for use in the subjugation of the Labyrinth thanks to an Alchemist Pact-Bearer, and there was no reason not to offer a potion to a close aide who had done a lot for the Forces. So Nierenberg received a high-grade potion as compensation for his particular duties, and he was able to heal his daughter, Sherry.

They distributed the victim list, swapped Sherry with an intelligence operative, and had Nierenberg's housekeeper leave early to make it easier to commit the crime. To ensure Sherry's safety, she was safeguarded at the Schutzenwald estate after her treatment, but Nierenberg's mood got worse as he continued to live with the intelligence operative day after day. Other than it causing the Labyrinth Suppression Forces' soldiers to become scared from the bottom of their hearts, it could be said things progressed as expected.

Robert had stooped to kidnapping Sherry to obtain information about the alchemist with so little resistance that it was anticlimactic. His psyche had probably long since worn away. The red and black magic medicine found in the cellar was that atrocious. And alchemists that the Aquinas family had been watching over for generations.

But the blame couldn't be placed entirely on the Aguinas family, especially considering the secret history of the alchemists, their unfortunate faith, and their resolve to continually supply potions until they were on the brink of death. And the question of dealing with the family, including the alchemists, was a headache of a problem.

With a sigh, Weishardt took a glass from a sideboard, used magic to put ice in it, and poured his favorite brandy. He gently held a sip of undiluted brandy in his mouth and recalled that night.

Why was Mariela, that alchemist, there...?

Even with his brilliant mind, this was the one thing Weishardt couldn't understand.

Her contact with Caroline Aguinas had been friendly and limited to within Sunlight's Canopy. In the unlikely event Caroline tried to take Mariela from the shop, an intelligence operative, Merle, would be contacted immediately, and a plan would be formed to stop it naturally. Who could have guessed the pair would meet by chance downtown, out of sight of the intelligence operatives, and manage to make their way to the Aguinas estate?

Weishardt excelled at deliberate intrigue and could hide the entirety of his emotions. He had complete control over his facial muscles through his own will. He had a wide field of vision and could observe the situation around him while pretending to look elsewhere.

If that weren't the case, everyone who happened to be present at that place would probably have noticed Mariela, because Weishardt was more surprised than he'd ever been in his life and gawked at her, which no one had realized.

When Weishardt first met Mariela in the corridor, he'd thought she was a delivery person from some shop. Since nobody friendly with the Black Iron Freight Corps had appeared in the City recently, though, Merle had been assigned to report on not only her movements, but her outward appearance, too.

She's too normal... I suppose she's more like a small forest creature than a unicorn...

He'd heard she was young. But that's what he'd heard about Pact-Bearers in general. He'd expected her to have a noble, extraordinary air due to possessing proper calmness and exuding intelligence despite her youthful appearance.

However, she was an ordinary person whom nine out of ten people passing her on the street wouldn't take a second look at.

It was a good thing he'd had her sit in a corner of the drawing room within his sight so the soldiers who didn't know the circumstances wouldn't be rude, though.

Why was she hopping...? Is she performing some sort of ritual from two hundred years ago? I've never heard of such a thing.

She'd been restlessly bouncing up and down in her chair until she was stopped by her escort standing behind her. Instead of intelligence, she exuded an air that made her seem even younger than she actually was, which was a bit disappointing.

If she was the same age she appeared to be, how could she make high-grade potions? And a hundred a day, at that. Weishardt had ordered potions in units of a hundred, but he'd only instructed to make the next order after the delivery of the first, and he'd never expected to receive daily deliveries.

He'd heard it was necessary to make over a hundred thousand mid-grade potions before being able to make high-grade ones. The bottleneck in creating potions was one's quantity of magic. Ordinary people needed a few decades until they were able to make high-grade potions. And what about the amount of magical power needed to make a hundred high-grade potions a day? Even with the maximum magical power rating of five, it was a wonder it could be done.

This was why he'd imagined she was a mysterious alchemist in the form of a young woman. When he learned one hundred high-grade potions could be delivered day after day, he secretly broke into a cold sweat as he felt thankful they'd been able to establish friendly relations with someone possessing such marvelous magical reserves.

He knew the method for raising the upper limit of one's magical power. Starting from under the age of ten, a child needed to keep using their magic until they ran out, day after day.

Easier said than done, as the pain caused by running out of magical power was greater than physical torment. It felt as though your mind had been sent into a frenzy as you were sapped of magical power.

It was common to hear of people beating up their bodies for the sake of training until they lost consciousness. However, how many people really had the ability to keep running until they passed out?

That was what it was like to keep using your magical power until you'd run out, an act accompanied by mental exhaustion and pain that could cause you to pass out. This was something children under ten years old did every day.

Even for people like Weishardt and top-notch mages who were discovered to have skills as children and taught to have high aspirations, it wasn't an easy thing to manage.

But alchemists endured harsh training from an early age and continued to make potions with one-track minds.

You might say this was a state of mind, the apex that only a handful of people could eventually reach. Why did a girl who reached that pinnacle at a young age appear so ordinary? Could she be camouflaging herself like Merle and the other intelligence operatives?

As a child, Mariela had been engrossed in the "game" of drying the rainbow flowers her master gave her into pretty colors, and she relentlessly dried every last bit of anything else she laid eyes on, from herbs in the area to weeds to washed clothes. She'd never thought of it as harsh or as training.

In typical fashion, her master had taught her things like "how to skillfully pass out while protecting your head" and "how to skillfully hide in a safe place before passing out," mingled with jokes, and treated fainting from magic exhaustion like it was hide-and-seek to entice Mariela. After Mariela did a good job fainting, she would wake up in bed after being found by her master, who said, "I found you agaaain" and tickled her while rolling around and laughing at her. As time went on, fainting from running out of magical power turned into something like getting tired of playing and going to sleep.

Weishardt, who didn't have a clue about this, explained the

situation to Caroline while watching Mariela like a hawk, assuming she had to be extraordinary.

He stationed a soldier who was fond of children near Mariela so he wouldn't do anything rude, but that had backfired. For some reason, the soldier had searched in his pockets, taken out a preserved cookie, and given it to her. It wasn't as if it had been nibbled on already, but since the seal was already broken, some people would probably get angry and consider it to be leftovers. Moreover, it wasn't a high-class pastry, but preserved food meant for tactical maneuvers. If he'd given it to the children in the area, they would have been delighted, but it wasn't something to be given to a noble person.

...Why...is she eating it...?

The sound of someone munching on a crispy, crunchy cookie with nuts could be heard in the drawing room where a serious topic had turned the place deathly silent.

Their conversation had been closed off from everyone else through magic, but they could hear Mariela's chewing.

Caroline giggled—"Hee-hee..."—at Mariela, who stuck out like a sore thumb, and then her face softened as she said, "This reminds me, shall we have tea as well?"

Because that preserved food probably made her thirsty...

Weishardt tilted his glass of brandy as he recalled that day and thought, *When we're in a state of confusion, people start reflecting on the craziest things.*

"It's rare to see you having a drink."

"Brother. I have been considering the situation regarding the Aguinas family."

Leonhardt had entered after knocking lightly. A whiskey man

himself, he poured his favorite drink into a glass and sat next to Weishardt.

"So what's your plan?"

"Robert's deeds were abhorrent, and he will be charged with the use of forced coercion through the illicit application of black magic, along with abduction, blackmail, and breach of faith with the Labyrinth Suppression Forces. Moreover, the involvement of the secret arts of the Sacrificials cannot be made public. Perhaps something along the lines of 'disinheritance due to illness' would be appropriate? Robert seems extremely tired, so it might do him so good to be placed on a leave of 'convalescence.' Even in light of his contributions to date, the Aguinas family could name Caroline as their heir and find her a suitable husband."

Weishardt took a sip of his brandy, continuing his report, which was mingled with a sigh.

"We will need to investigate whether that new medicine had any lasting effects on the soldiers who used it, as well as decide what to do with the Aguinas family's engineers involved in its manufacture and with the surviving slaves. Considering we also have a Labyrinth to conquer, it's all giving me a headache."

"What about the alchemist? You met her, right?" Leonhardt asked, groping for why his brother was so forlorn.

Dealing with the Aguinas family was a problem that could be solved, even if it would require a lot of work. However, the alchemist, Mariela, was a different story. The Aguinas family's alchemists had either remained asleep or woken up, but then either turned to salt or vomited blood and passed away not long after. There was no guarantee Mariela would be able to avoid the same fate.

The usefulness of potions in the subjugation of the Labyrinth had been proven with the previous King of Cursed Serpents and

Sea-Floating Pillar. And it had shown them that the potions the Forces needed might differ depending on the stratum.

Forcing her to endlessly make every type of potion possible was out of the question. What would they do if that shortened her life span? They couldn't afford to take foolish measures that would damage their friendly relations.

As Weishardt fell into an uncharacteristic worried silence, Leonhardt continued.

"I just remembered a story Father told me a long time ago, something a wise man of old once said: 'Drops of Life flow through ley lines and all the life that inhabits them. It is available whenever you most need it.' Maybe it was the ley line's guidance that led to those two girls to run into each other unnoticed by Merle."

Leonhardt's words were vague, with no basis nor proof to back them up, but they sank straight into Weishardt's heart.

There was only so much a pint-size person could do. In that case, they must do everything they possibly could for her.

"I agree. Let's toughen up her escort for the time being. You never know if some fool will make a pass at her after recent events. There's something about her that makes her seem unguarded."

Weishardt swirled the glass, making the ice clink around, and drank his brandy.

He wasn't the type that could get drunk on a few sips of alcohol, but he liked to savor the way the taste changed as the ice melted little by little. While they'd been talking, the ice had shrunk considerably, and the brandy was weaker than he liked. Still, it wasn't bad, and he drained the rest of the drink.

06

"Aaaah-*choo*!"

Mariela let out a spectacular sneeze in front of Sunlight's Canopy's living room fireplace. Her master once told her the number of sneezes meant different things: "One for praise, two for criticism, three for falling in love, four for a cold." In other words, someone, somewhere was praising her at this moment.

You're making me bluuush...

In the Labyrinth City, however, the saying seemed to be "One for criticism, two for praise, three for a cold," so when she sneezed once, she accepted her master's theory, and when she sneezed twice, the Labyrinth City's theory. Either way, Mariela interpreted sneezes as signs of praise. She continued to be praised every day. Gee, how flattering! But these inoffensive sneezes made Sieg extremely concerned.

"Mariela, did you catch a cold? I'll make you some hot cocoa. I think you ought to stop with the potion making today and get to bed early."

"I'm fine, Sieg. It's not a cold."

"But..." Not only was he extremely worried by a simple sneeze, Sieg also hesitated to speak.

"Sieg, what's wrong?"

This kind of behavior was proof he had something *serious* on his mind. Mariela had only recently realized that such thoughts were usually pretty trivial, and just reassuring him, "It's *fiiine!*" would settle things.

"Mariela... The alchemists sleeping in the Aguinas family's cellar... They all...died suddenly even after waking up..."

Aha, I knew it.

She'd never imagined Sieg would worry about a thing like that. "I'm fine!" she reassured him with a grin.

"You know magic circles don't activate properly if they're slightly crooked or off, right? There was probably something wrong with their magic circles. I used the one my master Imprinted in my head, which is why it worked like it was supposed to. So, there's nothing wrong with me. And I bet I'll outlive you!" Mariela spoke slowly, as if she were trying to persuade a little kid. Sieg's uneasy expression reminded her of a lost child.

"Really?" Sieg asked quietly, and Mariela beamed.

"Yeah, really. I just forgot to extinguish the lantern and over-slept. And because of that, I met you. And Lynx, and everyone else, too. I've been having so much fun every day. Actually makes me feel glad I forgot to put out the lantern."

That was the absolute, honest truth. Sieg, Lynx, Caroline, all her regular customers—each day was enjoyable with them in her life. *I wish things would stay like this forever,* she thought. But...

"*What does the margrave understand about the resolve those individuals had two hundred years ago, the hopes they had when they made those potions?!*"

Mariela could still hear Robert's scream from within that cellar, with the many coffins lined up inside. All the alchemists who'd slept in those coffins had felt death's close embrace as they whittled down their lives making potions that would be preserved until this very day.

Mariela felt guilty about her happy life surrounded by kind people.

"I'm fine. I'm gonna get to work making today's potions."

Wanting to at least make the potions that had been requested, Mariela stood up. Perhaps Sieg accepted what she said, because his uneasy expression disappeared and he followed her, saying, "I'll help." It wasn't like fetching materials or carrying completed vials up from the cellar was a big deal, but the potions were done slightly faster than usual, and they carried them to the cellar to wait for Lynx and Malraux.

Bang, bang, bang.

Clang, clang, clang-clang.

After the signal they'd predetermined, Lynx, who'd come through the underground Aqueduct, appeared.

"'Sup, guys? Hey, why the long face? Didya eat something bad off the ground?"

"I don't do that! I just harvest stuff."

"Aha, so you *did* eat something off the ground."

Mariela puffed up her cheeks indignantly as Lynx burst into laughter.

"All of Mariela's cooking is superb," said Sieg in an attempt to back her up while handing the day's potions to Malraux.

Over the two hundred years Mariela slept, there were alchemists continuing to struggle unbeknownst to nearly everyone.

She believed her current life rested on the foundation they'd built and maintained. After that one night at the Aguinas estate, Mariela grew absolutely certain that her present quiet, joyful days were absolutely precious.

The Flickering Shadow

This is a story from the short period of time between the destruction of the Sea-Floating Pillar and the incident at the Aguinas estate.

Mariela had made a point of emphasizing how "it sure was rough getting up super early every day to make all that holy water!" Malraux then met with Weishardt and subtly weaseled his way into a negotiation to secure her a special invitation as an "affiliate" of the Black Iron Freight Corps.

The destination for the invitation was the Labyrinth's fifty-fourth stratum, the beach cavern where the Sea-Floating Pillar had been.

"Wooooow! Sieg, look! It's the ocean! And a cave! It's so pretty and bluuue!"

Mariela was hyped up at seeing the ocean for the first time. And Sieg's gaze moved around restlessly at seeing Mariela in a swimsuit for the first time. Well, it was really just a pair of shorts and a tank top that revealed about as little as leather armor, but just the fact he could see her arms and legs, which were normally covered by her clothing, made it seem different than usual. Whether from wanting to cover her or wanting to look at her, he hung around holding a cloth as big as a sheet, so if everyone hadn't known him as her escort, he might have been arrested as a suspicious-looking person.

In contrast to Sieg's shady behavior, Lynx eyeballed Mariela and made all sorts of rude comments: "Mariela, you got cankles," "There's too much meat on those kneecaps," and "Those sleeves on your swimsuit? Oh, nah, it's just fat." She wanted to retort, but looking at his chiseled abs, she had nothing to retort with.

Only Sieg and Lynx were paying Mariela's swimsuit clad figure any mind, as the gazes of the Labyrinth Suppression Forces soldiers assigned as guards were glued to Amber's sacred peaks. Amber wasn't wearing anything like a swimsuit, and her divine mounds and deep valleys were hidden by a summer dress, but just the sight of her strolling along the water's edge like a lady was picture-perfect.

Captain Dick loitered around, trying to tempt her by saying things like, "Aren't you going to swim?" and "The water feels great," but he was shot down with a simple, "It's been so long since the two of us got to have a leisurely stroll together." Even the A-Ranker who dealt the decisive blow to the boss of this stratum lost face in front of Amber.

"Let's dive in!"

Mariela was ecstatic. To no one's surprise, she didn't know how to swim, so she'd prepared a swim ring made of creeper rubber just for this occasion. It was written in the Library's *Essential Alchemic Products to Make Your Life Easier*. She made it a little bigger so she could either get in it, put both hands on it, and swim by herself, or sit on it and be pushed around. She'd prepared for everything.

In any case, Sieg and Lynx were nearby. If both of them pushed her, she could move along the water's surface as if she were gliding.

Splash, paddle-paddle-paddle-paddle.

"Eeeek, so fast! Whee!"

Sieg and Lynx grasped the swim ring and alternated flutter kicks. The only one having a blast was Mariela, as it wasn't much fun for the two men pushing her.

"...Marielaaa, I'm tired of this. Let's get out of the water," groaned Lynx after a full hour of entertaining her. You could say he was quite service oriented. He was a really helpful guy.

"Oh, sorry for hogging it. I'll lend you the swim ring, so you two can have some fun!"

Mariela noticed she'd been the only one enjoying herself and tried to give the swim ring to them on the beach, but what part of two guys jostling around in it would be fun for either of them?

"...Nah, I've had my fill. Let's get a bite to eat, eh, Sieg?"

"...Yeah."

The trio went to have a light meal in the dining spot prepared by the Labyrinth Suppression Forces.

Apparently, soldiers got sleepy after playing in the water and filling their bellies, just like ordinary people.

The trio collapsed under a parasol erected on the beach. Mariela spread out the cloth brought by the overprotective Sieg as a blanket, and they all seemed to be in the same nap mode. Blue light reflected among the swaying waves, and although they were lying on the beach in the mystical cave illuminated with it, it felt like they were being rocked to sleep by the waves.

Dozing off and drifting through a pleasant nap, Mariela was suddenly pulled back to reality by a shadow in the blue light hitting her eyelids.

Huh? Was that...a person's shadow?

She thought she'd seen the shadow of a woman in the shade of a rock across the way.

She and Amber were the only women who'd come to the beach today. And Amber was enjoying a meal with Captain Dick at the dining spot, so whose shadow could that have been?

Looking around, both Sieg and Lynx appeared to be deep in dreamland, and Mariela couldn't bring herself to wake them. This stratum was safe, and the Labyrinth Suppression Forces were nearby, so she figured she'd likely be just fine wandering around on her own. Mariela took the swim ring in one hand and began to walk toward the shade of the rock.

When she got near it, someone's shadow dived underwater with a *sploosh* and swam in the direction of the open sea.

I wonder who that was..., thought Mariela as she clumsily got into the swim ring and entered the water.

She could hear someone singing from the direction the shadow had disappeared to. Even though Mariela had up and left all on her own, Sieg and Lynx both continued to sleep and didn't come for her. *I really shouldn't be going out to sea without waking them up first*, Mariela thought, yet this all felt like some sort of dream, like someone was luring her into the water.

Splish, splish, splash.

Mariela's kicks in the water were so weak that she should barely have been able to move forward at all, but the swim ring steadily carried her toward the open sea.

It's calling me.

The moment the thought crossed her mind, Mariela entered a small cave in the stratum wall.

"I'm sorry to call you here like this..."

Blue light filled the interior of the small, confined cave even more than the outside. The human shadow floating there addressed Mariela.

"I'm injured and can't go home... The pillar, the boss of this stratum, summoned me against my will, and although I hid, I was caught up in its collapse..."

The face that emerged from the water was that of a beautiful woman, no different from a human's except for her large pupils and her big, fin-like ears.

"Please, won't you give me a potion...?"

Blue hair that seemed to shine spread through the water. Mariela couldn't see the lower half of the woman's body, but there was webbing on the hand begging for a potion. Was the cave shining, or was this person's hair shining? To Mariela, the brilliance was like the butterflies said to inhabit the southern countries.

Mariela had high-grade potions in the small pouch at her waist. She'd started keeping them on her person out of habit since it would be troublesome for the soldiers who didn't know her situation to see them. She took one from the pouch and handed it to the blue-haired woman.

"Thank you. Thank you so much. Now I can return to the sea."

After countless thank-yous, she downed the potion, then dived back down into the depths of the water, making a small splash as she left.

The lower half of her body, visible when she dived, had the tail of a fish.

A mermaid, just like the legends said! They're actually real!

Somewhere between dream and reality, the figure of the mermaid was burned into Mariela's memory. Right when the mermaid headed for the bottom of the sea and disappeared, the tidal current changed, and Mariela was pushed out of the small cave and carried to the middle of the sea in the fifty-fourth stratum.

"There she is! Mariela!"

Sieg and Lynx, who'd woken up on the beach, spotted Mariela and dashed toward the water, where they dived right in. Mariela was being steadily carried toward the shore, but to them, it probably looked like she was just floating in the middle of the ocean.

"I'm fine," she was about to say when the water behind her swelled up with a big splash and something emerged from the sea.

Among the monsters known as krakens, there were those who had the shape of octopi in addition to the ones in the shape of squids. What appeared behind Mariela had to be...

"It's dangerous to go out on the open sea alone!"

Glint.

It was a dazzling man who diffusely reflected the blue light of the beach cavern.

Mariela would probably come across as uncouth simply by asking things like how could he stand up straight in the water without leg support while flashing a thumbs-up, or why he was in the beach cavern when it was by invitation of the Labyrinth Suppression Forces only.

All she needed to know was that Haage, who'd appeared from the water, was greatly enjoying his ocean swim, and that the top brass of the Adventurers Guild were probably very busy working while their guildmaster played around.

"I'll take you to shore!" proclaimed Haage, who pulled out a cord from somewhere, fastened one end to the swim ring, tied the other end around his torso, and began to swim to shore in a style where he moved his left and right arms symmetrically. The style was said to be like a butterfly. The hair of the mermaid had been beautiful like a butterfly from the southern countries, but the butterfly here was very dynamic. He moved toward shore with incredible energy. It had been fun to be pulled along while on top of the swim ring, but being pulled along while it was around her torso made Mariela feel like she was swimming herself, which was fun in its own way. Did that mermaid also part the waves like this as she swam?

After Mariela reached the shore, Sieg and Lynx were *incredibly* angry at her. They asked why she hadn't woken them and why she'd gone into the sea alone. When she answered she felt like she'd seen a person's outline, Haage, who'd appeared from the sea like a shadow, got a *terrible* scolding from the pair in her place.

Mariela thought maybe she should tell them about the mermaid, but she had a feeling the creature was a "person" like her in a different form, not a monster. The mermaid had simply gotten hurt and couldn't go home.

I shouldn't tell them about the mermaid. Better for them to stay legends, I think…

Mariela decided to remain silent and be scolded along with Haage.

In her pouch was a single mysterious, faintly transparent stone emitting a light like the moon, but Mariela decided to keep this locked away, too, along with her memory of the mermaid.

Appendix

Elmera Seele

♀ Age: **32**

The chair of the Merchants Guild's Medicinal Herbs Division, known to be prim and proper, serious, and stubborn. Appearances aside, Elmera is a sweet lady who's passionate about herbs and loves her two sons, and especially her husband, with her whole heart. Her secret identity is... Wh-whoa, the A-Rank adventurer Lightning Empress Elsee! Day in and day out, Elmera does her best to ensure she never works overtime. She uses lightning to defeat any monsters who stand in her way of getting home on time and threatens ruffians who try adding to her workload with a *pop*.

Haage

♂ Age: ??

A middle-aged man with too much free time who hangs around the Adventurers Guild— No, a practical training instructor! No... Actually, he's the guildmaster of the Adventurers Guild and an A-Rank adventurer known as the Limit Breaker. In order to build a system that can function even in his absence, he deliberately leaves his work to his subordinates, personally trains new recruits, and diligently strives toward maintaining public order by setting out into the Labyrinth City in a hooded cloak. At least, that's what he claims, but it seems to do him no good, as he's often caught by his subordinates.

Leonhardt Schutzenwald ♂ Age: 32

The eldest child of the house of Margrave Schutzenwald, overseer of the Labyrinth City among other territories. He was born with a rare skill called Lion's Roar, which boosts the abilities of any troops under his command, so from a young age he was raised first and foremost to subjugate the Labyrinth. His men consider him a preeminent warrior with strong leadership skills. As general of the Labyrinth Suppression Forces, Leonhardt continues to take on the Labyrinth to return the region to human control. The blades of the Labyrinth Suppression Forces will not bend as long as he continues to make strides in his quest.

Weishardt Schutzenwald ♂ Age: 27

Leonhardt's younger brother, who serves as lieutenant general of the Labyrinth Suppression Forces. In contrast to his brother, who excels in the art of war, he has outstanding intellect and supports Leonhardt in all aspects, from tactics involving the Labyrinth Suppression Forces to management of the Labyrinth City. As someone whose daily life is swirling with political intrigue, he tends to read into things too much. However, thanks to this, a certain sleepyhead alchemist has managed to achieve a proper work-life balance, so all in all things worked out okay.

Caroline Aguinas   ♀ Age: **17**

Daughter of the family of alchemists who have protected the secrets of potions in the Labyrinth City for two hundred years. She was raised as an aristocratic young lady befitting her lineage without being told the family's secrets, unlike her elder brother and Aguinas heir, Robert. She is a graceful beauty brimming with energy and curiosity, and her medicines are the top sellers at the Adventurers Guild shop even without the use of potions. She gets along well with Mariela, and together they make medicine as the pretty/itty-bitty girl duo at Sunlight's Canopy.

Jack Nierenberg   ♂ Age: **41**

A medical technician in charge of the Labyrinth Suppression Forces' medic team, who possesses the skill Probe Organism as well as one-on-one combat capabilities. Highly qualified and loyal to his professional duties, he's treated many soldiers' serious injuries with a smile and garners not only respect but fear from the Forces' troops. Nierenberg's beloved twelve-year-old daughter, Sherry, is lovely both in looks and personality, and the lack of any parent-child resemblance beyond her black hair proves a greater mystery than the Labyrinth itself.

Master* Mariela's
Alchemy Recipes

Mid-Grade Edition

* Unofficial title

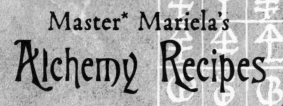

Mid-Grade Heal Potion

For those deep cuts that gush blood everywhere!

For wounds that just won't stop bleeding no matter what, don't panic and use this mid-grade potion.
Highly effective either taken orally or applied directly.

【Ingredients】 Apriore fruit: Harsh-tasting fruit. Delicious if you remove the astringency and mix it into cookies.

Curique: A medicinal herb that's effective for injuries and can be found just about anywhere.

Calgoran: A plant resembling a carrot. Use the roots.

Ogre dates: Available for purchase in dried form from street vendors.

Yurole flower buds: Found on trees that grow an abundance of long, thin, red flowers. Dry and use the bud before it blooms.

【Quantity】 Apriore fruit: 2 to 3 fruits; curique: 1 handful;
(per potion) calgoran: 1 piece; ogre dates: 1 half;
yurole flower buds: 5 to 6

Mid-Grade Cure Potion

Before you end up stuck in bed for a week!

Make that pain go away fast!
Easily and completely removes even the aftereffects of toxicants.

【Ingredients】 Jibkey leaves: A medicinal herb that grows in the shade. Dry at a low temperature.

Tamamugy seeds: Grain that grows in wetlands and bears fruit in the fall.

Fiorcus flowers: Rare mushrooms that resemble flowers.

Apriore fruit, curique, calgoran, ogre dates, yurole flower buds

【Quantity】 Jibkey leaves: 1 handful; tamamugy seeds: 1 spoonful;
(per potion) apriore fruit: 2 to 3 fruits; fiorcus flowers: A pinch;
curique, calgoran, ogre dates, yurole flower buds:
Half the amount used in mid-grade heal potions.

Holy Water

Sacred protection that stops curses in their tracks.

Take this to safeguard against curses.
Use in tandem with Holy Talisman for a perfect defense!

【Ingredients】 Sacred tree dew: Dew that falls from the leaves of a sacred tree. Infused with divine power that wards off evil along with morning light and the sacred tree's blessing.

Salt purified by a spirit's flames: Salt purified by a fire-attribute spirit.

Hair of a maiden: The younger and more tenderhearted the maiden, the stronger the effect.

【Quantity】 Sacred tree dew: Half a cup
(per potion) Salt purified by a spirit's flames: A pinch
Hair of a maiden: A pinch

How to Create Mid-Grade Heal and Cure Potions

1.
Remove the astringency from the apriore. Soak the shelled fruit in hot water with a dash of trona crystals overnight, or simmer over low heat.

2.
Extract the dried apriore and ogre dates from *Drops of Life*-infused alcohol, then extract the other ingredients in water mixed with *Drops of Life*.

3.

Thoroughly soak the yurole buds in the ogre date extract. Be careful not to soak too much.

4.

Mix the aqueous solution, then the alcoholic solution. Pay attention to the quantity and order you mix them in!

5.
Antidotes require a greater variety of ingredients, but the steps are the same.

A Word of Advice

The end result depends on how well the astringency from the apriore is extracted. They say carefully extracting astringency atop a magical heater is the perfect wintertime scene in an alchemist's workshop! Also, these potions use alcohol, so if your master is a heavy drinker, make sure they don't get their hands on it!

How to Create Holy Water

1. Do your best to gather the sacred tree dew...

2. ...and the salt purified by a spirit's flames...

3. ...and the hair of a little gi—er, a maiden!

4. Then just mix them all together!

! *A Word of Advice*

It's super-difficult to assemble these ingredients! Holy water is priceless.

Limit Breaker's Time

Kept ya waiting! This is the start of my story! There are several key words for Volume 3 hidden throughout the Life of Haage. It's a marvelous system where the words in bold are hints of the next book. That's what *Limit Breaker's Time's* all about!

The time is nigh, the moon is high, and the girl's figure grows round as a pie. Is the black figure floating in the portentous moonlit night a dragon, a demon, or a dark cloud? Could it be the Labyrinth, or human malice, that will bare its venomous fangs at Mariela and her friends…?

Snip, snip, snip.

The light sound of scissors could be heard from the washroom of the Adventurers Guild. Reflected in the mirror, the *full moon*… No, Haage lifted his chin and tilted it left to right to check the shape of his beard. Grooming his beard to elongate his jawline was his way of looking stylish. Behold, this curve like the wings of a *dragon*, that edge like the talons of a *wyvern!*

"Guildmaster, didn't I ask you to stop trimming your beard at work? Look at this mess! Hair is food for those *black things*, you know. Who do you think is going to clean it up?!"

A staff member, who at some point had snuck up to Haage unnoticed, coldly chided the guildmaster who stood gloating in front of the mirror.

"It's not as if I *love* accidentally getting it everywhere, you know…?"

Haage's excuse didn't fly. He had no choice but to *retreat* before the staff member's anger burst forth like a *volcano*. It

Limit Breaker's Time!!

was a total defeat. He had a hunch everyone was treating him coldly even though he was the head of the Adventurers Guild. Some *paradise* this was.

"Could it be that you…don't like me?"

"Don't worry. You're not as bad as *snakes* or *lizards*. Those creatures become more active when *spring comes* and grow *plump* when they eat their prey… Ugh, disgusting."

The reptile-hating staff's not-so-supportive support further deflated Haage. Still, whether it was because he looked pitiful, or whether it was just a coincidence, one of the top brass who was looking over a letter called out to him.

"Guildmaster, great work today as usual. This will also count as a guild request—how about taking it easy at a *hot spring*?"

A hot spring. Music to his ears. What a kind subordinate to suggest it.

"I'm touched… While we're at it, you all should join me!"

Convinced the suggestion was a *sign* from his subordinates that they wished to *deepen their friendship* with him, Haage flashed his blindingly white teeth and invited them along. However, they nonchalantly sidestepped his invitation with grins plastered across their faces.

"I'm quite all right, Guildmaster. After all, three promising young individuals will be going with you! One of them is from the Black Iron Freight Corps… *Lynx*, I believe? I hope you'll help them *grow* and improve! I'll send a reply to the Labyrinth Suppression Forces that the guildmaster himself will be coming."

"So where is this hot spring?"

"The *Ahriman Springs*."

With this, Haage's winter plans were settled, and the Adventurers Guild would have a *moment of peace*.

The Ahriman Springs were currently a *needle ape* paradise. No one knew whether Haage and his party would be able to take a *relaxing dip in the hot springs*.

Limit Breaker's Time!!

AFTERWORD

Thank you to everyone who has read up to this point and everyone from the website *Shōsetsuka ni Narō* who cheered me on from the very beginning. Thanks to you, I was able to put Volume 2 of *The Alchemist Who Survived Now Dreams of a Quiet City Life* out into the world. What's more, I'm happy I get to release this in the winter, just as it is in the story. It's the time of year where I want to nod off in a sunny spot, maybe even treat myself to a good book.

Now, Volume 2 covers Mariela and Sieg's day-to-day life in the Labyrinth City where they've settled in a place of their own, as well as the efforts of the Labyrinth Suppression Forces who help preserve this quiet lifestyle by subjugating the Labyrinth that's literally underfoot. This volume also reveals the secret of the potions preserved over the two-hundred-year period Mariela slept.

If this is your first time reading this volume, your view of Robert might have changed once the details of Estalia's life and death came to light. I wanted to write "a revelation that alters the way one appreciates and interprets the story," hence why I chose to keep Estalia asleep through the very end.

*   *   *

By the time Robert is introduced, Estalia has already departed this world. Robert's dramatics before her glass coffin may have been a hint that he had bound himself to her.

The two centuries following the Stampede have been like an extended winter for the Labyrinth City. The mysteries buried in the long winter come to light as the snow thaws and the season turns to spring. What kinds of changes will the springtime breeze bring Mariela and the others?

With spring comes giddiness and excitement, and yet the sky during this season tends to be cloudy and rainy. The turbulent shadows already beginning to smolder may bring forth dark clouds. I'm pleased to bring you such changes among the people of the Labyrinth City come Volume 3.

Finally, I'd like to express my heartfelt thanks to ox, the illustrator who so vividly depicted Mariela and the other characters; the manga adaptation and the advertisements; my editor Shimizu, who worked so hard to put this book out there; and everyone at Kadokawa.

Usata Nonohara

NIYARI (SMIRK)
シャリ

WHOOOA!

COOL!

......

HERE'S A LI'L BONUS FOR YA. REAL PRETTY, RIGHT?

A LEY-LINE SHARD!? YOU USE THESE IN SPECIAL-GRADE POTIONS!

AHHH!

I DIDN'T EVEN GET A GOOD LOOK AT IT YET!

KACHI! (CLICK)
カチッ

...AND TA-DAA, IT'S SEALED.

...INTO THE LOCKET...

POI (TOSS)
ポイ

YA PUT THIS LEY-LINE SHARD...

HA-HA. WELL, GOOD LUCK!

SIEG, DON'T YOU DARE HELP HER!

URGH!

IT WON'T OPEN! LYYYNX!!

THIS'S FOR YOU, MARIELA.

IT'S GOT A TRICK TO IT.

HERE.

GOTCHA AN EYE PATCH, SIEG. KINDA NIFTY, DON'CHA THINK?

...AND SEE, THE LOCKET OPENS.

YA JUST DO LIKE SO...

PAKA (OPEN)

'NOTHER THING...

GOSO

HUH? HOW'D YOU DO THAT? I CAN'T GET IT TO OPEN AT ALL...

I TOLDJA, LIKE THIS... SEE?

WANT ME TO COOK SOME SAUSAGES, TOO? ARE YOU OKAY WITH FRUIT JUICE?

GUESS I CAN'T SAY NO. SIEG, LET'S TAKE AN EARLY LUNCH.

OOH, SOUNDS GOOD. THANKS, SIEG.

NYURU (WRIGGLE)

NYURU

じゅうう

JUUU (HISSSS)

ぽい

POI (TOSS)

GOSO (RUSTLE)

OH, RIGHT. I FORGOT TO GIVE YA THESE.

OH, IT'S JUST LYNX.

WHADDAYA MEAN "JUST"?

I'M A CUSTOMER!

CHIRIN (DING)

WELCO—

LOOK, I GOT COCKATRICE EGG GALETTES.

DON'T BE SO STUFFY!

I BROUGHT SOME SOUVENIRS. LET'S HAVE A BITE TO EAT.

THIS ISN'T A CAFÉ!

ARE THE SMOKE BOMBS I ORDERED READY?

WHAT'S IN THE FIRST-AID SET?

THE STOMACH-ACHE MEDICINE HERE WORKS REALLY WELL!

KARAN (CLLINK)

OL' MAN GHARK, ARE YOU ASLEEP!?

"BARK-B-GONE"?

BE SURE TO GO "HIII-YA!" WHEN YOU THROW IT.

IT HAS A SMELL THAT DOG-TYPE MONSTERS HATE.

MARI!

EMILY, AMBER, WELCOME!

HFF...

HFF...

ALL RIGHT, THEN LET'S GET CRACKIN'!

MORNING! DOIN' SOME TRAINING?

GOOD MORNING. I JUST FINISHED.

HERE'S SOME WATER WITH DROPS OF LIFE!

BASHA (SPLASH)

COLD
...

MMM...

HFF!

......

HFF!

HAAH!

BUN

BUN
(SWISH)